The Skeleton King

KIRALYNN EPICS

The Silk & Steel Saga

Book One: *The Steel Queen*

Book Two: *The Flame Priest*

Book Three: *The Skeleton King*

Book Four: *The Poison Priestess*

Book Five: *The Knight Marshal*

Book Six: *The Prince Deceiver*

Book Seven: *The Battle Immortal*

Additional books by Karen L Azinger

The Assassin's Tear

Power Writing: Make Your Genre Fiction Soar

THE

SKELETON KING

BOOK THREE OF

THE SILK & STEEL SAGA

Karen L. Azinger

KIRALYNN EPICS

Published by Kiralynn Epics L.P. 2012

Copyright © Karen L. Azinger 2012
Second Print Edition 2017

First published in the United States of America by Kiralynn Epics 2012

Front Cover Artwork Copyright Greg Bridges © 2012

Celtic Lettering used with permission of Alfred M Graphics Art Studio

The Author asserts the moral right to be identified as the author of this work

ISBN   978-0-9835160-6-4

Library of Congress Control Number: 2012906988

ACKNOWEDGEMENTS

My dream of an epic fantasy continues, and like the first two books, it takes a lot of people to make the saga come true. First and foremost, to my husband Rick, who is always keen for the next adventure and always believes no matter the odds. To my best friend, first reader and sword sister, Danae Powers, who listened from the very first chapter. To my writer friend, Peggy Lowe, a critique circle of one. To my alpha readers, Mike, Nick, Diane, Mary, John, Stewart, Tanya, Chris, Cheryl, Bob, and Gina, your enthusiasm kept me going through all the bleak times. To Greg Bridges for the totally awesome front cover and the book spine. To Peggy Lowe, graphic artist extraordinaire, for the back cover, the two maps and the logo, well done! To all of my readers who eagerly followed the saga to the third book, I write for you. And to my mom, for everything, I so hope you know.

Prologue

The Mordant spoke not a word. He made no gestures and cast no spells. He merely stepped onto the gateway and the gargoyles awoke. Muscles rippling beneath granite, the gargoyles reared on their pillars, shrieking an unearthly wail. Wings unfurled and talons extended as the great stone beasts strained against their bonds. Twelve massive gargoyles towered overhead, each one a twisted nightmare of beaks and snouts, fangs and claws. Cast in stone and affixed to pillars, yet they *moved*. Infused with an unholy magic, they writhed in torment, clawing at the sky.

Trapped within his prison, Bryce felt their suffering as if it was his own. So much pain, so much torment, their shrieks flayed his soul, the damned calling to the damned. He saw them in his mind's eye. Stone wings beating against the sky, the great beasts struggling to take flight, but they remained fixed to their pillars, their souls forever trapped in granite sepulchers. Perhaps it was his healer's sensitivity, a blessing turned curse, but whatever the reason, their cries shattered his sanity, foretelling his own doom.

Bryce screamed but he had no mouth. Just a soul trapped within the Mordant, condemned to a living hell. *Release them! Set their souls free! Can't you feel their agony? Feel their madness?* He railed against the cruelty of his own existence, cursing the abomination that claimed his face...his body...his mind...but his struggles made no difference, a paper moth beating against a thousand years of evil. Bryce howled against his fate. *I'll not be trapped for centuries! I'll not be a thing possessed.*

Monk, you amuse me. Like a demon summoned from the netherworld, the Mordant's suffocating presence surrounded him.

Stunned to silence, Bryce made himself small, a mouse trying to hide.

So you sense the truth of my gargoyles, the souls of the damned trapped within stone. You have more value than I thought.

Bryce shuddered under the Mordant's scrutiny, desperate to hide a single secret.

Scream all you want, but like the gargoyles, you shall never escape. The Mordant prodded his prisoner with a lance of pain. *It is past time you willingly gave yourself to the Dark.*

Never! I walk in the Light!

I grow weary of your feeble chant. The Mordant's voice battered Bryce like a hand swatting a fly. *Soon you will feel the true power of the Dark Lord. Then you will know there is but one god worth serving.*

The Mordant withdrew, the walls of the prison slamming down. Bryce shivered with relief. The gray void was a cruel hell but the Mordant's scrutiny was worse.

Battered and bruised, Bryce curled into a ball. He could still feel the gargoyles, feel their soul-searing pain, but there was nothing he could do. Struggling for composure, he strove to keep his wits, needing to protect his one secret. The unexpected boon had come early in his captivity. To escape the monastery, the Mordant was forced to traverse the Guardian Mist. In the depths of the enchanted cloud, unbeknownst to the Mordant, the Guardian spoke directly to Bryce. Appearing as a star knight, with a winged helm and a face etched with wisdom, the Guardian whispered words of an ancient prophecy. And with the words came a gift, a pinprick of light, a spy hole onto the world. The gift gave Bryce a narrow glimpse of life, a way of eavesdropping on the Mordant, but it was a sterile view, without smell, or touch, or taste, yet the keyhole kept him sane.

At first, he tried to escape, after all, what shape did a soul have? Making himself tiny, he tried to slip through the eye of the needle...but he could not pass, as if a wall of mage-glass blocked the hole. Mind and will battered the barrier, a rage of purpose, all to no avail. Failure pushed him toward madness, till he recalled the words of the Guardian. Consoled by prophecy and the teachings of the monastery, he nursed his sanity, waiting for a chance to betray a thousand year old evil.

Come, monk, I desire a witness.

Startled, Bryce stilled his thoughts, burying his secret.

The gargoyles herald my return to power. Come and behold the first Trials of Return.

Pulled by the will of his jailor, Bryce rose from his prison to stare through the eyes of the Mordant. A rush of sensations overwhelmed him, a tidal wave of all that was lost. A breeze brushed his face, carrying the first bite of winter. Exposed to scent and touch, Bryce reveled in the wind's caress, swooning at the smell of sunlight striking the grasslands. Denied all sensations, he drank in every detail, wallowing in the sheer delight of the living world...but then the shrieks of the gargoyles intruded, their pain slashing at his soul, a reminder of his grim purpose. Embracing the pain, Bryce fought the ecstasy, forcing himself to think, to concentrate, to understand the enemy.

The Mordant stood beneath the rearing gargoyles, in the center of a short paved roadway that pierced the long gray wall. Bryce knew the wall divided the north from the south, marking the start of the Mordant's domain, but beyond the gargoyle gate, he saw nothing but golden grassland, the endless steppes stretching away to the north.

My soldiers come, summoned by the screams of the damned.

A patrol of horsemen galloped toward the gate. Clad in black armor laced with gold, a bristle of spears against the sky, they rode in disciplined ranks. A dozen great hounds raced in front. A pack of hunters seeking prey, the hounds howled for the kill.

Do you understand the risks? Clad in the maroon cloak and silver surcoat of the enemy, I wear a face none in my kingdom has ever seen.

Bryce trembled with hope.

Stand...or run?

Bryce knew it was a taunt, but he answered anyway. *Stand!*

The Mordant laughed, *I thought you would see it my way.*

Such an odd comment, but Bryce ignored his jailor. Staring through the Mordant's eyes, he watched the cavalcade gallop close. Two hundred strong, the soldiers leveled their lances and charged, a swath of death hurling toward the intruder. Transfixed with hope, Bryce willed them to come, praying for death, praying for release.

A thunderstorm of hooves converged on the gate. A dozen hounds led the riders, baying for the kill. Details became clear. Sunlight glinted on armor, gold pentacles on black breastplates, stern faces beneath dark helms. The surging line bore down on the gate, the horses' hooves churning up clods of grass. The leveled spears gleamed wicked keen, a promise of death, a promise of release.

Bryce watched them come, urging them on.

Somewhere behind him, the unmade knight gave warning, "They're not going to stop!"

A mere mortal would have run, but the Mordant stood his ground, his feet spread wide, his maroon cloak flaring in the breeze.

Sir Raymond screamed, "Run!"

But it was too late to run. The horsemen loomed large, a charging wall of spears. A horn sounded a sharp note. Riders hauled on their reins. Warhorses snorted and stamped, fighting their bits. The horsemen came to sudden stop, a thicket of spears bristling just beyond the gate.

Dazed, Bryce stared at the gleaming spear tips. So close...yet they'd stopped short. He reeled in disbelief, snatched from the brink of death.

The Mordant's voice boomed in his mind. *Behold the proof of my past! The shadow of fear cast by my last lifetime still holds sway.*

Bryce refused to listen. Fevered with desperation, he prayed to the Lords of Light, begging the gods to rouse the soldiers to a killing fury. Straining against his bonds, he fought to make a threatening gesture, to provoke bloodshed, but all he could do was watch, a prisoner trapped in his own body.

The soldiers stayed on their horses, a row of hostile faces staring down at him, silent and wary and full of judgment. Snarling against their chains, the hounds sniffed the air, slaver dripping from their jaws.

Something about the hounds snagged Bryce's attention.

From a distance, they looked like large, shaggy wolves, a motley of tan and black, but up close, they radiated wrongness. And then he got a good look at them. Like beasts sprung from the depths of hell, the hounds proved a living horror, a corrupted nightmare of jumbled features, the snout of a wolf, the curved teeth of a saber cat, the yellow eyes of an eagle...and something more, something twisted lurking deep inside. The twisted wrongness called to Bryce, compelling him to understand. He stared at the cruel yellow eyes...and something stared back...a fierce intelligence pulsing with hatred...*the twisted souls of men!*

The Mordant's laughter ripped through his mind. *You have a gift for sensing souls. These are my gore hounds, the perfect hunting beasts, a triumph of my last lifetime.*

Abominations! A crime against life!

Spare me your feeble judgments. To gain power you must be willing to wield it. Something your Order has long forgot."

The hounds erupted in a frenzy of howls. Fighting their chains, they snapped and snarled, as if trying to flee. Whips cracked as their handlers hurled oaths at the beasts, urging the hounds toward the intruder, all to no avail.

The Mordant stepped toward the hounds.

Their howls changed to a cringing whine, as if they'd caught the scent of something they feared.

The Mordant spoke a single command. "Sabolanth."

The hounds fell silent. Slinking low, their bellies scraping the ground in submission, they bowed before the Mordant.

Bryce shivered in his prison, realizing the twisted hounds knew their maker.

A ripple of unease ran through the soldiers. More than one made a strange hand sign.

Overhead, the gargoyles screamed a warning, writhing against their bonds.

An officer dismounted, a gold plume on his helmet signaling his rank. A black-robed priest joined him, a gold pentacle on a chain around his neck. The officer advanced with his sword drawn.

Bryce watched him come, a glimmer of hope in his heart.

The officer reached the shadow of the nearest gargoyle and stepped onto the stone roadway.

Silence fell like an executioner's axe. The gargoyles froze, cut off in mid-shriek. Beaks and talons stilled, they stood mute as statues. Their sudden silence seemed ominous, like an ill omen. Bryce shivered in his prison, knowing he witnessed the power of dark magic.

The officer and the priest closed the distance, stopping within a sword thrust of the Mordant. The priest, a sallow-skinned man with a curled mustache, began hurling questions at the Mordant. "Who are you? A deserter? A turn-cloak? A spy? An assassin? What brings a cursed knight of the octagon to the Gargoyle Gates?"

The Mordant held his silence.

"Answer the questions!" The priest sputtered, his face turning red. "Who are you? Why does a knight of the octagon wait here?"

"I've come for the Trials of Return."

The priest blanched, retreating a step.

The officer stood his ground, the point of his sword leveled at the Mordant's heart.

The Mordant ignored the threat, raising his voice loud enough for the soldiers to hear. "The first three conditions of the Trials of Return have been met. I wait alone beneath the screaming gargoyles. I have endured the charge of spears. And the gore hounds fall silent at my command. My actions prove my claim."

The officer nodded. "Put him to the question."

The priest made a curt gesture.

A pair of soldiers approached carrying a small ironbound chest. Setting the chest before the priest, they flicked wary glances at the Mordant, and then retreated to their horses.

The priest tugged on the chain around his neck, revealing a large skeleton key. "Once the chest is opened, your fate is bound to the secrets inside."

"Open it."

The priest cursed. "So be it." He knelt, inserting the key in the lock. Muttering a prayer, he opened the chest, revealing a scroll nestled in black velvet. Lifting the scroll, he held it toward the officer. The commander fingered the wax seals, as if checking their integrity, and then returned the scroll to the priest. "All is correct."

The priest broke the seals and read, "The gargoyles announce a single claimant to the Ebony Throne. The spears charge, answering the summons of the gargoyles, yet you refuse to run. The gore hounds scent a kill, yet you quell them with a single command. You have endured the first three trials, but your fate is now tied to the questions of this scroll. Knowledge from the past is the key to the future. A single wrong word and your life is forfeit, for no imposter shall ever gain the Ebony Throne." The priest lowered the scroll and glared, as if his stare would wilt the claimant. "Do you understand?"

"Ask your questions."

Bryce watched, praying for a mistake.

The priest read the first question. "What shape does Death take?"

The Mordant spread his arms wide. "Death comes in the shape of an enemy, in the maroon cloak and silver surcoat of the Octagon knights."

The priest nodded, a sour look on his face. "The gargoyles herald the return of a conqueror. What have you conquered?"

Do you understand, monk? The Mordant's voice whispered through the gray void. *The trial of words offers no riddles, no clues to be puzzled out, just a series of simple questions with a thousand different answers, a thousand ways for an imposter to find death.*

Bryce shuddered, his last hope crushed by the Mordant's certainty. *You wrote the questions...and the answers.*

Of course, signed and sealed before each of my deaths. The Mordant spoke aloud, his voice pitched to reach the waiting soldiers. "I conquer death with each new lifetime."

The priest checked the scroll, growing pale with each correct answer. "Who made the Gargoyle Gates?"

"Ten dead wizards buried beneath their last creation."

Sweat beaded on the priest's brow. "What do you claim?"

"I am the Mordant reborn."

"What are you owed?"

The Mordant smiled. "Your allegiance."

The priest blanched, his hand gripping the amulet at his neck. "What do you demand?"

"An escort to the Dark Citadel where I can finish the Trials and prove my claim to the Ebony Throne."

"Or die trying."

The Mordant completed the ritual. "Or die trying."

The priest gave a cautious half-bow and then turned to address the ranks. "The stranger has passed the initial Trials of Return. By the Darkness he is named a claimant to the Ebony Throne." He traced a rune through the air as if granting a blessing. "Behold the na-Mordant!"

Two hundred fists thumped against steel breastplates. *"The na-Mordant!"*

The storm of cheers rained like acid on Bryce's soul. He screamed inside his prison, railing against the Mordant's victory.

The officer sheathed his sword and saluted the Mordant. "Centurion Caylex, leader of the third border guard, at your command. My troops will see you safe to the Dark Citadel. I'll have a mount brought up for you." He glanced toward the unmade knight. "I assume your servant will ride the pale mare."

The Mordant raised a hand, forestalling the commander. "My plans cannot wait till my ascension. I claim the na-Mordant's boon."

The centurion gripped his sword hilt, his questioning gaze sliding to the black-robed priest. The priest stared wide-eyed, clearly forced beyond the comfort of his authority. "B-but surely this boon can wait till the high priests prove your claim?"

"Check your scrolls, priest. It is within my rights as na-Mordant to claim a single boon."

The priest hesitated, caught between risk and ritual.

Huddled in his prison, Bryce felt waves of Darkness lap around him.

"Look into my eyes, priest. Dare to meet my gaze." The Mordant's voice was a silken command. "Find the truth behind my stare."

The priest gasped a strangled sound. Felled to his knees, his face turned chalk-white, sweat beading his brow. Cringing, the priest raised his hands in supplication, shielding his eyes. "He's the one, the Mordant Returned!" Lurching to his feet, the priest grabbed the centurion's arm, panic written across his face. "By the Darkness, grant his boon!"

The Mordant's voice carried a sarcastic twist. "My first believer. I'll remember you, Tavros, priest of the border guards."

The priest quaked. "I n-never said my n-name."

"Darkness knows you, priest. Your soul shouts its secrets to me, the least of which is your name."

Trembling, the priest bowed low and backed away, clutching his amulet as if a mere metal trinket could save him.

The Mordant turned to the centurion, his words a command. "Cragnoth Keep is held by men loyal to the north. They wear maroon cloaks but serve the Darkness. Trask is their leader, an axe-wielding knight turned mercenary." He gestured to the ranks of spears. "Take two thirds of your men and ride hard for the keep. Relieve Trask and secure the stronghold against the Octagon."

"But your escort?"

"The true Mordant needs no escort."

The centurion saluted, his fist striking against his breastplate. "As you command."

The Mordant smiled. "And one more thing. Trask and his men were promised golds for their betrayal. Payment will be delivered once I ascend to the Ebony Throne. Make sure Trask lives. I have plans for the traitor-knight." He made his voice a command. "Ride hard and claim the keep for Darkness, securing a gateway into the south."

The centurion saluted, snapping orders to his men.

A soldier brought forth a black stallion. Another soldier knelt by the stirrup. The Mordant stepped on the soldier's back, mounting the stallion. Taking the reins, he turned the horse with a flourish. Raising his fist in triumph, the Mordant addressed the troops. "To the men of the third border guard, I give the honor of striking the first blow! Loose the gore hounds and bring war to the kingdoms of Erdhe!"

A cheer rose from the soldiers. Spears clattered against shields, horses stamped and snorted, and above it all, the gore hounds howled, the fearsome din of war.

In his prison, the monk wept for a chance lost, for a world teetering on the brink of war. He prayed to all the gods for a way to kill the Mordant, a way to kill himself, but his prayers went unanswered. Sick at heart, Bryce slumped in his prison, betrayed by the impotence of the gods.

The Mordant put spurs to the stallion, crossing the gate and galloping into the north. *Do you feel it, monk? Do you feel the gathering glory? I ride to claim a throne and all the power of the north, while you whimper in the dark, praying to a pack of useless gods.*

Bryce cringed, hiding in the corner of his prison.

You're a stubborn one, monk, but your gods will never answer. My rebirth is the ultimate proof of the Dark Lord's bounty. Forget the Lords of Light and spend your prayers on a god who answers. The Mordant's voice boomed through the gray void, a relentless goad. *What do you pray for, monk?*

Bryce swallowed his thoughts and shrank to insignificance, a moth hiding in the dark.

Answer me.

Darkness pressed around him like a threatening hand. *I was...* His voice faltered, snuffed by fear.

Come now, monk, your thoughts are mine to rape.

Bryce quaked in terror, knowing silence would be his undoing. *I was...* he forced the words out, *...praying for a chance to kill you.*

Mocking laughter rolled through the darkness. *Of course you were.* The Mordant's laughter intensified, beating against him, coming from all sides, like waves of acid. *But you will never get the chance. For you are a gift from the Dark Lord, mine to use or abuse, to reward or punish, my pet, my tamed monk, my servant for all eternity.* Darkness tightened around him, a fist holding him tight. *But keep dreaming of murder...of sweet revenge...and soon you shall be one with the Dark.*

The hand released him. The laughter receded. The darkness faded to gray.

Once more alone, Bryce curled into a ball. He stayed small and insignificant, afraid to move, afraid to think. But a single thought crept into his mind, *what if the Mordant was right?*

1

The Knight Marshal

King Ursus took the stairs two at a time. The knight marshal shadowed his king, keeping his hand on his sword hilt. Reaching the tower top, the king bulled through the outer doors, striding out onto the windswept battlement. A pair of guards snapped to attention but the king paid them no heed. A faint jangle of arms and armor marked their steps as the two men strode to the crenellated battlement. They'd come for the eagle's view. The great eight-sided castle stretched below, an invincible vision of martial splendor, but their gaze passed over the mage-stone battlements, drawn westward to the Dragon Spine Mountains. Dawn crowned the mountains in a glorious blaze of red and gold, the snowy ramparts dividing north from south. And there amongst the jagged peaks a signal beacon blazed bright.

"I knew it, Osbourne. I dreamt of it last night." The king gripped the merlon, staring west like a man seeing a vision. "Before my page ever brought word, I knew the signal towers would be lit."

The marshal's breath caught. The king oft displayed a sixth sense for war, as if an ancient battle magic flowed in his veins. But magic was anathema to the Octagon. The marshal banished the traitorous thought. "You dreamt of it, sire?"

"Lionel," the king spoke in a grave voice, "Lionel is in trouble. When the messengers come, they'll bring word of Cragnoth Keep."

It was too soon for messengers. "How can you be sure?"

"Do you trust me, Osbourne?"

Clad in scarred fighting leathers, his great blue sword looming like a threat over his right shoulder, the king remained a battle-keen warrior despite his years. The marshal bowed his head. "Always, sire."

"Then we gird for war." A cold wind snatched at their maroon cloaks, a bite of winter snapping at their faces. "I'll not tarry for messengers. We ride for Cragnoth Keep."

"A war in winter?" The one-eyed marshal shook his head as if he did not believe his own words, but his gaze was drawn to the proof, to the signal fire burning bright in the snowy heights. "The Mordant has never been so bold."

"Bold?" The king barked an angry laugh. "I call it devious. The Mordant is ever treacherous."

"Then you think it a ruse? A feint to draw us from Castlegard?"

"Tricks and traps are the hallmark of the Mordant, but either way the signal fire must be answered." The king's voice dropped to a low growl. "And Cragnoth is our weakest point. It makes sense for the first thrust to fall on the frozen keep."

The marshal countered the argument. "Cragnoth holds the fewest knights, but the keep is built strong. The tunneled pass-through could choke an army."

"But did it?" The king glared at the marshal, a fire in his eyes. "Did an army choke to death in the stone passageway or has the keep fallen, opening a door to the south?"

The marshal had no answer.

"Waiting only serves the Mordant." The king balled his gauntleted hands into fists. "Summon the knights. I'll lead a vanguard into the mountains to learn the truth of this threat."

The king's place was in Castlegard but the marshal's protest died on his lips. Ursus was too much of a warrior to wait while other men fought. "And if it's a trap?"

"Then we'll meet it with steel. Either way, the signal tower will be answered." The king turned to face his marshal, his gaze keen and sure. "Take a deep breath, Osbourne. Can't you smell it? War is in the very air. A great battle comes from the north. Our last war, our last chance for glory. This time we'll defeat the Mordant, ending forever the threat from the north." Conviction blazed from the king's face, the conviction of a man grasping a great destiny.

"You have my sword, sire."

The king clapped a gauntleted hand on his marshal's shoulder. "Then rouse the maroon. We ride for Cragnoth."

The marshal turned to obey, but the king was not finished.

"Do you think Lionel still lives?"

The king's voice held an odd timber, betraying a father's worry. The marshal hesitated. It was well known the king favored his youngest son for the throne. "Cragnoth Keep is well built and Lionel is a well-loved captain. Under his command, the Crag will never yield."

Dread flickered in the king's gray-green gaze. "Last night I dreamt of the signal towers...but I also dreamt of death." The marshal had no answer. The king scowled, his face mired in worry. "I can't lose another heir." Turning to stare up at the snow-capped mountains, the steel returned to his voice, the monarch replacing the father. "Summon the knights. Assemble a vanguard. We ride for the Crag."

The marshal saluted, leaving his king alone with his thoughts.

Castlegard thrummed with expectation, a hornet's nest set alight by the blazing beacon. Scores of knights clamored for a chance to wet their swords. The marshal chose the best of them, limiting the vanguard to two hundred knights and half a hundred archers. Provisions were drawn from the stores and parceled into saddlebags. Horses were brought from the stables, saddled and armored for war. The host assembled in the great yard, a gleaming swirl of burnished steel mounted on snorting warhorses.

A cheer thundered through the yard, announcing the coming of the king. Bold and bright like a hero of old, the king wore a helm crowned with gold, his breastplate gleaming silver in the morning light. A squire held the king's warhorse, a dappled gray stallion caparisoned in maroon. King Ursus swung into the saddle like a young man, defying the weight of his armor. A double line of mounted knights formed behind the maroon banner. The marshal nudged his mud-brown gelding forward, taking his place at the king's right hand. A trumpet sounded and the king led them out at a slow trot, a clatter of hooves drumming across the drawbridge. Knights, squires, and men-at-arms lined the castle walls, cheering the vanguard to victory. The marshal turned in the saddle, drinking in the cheers and the sight of the mage-stone walls. The view was grand enough to swell a man's pride and melt away the years, yet he could not shake a nagging sense of doom.

The king set a blistering pace but the marshal insisted on outriders, always leery of a trap. The countryside proved peaceful, fallow farmland teetering on the edge of winter. They spent long days in the saddle, always pressing for speed. Farmland gave way to a cedar forest skirting the steep mountain trail. Single file, the horses forged upwards, snowflakes swirling down from the ice-bound heights. The trail narrowed to a series of knife-edged switchbacks, a long line of maroon snaking up the mountainside. Cold winds blew down from the pass. Riding behind the king, the marshal huddled under his wool cloak, seeking refuge from the wind's bite.

The king's squire saw it first. *"There, Sire!"*

A square, blockish tower squatted at the top of the pass like a stone fist. Crusted in ice, Cragnoth Keep was an ugly lump of stone, yet a maroon banner still flew atop the ramparts.

The king turned in the saddle, snowflakes crusting his beard. "The Crag is still ours."

The marshal spurred his horse forward. "Sire, beware! Look to the sky." Eagles circled the keep, dark wings carving lazy circles in an iron-gray sky. In the flatlands, crows and ravens were ever the first to spy a carrion feast, but eagles ruled the snowy heights. "Something's wrong. Beware a trap."

The king nodded, his eyes like chips of flint. "If it's a trap, then we dare not linger." Unsheathing his blue sword, the king stood in his stirrups, raising a flash of sapphire to the heavens. "For Honor and the Octagon!"

"*Honor and the Octagon!*" The war cry echoed down the long maroon line. Weapons gleamed in the afternoon light. The marshal unsheathed his sword and spurred his horse to a gallop, determined to protect the king. Trumpets blared as the war host thundered up the switchbacks. Rounding the last bend, they charged the keep.

An angry shriek split the courtyard. A pair of eagles fought over a severed hand. A feast of corpses lay strewn across the ground. The courtyard was empty...except for the dead...and all the dead wore maroon cloaks.

The marshal hauled on the reins, pulling his gelding to a stop. Behind him, the war host ground to a halt. Weapons in hand, the knights stared slack-jawed from their horses, nothing to fight but death.

A second eagle screamed a warning. Dark wings beat into the sky, carrying off the severed hand. A cold wind swirled through the courtyard, raising the stink of the dead.

The stench was like a slap in the face. The marshal dismounted, spewing orders. "Sir Winton, take forty knights and secure the tower. Sir Abrax, protect the king." Men leaped to action, swords held at the ready. An honor guard circled the king, while a troop of knights dashed for the tower. "Sir Ambrose, another forty with me." The marshal led them toward the tunneled pass-through, the key to defending the keep. Legends said a single knight could hold the passage against all the hordes of the north. But legends seldom proved true. "Light some torches and be wary of a trap."

Dark and cold as a cave, the tunneled passageway gaped open, waiting to swallow the unwary. The marshal advanced with naked steel, swords bristling around him. A rotten stench slammed into him, demanding a gag. A veteran of many battles, he'd smelled carrion before but the narrow passage magnified the reek. Swallowing hard, he pressed forward, torchlight glinting on rough stone walls. A third of the way in, he found the source of the stench. Bloated and ripe, a half-dozen corpses lay jumbled around a fallen warhorse, a clog of death. Like the courtyard, all the dead wore maroon cloaks, not a single enemy among them.

Behind him, Sir Ambrose hissed, "By the nine hells, what evil did this? They died facing the north, but where's the enemy?"

The marshal pressed forward, stepping around the dead, seeking an answer to the riddle. A trail of corpses littered the passage, all of them knights, many feathered with arrows. He knelt to pull an arrow from a corpse. All the fletchings were the same, black feathers, without a speck of gold. Another mystery.

The trail of corpses ended two thirds of the way down the passage; clumps of horse dung the only other clue. Needing to see it all, the marshal continued to the end. They found the outer doors closed and barred, no sign of any struggle.

Sir Ambrose pounded his mailed fist against the ironbound gate. "How can this be? They must have repulsed the invaders in order to seal the gates, but where are the victors? And why do all the dead wear maroon cloaks?"

The marshal had no answer. The passageway stank of treachery.

Sir Ambrose stared at the gate. "Let's see what lies beyond."

Two knights moved to shoulder the heavy bar aside, but the marshal stopped them. "Leave it. We'll check the far side from the tower ramparts." He gripped the hilt of his sword. "I'll not open the gates to ambush."

They retreated back down the grim passage, a clank of armor and weapons. The marshal paused at each body, putting names to the bloated faces, praying the king's son wasn't among them. He recognized most of the fallen. Men he'd trained, men he'd led, brothers-in-arms, ruined by battle and ravaged by decay, they stared up at him with vacant eyes. The marshal wondered if they'd died with honor. If only the dead could talk. Reaching the last corpse, he turned to Sir Ambrose. "Get the passage cleared. If this is a trap, I'll not have our men tripping over corpses to hold the tunnel against the north."

Sir Ambrose saluted, his face grim.

The marshal left them to the task. Stepping from darkness into the windswept courtyard, he took a deep breath to clear his lungs, but the stench clung to his wool cloak, the putrid smell of rotting corpses. He flicked the cloak behind him, preferring the cold.

The courtyard was a hive of activity. Surrounded by a ring of knights, the king took reports and issued commands. King Ursus met the marshal's stare. Waving the others away, he asked a single question. "Lionel?"

The marshal shook his head. "No sign of the prince."

The strain on the king's face eased a fraction.

The marshal made his report. "They fought in the tunnel. The outer gates are barred from inside but the passage is clogged with corpses...all of them knights. They died facing the north but there's no sign of the enemy." He held an arrow aloft. "Many were feathered with arrows, but the fletchings are pure black, not the black and gold of the Mordant." He stared at his king. "More riddles without answers."

The king tugged at his beard, a grim look on his face. "Cragnoth stinks of treachery. Come look at this." The king led him to one of the dead, a massive knight lying on his back, a battleaxe locked in his fist.

Size alone was enough to name the dead. "Trask."

The king nodded. "Look at the death wound."

A single sword thrust pierced clean through the breastplate, through chainmail, through flesh and bone, straight to the heart. A remarkable death-stroke, requiring immense strength and skill, but the marshal needed to see Trask's back to be sure. He bent to roll the body, but the king stayed his hand. "The wound goes all the way through, skewered by a single thrust. Armor cut like butter." The king scowled. "I've seen wounds like this before. Made them myself in battle."

"*Blue steel!*"

"Just so." The king voice dropped to a low growl. "But none were posted to Cragnoth...and only one blue blade is unaccounted for."

"*Blaine.*"

"He deserted his post and now he's killing knights."

The marshal could not believe it. "There's more to this riddle than meets the eye." Seeing another knight approach, the marshal held his thoughts.

Sir Winton strode from the tower door and saluted the king. "The tower is secure. We found more dead inside, eight in total, seven knights and one steward. The steward was hanged, looks like he did it himself. The others died fighting. But there's no dead except our own, no sign of the enemy."

"And Prince Lionel?"

"Not among them. But it seems they used the signal fire as a funeral pyre. There's armor and bones among the ashes." Sir Winton gave the king a hesitant look. "I found a scroll pinned to the door of the signal tower with a dagger. It bears the seal of a hawk in flight." He handed the scroll to the king.

The king gave the marshal a piercing stare. "It must be from Lionel, but none of this makes sense." The king broke the seal, reading in silence. His face remained stoic, but his eyes flashed with anger...and something deeper, something the marshal refused to see.

Crumpling the parchment in his mailed fist, the king sheathed his sword. "I'll see this funeral pyre for myself." He glared at Sir Winton. "Lead the way."

The knight saluted, leading the king and the marshal into the tower. A narrow staircase spiraled up through the keep's stone heart. The steps were worn deep, carved by centuries of honor. The Crag was old and never defeated, and now this. The marshal scowled, his hand gripping his sword hilt. Halfway up, smears of blood marked the walls, more signs of battle, but the bodies had already been removed. They rounded five spirals before the staircase opened to the great hall. An appalling stench hit them in the face, a foul mix of stale ale and rotten bodies. A bloated corpse swayed on a rope hung from the rafters. An overturned bench beneath the dangling feet told the tale.

The king growled, "Cut that body down and take it outside with the others."

Two knights leaped to obey.

Sir Vardine approached, a length of charred rope in his hands. "Sire, we found this tied to the catapult on the lower parapet. They left the burnt length dangling over the battlement."

The marshal took the rope and sniffed the burnt end. "Soaked in oil." A piece of the puzzle fell into place. "After the battle, they barred the gates and climbed down the rope, escaping into the north." He handed the charred rope back to the knight. "But why the battle? And why leave the keep secure?"

A thunderstorm raced across the king's face. "Osbourne, with me." The king strode toward the spiral staircase, climbing the stairs two at a time. The marshal followed, past the sixth floor and up to the windswept parapet. He stepped from the doorway, into the biting cold.

A signal platform dominated the tower top.

The king stood next to the platform, studying the charred remains.

The fire must have been fierce. Most of the bones were consumed, but the armor remained, forming an outline of a knight. A melted half-helm, blackened chainmail, the hilt of a great sword, the steel edging of an oak shield, all burnt and blackened, lying ruined amidst the ashes. The marshal stared at the burnt mystery, waiting for the king's explanation, hoping it wasn't Lionel. The silence stretched.

"It was Katherine."

"What?" The marshal turned to gape at his king. "Your daughter?"

"If the note is to be believed."

"But the battle? All the dead knights?"

"Blaine and his blue sword, and Sir Tyrone, and perhaps a handful of archers." The king shook his head. "And now they've gone into the north, corrupted by the monks."

The marshal struggled to understand. "But why?"

"They found Trask in charge and bloodstains on their beds. Suspecting murder, they tried to flee but were discovered and had to fight their way out." He gestured toward the funeral pyre. "The dead knight is Sir Tyrone. The note claims he died a hero, trying to hold the passageway while the others escaped."

Murder! The marshal found it hard to believe. "No knight would draw steel on the king's own daughter!"

King Ursus' gaze was glacier-cold. "Katherine spins a foolish tale of the Mordant."

The marshal could only stare.

"I know. Hard to believe the rantings of a misguided girl." The king crumpled the note in his mailed fist. "I should have taken Katherine to hand long ago."

The marshal considered the evidence. All the pieces fit save one. "And Lionel?"

"Murdered." Grief burned in the king's steel-green eyes. "Send men to look for the slain below the tower." His voice betrayed the faintest quaver. The king turned his back on the marshal, staring into the bitter north.

The marshal waited. King Ursus was a stern man but he loved his sons well, especially Lionel. "My lord, I am sorry."

"First Tristan and now Lionel, both slain, both stolen from me. The gods take the best of my sons. How can they be so cruel?" The king shook his head, his silver hair shimmering like the mane of an aging lion. "Lionel would have worn the crown well. And now he lies murdered, killed by traitors in maroon cloaks. Dark times are upon us." His mailed fist slammed against the battlement, once, twice, and then a third...but when he turned, his face was a mask of steel. "My son's body will be found and the Octagon will be purged of any taint."

The marshal nodded. "I'll see to it myself. And then?"

A grim smile graced the king's face. "War."

"And what of Katherine? Should I send a patrol after her?"

"Daughters are naught but a disappointment." The king shook his head. "Thank the gods that crowns depend on the strength of our sons, not the weakness of our daughters."

"But should I send a patrol?"

"No!" The reply struck like a sword stroke. "My daughter is lost to me. She does nothing but disobey. Perhaps Lionel would still be alive if she hadn't meddled in the affairs of men." He shook his head like a wounded bear. "Katherine is a fool and I'll not risk good men chasing after her." Turning, he strode towards the door, his back as straight and stubborn as a sword. "Trouble me not with daughters. I have a slain son to find."

The door slammed shut and the marshal was left alone on the tower top. He stood at the foot of the charred platform, the king's words etched in his mind. Pieces of the puzzle fit together but he felt like something was missing, some deeper understanding lurking just beyond reach. Images of the carnage in the tunneled passageway flooded his mind, a fierce battle, a few fighting against many. He studied the charred remains, wondering what answers Sir Tyrone might have held. "Did you die a hero...or a fool?"

His whispered words were snatched by the wind.

He stared at the melted chainmail and the empty half-helm, but he found no answers, nothing but blackened ruin and the silence of the grave.

A sudden gust howled out of the north, sweeping away the ashes, leaving only ruined armor and charred bones.

And then he saw it, revealed by the wind, a long gleam of bright steel. Untouched by fire, Sir Tyrone's sword remained straight and true. Everything else was blackened, melted and twisted, charred to ash, but not the sword...as if the gods gave answer to his question.

"So, you died a hero." Bowing low, he honored the dead knight...and then he turned his gaze toward the north, wondering if his king might be wrong. Surely the gods worked in strange ways. Katherine was only a daughter, yet she carried the blood of kings, the blood of Castlegard. Perhaps Ursus discarded his daughter too easily. Shaking his head at the mad thought, he quelled the strange notion. Having faced the northern hordes in battle he knew the girl rode to certain death, yet he whispered a prayer anyway. "May Valin guard you though you trod the path of death." The marshal turned from the parapet, seeking his king.

2

Katherine

Dark wings flashed into a steel-gray sky, a murder of ravens taking flight, an ill omen for a god-cursed land. The plume of wings rose from a point farther down the trail, harsh caws echoing against the mountains. Kath assumed it was another horse, still saddled, ridden to death, cast aside, broken. If the ravens held true, this would be the second carcass since Cragnoth Keep, more proof of the Mordant's passing. The grisly remains marked a trail down the Dragon Spine Mountains, taking the five companions beyond the reach of the southern kingdoms...beyond the protection of the Octagon. They rode into the unknown, death as their only guide.

A cold wind blew out of the Spines, a breath of winter pushing at their backs. Huddled beneath wool cloaks, they kept their weapons close, riding single file down the steep mountain trail. Kath led the way, holding her sorrel warhorse to a trot, a pair of throwing axes strapped to her back, a short sword belted to her side. Duncan rode close behind, his longbow strung, a quiver of arrows ready. Zith carried a quarterstaff, the preferred weapon of the monks, while Blaine rode at the rear, his great blue sword looming over his right shoulder. Danya rode in the middle, the only companion who didn't carry a weapon. Bryx, the great mountain wolf, stayed close to the girl's side, a vigilant threat of claws and fangs.

Twisted conifers crowded close to the trail, a sweep of dark forest cloaking the foothills. An owl hooted somewhere in the shadowy depths, a mournful sound that echoed Kath's mood. Swiveling in the saddle, she stared back at the jagged peaks, searching for a glimpse of the signal fire, but Cragnoth Keep was lost to the clouds. A part of Kath could not believe they'd crossed into the north. So much had happened, so much had changed. She'd fled her home, escaping Castlegard only to find traitors holding the frozen keep. *Knights of the Octagon turned to the Dark,* Kath shivered at the memory. They'd fought their way out, with Sir Tyrone paying a hero's price, another bitter loss. Using the signal tower as his funeral pyre, they sent warning to the Octagon. Kath prayed her father understood but she feared her actions made her an exile. The loss weighed heavy on her soul. And now they rode north, into the land that birthed all her childhood nightmares. Five companions dared the wrong side of the mountains, chasing an ancient evil into the north. It sounded like a bard's ballad, but Kath knew the dangers were all too real, the odds deathly grim. She gripped the crystal dagger, praying the gods lent their hand to the trials ahead.

The horses trotted around a bend cast deep in shadows. A rotting stench slapped Kath in the face, the stink of carrion. Jerked from her reverie, she stared at the dead horse.

"Caw!" A lingering raven squawked a warning and then launched into the gray sky.

Kath steadied her stallion, holding her breath against the stench. Still saddled with the Octagon's maroon livery, a confusion of tracks surrounded the rotting feast. Mountain lion, wolf, bear, and a few she didn't recognize, come to claim the prize of easy meat.

Duncan swung down from his gelding. "Not much meat left, just skin and bones." Slapping away the shroud of flies, he knelt to examine the saddlebags. "Judging from the smell, I figure the Mordant has more than a fortnight lead on us."

Bryx trotted close, nosing the carcass, issuing a low growl.

Danya patted her mare and looked pale, her voice flushed with anguish. "He doesn't even unsaddle the poor beasts."

Blaine nudged his warhorse close, concern on his face. "He runs them into the ground and then discards them. Horses and people make no difference to the Mordant, just tools to be used."

"No, you're wrong." Kath shook her head, remembering the bitter fight at the Crag. "To the Mordant, people are bears in a pit, goaded to fight. He incites kingdoms to war and then sits back to enjoy the bloodshed. When the fighting's done, he claims the spoils from both sides." She looked back at the ruined carcass. "In the Mordant's world, the horses get off light."

The monk murmured, "She has the truth of it."

Duncan finished his search, wiping his hands on a patch of ferns. "Saddlebags are empty, no clue to the Mordant's intent, just like the other horse." He vaulted into the saddle, fluid grace beneath black leather. "The dead horse is message enough." His mismatched gaze found Kath, one cat-eye golden and the other sapphire-blue. "The Mordant races to reclaim his power. His lead is too great for us to stop him."

The truth could not be denied, yet it did not change her need to put an end to the ancient evil. "Then we'll just have to follow and find another way."

Duncan nodded, "Just so," but his smile did not reach his eyes.

Kath turned her stallion downhill and asked for a trot. A clop of hooves followed. The rotting stench fell away, replaced by the crisp scents of cedar and pine. Trees twisted by the wind crowded close. Kath peered beneath their boughs, wary of ambush. Everything seemed sinister north of the Spines, the steel-gray sky, the gloomy forest, the winter-cold wind, and the ever present ravens, as if the land held its breath, waiting for evil to strike. Chiding herself for such dark premonitions, she gripped her sword hilt, reassured by the feel of good Castlegard steel.

Strung out in a line, they rode down through the foothills, the shadows stretching toward twilight. Kath yearned for the sunlight. Her warhorse must have sensed her unease, pulling ahead of the others. Only Duncan kept pace, his dark gelding matching strides with the sorrel stallion.

The trail curved out onto a rocky promontory, offering the first unfettered view of the north. Kath pulled the stallion to a halt. A sea of grass stretched to the horizon, golden grains rippling in the wind. Untamed by trails or roads, the vast steppes of the north almost seemed benign.

Duncan joined her on the overlook, the wind tugging at his dark hair. "Don't let the grasslands fool you."

Kath gave him a questioning look.

"It looks peaceful enough, but it's really a trap."

Kath studied the north, judging the vast grassland with military eyes. "No trees, no high ground, no chance for stealth or strategy." She nodded, seeing the trap beneath the stark beauty. "It's like a great greensward, a moat of grass. Naked and exposed, numbers and speed are the only advantages. And the Mordant always has the numbers."

"So they say." Duncan leaned forward, patting the neck of his gelding. "The forest looks threatening but we're safer here, hidden by leaf and bark." He stretched in the saddle, muscles taut beneath black leather. "We'll be out of the foothills by tomorrow afternoon. Then we'll be thankful for the dead horses. The ravens will be our only guides, bellwethers for the Mordant."

"A trail of death and evil."

"We've been following it all along, ever since the monastery."

Kath thought about their journey across the kingdoms of Erdhe and knew it was only a taste of things to come. "Just so." Struck by a sense of foreboding, she pointed toward the steppes with her chin. "My brother, Tristan, died in the steppes." Her voice dropped to a hush. "My father's favorite."

"Why was he favored?"

Kath smiled, her voice wistful. "Tristan had a way about him. Good with a sword, good with his command, gallant and honorable, the perfect knight...till he was caught in the steppes, out-numbered, slaughtered with all his men." She stared out at the unforgiving grasslands. "I wanted to be him."

"You're better than that."

"What?"

"You'll not die outnumbered in the steppes. You're better than that." His gaze held hers, strong and unwavering. "You'll find a way to out-wit your enemies...and you'll out-heart them as well."

His voice was certain as steel. *He believes in me,* a rare gift she'd longed for but never really found...till him. Wrapping his words around her like a wool cloak before winter, she thanked the gods for Duncan.

"We should find a campsite for the night."

His words snapped her back to the practicalities of the north. Noting the hint of twilight in the sky, she said, "Here?"

"No, the cliff is too exposed. A campfire would serve as a beacon to whatever lurks ahead."

She heard the worry beneath his words. "Then you feel it too?"

He shrugged. "We're only five against the north. We'll need to keep our wits sharp and our weapons close." He rubbed the dark stubble on his chin, his face thoughtful. "And we'll need to keep our advantage."

Hearing the irony in his voice, she studied his face, a hawk's piercing gaze over a suggestive smile, the shadow of a beard only making him more attractive. "What advantage?"

"Whatever the Mordant expects," he flashed her a wry grin, "it won't be the five of us."

"Ah, the element of surprise." She met his gaze and shared his laughter, loving the glint of daring in his mismatched eyes.

He gave her a quicksilver smile and wheeled his gelding back toward the trail. "Come on!" Drumming his heels against the horse's flanks, he yelled a challenge, "Or I'll leave no enemies for your sword!" The gelding exploded into a gallop, hooves flying down the trail, sending up a spray of stones.

Kath glanced up the trail and waved to Danya, then wheeled the stallion to follow. The big warhorse surged to a gallop, a charge of hooves racing after the gelding. Kath leaned low in the saddle, her long blond hair streaming behind, glorying in the thrill of the chase. Ahead, the black gelding pulled around a curve. The gelding was quick but the sorrel stallion was powerful, she settled into the race, certain the stallion would close the distance. The trail snaked down through the forest, a series of twists and turns, a clatter of hooves on stone. She lost sight of Duncan but held to the trail. Her warhorse thundered around a curve, charging into a long straightaway...but the trail was empty, no sign of the leather-clad archer. Kath hauled on the reins, bringing the stallion to a stop. The warhorse stamped and snorted but stood his ground. Unsheathing her sword, she studied the forest, searching for a threat. She nudged the stallion forward, holding him to a walk. "Duncan?" Her voice echoed against the mountains.

"Down here."

Relief washed through her.

"Take the side trail."

She followed his voice to a narrow side-spur, branches of cedar and pine obscuring the turnoff. Deliberately breaking a branch, she left a marker for the others before descending the tree-cloaked trail.

Her stallion's hooves skittered on loose stones, a steep descent into the depths of the forest. Branches beat against her, releasing a breath of pine. A hushed stillness cloaked the forest, fallen needles muffling the drum of hooves. Her eyes adjusted to the gloom, her hand still gripping her sword. Trees crowded close, curtains of moss hanging from low branches. But something else hung from the lower limbs. She got a better look and gasped with understanding. Shields hung from the lower branches, old and weathered, cracked and dented. Most were so blackened by time that the heraldry was hidden...yet she knew with certainty what device they all bore. She'd heard legends of such places. Between the trees, impaled in the ground, she saw the swords, their hilts rusted dark red, marking the graves of fallen heroes. A forest of shields, so many men lost to the north, their lives traded for the peace of the southern kingdoms, their bodies laid to rest in hallowed ground. She rode beneath the octagon shields, thinking of Sir Tyrone and his valiant stand at Cragnoth Keep. "For Honor and the Octagon." The words whispered out of her, a token of reverence for the honored dead. She sheathed her sword, feeling safe among the fallen heroes. Awed by the number of shields, she sent a prayer to the Lords of Light, giving thanks for the maroon knights.

Ducking beneath a curtain of moss, she emerged into the last light of day. The forest gloom gave way to a small glade and the cheerful sound of a brook. Kath shivered, feeling as if she'd ridden from the stillness of the grave back into life.

Duncan waited for her by the stream. Tall with broad shoulders and a tapered waist, muscles beneath black leather, he leaned on his longbow, watching the gelding drink. He looked up as she approached, a greeting in his mismatched eyes, a warm smile on his sun-tanned face. "I found our campsite."

Kath slipped from the saddle. "What will we do when this is done?"

"You mean after we beat the odds and kill the Mordant?" His tone was playful but he held her gaze.

Nodding, she secured her horse.

His hand caressed the polished wood of his longbow. "I suppose we'll live happily ever after."

Kath watched his hands, envious of the yew wood. For a rare moment, the two of them stood alone. Like iron pulled to a lodestone, she moved towards him. He reached for her, pulling her close. Her arms wrapped around him. Nestled against his chest, enfolded by his musky scent of leather on skin, she shivered with need. He tilted her chin and kissed her. Tender at first, but then his kiss deepened. His lips burned into hers, a whole world of wanting. Closing her eyes, she shuddered against him, yearning for more. Beneath his leathers, his manhood reared against her. Instead of pulling away, she pressed close, a desperate mix of fear and wanting. He broke the kiss, his voice ragged. "We'd best not..."

She looked up at him, daring to speak her heart. "I don't want to wait."

His eyes widened. "But I thought?"

"We're north of the Dragon Spines."

He held her stare.

Kath struggled to explain. "Everything's changed. I've lost my home, forced to escape Castlegard, forced to flee from my own father. I've slain knights of the Octagon, traitors to be sure, but I never thought to slay a knight. Sir Tyrone is dead and my brother murdered. And now we follow the path of death, chasing the Mordant into the north." She struggled to find the right words. "We've crossed the Dragon Spines, passing into nightmares. Whatever happens, whatever lies ahead...I can't lose you too."

His fingers caressed her face, his voice full of reassurance. "You'll never lose me."

"It's more than that. In Cragnoth Keep I faced death without ever having tasted love." She met his mismatched stare, willing him to believe. "I need you...all of you."

His breath caught. "As my wife?"

She felt his heartbeat racing beneath his leathers, and knew her own raced at the same breakneck pace. Kath dared to follow her heart. "Yes."

He lifted her into his arms, kissing her with the ardent promise of more.

Horses clattered into the glade, the sound of voices emerging from the trees.

They pulled apart, a quick distance that was suddenly painful.

Duncan sent her a fervent whisper, *"Tonight, beneath the trees, while the others sleep."*

Nodding, Kath felt her face flame red, her loins liquid with need. She turned away, busying herself with her horse's tack, hoping the others did not notice. Her hands shook as she worked the buckles. A part of her could not believe her own audacity...but another part, her heart, soared at the thought of finally knowing Duncan. She clung to his words, repeating them like a prayer. *Tonight...beneath the trees...while the others sleep.* Kath stared at the sky, willing the moon to rise.

3

The Mordant

The Darkflamme flew overhead, snaking against a steel-gray sky, twelve feet of black silk ending in two silken tails of bright red flecked with gold. The forked banner snapped like a serpent's tongue, creating the illusion of darkness on fire, a threat of terror to the Mordant's foes, a promise of victory to his legions. Unfurled above the gathering host, the battle banner announced his return, the na-Mordant, the ruler of the Dark Citadel, the claimant to the Ebony Throne.

Like the useless skin of a molting snake, the Mordant shed the maroon cloak and silver surcoat of the enemy. Clad in his true colors, black adorned with gold, he chose the trappings of a soldier over the robes of a priest, sending a message to his followers. Black gauntlets, a black cuirass emblazoned with a gold pentacle, black leather pants tucked into knee-high boots, and a sweeping cape of the finest black wool, but he kept his head bare, awaiting a crown.

Riding at the head of the gathering host, he held the dusky stallion to a slow trot, turning the journey north into a stately progress, a monarch surveying his domain. Word of his return raced ahead, spread by mounted couriers, carrier pigeons, and rampant rumors. With every passing league, the Mordant's entourage grew. Officers, soldiers, and priests, dispatched from every unit and outpost of his army, they flocked to his standard. Some came to bear witness; others came to enjoy the spectacle; but most came to curry favor, to gain a place in the new court of a dictator-king.

He welcomed them all with an open smile, keeping the weight of his years hidden, his glorious darkness buried deep beneath the facade of a young monk's face. His youthful countenance served him well. Cloaked in the illusion of inexperience, his appearance emboldened his entourage, inviting advice, and boasts, and whispered secrets. Only the graybeards remembered, hanging back, wary with their words, a glint of fear in their eyes. The Mordant listened and watched, hiding his amusement, studying his subjects.

The bold and the ambitious competed for his time, jostling to ride next to him. The Mordant spent his days in the saddle, listening to schemes and petitions without giving a single promise. His silence never deterred the flood of ambition...or his steady progress into the north. Crossing the grasslands at a trot, they eventually reached the sprawling farmlands of his inner domain, the black soil lying fallow for winter. A song of praise erupted from the host at his back, now swelling to the size of a small army.

Each night, he held court in his pavilion, a sumptuous tent lavish with wine and sweetmeats. Beneath the billowing silk, they came before him, some to bow allegiance, others to stand stiff-kneed, reserving fealty till the Trials were complete. He accepted them all, the stubborn and the compliant, plumbing their souls, weighing their worth.

He plied his dark powers with subtlety, putting a name to each face and a value to each soul. Nearly a quarter of those who flocked to his banner were closed to him, honest men who lacked sufficient darkness in their souls. He probed the honest ones with words instead of magic, but he judged them all, each according to their worth. Most served with their swords, fodder for the coming war, but a few had value beyond the killing fields. Memorizing their names, he kept a secret tally, noting some for promotion to his personal guards, others for positions in the Citadel. But not all of the petitioners were faithful. Some harbored the seeds of treachery in their souls, mostly among the priests. Those he marked for death. Their treachery did not surprise him. After all, the Ebony Throne had sat vacant for more than thirty-two years, long enough for men to forget their fear, for treason to breed and plots to hatch. But even the traitors would serve, providing an example to others.

Growing bored with the fawning prattle, he waved them all away. A handful of priests lingered. He made his wish a command, a touch of darkness lurking in his voice. "Leave me." Finally alone, he settled into a camp chair, the charcoal braziers dispelling the night chill. Sipping a fine merlot, he studied the campfires spread across the fallow fields, knowing it was but a fraction of those who served the Ebony Throne.

Seeking amusement, he reached for the one soul who knew the truth of his Darkness. *Come, monk, attend me. I appoint you my court jester, a foil for my royal thoughts.*

But the monk did not reply, a brooding prisoner locked in the Mordant's mind.

He could have forced the monk to his will but a taste of freedom long denied often proved the cruelest torture. *Come, I give you leave to see through my eyes, to feel the brazier's warmth, to smell the soil's rich loam, to taste a full-bodied wine. Come and remember what it means to be alive.*

He felt the monk rise to the temptation, looking through his eyes, swooning over the wine's lingering taste. The damned were so predictable. Chuckling, he prodded the captured soul. *I've felt you brooding, monk, ever since the Gargoyle Gate. Have you finally decided to renounce your useless Lords of Light?*

Never!

He laughed. *A pity I cannot dress you in motley and have you caper before me, the perfect court jester.* His laughter turned to a chuckle. *But let me guess at your discomfort. You thought I would be served by rabid monsters, not mere men, and certainly not by men free of the taint of Darkness.*

A brooding silence was the only reply.

Answer me, monk, or the taste of life will be revoked.

You deceive them.

No, they wallow in their own delusions. If there is one thing the centuries have taught me, it is that mortals are masters of self-deception, even disbelieving their own mortality. Thousands of men have died by my own hand and all of them had one thing in common. Shock always filled their faces as the dagger pierced their hearts.

That proves nothing.

Then look at the faces of those who serve me. Raised under the Pentacle, they believe their cause is just, that the Dark Citadel is the pinnacle of civilization, enduring against the threat of the barbarous south. Trapped by myths of their childhood, honest men make the most loyal soldiers. He laughed. *Mortals are victims of their own delusions...a boon to any tyrant who has the good sense to use them.*

No! You are the Deceiver. I won't listen. I walk in the Light. I walk in the Light.

See, you prove my point. You stubbornly cling to your own delusions, believing in gods who ignore you, while proof of the Dark Lord's bounty surrounds you. What will it take to break your mortal delusions?

Footsteps approached from the dark.

The Mordant suppressed the monk, letting him share his eyes, but nothing more.

A black-robed priest crept to the edge of the brazier's light. Red hair and a pudgy face splashed with freckles, Fenthane was a minor priest serving a bishop of the border guards. So this is how they would come at him, sending the young and the unsubtle to test his skills, more proof of the potency of his youthful disguise. "Fenthane, why have you returned?"

Bowing low, the priest took mincing steps into the light. "To offer a gift from my lord bishop," he proffered an amber flask trimmed in silver. "A flask of rare Urian brandy for your pleasure."

Draining the last of the merlot, the Mordant extended his goblet. "A thoughtful gift. It has been too long since I've tasted a fine brandy."

The priest's hands shook as he uncorked the flask, filling the goblet with amber liquid.

"Why so nervous, Fenthane?"

"It is an honor to serve you, Lord."

"No doubt." The Mordant swirled the brandy and raised it to his face, inhaling the rich aroma. Autumn apples fermented to the fiery scent of alcohol, aged in oak barrels to provide a woody base, but he caught no hint of any taint. At least the poison was subtle if not the hand that delivered it. *Shall I drink, monk? It would kill this body but one of us would be reborn.*

He felt the monk tremble, hungry with hope.

Setting the cup to his lips, he watched triumph bloom in the young priest's eyes...but he did not drink. Lowering the cup, he gave the priest a charming smile. "Tell me, Fenthane, what are your dreams, your ambitions?"

"M-my dreams, Lord?"

The Mordant swept his hand toward the campfires glittering like stars against the night. "Surrounded by followers, I am constantly plagued with petitions and requests, why should I not hear yours?" He raised the goblet in salute. "Especially given your princely gift."

The young priest swallowed, his hands fumbling with the amber flask. "I long to leave the border priests, to serve in the marbled halls of the Citadel."

"An ambition as small as the man."

The priest retreated a step, his face suddenly fearful. "W-what do you mean, Lord?"

The Mordant called the Darkness, summoning the weight of his years. Darkness rushed to fill his gaze. He stared at the priest, drilling into his mind. Like a flock of starving vultures the Darkness struck, shredding the man's soul. The priest screamed. He fell to his knees, but he could not look away. The Mordant made it rape, taking what he wanted and then flooding the man's mind with visions of torture, the brutal death of a traitor. The priest whimpered a strangled sound, the smell of hot urine flooding the pavilion. Satisfied, the Mordant withdrew, burying the Darkness beneath a mask of youth.

Released, the priest crumpled to the ground, a puppet without strings. Drenched in sweat, the young man groveled at the Mordant's feet. *"Forgive me, Lord! I did not know!"*

Guards rushed to surround the priest, their swords drawn.

The Mordant raised his hand, forestalling bloodshed. "There is no danger, only a lesson. Sheathe your swords and watch."

The guards obeyed, steel sliding into scabbards.

Making his voice soft and soothing, he nudged the priest with his booted foot. "Sit up. Let me see your face."

Sobbing, the priest obeyed, his face streaked with a river of tears.

"It is always the weak who are first sent against me."

"But they told me..."

"Shhh..." The Mordant kept his voice soothing. "There is no need for words. All the answers are written upon your soul."

The priest shuddered, a hint of hope in his gaze. "Then you'll forgive me?"

"You know what you've done...and now you must atone for your sin."

"But I did not mean to, Lord, I did not know it was truly you!"

The Mordant gestured and the priest fell silent. "I've shown you the fate of traitors."

The priest made a low whining noise, like an animal caught in a trap.

"I offer you a choice."

Choking on a sob, the young man sat back on his heels, staring up at the Mordant, his face ghost-pale. "A c-choice?"

The Mordant extended the goblet. "Drink."

The priest shrank back, his eyes wild.

"The cup or a traitor's death, yours to choose."

"Is there no other way?"

The Mordant waited.

Trembling, the priest took the goblet, his face flushed with fear.

The Mordant hid his smile, the power of fear was intoxicating to behold. "Drink it. Every drop."

The priest stared into the cup, slowly raising it to his lips. Tipping the goblet, he drained it in one long draught. Empty, the golden goblet fell from his hands. A single drop of amber liquid gleamed like a deadly jewel on the young man's lips. Shaking, the priest sat back on his heels, staring up at the Mordant, his face as pale as death.

The Mordant settled back in the chair, savoring the entertainment. "Now we'll see the true nature of your gift."

He did not have long to wait. The priest groaned, bending at the waist. Wracked with sudden convulsions, he fell to his side, writhing like a snake. Arching his back, he clawed at his throat, fingernails gouging bloody rents in the pale flesh, his mouth contorted in a rictus of pain.

Drinking in the details, the Mordant felt his manhood stiffen.

The priest flopped like a landed fish, foam flecking his lips. His eyes rolled back in his head, his back bent to an impossible angle. Uttering a final strangled gasp, he fell still, the smell of death hanging in the air.

A hush settled over the pavilion.

The Mordant studied the faces of his guards, his voice calm. "Treachery gains its just reward. Remember the lesson."

The guards saluted, fists thumping breastplates.

The Mordant nudged the corpse with his boot. "Return this to Bishop Tynes. Have the body stripped naked and staked in front of his tent, an offering to the ravens and a warning to traitors."

The guards saluted, reaching for the corpse.

"And captain," the Mordant smiled, "bring me a clean goblet and find me a woman."

The captain saluted, overseeing the removal of the corpse.

The Mordant leaned back in the chair, eager for the woman, hungry for release. Foiled treachery always sharpened his appetites. Power and youth made for such a heady combination. His hand worked the stiff ache at his loins, enjoying the vigor of a body in its prime. He had much to look forward to. Centuries of planning would finally come to fruition. This lifetime promised to be glorious, full of retribution, deceit, and war.

A woman approached. Dark haired and dark eyed with a full and buxom figure, she was just the sort to quench his need. "Drop your robe and kneel. I have much to celebrate."

4

Katherine

Blaine's voice carried across the glade. Riding next to Danya, he regaled the dark-haired girl with tales of ancient battles. Zith rode close behind, leading the packhorse. Kath ducked behind her horse, fumbling with the saddle, her mind ablaze with thoughts of the coming night. Unable to resist, she risked a glance at Duncan.

He flashed her a secret smile. *"Tonight."*

Her face blazed like a sunset. Struggling for composure, she staked the stallion and rubbed him down with handfuls of grass. While the others settled their horses, she slipped downstream seeking privacy behind a bush. She longed for a proper bath, but a quick wash would have to do. Crouching by the stream, she pulled off her shirt, shivering against the biting-cold water. A small lump of amole root served as soap. Leaning forward, she peered into the water, trying to catch her reflection, but the rushing stream held too many ripples. Her boots slipped and she nearly took the plunge. Regaining her balance, she laughed at herself. If she'd stayed in Castlegard her wedding night would have been so different. Scented baths, silken finery, and a sumptuous feast in the great hall...but the man waiting at the altar would never be of her choosing. Far better to wash by a stream and marry Duncan beneath the trees. Eager for the night, she finished and returned to the others.

A crackling fire drew her back to the glade. Six fire-rings of blackened stones proved the glade was an old campground, a staging area for the knights before they sallied into the north. Kath found her companions gathered around the ring closest to the stream, bedrolls spread in a circle around the fire pit. Duncan had set his bedroll next to hers, the same discreet distance as always, but Kath blushed to see it. She ducked her head, hoping the others would not notice.

Busying herself with work, she went to gather kindling, but pinpricks kept dancing down her spine. She whirled to find Duncan staring. The man was driving her to distraction, but she could not repress an answering grin.

Returning with an armful of kindling, she found Zith had assumed the role of cook, taking over from Sir Tyrone. Rabbits spitted on sticks sizzled above the flames. The smell made Kath's mouth water, sparking a sudden hunger.

They shared the rabbits, licking grease from their fingers. Bryx chuffed, gnawing on the bones. Sitting circled around the fire, they leaned on bedrolls, sipping mugs of tea, the warmth chasing away the evening chill. Kath smothered her impatience, wishing the others would sleep, but Blaine nattered on about the forest of shields and the heroes of old. Kath had never seen him so talkative. She studied the blond-haired knight and the wolf-girl, wondering if the attraction was mutual. Blaine was clearly smitten, showering the girl with attention, but Danya seemed distracted. Huddled beneath a cloak of brown wool, her hair bound in a long braid, she sat cross-legged, staring at something in her hand, a dreamy look on her face.

Magic spiked through Kath, creating an irresistible pull. Kath gasped, feeling a magic she'd thought long lost. She gripped her gargoyle, but it was not the source. A strange certainty ran through her. Sitting up, she stared at Danya, her voice hard with mistrust. "What's in your hand?"

The conversation stilled.

The wolf growled a low warning.

Danya blinked like an owl woken from sleep. "My hand?"

Kath stifled the urge to leap across the fire and take what was hers. "What are you holding?"

Understanding seemed to break across the wolf-girl's face. "Is it yours?" She opened her hand and held it out. A small amber pyramid nestled on her open palm.

Kath gasped, fighting the urge to rip the focus from the girl's hand. "Where did you get that?"

Danya extended her hand. "If it is yours, then take it." Her voice fell to a hush. "I don't think I need it any more."

Kath circled the fire, her gaze locked on the amber pyramid. Her right hand gripped her sword hilt, unable to believe that Danya would give up the focus without a fight, but the brown-haired girl did not waiver, the amber pyramid offered on her open palm.

Kath snatched the focus from her hand...and staggered backwards, as if released from a spell.

Duncan leaped to catch her, concern in his voice. "Are you well?"

Kath shuddered, released from the compulsion. Sinking onto her bedroll, she stared at the amber pyramid and then at the wolf-girl. "I'm sorry." She shook her head, struggling to understand. "I don't know what came over me." Clenching her fist, she held the pyramid tight. "I somehow knew you had this...and I had to have it back."

"The bond of the focus re-asserts itself."

They all stared at Zith.

Wrapped in his midnight-blue robes, the monk tugged on his silver beard, his voice thoughtful. "A magical bond is created between the focus and the wielder. It usually displays as a compulsion to touch or fondle the focus, to always keep it near, to never let anyone else have it." He stared at Kath. "The bond called to you, demanding to be reclaimed."

Kath opened her fist and stared at the pyramid, disliking the compulsion, but unable to give up the small amber carving. "But why now? The pyramid has been missing since I woke from the gray space." She stared across the fire at Danya, questions in her gaze. "I lost it in the Deep Green. Why didn't I sense it before?"

The wolf-girl nodded, her face pale. "I found it in my pocket when I woke from that awful nightmare." She shivered, her voice holding a note of apology. "I never knew it was yours."

Kath stared at Danya, relieved to hear the honesty in her voice. She turned to Zith, needing answers. "Why didn't I feel it before? Why now?"

The monk held up his hand, forestalling her questions. He turned to Danya, his voice full of soft inquiry. "Did you bond with the focus? Do you know its purpose?"

Kath held her breath. She'd carried the amber pyramid since the monastery but she'd never learned its secret.

Danya nodded, her face hesitant. "I think so."

"Can you tell us what it does?" The monk's voice was soothing, a gentle prod.

Danya lifted her left arm, slowly rolling back the sleeve to reveal a gleam of silver. An ornate silver cuff covered her arm from wrist to elbow, silhouettes of animals incised along its length. "It taught me how to use this."

The monk gasped but Kath's stare remained locked on Danya.

"Before, I could only talk to Bryx. Sometimes I'd catch a few stray thoughts from the horses, just bursts of emotions." Danya stared at the cuff, turning it so the firelight flashed along its silvery length. "But at Cragnoth Keep, I could feel the eagles. I knew why they circled overhead. I saw the dead as they did, bodies broken on the rocks, discarded carrion, food for eagles." She stared at Kath, her dark eyes begging for understanding. "And today, when you raced ahead, I felt the horses. I knew they ran for the joy, not fear, so I knew there was no need to follow, no need to rush and catch up."

Zith whispered, "A *Beastmaster*," his voice full of awe. "You've become a Beastmaster."

Kath said, "Why didn't you say something?"

Danya shrugged, her face flaring red. "I was so overwhelmed...I didn't know what to think." She shook her head, a bewildered look on her face. "At first I did not believe. And then I didn't know what to say." She shivered, a glimmer of fear in her dark brown eyes. "In the village where I grew up, those who consorted with beasts were hunted down and killed," her voice fell to a hush, "burned at the stake. I've had nightmares."

The wolf whined, pressing close to the girl, as if offering comfort.

"You're among friends." Kath stared at the dark-haired girl, willing her to hear the truth in her voice. "We'd risk our lives for you."

Blaine unsheathed his blue sword, his silver surcoat shimmering in the firelight. "By my sword, I swear to protect you."

Danya stared at Blaine and then back to Kath, a mixture of relief and gratitude on her face. "I could not ask for better friends."

Duncan leaned toward the fire, his voice intense. "This proves we are *all* outcasts, each in our own way." His single cat-eye glowed golden in the firelight, a reflection of his mixed heritage. "Perhaps that is why we've been chosen for this task. Those who are overlooked may yet make the greatest difference."

The archer's words fell like a mantle across the five companions, binding them together, a promise and a geas.

The monk broke the silence. "The gods work in mysterious ways."

A shiver raced down Kath's back. "What do you mean?"

"More raw power sits around this fire than any dared hope for." Zith stared at Danya. "There has not been a true Beastmaster since before the War of Wizards." He turned his gaze to Kath. "And in addition to the crystal dagger, you now carry a Quickner."

Kath shook her head, confused.

"Danya's growing talent reveals the truth of the amber pyramid. Much more than a simple focus, it is a higher magic, long thought to be lost. A Quickner creates and strengthens the bonds between a focus and the wielder. In essence, it quickens magic." His face turned thoughtful. "If the Grand Master had known of the pyramid's power, he would not have let it leave the monastery." He gave Kath a penetrating stare, his voice earnest. "You can never let the pyramid fall into the hands of the Mordant...or any other harlequin."

Kath tightened her fist around the pyramid. "Why?"

"The Mordant hoards magic."

His words brought back memories of her kidnapping, her ordeal in the woods.

"Given a Quickner, he could bond with every focus in his hoard, achieving the powers of the wizards of old."

Duncan gasped, "By all the gods!"

A shiver of fear sliced through Kath. She opened her palm and stared at the amber pyramid, reluctant to lose it, but she said the words anyway. "Perhaps we should send it back to the monastery?"

Zith shook his head, pulling his midnight-blue robes close. "No. Sometimes magic seeks the wielder. The Quickner found its way to Danya, to waken her powers, and now it has found its way back to you." He stared at Kath, his face thoughtful. "The Quickner chose you for some purpose. We must trust in the gods...and in our own abilities."

Duncan's voice was hard. "The gods have a habit of being absent when they're most needed."

The monk nodded. "Just so. But more than coincidence is at work here."

Kath shivered, feeling the weight of prophecy...or the threat of doom. Sometimes it was hard to tell the difference. She stared at the amber pyramid, wondering that so much power could be contained in such a small thing. "But why did it leave me? And will it leave again?"

Zith had a strange look on his face but he did not answer. Kath wondered if he did not know...or if he did not want to say. She pressed for more. "Does it serve the Light or the Dark?"

"Magic is like a sword. It serves the one that wields it."

A stillness descended on the companions, each to their own thoughts.

Blaine broke the tension, throwing a log onto the fire, releasing a spray of sparks. "I'll take the first watch."

His words jarred Kath's thoughts back to Duncan. "No, I'll take first watch."

Blaine gave her a searching look.

Realizing her words were too eager, Kath scrambled for an excuse. Opening her palm, she revealed the amber pyramid. "I have much to think about."

Duncan said, "I'll take second watch."

Blaine shrugged. "As you wish."

Kath settled by the fire, watching the others slip into their bedrolls, their weapons close at hand. She clenched her fist around the amber pyramid, the words of the monk running through her mind. The Quickner seemed like a boon...and a perilous burden. She wondered if they dare take it into the north. Staring up at the sky, she searched for answers, but the stars were hidden. A full moon hung low in a cloud-choked sky, a single smudge of light against the dark. So dark the sky, it seemed an ill-omen.

Blankets rustled beside her. Kath felt Duncan's steadfast gaze, tugging her thoughts in a different direction. She met his mismatched stare, a rope of emotions tethered between them. He leaned towards her, his voice a low whisper, pitched for her alone. *"Yours to decide."*

A choice, he gave her a choice, the most precious gift of all. Warmth rushed through her, confirming the rightness of her choice. She held his mismatched stare, a flood of emotions in her voice. "Yes."

He smiled like a burst of sunshine at the dawn. "Then I best get some rest." He flashed her a rogue's grin before pulling his blankets close.

Kath's face flamed red. One glance and he brought her blood to a boil, a promise of the pleasure to come. She bit her lip, finding it hard to wait, but they could not leave till the others slept. Feeling the amber pyramid in her fist, she buried it in her deepest pocket. The gods alone knew what they'd face tomorrow, but for this one night, she would think of nothing but Duncan.

5

The Knight Marshal

Cold seeped into his bones, waking the pain of old war wounds, yet the marshal felt drawn to the tower. Wrapped in his maroon cloak, he paced a circuit around the signal platform, another man's great sword looming over his right shoulder. Before coming to Cragnoth Keep, he'd always carried a saber, his First Weapon, but he'd felt compelled to take up Sir Tyrone's blade, reclaiming it from the ashes. Kissed by fire, yet the blade was not blackened or dulled, as if the gods offered their blessing...as if the blade still held a greater purpose.

He shrugged his shoulders against the harness, unaccustomed to the weight. A cold wind battered his face, a bitter squall from the north. Storm clouds threatened to break but at least the gray sky was empty of eagles. All the dead were buried or burned, yet a pall still hung over the tower, a lingering stench of treachery.

Rusted hinges squealed in protest as the tower door opened. The marshal turned, hoping to see the king, but it was just a pair of squires laden with wood. Sir Tyrone's remains were gone, given honorable burial with the prince and his men. Swept clean of ash, the stone platform held layers of chopped wood carted up from the valley below, fuel awaiting the next signal fire. The squires hesitated when they saw him but the marshal waved them toward the platform. "Stack it tall and stack it well, lads, for the signal fire's sure to burn a warning ere winter's end."

Iron-shod hooves clattered into the courtyard below. He leaned over the parapet to spy the new arrivals, a party of six, their horses sweat-streaked from a hard ride. One in particular was familiar, Sir Lothar, the captain of the Salt Tower, the farthest to ride and the last to arrive for the king's council.

Keen to greet his old friend, the marshal abandoned the tower top. Descending the spiral stairs, he paused on the sixth level, but the king's door remained shut as it had since Lionel's burial. Except for morning arms practice, the king kept to himself, wrapped in his grief. But too much grief could erode a man's soul. The marshal hesitated, his hand raised to the door, but his resolve bled away. After all, what did he know of a father's loss?

He passed the door and descended to the great hall. Like stepping from winter into summer, the hall brimmed with light and life. Heat blazed from both hearths, the smell of roast lamb teasing his hunger. Every table was crowded. Knights in maroon cloaks sat shoulder to shoulder on the long benches, sharing an ale and a jest. Gray-garbed squires scurried between tables, helping the stewards serve heaping platters of spit-roasted lamb. Laughter erupted from a far table, echoing a line from a bawdy joke.

The marshal forged a path between the benches, making note of names and faces. A man's choice of drinking partners often revealed his alliances. Even within the maroon, politics played a part.

Like a ripple in a pond, men raised their heads as he passed, some nodding greetings while others stared at the great sword looming over his shoulder. The marshal kept his face closed, ignoring their stares. Command had its privileges and its burdens. His true friends were few, his responsibilities many. The marshal eavesdropped as he walked, regretting that he hadn't paid closer attention to Trask and his cronies.

Six knights trooped into the hall, a dusting of snow on their maroon cloaks. The marshal's gaze snapped to their captain, Sir Lothar, his weather-beaten face sporting a long mustache, his dark gaze full of questions. The marshal crossed the hall to greet the newcomers. "Well met." Sir Lothar clasped the marshal close, his voice a low whisper, "Are the rumors of treachery true?"

"Too true."

"And the king?"

"Locked in his grief."

They parted with a knowing look. The marshal said, "Come and share meat and mead with me. There is much to discuss." He led Lothar to the high table. Most of the chairs were already taken, filled with captains come to pay court to the king's three remaining sons. The princes dominated the table. Ulrich and Godfrey sat in the center, supping on ale and lamb and roasted potatoes, while Prince Griffin sat sprawled at the far end, his hands curled around a tankard. All three were fierce warriors and able swordsman, captains in their own right, commanding strongholds along the Domain. Big blond men, well muscled and bold, the princes echoed the king's bearish physique. They struck an uncanny resemblance, especially Ulrich. The king's first-born wore scarred fighting leathers, the hilt of a blue steel sword looming over his right shoulder. For half a heartbeat the marshal hesitated, like staring into the past. Yet there was something missing, some indefinable quality that made the son a pale imitation of the father.

Ulrich broke the spell, his booted foot pushing an empty chair toward the marshal. "So the one-eyed eagle comes down from his aerie. It seems even the knight marshal must eat."

A forced chuckle circled the high table, the sound of men currying favor.

The marshal shrugged his cloak over his shoulder, taking a seat across from the prince. Lothar took a chair next to the marshal.

Ulrich's stare fixed on the hilt of the marshal's great sword. "So it's true, you've taken up a dead man's blade?"

He didn't explain; he wasn't sure he understood it himself. "Good steel should never be wasted."

"But you've always been a saber man. Why take up the great sword when there's gray in your hair?"

So the princeling flexed his muscles, reaching for Lionel's place. The marshal flashed a predator's smile, rising to the challenge. "I wanted a sword with greater reach. You understand the value of reach?"

The prince never broke eye contact, but he eased back in his chair. "We've seen little enough of you these past few days, and even less of the king. What draws you to the tower top?"

"Snow, rock and more snow." Gesturing for a squire to bring a plate for himself and Lothar, the marshal tugged the leather gloves from his hands, tucking them into his belt. "It'll likely be a long winter."

Ulrich grinned, the right side of his mouth twisted by an old scar. "But if the signal towers hold true, it'll be a winter full of war. A chance for honor and glory, else why call the captains to council?"

Griffin, a leaner version of Ulrich, answered from the far end of the table. "For the sake of treachery, brother."

Ulrich scowled and Godfrey shook his head but Griffin's hooded gaze never wavered. "And then there's the question of the crown."

Prince Griffin's words hung across the table like a battle axe.

The marshal glared, "Prince Lionel's grave is still fresh-turned."

Griffin held his gaze, "Yet it is the duty of king's to have an heir...and our lord father is ever fond of duty."

Ulrich intervened, wielding his birthright as the eldest. "Rest assured, brother, the king will name an heir, else why has he summoned us to council?"

The marshal knew the princes well, having trained all three to the sword. Ulrich fought like a bull, rushing in at the slightest hint of an opening, while Griffin showed a cautious shrewdness, preferring a slow dance of parries and feints. Godfrey, the third-born prince, was a follower, always mimicking his oldest brother. "The council is called for treachery...and for war."

Ulrich flashed a wolfish grin. "So there'll be war then."

"As sure as winter."

"And the traitors?" The question came from Sir Gravis. Bald as an egg, his face as tough as boot leather, Gravis was a stern captain and a staunch friend to the king.

"All dead."

More than a few made the hand sign against evil.

"Does the treachery stop at Cragnoth?"

The marshal met Godfrey's stare. "That's the question, isn't it? How far has the Darkness spread?" A murmur of unease ran the length of the table. "It's hard to hold a castle when a traitor mans the drawbridge." The marshal reached for a tankard of ale. Talk of treason left a bitter taste in his mouth.

"They say there was a note," Prince Griffin's voice cut like a well-polished sword, "a note pinned to the tower door, sealed with a red hawk."

Rumors were hard to contain. The marshal nodded, reluctant to speak of the king's daughter; a mere girl had no part in war. "The note told of Trask's corruption to the Dark."

Sir Gravis nodded, "A message from Lionel, no doubt, before they murdered him."

Ulrich's stare smoldered. "Yes, the king's chosen successor, struck down by his own men." Scorn filled Ulrich's face, an ugly mix of ambition and jealousy. "Death by treason. That must have been a mighty blow to the king."

The marshal speared the prince with his gaze. "The king mourns his son."

"But would he mourn half so much for the rest of us?" Ulrich's face hardened like tempered steel. "Or aren't we shiny enough for his liking?"

Ulrich talked like he fought, with broad smashing strokes, but for once his words struck true. The marshal looked away, unable to deny it. The king's younger sons had been made of finer stuff, something shiny and noble. Tristan and Lionel both carried heroic glows that made other men rise above themselves, willing to dare the fiercest odds. Somehow that shining characteristic had passed over the older sons, as if the mold had been set but the metal wasn't quite right, leaving men of blunt iron instead of bright steel. The marshal shook his head, mourning the loss. The promise of the younger sons was gone, snuffed out like a bright-burning flame. Sometimes the gods were cruel. He reached for his tankard. "The king needs all his sons."

"Some more than others." Ulrich scowled. "They tell me Lionel has his own shield grove, set on the south side of the mountains so that all travelers from Castlegard to the Crag can pay homage as they pass. Seems like a lofty honor for a murdered prince."

The marshal's voice held a cutting edge. "The king loved Lionel well."

"I'll not begrudge the dead their due...but he *is* dead." Ulrich's gaze narrowed. "The king must name a new successor." He leaned back in his chair, a warrior in his prime. "I've always been the strongest, the best sword among my brothers. In times of war, it's strength that matters most. It's past time the king chose his first-born to rule."

"Ayes" circled the table...but not from everyone. Gravis kept silent and so did Sir Mellott and Sir Lothar, while Prince Griffin merely watched through hooded eyes.

The marshal crossed stares with the first-born prince. "The royal house of Anvril has ever ruled the maroon, but it has not always been the oldest who gains the throne." He lowered his voice, a warning and a threat. "The king alone decides his heir."

A low murmur rippled through the great hall.

The marshal turned to find the king standing on the stairwell. New lines of grief were graven on his face but his eyes sparked like flint.

Benches scraped against stone. Almost as one, the knights rose to greet their king. "The Octagon!" The shout echoed through the hall. King Ursus moved among them, nodding greetings and exchanging a murmur of words. Even in the winter of his years, the king roused a fierce loyalty among his men. Like a blazing hearth, the warmth of brotherhood swept through the great hall. The marshal stood with the others, proud to serve such a king.

The press of maroon cloaks parted and the king reached the high table. He nodded to the marshal, "Osbourne," and then took a seat next to Ulrich. His gaze circled the table, keen as sharpened steel. "The signal fires have been lit. The council of captains is summoned for war."

Knights of lower rank took their leave, nodding to the king before moving from the high table. The great hall began to clear. The other captains joined them at the high table, Sir Boris of Holdfast Keep and Sir Dalt of the Ice Tower. Each captain commanded a tower or a keep along the Domain. They filled the high table, five captains and three princes, with the marshal seated beside the king. One chair remained empty...the chair of a dead prince.

Stewards poured tankards of ale and offered plates of roast lamb smothered in gravy. Baldwin, the king's squire, spread a map of the north across the heart of the table, tankards set at the four corners. Their work done, the stewards retreated to the staircase. Logs snapped and crackled in the two hearths, the only sound in the great hall.

The king surveyed his captains. "I led a war host to Cragnoth expecting battle...but instead found only treachery and murder. The Mordant found a way to corrupt Trask and some of his knights. It seems he sought a back door for his army, an easy way into the southern kingdoms."

The marshal eased back in his chair, watching the faces of the captains. Only Lothar and Boris, the last to arrive, looked surprised.

The king clenched his fist. "This treachery cost us dear, the death of Prince Lionel and a score of loyal swords, but Cragnoth is ours once more. The back door is closed, secured against the north." His stare circled the table. "But I expect the Mordant will try again, the Octagon is summoned to war."

Sir Lothar scowled. "A war in winter. The Mordant strikes when it is least expected."

"Exactly." The king leaned forward, like a hawk stooped to the hunt. "We must snatch advantage from treachery, heeding the warning."

Ulrich grinned. "Then you expect another strike at Cragnoth?"

"Of a certainty," the king cast a sideways glance at his son. "The Mordant never wastes an opportunity. He'll send a force against Cragnoth to collect the wages of treason." His fist settled on the map, covering the painted symbol of the keep. "When the Mordant finds his way blocked, he'll seek another route across the Spines." His hand swept the length of the Domain, from Castlegard in the east to Salt Tower perched on the edge of the Western Ocean. "With so few men, we must anticipate the strike." He turned to study his first-born. "If the Octagon was yours to command, where would you wager the bulk of our strength?"

Ulrich leaned over the map, casting a furtive glance toward Griffin, but the second son remained impassive. "Cragnoth is our smallest garrison. By attacking the Crag, the Mordant proves he strikes at weakness, so I believe he'll try for a quick victory at Holdfast Keep or the Ice Tower."

The king turned his gaze toward his second son. "And you, Griffin?"

The prince did not hesitate. "The mountain trails are perilously narrow at Holdfast and treacherous with snow at Ice Tower. An army would take the better part of a month to cross at either point." The prince's gaze narrowed, a thin smile on his face. "Since the subtly of treason failed at Cragnoth, I believe the Mordant will abandon a dagger in the back in favor of a battering ram." He fingered his close-shaved beard. "I believe he'll empty the north, bringing his full force against us at Raven Pass."

A murmur of unease circled the table.

"A full assault in winter," Sir Gravis shook his head, his voice skeptical, "the Mordant has never been so bold."

Prince Griffin answered. "Winter is the perfect cloak for trickery. While most men sit by their hearths, polishing their swords, the Mordant will march in full strength against us."

Sir Gravis persisted. "But in the dead of winter? His supply train will triple in size just to keep his army in wood for fires, let alone food."

"He'll not bother with a supply train." Every stare turned toward the king. "He'll use the winter as a goad to his army."

Sir Lothar tugged on his mustache, a frown creasing his face. "Victory or death. They'll have to punch their way south or freeze to death in the steppes."

The king nodded. "Exactly."

"Ruthless, very ruthless," Lothar chuckled but the sound held no mirth. "And the Octagon will bear the brunt of the madness."

"As always."

"Where will he strike?"

"Castlegard will never fall. He'll not wager an army against mage-stone walls. And all the other trails are too narrow." The king's gaze settled on his second-born son. "I agree with Griffin, he'll strike at Raven Pass."

Ulrich scowled but he did not argue.

Sir Gravis leaned forward. "Then you'll be wanting our men."

"Your men, your spare arms, and your supplies." The king swept his hand across the map, his fist coming to rest on Raven Pass. "We'll gather our strength at the pass, leaving skeletal forces everywhere else except Cragnoth Keep."

Sir Lothar frowned. "A dangerous gamble."

"A calculated risk." Confidence filled the king's words, but the marshal saw the worry shadowing his eyes. "We'll make our stand at Raven Pass."

Ulrich grinned. "As captain of the pass, I pledge to lead that stand to victory."

The marshal caught his breath, the prince presumed too much.

The king turned toward his oldest son. "Cragnoth Keep needs a captain. You'll take command of the Crag while I lead our forces at Raven Pass."

"But Raven Pass is mine to command!" Ulrich bristled, his fists clenched. "And besides, the Crag is insignificant."

"The Crag was good enough for your brother." The king's eyes darkened with anger but Ulrich was blind to the warning.

"You steal my chance at glory...and the crown."

The other captains pushed back from the table, gaining a safe distance.

The king stood, a thunderstorm on his face. "Every son of mine must serve before he's given the honor to lead." He loomed over his first-born, his voice brimming with anger. "Have you forgotten how to serve?"

Ulrich weathered the king's stare, but his voice was sullen. "No, Sire."

"Remember your oath. You swore to serve the maroon."

A spark of rebellion kindled in Ulrich's eyes. "I swore to *fight*."

"And so you shall. You'll have your fill of it." The king's voice struck like a slap. "Tell him, Griffin."

"The first battle will be fought at Cragnoth, when the Mordant comes to harvest his deceit."

Mollified, Ulrich nodded. "Then honor of first blood is mine."

The king turned his back on his first-born, stepping toward the blazing fireplace. "You'll take command of the Crag and crush the attack. Then bring the bulk of your men to Raven Pass to reinforce the wall. If the Mordant turns his full might against us, every sword will be needed."

"And the crown?"

The king stiffened, his broad shoulders cloaked in maroon. For half a heartbeat, the marshal thought he'd turn and strike his son, but the king chose to answer, a touch of weariness in his voice. "The crown is earned by deeds not bluster. Leadership, strategy, honor and courage, these are the measures of a king of Castlegard."

A hushed stillness settled over the great room. Pine logs snapped and crackled, releasing a pungent scent. The king kept his back to them all, facing the fireplace, casting a long shadow across the room. "More questions?"

A chorus of "no's" rippled around the table.

"You have your orders. There's no time to waste. See that it's done."

The captains stared at the king and then nodded to the marshal. Wood scraped against stone as they pushed back from the table and took their leave. Ulrich hesitated, staring at the king's back, but he turned without saying a word. Sir Lothar lingered the longest. Nodding to the marshal, he followed the others.

The marshal remained alone with his king, the only sound the crackling of the hearth fire. "What troubles you, my lord?"

"I felt this coming, Osbourne, felt it in my very bones, yet the warning did not come in time to save Lionel."

The king turned, a haunted look in his eyes.

"And now you feel it again?"

The king nodded, "Something worse comes. A great doom from the north."

"And the hammer blow will fall on Raven Pass?"

"Even Griffin can see it. He sees it but he cannot sense it." The king's voice sounded weary. "My sons tussle for a crown when so much more is at stake...proving none are worthy." The king stared at his marshal, a strange mixture of grief and iron conviction writ upon his face. "We must anticipate the attack, Osbourne, throwing the full weight of the maroon behind a single bulwark. A desperate gamble...the gods help us if I'm wrong."

"You're never wrong, sire, not when it comes to war." The marshal drew a slow breath. "Then we fight at Raven Pass. And the fate of the southern kingdoms will turn on a single battle."

The king stared into the fire. "We gird for war, Osbourne, and we dare not lose."

6

Katherine

Kath added kindling to the campfire, needing to be sure the flames would not die. The others slept, soft snores coming from their bedrolls. Duncan had already slipped away, but she'd promised him a half turn of the hourglass before she followed. She knew what to expect...or at least part of it. In the Deep Green she'd peppered Duncan with questions about the customs of his people. Weddings were simple affairs, two people pledging their lives before an old growth tree...and then they slipped away into the forest, both coming to the wedding bower...*naked*. Kath's heart raced just thinking of the last part. A wild excitement engulfed her but beneath it ran a current of fear. She knew she was being skittish but she could not help it.

Moonlight broke through the clouds, silvering the glade. Kath smiled, taking it as a blessing from the gods. Deciding she'd waited long enough, she took a deep breath and cast one last glance at her sleeping companions. Only the wolf remained awake. Bryx grinned at her, making a soft chuffing sound, as if he knew her intent. She bowed toward him, trusting the wolf to stand guard. Shrugging her axes from her shoulders, she decided to keep her sword. Kath blushed at the thought, knowing a bride should never bring a weapon to her wedding, but the sword was too much a part of her. Turning her back on the campfire, she stepped toward the forest.

Bright moonlight lit her way across the glade. Stepping past a curtain of moss, she entered the forest. Her eyes adjusted to the gloom. A tangle of branches shrouded the moon, leaving barely enough light to see by. Kath shuffled forward, avoiding thick-trunked trees and low hanging shields, and then she saw it. A single candle glowed in the forest. *Duncan!* He could see in the gloom but he'd brought a candle just for her, a beacon in the darkness. The simple gesture melted her heart. She followed the candlelight and found him waiting by a gnarled oak tree.

"Beloved," he held his hand toward her.

He'd never called her that before. The single word shimmered in her soul. Kath stepped into the candlelight and took his hand. At first touch, a jolt raced through her. She knew he felt it too, a promise of the pleasure to come. Clasping his hand tight, she stared into his mismatched eyes.

Duncan smiled. "I found the oldest grandfather tree in the forest. My people believe the older the tree, the deeper the roots, the more binding the vows." He voice was laden with meaning. "The roots of this tree delve deep."

Kath tore her gaze from Duncan to look at the tree. An immense live-oak, the trunk was wide enough to hide a horse, the branches thick and gnarled, and amongst the branches hung half a hundred shields. Tears crowded Kath's eyes, as if the heroes of the Octagon had come to witness her vows. "It's perfect."

Duncan nodded. "As if the gods arranged it, your people and mine."

She gave him a solemn smile. "What must I do?"

"We keep one hand clasped," his grip tightened on her left hand, "and place the other on the tree."

Kath mirrored Duncan, the oak's bark rough beneath her right hand.

"Now I sing the tree awake." He closed his eyes, and began to hum a deep wordless tune that shivered with ancient meaning. Masculine and strong, the melody wove around Kath like an embrace. She strained to listen, seeking to understand, but the meaning beneath the melody remained out of reach, a primal language of leaf and bark. The humming came to a sudden stop and Duncan's eyes snapped open, holding her with a burning gaze. "And now we say the words that bind us."

Kath stared at him, feeling as if she stood on the threshold of a dream.

Duncan's voice was clear and certain. "By Leaf and Bark, by Tree and Root, I, Duncan Treloch, pledge my life, my love, and my body to you, Kath of Castlegard, forever wed in the sight of the trees."

Kath took a deep breath, knowing it was her turn. "By Leaf and Bark, by Sword and Shield, I, Kath of Castlegard, pledge my life, my love, and my body to you, Duncan Treloch of the Deep Green...forever wed in the sight of the trees."

In the back of her mind, Kath heard a chime, as if the gods sealed their vows.

Duncan stepped toward her. "It is done." His arms captured her, pulling her close. His mouth sought hers, a tender kiss that deepened to more. She melted against him, feeling the pounding of his heart. But then he pulled away, leaving her confused. His voice was rough with wanting, "Now we seal our words with our bodies. I'll light a second candle to guide you. Come to me in the depths of the forest." He gave her a hungry glance and then slipped into the velvety darkness.

Kath stood alone in the candlelight. Now came the moment she both longed for...and dreaded, but their vows would not be complete until their bodies were joined. She fumbled with the ties of her clothing. Jerkin, shirt, pants and small clothes, it all came off, including her gargoyle. Bundling everything into her cloak, she tied it tight. Lastly, she unbound her hair, the tangled tresses falling just below her breasts. Naked and exposed, she shivered against the night chill. Her face flushed, but she refused to hide. Holding her sword belt and her bundled cloak in one hand, she lifted the candle and stepped barefoot into the forest.

A second candle glimmered nearby.

Her skin prickled in the cold. Taking a deep breath, Kath went to her marriage bed. Stepping carefully past gnarled roots and rusted swords, she walked with her head held high, her hands away from her body, determined to show Duncan there was no doubt.

He stood in the light of the second candle. Her gaze drank him in. Broad shoulders and a chiseled chest, a line of dark hair traced a path to his tapered waist and down to his loins. Her gaze followed the path, needing to see all of him. His manhood stood rampant and proud like a battering ram. Kath quailed at the sight.

His voice was soft and soothing, "There's nothing to fear. The first time is always the hardest for a woman, but I promise you the pain will be slight, outweighed by the pleasure."

Kath quivered, unable to answer.

He took the candle from her hand and set it by the other. And then he took the sword and the bundle. Divested of both, she felt even more naked. And then he was standing before her, so close but not touching. "Kath, my lioness, my wife." He cupped her face, his fingers stroking her cheeks, caressing her lips, as if memorizing her features, and then his hands moved down, drawing her blond tresses away from her breasts. Exposed to the cold, her nipples grew tight and tender as buds. He warmed them with his hands, an agony and an ecstasy. His lips found hers. He lifted her against him and then laid her on the bower of his cloak, a rustle of leaves beneath. She stiffened for a moment, a sudden stab of fear, but then his lips and hands roused her. They kissed forever, tasting and touching. Every caress ignited pleasure within her, like nothing she'd ever felt before...but then his hand slipped between her legs. Her breath caught, a wild mix of fear and hunger. He opened her with a single finger. Shallow at first but then deeper, she gasped at the secret touch. Wet and warm, her back arched with need. His touch became insistent. Heat flashed through her. And then he rolled on top. His weight pinned her to the ground, his breath harsh against her face. *"Beloved!"* She felt him poised at the gate, rampant and hard. The first thrust hurt...but then the pleasure came in waves. She moaned against his shoulder, holding him tight, riding the ecstasy.

#

Later, much later, she lay nestled against him. Sore but sated, Kath could not believe it was done. Her fingers teased the hair on his chest. "Duncan...my *husband!*"

"I am that." He captured her hand and kissed it.

"You chose the perfect tree."

"Deep roots and many shields, the perfect melding of our two peoples."

"So now I too belong to the Deep Green?"

"As much as I do."

She heard the catch in his voice and regretted her question.

"The deep roots will carry and hold our vows. The Treespeaker will know of our marriage."

She hadn't thought of that, but she liked that the Treespeaker would know. "I'm glad." Warm beneath his shared cloak, Kath stared up at the branches, a lattice silvered by moonlight. "I don't want this night to end."

"Nor I."

"I never thought it would be like that."

"And how was it?"

"So...consuming."

He laughed, a deep rumble in his chest. "It's only the first taste."

Her imagination failed her...but her interest was piqued. "How else does it taste?"

Duncan rolled to his side, staring down at her. "Wild like summer lightning," he kissed her, "tender as a rain shower," another kiss, "soft and slow as a falling leaf," he nibbled her lip, "hard and pounding like a horse's hooves," he pressed his manhood against her, "quick and sharp as a horn thrust," his hand went lower, "reckless as a ram in rut...as many different flavors as there are leaves in the forest."

Kath could not imagine it, but she grew warm with each kiss, each touch. "I want to taste them all."

He gave a throaty laugh, "My lioness!"

"But is it always so sticky?"

"My seed, your blood, our marriage bed." Duncan rolled on top and took her again. This time there was only pleasure.

#

Duncan woke her with a kiss. "Kath, it's time."

She clung to the sweet dream, the memory of his touch, his taste.

"Kath!" his voice prodded her with urgency, "if you want to keep our marriage secret, we must go."

She startled awake. "So soon?" Clothed in black leathers, he knelt beside her. "But you're already dressed?" Her voice was laden with disappointment.

He grinned. "You would not wake. I gave you as much time as I could."

She looked past his shoulder, through the tree limbs, ambushed by the brightening sky. Her breath caught. "We need to get back."

He leaned over her, capturing her gaze. "I would tell them if you would."

Tempted and touched, Kath considered it, but then she shook her head. "No, this night was just for us." Somehow she felt if they kept their marriage secret, kept it just for themselves, then no one, not even the gods, could take it way. She caressed his face, enjoying the rugged stubble beneath her fingertips. "A promise of love before we engage the Dark."

He kissed her, deep and ardent...and then he pulled away. "As you wish." He stood over her, gazing down. "I brought a water skin. If the others wake before you return, I'll say you've gone to wash."

"Thank you...for everything."

"My wife." He gave her a loving look and then turned and strode through the forest, a shadow in black leathers.

Naked, Kath stayed within the warmth of his cloak, clinging to memories of the night. But the dawn was insistent. Sighing, she reached for the water skin, making a quick ablution. Kath soon discovered she was more than sore. Blushing, she wiped away the blood, no longer a maid. She dressed with care, settling her gargoyle around her neck and the amber pyramid in her deepest pocket.

Buckling her sword belt, she shook out Duncan's cloak, claiming a single autumn leaf from their marriage bower, a keepsake of the night. Tucking the dried leaf beneath her jerkin, she pocketed the two melted candle stubs and retraced her steps, eventually finding their wedding tree. Dawn's light filtered through the branches, prodding her to hurry yet she paused before the tree. Laying a hand on the old oak, she whispered, "Thank you." Bowing to the tree and its burden of shields, Kath hugged Duncan's cloak close and made her way back to the glade.

7

Katherine

Dawn lit the sky as the companions rode out of the foothills and into the steppes. Kath regretted leaving the forest, but duty drew them northward. She swiveled in the saddle for a last look, holding the memories of her wedding night close to her heart.

Duncan rode beside her, his voice pitched for her alone. "The trees will remember...and so will I."

She felt a blush heat her face. "Last night was...perfect."

Hoofbeats came from behind as Zith and the others drew close. Unwilling to share the morning, Kath urged her stallion to a trot. Golden grasses rippled in the wind, stretching to every horizon. Unmarred by roads or trails, the north seemed beautiful at first, an endless sea of sun-kissed grasslands, but then the dull sameness began to wear on Kath, a sixth sense adding to her unease. The openness of the steppes made her nervous, too flat, too exposed, too vulnerable for a party of five. Feeling as if she rode into a trap, Kath gripped her sword hilt, pinpricks of unease dancing down her spine. The wolf seemed to sense it too, disappearing into the tall grass for hours at a time and then returning to Danya's side.

They rode without talking, the threat of the steppes dampening even Blaine's enthusiasm.

A pillar of dark wings loomed ahead, an exclamation mark punctuating the golden grasslands. Ravens wheeled in tight circles, always the first to arrive and the last to leave, the handmaidens of death. Kath steered her stallion toward the dark pillar. At least the ravens served as good guides, marking the trail of dead horses.

A rotting stench heralded another carcass. A rush of black wings scattered at their approach, raising a cacophony of harsh caws. Danya hung back but Kath needed to see. Mauled by predators, the dead horse was little more than skin and bones and saddle. Duncan dismounted, disturbing a legion of flies. "Maroon trappings emblazoned with the Octagon, the same as the others."

Kath scowled, a grim reminder of the Mordant's treachery.

"There's nothing here. The Mordant leaves no clues." Duncan swung into the saddle, his longbow in his hand.

Kath nodded, urging her sorrel stallion to a canter, eager to be away. The others followed. Bunched close, they pressed on into the north, searching for the next plume of ravens.

For six days they rode north, following a trail of dead horses. Camping at night, they slept fitful without a fire. Rising at first light, they spent long days in the saddle, chewing dried venison for meals. They made good progress, but for every league north, Kath's unease grew.

The wolf loped alongside Kath's stallion, looking up as if he heard her thoughts. Bryx chuffed and then darted away, melting into the tall grass like a dark ghost. Kath watched him disappear, wondering what he'd find.

Duncan's gelding pulled even with her. "Trust the wolf."

Kath shrugged, but the tightness of her shoulders would not go away.

"The wolf has a better sense of smell than any of us."

"Even you?"

"Perhaps." He flashed a grin but his voice was serious. "If there's any danger, the wolf will spot it first."

Kath nodded, knowing he was right, but she kept searching the horizon, expecting a threat that seemed just beyond sight. The sun climbed to the noon zenith, a pale disc in a winter-gray sky, providing little warmth against the chill wind. By unspoken agreement they kept riding, wrapped in wool cloaks, their appetites ruined by another dead horse.

Kath rode next to Duncan. "Do you suppose the trail leads straight to the Dark Citadel?"

"This trail leads to trouble."

His words echoed her feelings.

"The Mordant will find a patrol of soldiers long before he reaches the Dark Citadel." His stare met hers, his face hard. "That's when trouble will find us."

She tightened her grip on her sword hilt.

Duncan steadied his horse. "Back in the monastery, the monks had maps of the far north. Brittle and faded with age, the maps all showed the same thing. A great wall divides the steppes, marking the southern boundary of the Mordant's domain. Ten gates, spaced leagues apart, provide the only breach in the long wall." He gave her a piercing stare.

"The maps all carried the same warning. The gates are guarded by a foul magic."

Kath sketched the hand sign against evil, recalling nightmares from her childhood. Weaned on tales of valor, she'd heard wild stories about demon-guarded gates in the far north, but she always assumed the knights had been too far into their cups, the ale twisting the truth to a nightmare. But that was before she believed in magic. She reached for her gargoyle, needing to be sure the small figurine was safe. "Walls we can deal with, but we might want to avoid the gates."

He nodded. "I'm betting the trail of dead horses leads to a gate."

"Then we'll need to veer away at the first sign of the wall."

"Just so."

They rode in silence, carving a path through the deep grass. Kath scanned the horizon, searching for a first glimpse of the wall, but the steppes remained unbroken, a never ending sea of grass.

A lone wolf howled in the north.

The sound spiked through Kath. She threw a warning glance at Duncan, her unease mirrored on his face.

A woman's scream split the sky.

Kath pulled the stallion to a halt, her sword flying to her hand.

Danya clutched her horse's mane, her face pale, her eyes glazed. *"From the north!"* She shuddered, shaking her head. "Something evil comes!" She writhed in the saddle, her stare wild and unfocused. *"Abominations!* They claw at my mind!"

Blaine unsheathed his blue steel sword, urging his horse next to Danya. "I'll protect you!"

Zith struggled to control his horse, his mare turning skittish.

Kath and Duncan stood in their stirrups, staring north, searching for the threat, but the horizon seemed empty, nothing but an unbroken field of grass.

"There!" Duncan pointed. "See the ripples in the grass, like arrows racing toward us!"

Kath saw them, six long furrows speeding toward them, one leading the others. "What is it?"

A howl ripped from the north, a twisted wail, like hounds loosed from the bowels of hell. The sound clawed at Kath's soul, a shiver of fear.

Danya screamed, *"They're hunting us!"*

Duncan nocked an arrow, steadying his horse with his knees. "Get the others away!" He drew the great bow to a kiss.

Kath yelled a warning. "One of those might be Bryx!"

The bowstring thrummed. "I know." Duncan reached for a second arrow. "*Ride!*"

Kath spurred her stallion to a gallop, herding the others toward the southeast. Her sword in her hand, she swiveled in the saddle, looking for Duncan, looking for the threat.

The longbow twanged, black-fletched arrows arcing into the sky.

A snarl of pain erupted from the north, a tortured cry that seemed half-human.

Her horse leaped forward, finding extra speed, running in a blind panic.

A deep-throated baying followed, the hounds of hell loosed to the hunt.

Hoof beats came from behind. Duncan rode low in the saddle, racing to catch up.

Kath urged her sorrel stallion for more speed. Racing behind her companions, she drove them forward, a prickle of fear lancing her back.

Another howl, closer than before, the hounds narrowed the gap.

Her stallion surged forward, ears pinned back, foam flecking his mouth, but Kath knew the race was already lost. She scanned the horizon, desperate for a defensible position, but the steppes were a trap, flat and vulnerable with nowhere to hide.

A black-fletched arrow thrummed past her, skewering the rump of the packhorse. The horse's rear leg crumpled. Squealing in pain, the packhorse fell, hooves churning in terror.

Zith turned in the saddle, shock on his face.

Kath screamed at the monk, "*Ride!*" She knew what Duncan was doing, offering the hellhounds easy meat. Lashing her stallion past the flailing horse, she prayed for the sacrifice to work.

Wild baying drew near.

Duncan pulled alongside her, the black gelding streaked with sweat. Neck and neck, the horses stretched for speed. Kath risked a glance behind, catching a glimpse of dark forms racing through the grass. "*They're coming!*"

The baying deepened, close and hungry, like a hot breath on the back of her neck.

Kath cursed their ill luck, asking the stallion for more speed.

The wild baying stopped. A sudden eerie silence descended, loosing a threat that shivered down her spine.

The horses kept at the gallop, eyes showing white, sweat soaking their flanks. Kath crouched in the saddle, feeling death at her back.

A dark streak raced past. Shaggy fur, tan and black, larger than a wolf, the beast ignored the other riders, closing on the lead horse.

Fear knifed through Kath; *the beast hunted like no natural animal!* Wolves always culled the weak, taking the easy meat...but these hounds sought the leader. Kath screamed a warning, "*Danya, lookout!*"

Blaine swiveled in his saddle, but the hound raced past, leaping onto the hindquarters of Danya's mare. Teeth and claws ripped into horseflesh. The mare skidded to a halt, kicking and squealing in terror. Danya clung to the saddle, staring back at the beast, her face twisted in fear.

An angry snarl raced through the deep grass. Bryx vaulted onto the tan beast, teeth flashing. The two predators tumbled into the grass, a snarling ball of hate.

"*Kath, behind you!*"

Kath whirled to see a second beast leap onto her stallion. A snout like a wolf and teeth like a saber cat, it lunged for her face. Her sword flashed a cutting stroke. The beast snarled and fell back, claws raking her stallion's flanks. The warhorse squealed, a kick of iron-shod hooves dislodging the hound. Kath wheeled the stallion, controlling him with her knees. Trained to war, the horse reared. Iron-shod hooves lashed out, but the beast evaded the stallion. Kath sheathed her sword and reached for a throwing axe. The hellhound circled, keeping low to the ground, trying to flank the stallion. The warhorse pivoted, a dual of hooves against claws. Kath saw an opening and loosed the axe. Her steel bit deep. Blood gushed from beast's throat. Her warhorse plunged for the kill, smashing the beast's head to a bloody pulp.

Kath reined the stallion to a stop, trying to make sense of the chaos. Zith fought on foot, retreating from a snarl of fangs. His quarterstaff whirled, barely keeping the beast at bay. But as she watched, the monk *slipped!* The hellhound pounced. Zith screamed.

Kath reached for her second axe, a whirl of steel...but the timing was off. The axe struck a glancing blow.

Unharmed, the beast whirled, a snarl of saber-sharp teeth. Kath urged her warhorse to attack. Rearing, her stallion lashed with iron-shod hooves, but the hellhound leaped away. The warhorse pivoted but the beast moved lightning-quick. For half a heartbeat, she lost it in the tall grass.

Slavering teeth rushed toward her. The hellhound leaped on her stallion's flanks, attacking the rider instead of her horse. Claws scrabbled against horseflesh. A slaver of jaws snapped at Kath's face. She jerked away, trying to pull her sword from the scabbard. Pain lanced through her left thigh, the hellhound's claws piercing leather. The stallion bucked and plunged, squealing in panic, desperate to dislodge the beast.

Kath pulled her sword free. Bright steel slashed down. She stabbed at the hound, frantic to hold the teeth at bay. An arrow thunked into the beast. She felt the hellhound shudder, a gleam of hate in its yellow eyes. A second arrow confirmed the kill. Kath pushed the carcass away, shaking from the fight, her stallion quivering beneath her.

Horses whinnied in pain but the snarl of the hellhounds had fallen silent. All around them, the grass was beaten flat and bloody. Three horses were down, hooves flailing in agony...but Kath's gaze sought the leather-clad archer.

Duncan strode towards her, his longbow in his fist. "Are you harmed?"

Relief washed through her, "Is it over?"

"For now." Reaching up, he drew her from the saddle. Pulling her to his chest, he held her close, as if needing to prove she lived. They clung to each other till her heartbeat slowed...and the squeals of the horses intruded.

Kath whispered, "The others."

Duncan stepped away...but Kath's left leg crumpled beneath her weight. Duncan caught her. Kath swayed, biting her lip. "That fight took more out of me than I thought."

"Let me see."

"It's nothing." Kath shook her head. "The others may need help." Taking a steadying breath, she limped across the bloodied grass, pain lancing her left thigh. Gritting her teeth, she made her way toward Blaine and Danya, avoiding the thrashing hooves of Danya's mare. "Are you two hurt?"

Blaine leaned on his blue sword, a decapitated hellhound at his feet. Danya sat nearby, hugging the wolf, blood smeared on her face. Bryx had a tattered ear and a bloody gash along one flank, but he looked as if he'd survive. Danya hugged the wolf, a half-crazed look on her face. "The horses! They hurt! Can't you ease their pain!"

Duncan pulled his dirk. "I'll take care of the horses."

Kath nodded. "Where's Zith?"

The monk groaned, "Over here." He struggled to rise, his dark-blue robe torn to bloody shreds, a claw mark slashing his chest. "That beast almost had me." He looked at Kath, his face pale. "My thanks."

She nodded, relieved her throw had been in time. Sheathing her sword, she checked to make sure the amber pyramid and the gargoyle were both safe, and then grabbed her saddlebag and a water skin and began tending the monk. "What were those things?"

Zith grimaced as she cleaned the wounds on his chest. "Abominations."

"I've never seen anything like it."

"*Soul magic*," The monk spat the words, making the hand sign against evil. "The Mordant plies the worst sort of magic."

Quick as a dagger stroke, a squealing horse fell silent.

Zith hissed in pain as Kath poured a measure of brandy on his wounds. "Do you have another robe?"

He nodded, gritting his teeth.

"Good, because this one's slashed to rags." Kath tore strips from his robe, using them to bind his wounds.

A third horse fell silent. Duncan returned, striding through the long grass, silent as a shadow. He helped Zith to his feet. The monk leaned on his quarterstaff. They limped back to the others.

They found Blaine cleaning blood from his blue steel blade. The blond-haired knight seemed unscathed. He prodded a dead hellhound with his boot. "They're ugly but they die like any other beast."

Danya looked up, tears streaking her face. "I'm sorry I couldn't help." She shook her head, her voice breaking. "But those things clawed at my mind." She shuddered, hugging the wolf, her dark gaze full of sorrow. "The poor horses, they did not deserve such pain."

"Duncan gave them mercy." Kath handed Danya the water skin and then knelt, studying one of the dead beasts. Larger than a wolf, the shaggy fur was an ugly motley of tan and black, but the true horror was the head. Snout of a wolf, the curved teeth of a saber cat, and the cruel yellow eyes of a bird of prey, all combined into a single nightmare. She clutched the crystal dagger, her words a whisper. "By the nine hells, what are they?"

Danya answered, her voice grim. "It felt unclean, like something corrupted, twisted beyond the touch of nature."

Zith said, "Abomination."

Kath nodded, her voice full of dread. "It didn't fight like a beast. It knew to avoid the easy meat and go for the lead rider...almost as if it could *think*." She shivered. "Truly a hound loosed from hell." Kath realized it was the second time she'd been hunted by the Mordant's creatures. First the magic-sniffing goblin man and now the hellhounds, she did not like being prey.

Blaine sheathed his blue steel sword. "We haven't even reached the Mordant's domain and we've already lost most of the horses. Five riders, two horses, it will be a long walk either way. And Valin only knows what other nasty surprises await." He stared at Kath, a question in his gaze.

The horses were a major loss but they could not give up. "We bind our wounds and retrieve what we can from the horses." Unease pricked the back of her neck. "We'll head north. But we'd best leave before the scavengers come, before the ravens betray us."

Duncan stared north. "Too late."

His words froze her. "What?"

He pointed north. "Hunters follow the hounds."

Kath stared at the horizon, a cold hand gripping her stomach. A line of riders approached at a gallop, a hundred spears bristling against the sky. Their armor gleamed black and gold in the waning sunlight, *soldiers of the Mordant*. A horn blared, a call to arms. Death rode towards them.

8

The Mordant

The Dark Citadel thrust up from the land like a mailed fist. Built around a massive rock, the citadel's dark ramparts dominated the steppes. Black granite walls spiraled nine times around the central monolith, creating eight tiers of city streets crowned by the royal palace, a stone beehive swarming with slaves, servants, soldiers, and priests, all awaiting their rightful lord.

The Mordant smiled, surveying the seat of his power. Thousands had perished raising the tiered city, a marvel of human toil, but the true wonder lay in the foundation, in the secret heart of the monolithic rock. Buried in the ancient depths, a doorway opened to Darkness. Even leagues away, he could feel the Dark Lord's summons, a hungry pulse tugging at his soul, the same summons that had first drawn him to the monolith so many lifetimes ago.

Keen to reclaim his destiny, the Mordant urged his stallion to a gallop. Surging ahead of his entourage, he gloried in his youth and his vigor. A cold breeze blew from the west, a tang of sea salt heavy in the air. Seagulls roiled overhead, their forlorn cries heralding his return. Nearly invisible from the farmland, the ocean pounded against cliffs three hundred feet high, eating away at the land, an abrupt end to the northern steppes. The jagged coastline came within a few hundred feet of the Dark Citadel, the rocky cove providing access to the Western Ocean, a source of power and intrigue.

Five leagues to the east lay another wellspring of power, a triumph of an earlier lifetime. Wooden towers reared into the sky, perched on the edge of the pit like giant praying mantises. A remnant from the War of Wizards, the pit had proved an unexpected boon, providing a fertile breeding ground for a twisted army.

Centuries of toil and achievements surrounded him, his great grand design finally coming to fruition. The Mordant spurred his horse, a feeling of triumph simmering in his soul.

His gaze snapped to the citadel. The dark heart of the north called him home. He galloped across the remaining leagues, his long black cape streaming behind, the cold wind raking his blond hair.

A delegation of black-robed priests stood in the citadel's shadow. Keepers of ritual, the priests of the pentacle administered his city, as well as the Trials of Return. Reining his stallion to a halt, the Mordant studied their faces, all of them strangers, too young to remember his last lifetime.

His guards arrived in a thunder of hooves. Stern faces under dark helms, they formed a crescent of steel at his back. The Darkflamme snapped overhead, a forked banner of black silk writhing in the wind.

The Mordant eased his stallion forward, his words conforming to ancient ritual. "Death has once more been defeated. The Mordant returns to claim his throne."

A bearded bishop met his gaze. Leaning on a wooden staff tipped with a golden pentacle, he stared up at the Mordant, his face wary, his words full of ritual. "The Trials of Return will prove your claim...or see you *dead*." He waved his hand, summoning a priest holding a velvet pillow, a simple iron circlet nestled on velvet. "Dare to wear the na-Mordant's crown and your life will be forfeit if you fail."

The priest approached, holding the pillow like a holy offering.

The Mordant claimed the iron crown. Raising the circlet with both hands, he made his voice loud enough for all to hear. "*I am the Mordant reborn*." He crowned himself, settling the circlet on his brow. "By deeds and words I will prove my claim ere the sun sets this day."

The bishop raised his staff in benediction. "Let the Dark Lord's will be done."

The ritual completed, the Mordant flashed the cleric a confident smile. "Is everything prepared?"

"All according to ritual."

"And High Priest Gavis?"

"Awaits you on the top tier."

"Good." The Mordant wheeled his stallion toward the citadel. "Then let the Trials be finished." He spurred the stallion to a canter, hooves clattering on the long stone ramp. The citadel towered above, black banners streaming from crenellated ramparts. A square gatehouse straddled the ramp, the ironbound doors thrown open wide like the maw of a hungry beast. Soldiers crowded the ramparts, straining for a view.

The Mordant slowed his stallion to a stately prance, passing beneath the stone arch. Emerging from the gate's shadow, he entered the citadel to a triumphant roar. Trumpets blared and people cheered.

Young and old lined the cobblestone street, black-armored soldiers holding back the crush. In the center of the street stood four young pages burdened with baskets of fresh baked bread and pouches bulging with coins. By long-standing tradition, the Mordant's largess summoned the people to the Trials of Return.

Burdened with bread, the pages preceded the Mordant, tossing small loaves and copper coins to the waiting crowd. People surged forward, hands outstretched, grasping at the bounty. Spear-wielding soldiers held the crowd in check, keeping the street open.

The Mordant kept his stallion to a walk, studying his people. Faces lean with hunger stared up at him, fighting for crusts of bread and copper coins. Most looked half-starved, their clothing threadbare. Little had changed in the ninth tier. By design, the citadel's lowest level held society's dregs. Barely more than slaves yet they clung to their positions with a rabid ferocity. Stewed in their own misery, they fought to survive, fermenting the feral qualities the Mordant prized in his assassins. He nodded in approval, pleased that nothing had changed, all part of his grand dark design.

People cheered as he passed, reaching for the Mordant's bounty. Dancing in the street, they held loaves of bread aloft. A frenzied, festive feeling prevailed. The Mordant smothered a smile. By beginning each reign with a veneer of benevolence, he gave his people a leader to revere, a hope for a better life, a grand delusion that ensnared their loyalty. And all the while they blamed their misery on the priesthood, the ruthless administrators of the citadel's harsh laws, the cruel taskmasters who separated the people from their god-monarch. The Mordant laughed, enjoying the beauty of the delusion. Mortals were so easily deceived.

A young boy ducked between two solders, his gaze fixed on a fallen round of bread. Oblivious to the Mordant's warhorse, he darted toward the crusty loaf. Startled, the warhorse reared, lashing out with iron-shod hooves. The boy tripped and fell, cowering beneath the rearing horse. The Mordant yanked on the reins, forcing the stallion to settle, turning the horse away from the boy.

A guard grabbed the boy, slapping him across the face with a gauntleted hand.

"No!" The Mordant stayed the guard. "Give him a loaf of bread and return him to his mother. See that he is not harmed."

Saluting, the guard leaped to obey.

A roar of approval echoed through the street.

The Mordant smiled, another delusion of benevolence.

The procession resumed its stately march, slowly spiraling toward the upper tiers. Gatehouses divided each tier, but on this day, all the gates were thrown wide open. As the street spiraled upward, the Mordant rode from poverty into prosperity. Dirt and grime gave way to gleaming polish. Colors appeared in the crowd, crimson and sapphire and malachite, bright silks and warm furs replacing drab wools. Each tier had its purpose, from the lowly rabble, to the servants, the craftsmen, the soldiers, the armorers, the acolytes, the officers, and the priests, each according to their worth. By its very nature, the tiered city enforced a soul-numbing stagnation designed to feed the Dark Lord. Sons were condemned to the trade of their fathers and daughters were raised to bear more sons. The rare few who advanced beyond their birth station, did so by climbing on the backs of others. And above all, everyone sought the intercession of the Mordant, seeking a chance to vault above their station.

Shadows lengthened, cloaking the citadel in shade. The streets became steep, slowly spiraling to the palace. With each passing tier, the Mordant's largess changed. By the time he reached the top, the four pages threw coins of silver and gold. Even in the upper tiers, the people pushed and shoved, scrambling for every coin. Greed remained pervasive in the citadel, a mortal trait the Mordant encouraged.

Rounding the final bend, he found the way forward blocked by immense doors clad in gold reliefs, the gatehouse to the first tier. A flurry of trumpets announced his arrival. An honor guard snapped to attention, black banners fluttering in the wind. The Mordant nudged his horse toward the final gate.

Four times the height of a tall man, the golden doors displayed triumphs from his past lives. The cataclysm of Azreal, the creation of the Pit, the destruction of the Star Knights, the battle at Breanth, the raising of the Dark Citadel, the completion of the Gargoyle Gates. Victories, betrayals, feats of dark magic, the gates displayed the legacy of his past lives, all done for the glory of the Dark Lord. The Mordant smiled, knowing this lifetime promised to eclipse them all, the final culmination of age-old plans. Eager to begin, he made his voice a command. *The Mordant has returned. Open the god gate.*

A pair of black-robed priests slowly pushed the great doors open, revealing the wonders of the first tier.

Behind him, the crowd jostled for a view.

Dismounting, he threw the reins to a waiting page and strode beneath the shadowed archway.

An ambush of crossbowmen stepped from the shadows, their loaded weapons trained on his chest.

The Mordant stared at the soldiers, his arms held wide. The soldiers lowered their crossbows and sank to their knees. Had he dared defy the laws of the citadel by riding a horse through the golden gates, they would have skewered him with quarrels, proof of an imposter, another deadly test.

Walking past the soldiers, he strode to the heart of the first tier, to the great circular courtyard. Fashioned from silvery granite, the stones of the courtyard were inlayed with runes carved from black marble. Written in a language long forgotten, the runes spiraled out from the center, imbuing the citadel with dark cantrips of endurance and strength. At the very heart of the runic spiral, the peak of the monolith thrust up to the sky, revealing the dark doorway to below.

The Mordant stared at the shadowy doorway, breathing deep, feeling the rush of Dark power, the age old summons. He bowed low, his words hushed, "Soon, my Lord" and then he turned and strode across the courtyard.

The royal palace dominated the far side, a crescent-shaped edifice made of gilded columns and black marble. Burnished bright by the fading sunlight, the twisted columns glowed golden.

Arrayed in all of their finery, the citadel's elite stood on the palace steps, a bejeweled spectacle of bright silks and polished armor. High priests, generals, and stewards, the mortals who risked the most by his ascension, stood ready to witness the Trials. Most yearned to watch an imposter die a horrible death, remaining secure in their borrowed power. Staring down at him, they kept their faces stone-closed, their eyes wary, but they could not hide their souls. Darkness rolled down the steps in waves. The Mordant breathed deep, sorting through the tangled scents. Most reeked of boundless ambition, ruthless cruelty, and cold-blooded murder, the common tools of statecraft in the citadel...but underneath the petty acts of Darkness, he caught a hint of rarer fare, the taint of treachery...and a tantalizing thread of fear. Only a rare few had the wisdom to fear, mostly the graybeards, the ones who remembered.

The Mordant hid his smile. Fear was useful; it led to obedience. He searched the faces of the elite, making note of those he'd known in his last lifetime. Old and gray, the few who survived were ravaged by time. So many more were missing, conquered by death or the ambitions of younger men; the politics of the Dark Citadel were not for the faint of heart.

He breathed deep, taking their measure. Of all the flavors of Darkness, treachery spiked the Mordant's attention like no other. He smelled it now, staining the steps of the palace. More than a few souls carried the taint...but it swirled the strongest around one man, the High Priest, the keeper of rituals, the administrator of the citadel, the one man who ruled in the Mordant's absence. Dressed in rich robes of the blackest velvet, High Priest Gavis wore a tall conical hat, a golden chain of linked pentacles around his neck, a staff encrusted with black diamonds held in his right hand. A robust man in his mid-fifties, he had long auburn hair, a hawksbill nose, and a majestic beard. Gavis had done well for himself. At the time of the Mordant's last death, he'd been nothing more than a freshly sworn acolyte, newly dedicated to the priesthood. Wielding a sin-dark soul full of boundless ambition, Gavis had climbed far and fast, but now he teetered on the knife-edge of treason.

The Mordant studied the elite, sensing the swirling undercurrents of threats and possibilities. Clearly the young needed a lesson in fear, a demonstration of his power, another reason for the Trials of Return. The Mordant turned a cold stare to the High Priest, his voice ringing with challenge. "I am the Mordant reborn. I come before you to complete the Trials of Return and claim the Ebony Throne."

"We hold your life in our hands." The High Priest made the sign of the pentacle with his staff. "Let the Trials begin. May the Dark Lord judge the truth of your claim, for no imposter shall ever rule the Ebony Throne."

Trumpets blared and drums thundered, announcing the start of the Trials. Thousands streamed through the golden gate into the courtyard, soldiers from his entourage mingling with citizens of the upper tiers, come to witness the spectacle. An honor guard formed a crescent at his back, the Darkflamme snapped overhead. He flicked a glance at their faces, knowing they'd take his head if he failed, or be among the first to swear their loyalty if he succeeded.

Turning his back on the crowd, the Mordant stared up at the palace steps.

The High Priest gestured and a second trumpet sounded a volley of notes.

The elite of the citadel parted, opening a path to the palace doors. Six black-robed priests emerged, each pair bearing a coffin-shaped box. Made of silver embossed with runes, the three coffins were placed in front of the Mordant. The priests made a ceremony of unlocking the boxes, slowly opening the lids.

Lined with purple velvet, each box contained three staffs, all of them made of the blackest iron. At first glance, they seemed much the same. Six-feet in height, each was topped with a five-fingered iron claw clutching a red crystal. The crystals' color and facets varied slightly, as did the rune markings inscribed on the long shafts, but the true difference lay in their hidden power.

The High Priest gestured toward the boxes. "Choose correctly or die."

The Mordant stepped toward the boxes. Nine staffs to choose from. Three resonated with power...but only one called to him, the most treasured focus in his hoard of magic. The Staff of Pain sang to the Darkness in his soul. The Mordant made his choice, the red crystal glinting as he lifted it into the fading sunlight. His hands caressed the rune-carved shaft, his blood thrumming with Darkness, forging an instant bond.

Footsteps whispered from behind.

The Mordant whirled, summoning the staff's power.

A guard lunged, his sword raised for a killing strike.

The Mordant unleashed the staff, loosing a burst of pain.

The soldier froze in mid-stride, his face contorting in agony. His sword clattered to the pavement. Crumpling to his knees, his hands scrabbled at his groin as if seeking a dagger that did not exist.

The Mordant twisted the power, deepening the torment.

Screaming, the attacker writhed at the Mordant's feet. *"Please, lord!"* His back arched, his head nearly touching his buttocks, and then he fell still, a trickle of blood dribbling from his open mouth.

The Mordant swayed, his vision suddenly blurred. Leaning on the staff, he struggled to hide his weakness, his new body not yet accustomed to so much magic. Taking a deep breath, he turned to face the High Priest, his voice a low growl. "Treason can be a lesson. Does your ambition outweigh your sense of survival?"

The High Priest did not even blanch.

The Mordant smiled, this one had steel nerves. Gavis would make a fine High Priest...or a fresh corpse.

"The Ebony Throne is not *yet* yours." The High Priest gestured and five men were brought forward. All five wore the black and gold armor of citadel guards, but their faces were worn by age, their hair faded to varying shades of gray. They dropped to their knees, their heads bowed.

"It is said that the Mordant can weigh a man's soul with a single glance." The High Priest gestured to the five. "One of these carries scars from the past, name him and his deed or fail the fifth Trial."

The Mordant stepped towards the five. A single breath told the tale. The fourth kneeler reeked of fear, a special fear that few mortals lived to bear. He pointed toward his choice. "This man served as a guard for the Door."

Soldiers rushed forward to grab the Mordant's choice. They stripped him of armor and clothes, till he stood bare-chested in the waning light. The proof was writ across his chest for all to see. Tattooed above his heart was the rune of the Dark Lord. But unlike all other tattoos, this one was inked by dark magic, inscribed *beneath* the guard's skin.

Darkness called to Darkness.

The Mordant stretched out his hand, holding his palm a foot above the man's chest. "You witnessed my death in the Dark Chamber...and now I've come to witness yours."

The old soldier stared wide-eyed, but the others held him captive.

"*Salra cathra abendt.*" The Mordant called the rune.

Shuddering, the soldier's face convulsed with fear. Sweat erupted across his skin...and then his chest began to bulge outward, as if something sought to escape his flesh. He screamed in agony, but the others held him rigid.

The Mordant flexed his power, calling the dark rune. "*Salra cathra abendt.*"

Blood erupted from the man's chest, like a spear thrust from within. The dark rune burst from beneath the guard's skin, flying to the Mordant's hand...and with it came the beating heart.

Screams ripped through the crowd. Women swooned, soldiers quailed, and the elite drew back. Fear and terror claimed the courtyard.

The Mordant breathed deep, such intoxicating scents, such an important lesson. He raised the blood soaked heart aloft. Revealed by the power of Darkness, his voice thundered, "I *am* the Mordant Reborn!"

Behind him, soldiers and the low-born clattered to the ground in homage...but the elite were made of sterner stuff. They shrank back, their faces pale, but they did not cower. One man pushed to the front, a hatched-faced general in gilded armor. Tall and imposing, the general made his way down the steps, daring to approach. Despite the assault of age, the Mordant recognized his face. His body was still warrior-lean but his hair had gone silver and his face bore a ragged scar running from his right eye to his chin. Thumping his fist to his breastplate, he bowed low. "I always knew you'd return, Lord."

Pleased by the show of faith, the Mordant said, "General Haith, it has been a long time."

"A lifetime, lord, yet I never doubted."

"Come and stand with your sword at my back. Your faith has earned you that privilege." The Mordant turned his stare to the High Priest. "Where will you stand, Gavis?"

"The Trials are not yet complete."

"How many Dark miracles will you need before you believe?"

"Only as many as prescribed by the Trials."

Such a careful answer, the Mordant nodded. "So be it."

Black-robed priests scurried forward to claim the heart and clean the blood from the Mordant's hand. Other attendants removed the ruined body, blood sopping onto the granite pavement. One attendant knelt, using his robe to wipe at the blood.

"Leave the blood. The stones will drink it."

Blanching, the attendant scuttled away.

The Mordant faced his high priest. "Finish it."

Gavis thumped his staff against the stone courtyard, his voice ringing with command. "Bring forth the final Trial."

Once more, the doors of the palace opened, disgorging a gray-haired bishop wearing a flowing black robe and a black miter. He bore a small golden casket aloft. Descending the stairs, he opened the casket, offering its contents to the High Priest.

Making the sign of the pentacle, Gavis addressed the waiting crowd. "The Dark Lord is the final Trial, for no imposter will ever sit on the Ebony Throne." He reached into the casket and withdrew a single shard of crystal, eight inches in length and straight as a dagger. "By the light of this sacred crystal, the truth will be known." Gripping the shard in his fist, he raised it so all could see. "In the hands of a mortal, the crystal remains dormant. But in the hands of the true Mordant, it will glow bright red, revealing the Dark Lord's favor." He turned so all could witness the quiescent crystal, a pale shard of milk white, unsullied by red. "Let the Dark Lord's will be known." He extended the crystal toward the Mordant, offering it on his open palm.

The Mordant stifled a secret smile, enjoying the irony. A tool of his oldest enemies now served to protect his throne. Steeped in magic, the Dahlmar crystal was used by the Kiralynn Order to detect the reborn. Taken from a captured monk, the Mordant had long ago subverted the crystal to his own use, making it part the Trials of Return.

He reached for the shard and raised it high. "Let the truth be known."

The crystal blazed to life, glowing with the red light of Hell.

Compelled by the crystal's magic, the Mordant's eyes revealed his true nature. Like twin lanterns, his gaze filled with a fiery red glow, revealing the oldest of the harlequins. "I *am* the Mordant reborn." He turned toward the crowd, his voice booming across the courtyard. "The power of the Dark Lord flows in me. *Kneel before me and obey!*"

Thousands fell to their knees. Lying prostrate on the cold stones, they groveled before him.

The Mordant turned his fiery gaze back to the citadel's elite. All sank to their knees...except for the High Priest. Unlike the others, Gavis had tasted the rulership of the citadel. Sometimes stewards needed to die before they were deposed. "Which will it be, Gavis, service or death?"

The stiff-backed priest slowly sank to his knees. "Yours to command."

"A wise choice." The Mordant returned the crystal to his High Priest, extinguishing the red light. "This will be a glorious lifetime." Climbing the palace stairs, he turned to accept the adoration of the crowd, the ruler of all he surveyed.

9

Katherine

Death galloped towards them. Still leagues away, the soldiers rode in disciplined ranks, bristling with spears. Hunters following the hellhounds, the threat of steel chased the savage bite of fangs. Kath guessed they numbered a hundred or more, too many to doubt the outcome.

Duncan stood beside her, his voice calm. "Fight or flee?"

Kath shook her head. "With only two horses, we won't get far. And there's nowhere to hide in the grasslands." She shuddered, recalling tales of torture from the north. "I'd rather die fighting." She stared at each of her companions, seeing her own grim resolve etched on their faces. Even Danya, the girl who never carried a weapon, gave a solemn nod. Kath gripped her sword hilt. "Then we fight. Let's use what time we have."

She studied the steppes, cursing the flat openness, realizing the slain horses offered their only cover. Two of them lay close together, forming a rough vee. "We'll make our stand here, using the dead horses as a bulwark. Get your weapons. We have little enough time to prepare."

Ignoring the pain in her left thigh, she hurried to recover her throwing axes, not bothering to wipe the blood from the blades. Next, she approached the sorrel stallion, searching her saddlebag for the chainmail shirt at the bottom, carried all the way from Queen Liandra's kingdom. Burnished bright, the chainmail gleamed in the sun, but what good would it do against a hundred spears? Banishing the grim thought, she pulled on the quilted jerkin and then shrugged into the chainmail. Her harness with her throwing axes went over the chainmail, her shoulders tightening beneath the added weight. From the rear of the saddle, she unbuckled a small octagonal shield she'd found in Cragnoth's armory. Lastly, she unwrapped Sir Cardemir's princely gift, setting the gleaming garnet helm on her head. Girt for battle, she stripped the saddle from the stallion and beat his rump with the flat of her sword. "Run!" Snorting, the warhorse sprinted south. She prayed he'd make it home to the Octagon; the valiant steed deserved a better end than death in the god-cursed steppes.

Armed for war, she had one more thing to attend to. Reaching into her deepest pocket, she removed the amber pyramid. To the victors went the spoils, but she dared not let the Mordant claim the Quickner. Kath scanned the trampled grass for a hiding place. Knowing pockets and saddlebags would be searched, she knelt by one of the dead horses. Taking a last look at the small amber focus, she pried open the horse's mouth.

A shadow fell across her. She looked up, meeting the monk's stare. "You said the amber pyramid should never fall to the Mordant."

Zith nodded, his face solemn.

"Then I'll give it to death." She shoved the pyramid into the horse's mouth. "Let the gods and the ravens fight over it."

A muffled thunder came from the north, a warning that the enemy drew near.

Wiping her hands on the grass, she joined her companions.

Duncan gave her a lingering look. "Armor becomes you."

Kath felt her face flush...but the pounding hooves intruded, drawing her back to the threat at hand. "We'll make our stand behind the dead horses."

They stood behind the vee formed by two dead horses, a pitiful bulwark but it was all they had.

Blaine unsheathed his great blue sword.

Duncan nocked a black-fletched arrow, three full quivers tied to his belt. He stared at Kath, his voice steady. "They're almost within range." He quirked a half smile. "Shall I let them know we intend to fight?"

She looked at her companions, giving each of them a last chance to retreat. "There's one horse left."

Blaine hefted his sapphire blue sword, sunlight glinting on his silver surcoat, looking like a hero of old. "What else are blue swords for?"

She gripped his arm, grateful for his lighthearted bravado. Releasing the knight, she turned to the others, a question in her stare.

Zith leaned on his quarterstaff, his voice grim. "The gods' willing; I'll see this to the end."

Danya stood further apart, a dagger awkwardly clutched in her right hand, her left hand on the wolf. She gave Kath the smallest of nods, her face pale but determined. The wolf pressed close to the girl, issuing a throaty growl.

Pride rushed through Kath. "So be it." She turned to Duncan, memorizing the lines of his face, wishing they had more time. "Make every arrow count."

He smiled, his voice full of meaning. "And every sword stroke." He pulled the bowstring to a kiss, a fluid motion, and then released.

A black-fletched arrow arced into the steel-gray sky. It soared for a small eternity...and then plummeted into the spears, a declaration of war.

A cry erupted from the enemy.

"Now they know we have teeth." Kath's hand tightened on her sword hilt, determined to make a difference.

Beside her, Duncan pulled and released, a thrum of arrows arcing skyward, a steady rain of death.

A horn sounded and the dark riders spread out. A long line of spears swept south across the grasslands, a scythe of death.

Kath watched them come, their lances leveled. "If anyone has a brilliant idea, now would be a good time." She looked at Zith, half-hoping the monk had some secret magic, but he shook his head, his face grim, his hands white-knuckled on his quarterstaff.

Danya moaned and sank to her knees, her face ghost pale, her eyes glazed, the dagger discarded on the ground.

Kath felt sorry for the wolf-girl, but there was nothing she could do. She raised her sword to the heavens, shouting loud enough for the gods to hear. *"For Honor and the Octagon!"*

The wolf loosed a howl, as if echoing her cry.

Blaine lifted his blue sword, "Honor and the Octagon!"

Hoof beats thundered from the north, a long line of death. Details became clear, gold pentacles on black armor, stern faces beneath dark helms, black battle banners snapping in the wind. She watched them come, a dark wave racing across the golden grassland, a destiny of spears.

Duncan's arrows thrummed a constant rhythm, poking holes in the long line, like bees stinging a raging lion...but the beast kept coming.

Kath counted their numbers, still too many. The ground shook with the threat of hooves. A cold hand seized Kath's stomach, the grim certainty of impending death. She gripped her sword hilt, sending a prayer to Valin, hoping her courage would not fail.

Thunder pulsed beneath her feet, a looming wall of spears. The enemy drew close, a tidal wave of death.

Kath set her shield, bracing for the clash, sweat dripping from her forehead.

Then the screams started.

Squeals of terror erupted from the horses, a chaos of thrashing hooves. The disciplined line shattered. Warhorses bucked and bellowed, throwing their riders. A wild madness gripped the horses. Rearing, they turned on their fallen riders, lashing out with iron-shod hooves. Kath watched as a foam-flecked stallion trampled his rider, crushing the man's head like a ripe melon. The rider lay still as death, yet the horse kept stamping, churning the body to a slushy red gore. The grisly scene repeated across the battlefield. Enraged warhorses fought like demons on four legs, biting and kicking, a frenzy of hooves slashing in all directions, pounding their riders to a bloody pulp. Soldiers fought against their own mounts, a desperate slash of steel. Hamstrung horses bellowed in pain, struggling to stand. Screams of the dying mingled with the squeals of the maimed. The grasslands became a killing field, a blood-soaked horror.

Kath and her companions gaped in shock, held spellbound by the carnage.

A battle horn sounded, a wild trill of notes.

The slaughter began to slow, the numbers thinned by death. A stallion reared, bellowing a challenge. A lone officer answered, raising his sword in defiance. A straggle of soldiers formed a circle, fighting back to back, a desperate bristle of spears holding the horses at bay.

Quick as summer lightning, the madness fled. Blood-spattered horses stamped and snorted, milling across the field but they did not fight. A foam-flecked stallion reared and whinnied, issuing a clarion call. The remaining horses answered. Together, they fled into the steppes, galloping as if chased by hell-damned demons.

A harsh stillness settled over the battlefield. Mangled bodies covered the field, blood and gore soaking the steppes. Only seventeen soldiers remained standing, seventeen out of a hundred, all of them wounded. Surrounded by a sea of carnage, the survivors turned their weapons toward the companions. Issuing a guttural growl, they threw down a gauntlet of hate.

For a moment, neither side moved.

Duncan's voice broke the spell. "Finish them." Lifting his longbow, he loosed a shaft. His arrow whistled straight for the enemy. A lone scream marked another death.

The enemy charged, releasing a blood-curdling yell.

"Stand your ground! Let them come to us!" Kath waited, letting the enemy come, letting the arrows do their work.

They charged like berserkers, racing across the bloody ground. Arrows thinned their numbers, but still they came, screaming a wild howl of vengeance.

Kath reached for a throwing axe, waiting till she could see the hatred in their eyes. She picked a worthy target. A big brute towered above the rest, wielding a sword in each hand, his face a snarl of rage. She threw her axe and reached for the second. Two whirls of steel flew towards the brute. He deflected the first, but the second took him in the face, one less enemy for her sword.

The charging line was nearly upon them, black-fletched arrows sprouting from shields.

Kath unsheathed her sword. Crouched behind a dead horse, she hurled a prayer to Valin.

Five strides and the battle was joined. The first blow struck her shield, a mighty sword stroke that nearly drove her to the ground. Struggling to keep her footing, she dodged sideways. Her shield arm went numb but she kept her sword raised. Seeing an opening, she lunged under the man's guard, stabbing at a weak point in his armor. A sword blocked her thrust. Steel clanged against steel, locked in a dance of death.

Beside her, Blaine bellowed, *"For the Octagon!"* but Kath kept her stare on her opponent, her world narrowing to the clash of swords.

Parry and thrust, she fell into the wild rhythm of war. More than once, the chainmail saved her life, deflecting a fatal blow. The wolf fought beside her, snapping and snarling, darting in to hamstring her opponent. As the soldier's leg crumpled, she lunged for the kill. Wrenching her sword free, she pivoted to face the next threat. Another sword sliced toward her face. She ducked and parried, striking the enemy across the face with her shield. The fight became a blur, a flurry of sword thrusts. Her muscles began to ache, her lungs gasped for breath, locked in a desperate struggle.

The footing became treacherous, the ground slick with blood. The battle seemed never-ending, a test of endurance. The chainmail weighed her down. Her sword arm ached. Her left thigh throbbed with pain. Wiping the sweat from her eyes, she parried a sword thrust but lost her footing, slipping to the ground. The soldier leered above, a big man with a beard, moving in for the kill...but a blue sword took his head in one mighty stroke. Headless, the body staggered for two steps then toppled at her feet, releasing a gush of blood.

Stunned, Kath lay on the bloody ground, gasping for breath. A man screamed and another yelled a curse and then the clash of steel fell silent. She gripped her sword, looking for the enemy. Struggling to rise, she slipped in the bloody muck.

Blaine loomed over her, offering his hand, bloodstains on his surcoat.

"Is it over?"

He nodded, pulling her to her feet.

Weariness hit her like a war hammer. She could hardly stand.

Blaine steadied her. "Are you harmed?"

Everything ached, especially her left thigh, but she was alive. "I'll live." She gave him a weak smile. Struggling for breath, she tried to make sense of the blood smeared field, a nightmare from hell. The sounds hit her first, wounded men crying for mercy, the faint nicker of dying horses. Bodies lay everywhere, the dying next to the dead, men next to horses, a bloody swath of carnage. Kath shuddered, amazed to be alive...but then a new fear seized her. "Duncan? The others?" She gripped Blaine's arm, terrified of the answer.

"This way." He turned her around, leading her back toward the vee of dead horses.

Limping, she clutched his arm, amazed that she'd come so far into the killing field. Her memory was a fog, full of blood and steel. Kath shook her head, struggling to clear the fog of war. But then she saw him, broad shoulders in black leather, kneeling with his back toward her. "*Duncan!*"

She half-ran, half-staggered toward him, needing to know he was unharmed.

He turned, a smile lighting his tanned face. "Kath."

His voice was a balm, easing a weight from her heart. But then she saw the blood...and the body lying on the ground. She gasped, "Will he live?"

Duncan's face turned grim. "That remains to be seen."

Her heart hammered. "What can I do?"

"I need a fire, two strips of leather, flasks of wine, and some blankets."

Blaine said, "I'll get the blankets."

Kath nodded. "I'll look for the rest." She turned to survey the battlefield. Their packhorse was long lost, sacrificed in the mad flight from the hellhounds, but the field was strewn with the enemy's slain horses, a battlefield of supplies waiting to be harvested. She sheathed her sword and walked out into the killing field, searching for dead horses with fat saddlebags. Finding a likely candidate, she knelt, fumbling with the buckles, cursing her fingers for their slowness. Slicing the strap with her dagger, she tumbled the contents onto the bloody grass. Searching through the jumble, she tried to ignore the personal items, preferring to think of the slain soldiers as enemies instead of men.

A hand grabbed her ankle, yanking her off balance.

Kath spied a flash of steel as she fell. Kicking sideways, she knocked the dagger from his hand. The ground hit hard, stealing her breath. Gasping, she reached for her sword but the soldier rolled on top, his weight crushing her down. He pinned her sword hand with his knee and wrapped his hands around her throat. A veteran with gray in his beard, he glared at her, his face contorted in hate. "*Die, witch!*"

She bucked beneath him, trying to win free, but his weight was too much. His hands tightened to a deadly choke. She pounded him with her left fist, but he only sneered, his hands squeezing harder. Desperate for air, she stretched her left arm, reaching for a gleam of steel.

His rank breath hissed in her face. "You *bewitched* the horses. You *murdered* my men."

Darkness threatened. Her hand reached the dagger. She plunged it into his neck, all the way to the hilt. His eyes widened in surprise. She jerked the dagger free, releasing a fountain of hot blood. His hands went to his neck, as if he could hold back the tide of life. Gasping, she pushed him away, and rolled to her feet.

Blaine rushed to her side, his blue sword in his hands. "Are you hurt?"

Kath struggled to keep her voice steady. "Be careful of the dead."

He nudged the dying soldier with his boot and then swung his great sword in an overhead arc. Blue steel descended in a rush, severing the head. "Good advice."

Shuddering, she took a deep breath and resumed the search, careful to make sure the nearest bodies were truly dead. Keeping the dagger in her fist, she ransacked the saddlebags. It took six horses before she found everything she needed.

She carried the load back to Duncan. "I found a surgeon's set of tools." Unwrapping the leather bundle, she displayed a set of sharp knives and bone crackers, instruments fit for a torturer.

"Good. I'll need them." He sent a passing glance toward her but then his eyes widened, staring at her blood drenched chainmail. "Are you hurt?"

"One of the dead got rowdy."

He studied her face and then nodded, reaching for a flask of wine. "I need a fire."

Zith moaned in pain.

Kath shuddered, afraid of losing another companion. "Where's Danya?"

Duncan's voice was weary. "She seems unharmed, no sign of any wound, but I could not wake her." He shrugged. "The monk needs our help or he'll surely die."

"I'll start the fire." Numb with worry, she ripped up fists full of dry grass, using her dagger to dig a shallow pit. One of the dead horses had carried a bundle of fagots, a stroke of good luck. She retraced her steps, dragging the bundle back to Duncan. Stacking the wood in the bottom of the pit, she added bits of dried grass for tinder and used a flint to strike a spark. It was the first fire they'd had in many days. Kath stared at the flames. "A beacon for our enemies."

"It can't be helped." Duncan worked to staunch the flow of blood.

She nodded. "What now?"

"I've tried to get some wine into him but it won't be enough." He set a dagger in the fire, placing the blade in the heart of the flames. "Get a stick for him to bite on, and keep it in his mouth." He looked at Blaine. "Do your best to hold him still."

They moved into position. Kath cradled the monk's head in her lap, working the stick into his mouth, while Blaine pinned his shoulders down. The wound was wicked. Splintered bone protruded from the torn flesh of his left arm, only a strip of muscle holding the hand to the forearm. Kath stared at the wound, knowing it could well cost his life.

Duncan doused the wound with wine.

Zith writhed in pain, a muffled scream.

Kath held the stick in place, her stomach churning.

Duncan selected a knife from the surgeon's tools. "Hold him still."

Kath looked away, unable to watch.

The monk bucked and screamed, his gaze wild, his face ashen.

Duncan hissed, "Keep him still!" the rasp of a blade cutting bone.

Blaine pressed the monk's shoulders into the ground while Kath held his head. A scream bubbled from the monk's throat...and then he lay still. Duncan finished cutting, discarding the severed hand in the flames. The fire snapped and sizzled, releasing the stench of burnt flesh.

"And now to seal the wound." Duncan retrieved the dagger from the flames, the blade glowing cherry-red.

Kath closed her eyes, sending a prayer to Valin.

Hot steel hissed against flesh. Kath's stomach roiled, but mercifully the monk never woke.

"It is done." Duncan sounded weary to the bone. "Now it is up to the gods."

Unable to keep the bile down, Kath staggered away from her friends. Kneeling in the grass, she bent double as her stomach convulsed. The horror of the day swept over her, so much blood, so much death. She heaved till her stomach was empty, and then lay spent in the grass, too tired to move.

The sun set in a blaze of red, a bloody sky for a bloody day. The moans of the dying fell silent, muted by death or the mercy of a dagger. Weariness claimed her. She lay on her back, searching for the first star, for a ray of hope in the darkening sky.

"Are you well?"

She hadn't heard him approach, a shadow in black leathers. Embarrassed to be seen wallowing in her own stink, she tried to rise, but the chainmail weighed her down.

Duncan knelt beside her, his hands gentle. "Let me help." He eased the harness for her throwing axes from her shoulders and then helped her out of the chainmail. She sighed, relieved to be free of the weight. He pulled her to her feet. Pain lanced through her left leg. She bit back a scream. Her left leg crumpled under her weight. Duncan caught her, a pillar of strength. "Are you hurt?"

Suddenly slick with sweat, Kath shuddered. "One of the god-cursed hellhounds clawed my thigh. I'll be all right." A strangled laugh bubbled out of her. "Was it only this morning that we fought the hounds?"

"A hell of a day," he lifted her into his arms, "and a lifetime ago."

He carried her back to the fire, a single blaze holding back the night chill. The others surrounded the fire pit. Zith lay swathed in blankets, pale as death, but at least he slept. Blaine lay on the far side of the blaze, huddled next to Danya, his arms wrapped around the dark-haired girl.

Duncan whispered, "Is she awake?"

Blaine shook his head, his face lined with worry. "She hasn't moved or made a sound since the battle." He tucked a blanket under her chin. "She's pale as a ghost and cold as death but she still breathes."

The wolf whined, burrowing next to the girl.

"Keep her warm. Perhaps she'll wake with the dawn." He eased Kath down onto a bedroll. "Now let me see this wound of yours." He pulled her boots off and then used a dagger to split the leg of her pants, peeling the leather away from the wound.

Kath gasped with pain, surprised by the ugliness of the wound. Five claw marks ran the length of her thigh, puffy and raw, surrounded by bruised skin.

Duncan hissed, "You fought on this?"

"There wasn't much of a choice." She shrugged. "Besides, it didn't hurt so much before."

"Well it's going to hurt now. Those claw marks are shallow but they have to be cleaned." He handed her a flask. "Have a swig of this, but don't drink it all."

She took a sip and almost choked, liquid fire burning down her throat.

"More."

She tipped the flask and forced herself to swallow, tears crowding her eyes.

"Good." He took the flask and handed her a strip of leather. "Bite on this."

She tried to make light of it. "At least the scars will be interesting." She bit the leather and closed her eyes. The strap tasted foul, almost as bad as the liquor.

Agony exploded in her thigh, a searing sting. She arched her back, biting the leather, fighting a scream. Pain pulsed through her, seeming to last for an eternity, but then it faded to a dull ache. Spitting out the leather, she lay still, breathing hard, drenched in sweat.

Duncan tore long strips from a blanket, doused them in brandy and bound the wound. "Now let me see your arm."

She tried to sit up but her head spun. "My arm?"

"You've got a sword cut on your right arm but it doesn't look deep."

She stared at the shallow cut. "I never noticed." She lay back and let him work, staring up at the night sky, too many clouds to see the stars. His hands were gentle but she hissed when he cleaned the cut. "Where did you learn to do this?"

"Growing up in the Deep Green, you see a lot of wounds from clashes with the white eyes." He shrugged. "We all learned."

Prejudice again. She regretted the question.

"Are you hungry?" He finished binding the cut.

"No." She closed her eyes, remembering the gore of the battlefield. "Not after today."

"Tea then." He crushed leaves into two mugs, lifted a kettle from the fire and poured, releasing a billow of steam.

She struggled to sit up, wrapping her hands around the mug, grateful for the warmth and the soothing taste. They sipped in silence, sitting inches apart, heavy with thought. The truth of the day hit hard. "We should have died today."

"Yes."

In her mind's eye, she saw warhorses running amok, trampling bodies beneath iron-shod hooves. "Their horses became demons, death on four legs."

He nodded, his voice a whisper. "The power of a Beastmaster revealed."

A shiver raced down her spine. She glanced over at Danya but the wolf-girl lay still as death. Kath shook her head, her words a whisper. "They fought like something possessed." Images of the battlefield clashed in her mind. "They didn't just kill, they destroyed." Shuddering, she made the hand sign against evil. "Little wonder Beastmasters are so feared."

"She saved us all."

Kath stared across the fire at Danya's pale face. "Just so"

"And now we have to protect her."

Something in his voice caught at her heart, a warning she did not want to hear. "What do you mean?"

"There were survivors. Some of the soldiers ran."

She nodded, afraid to follow his logic.

"They must be hunted down and killed." He raised a hand forestalling her argument. "Tales of this battle can never reach the Mordant." He lowered his voice. "Five stood against a hundred. It is the stuff of legends."

She shivered, feeling the touch of the gods.

"The Mordant is sure to see the magic behind the defeat." Duncan leaned toward her, his voice a whisper. "What will the Mordant do to claim such a power?"

Her mind balked at the question.

"If word reaches the Mordant, all the might of the north will be arrayed against a small band of five."

Her heart thundered. "I'll go with you. We'll hunt them together."

"My Lioness." He gave her a slow smile. "Your courage is without measure but with a wounded leg you will never keep up. And besides, the others will need you." Firelight danced on his face, his golden cat-eye glowing in the dark, his difference and his strength. "This task is mine." He leaned toward her, his voice soft. "You know I am the one to do this."

The fire snapped, a spray of sparks. "I don't want to lose you."

"You will never lose me." His hand cupped her face. "My wife."

She leaned into his touch. "Promise?"

Fingers brushed her lips as if to seal the words. "Promise."

His hand withdrew and she felt bereft.

Duncan stared at her. "What will you do tomorrow? Will you go north or south?"

Kath rocked back, ambushed by the question. She hadn't thought beyond surviving the day. "I don't know."

"You have to decide. I need to know how to find you."

She tried to concentrate, pushing past the weariness of battle. "It seems hopeless to go north." She shook her head. "Yet to go south is to give up, to admit to defeat, when the whole of Erdhe is at stake." She stared at his mismatched eyes, looking for answers. "We've come too far to give up." It was as much a statement as a question.

He nodded. "Then you'll go north."

The surety of his words convinced her. "Into the north." She nodded. "And the gods will just have to help."

He smiled. "My Lioness."

She swayed, suddenly dizzy, as if the decision had robbed the last of her strength.

"But now you should sleep." He helped her into her bedroll, tucking the blanket around her shoulders, his hands gentle. And then he surprised her, lying next to her, pulling her close. She nestled against him, her head on his shoulder, surrounded by warmth and the smell of leather. "I don't want you to go."

"I know." He brushed a wisp of hair away from her face, tucking it behind her ear.

She pressed her face against his chest, wanting the night to last forever, but she had to ask. "When will you leave?"

"Before the dawn. The night is my ally."

The truth was cruel, a sword at her heart. She sighed and held him close, listening to the steady rhythm of his heartbeat, wanting the moon to stop its trek across the sky. But her own body betrayed her. Weariness claimed her, stealing the night. Exhausted, she fell into a dreamless sleep.

10

Duncan

An eerie stillness filled the night, as if the spirits of the slain hovered close. Plagued by worries, Duncan eased from the bedroll, careful not to wake Kath. He tucked the blanket around her shoulders, relieved that she slept. The other companions lay still as death, felled by exhaustion. Stretching, Duncan shrugged off his own weariness, knowing the battle could still be lost. He reached for his longbow, hung a full quiver on his belt and strode towards the killing field.

Clouds hid the moon, a pale smudge in the midnight sky, but there was more than enough light for his golden eye. He walked among the dead, reading the signs. Faces stared up at him, frozen in masks of horror. Horses lay twisted and broken, impaled on spears. Mangled bodies littered the grassland, torn apart and trampled to a sea of gore. He shook his head at the carnage. So many dead, a hundred defeated by five, a slaughter written in blood, yet all the dead wore the same armor, bore the same foul symbol. The truth was easy to read, too easy. The battlefield screamed of magic, a truth that could damn them all. Urgency gnawed at his mind; the survivors needed to be hunted down and killed, stopping the tale before it spread. He shivered feeling the hand of fate, knowing this was his task.

A shadow in dark leathers, he prowled the killing field, reading the fall of trampled grasses. Sorting a confusion of footprints, and telltale signs of blood, Duncan searched for his prey. The first trail was easy to spot, three men cutting a fresh swath through the grasses, fleeing northwest, at least one of them wounded. They ran in a wild panic, flailing through the waist-high grass, leaving a trail a blind man could follow. But the second trail was more subtle, obscured by hoof prints, a hint of blood giving it away. Crouching low, Duncan studied the signs. The second group was smart, retracing the trampled path of the charging horses. An occasional boot mark imprinted the hoof prints, proving men on foot traveled north instead of south. The cavalcade of iron-shod hooves made the trail hard to detect and harder still to read but Duncan persisted.

Needing to know their numbers, he loped along the trampled grass, crouching now and then to check for signs, looking for differences in the boot prints. He backtracked twice to make sure, cursing the answer written in the ground. Six perhaps seven men traveled north at a jog. Two groups fled the battlefield...heading in two different directions. The task would be harder than he thought, but there was no one else to do it.

Needing supplies, he returned to the others. The campfire still blazed, a beacon in the night. The wolf chuffed a greeting, green eyes glowing in the firelight, and then settled next to Danya. Duncan nodded, grateful for the wolf's vigilance.

The others slept, exhausted from the fight. He crossed to the far side of the campfire, drawn to Kath like iron to a lodestone. Standing over her, he stared down. Exhaustion etched her face. Even asleep she looked determined. She'd fought like a lioness despite her wounded thigh, doing her best to save them all...and now it was his turn to do the saving.

She sighed and turned, caught in a dream, a lock of blond hair falling across her face, her right hand reaching beyond the blanket.

He fought the temptation to tuck the wayward hair behind her ear and take her in his arms, knowing she needed every moment of sleep. A sense of urgency pulled him away.

Knowing time was against him, he quickly gathered a few supplies, a water skin, a flint, and a small pouch of dried meat. He checked the water skin to make sure it was full. With two groups to track down, the task would take longer than he'd like. Determined to travel light, he left his bedroll and his saddlebags, keeping stealth and speed as two of his greatest weapons. A second knife slid into his belt and then he checked to make sure he had a spare string for his longbow. Slinging the water skin over his shoulder, he strode to the edge of the firelight and then paused.

He turned back for a last look at Kath. Crossing the distance in three strides, he pulled the silver warrior ring from his long hair. Engraved with Aspen leaves, the symbol of his clan, it was the one token he carried from the Deep Green. Kneeling, he set the ring in Kath's outstretched hand, his voice a hushed whisper. "Till I return."

Her hand tightened around the ring yet she did not wake.

Even asleep, she claimed her own. "My Lioness." He took a last look, memorizing her face, and then turned and strode into the night.

11

The Knight Marshal

Sir Lothar leaned on the rampart, counting the newcomers. "Will it be enough?"

A cavalcade of mounted knights thundered into the yard below, a proud flurry of maroon cloaks and battle banners come to man the walls at Raven Pass. The marshal did not hesitate, "It has to be." Morale was as much about words as numbers so he kept his voice confident. "One knight is worth three of the enemy."

"Only three? I'd heard it was five." Lothar flashed a grin, his dark eyes gleaming in a weather-beaten face. "Or perhaps the young ones aren't as good as we were in our prime."

"They're good enough." The marshal flexed his shoulders, still unaccustomed to the weight of the great sword. "They just don't brag as much as some."

"Bragging is a hero's art. It takes more than a hint of truth to be good at it." Lothar tugged on his mustache, his right hand fingering the battleaxe strapped to his side.

"You should know, my friend. When you're in your cups I'm never sure where the truth ends and the tale begins."

Lothar chuckled. "Just as it should be."

A cold wind blew out of the north, snatching at his words, as if the wind begrudged them a moment's respite. So cold, the first breath of winter, the marshal turned his back on the north. Wrapped in maroon cloaks lined with fur, the two men walked the battlement, watching the tide of new arrivals. Warhorses churned the muddy yard below, a column of mounted knights newly come from Castlegard, answering the summons of the king. Each day, men and arms arrived from all points of the Domain, swelling the ranks at Raven Pass, but the marshal feared it would not be enough.

"How many?" Lothar worried the numbers like a man with a bad tooth.

"Should be nigh on three thousand knights and twice as many foot. More than enough to man the walls. And winter will fight beside us, an ally in white. The enemy will freeze on the steppes before he ever breaks our gates." The marshal cast his gaze along the valley. Steep granite walls reared up on either end of the battlement, snow-capped mountains looming overhead. Raven Pass cut a swath through the heart of the Dragon Spines, an open invitation to the Mordant were it not for the Octagon. Three walls blocked the pass, stout and strong with ironbound gates. The first sealed the entrance to the valley, a thirty-foot wall, topped with crenellated battlements. A killing field of three hundred feet separated the first from the second. Beyond the muddy lane, the second wall rose to a height of fifty feet, a pair of drum towers guarding the central gate. The third stood half a league south, a stubby twelve-foot wall serving as the last line of defense. The two men walked the second wall, gazing out over the steppes. "Not mage-stone but the builders wrought well. The walls will stand against the north."

"By Valin's sword, they'd better." Lothar kept pace beside him. "Have you heard their new names?"

"What?"

"The walls." Lothar ran a gloved hand along the granite battlement. "The men dubbed the first wall Shieldbreaker. And this one Swordbreaker. Venture a guess on the third?"

From the wry grin on his friend's face, he knew it must be something lewd. "*Ball*breaker?"

"Ha!" Lothar barked a laugh. "Spoken like a drunken bard!" His face sobered, his voice dropping to a throaty growl. "No, they've named the third the Whore. 'Cause if we have to retreat that far, we're well and truly screwed."

Both men fell silent, considering the odds.

"It doesn't help that the men are divided."

The marshal shot a searing glare at his friend. "You mean the succession?"

Lothar nodded. "With war looming, the king should name his heir. The men fret at the question like hounds with thorns in their paws."

The marshal swore, knowing morale was ever a fragile thing. "What are they saying?"

"Some want Ulrich, they see him as a strong warrior, a champion of the sword, but others fear he'll rush to battle without thinking, spilling blood like water."

"And Prince Griffin?"

"Too shrewd for most. They see him as a plotter, a schemer, not one to lead from the front, not a monarch they can trust." Lothar shook his head. "King Ursus casts a long shadow. He rules too well. His sons suffer by comparison. Yet the king grows old," he snorted in disgust, "as do we all."

"You could have stayed at Salt Tower. The captains were not expected to answer the king's summons."

Lothar snorted. "And leave all the glory to you? I think not." He tugged on his mustache, stopping to stare across the steppes. "Will the Mordant come? And how many will he bring?"

"The king says they'll come. War is certain as winter. But only the gods know how many ride under the Darkflamme." The marshal shrugged, adjusting the harness of his great sword. "The king has an uncanny sense for battle, so we have a chance to prepare. Better to meet them here on the walls than out on the grasslands. Walls have a way of leveling the numbers." He quickened his pace. "Come, we still have the trebuchets to inspect."

"Filthy contraptions." Lothar spat. "Knights should fight steel to steel, so we can stare into each others eyes. Battle is as much a test of will as strength. There's no honor in these infernal engines."

"You'll thank Valin for these engines once the Mordant comes."

They reached the first trebuchet, a monstrous wooden beast crouched on the edge of the battlement. Routinely used to destroy walls rather than protect them, the king had ordered it disassembled and carried to the topmost battlement. It looked like a long-necked dragon, a thick beam of wood rearing up into the sky, a massive counterweight squatting on the short end. A leather sling dangled from the top like a noose awaiting a murderer. The marshal scowled, the trebuchet was an ugly thing, a cold cruel killing contrivance, but the Octagon needed every advantage.

A gray-cloaked sergeant spied the marshal and snapped to attention. "Everything's in working order, sir."

The marshal nodded. "Then let's see how far it throws."

"Yes, sir!" The sergeant yelled a stream of orders. A team of twenty men rushed to service the beast. Soldiers worked the windlass, cranking the counterweight into the air. As the weight rose, the great arm slowly sank, bringing the sling to the rampart floor. Timbers groaned, protesting against the strain. Men swore, struggling with the final turn of the windlass. A soldier rushed to set the slip-hook, securing the counterweight. Four men wrestled a boulder into the leather sling. The sergeant barked an order, and the men leaped away.

Timbers flexed and groaned. The counterweight crashed down as the massive arm jerked upright. Snapping like a whip, the sling unfurled, hurling the boulder into the air. As if lobbed by a giant hand, the boulder tumbled upward, rising over the first wall and sailing out over the steppes. The men roared a cheer, urging it higher. The boulder seemed to tumble forever, finally landing with a bone-crushing thud. A cloud of dirt marked the new-formed crater. The marshal figured the distance at more than two thousand feet. "Impressive. But the engine is only worth the number of boulders ready to throw." He glanced at the stack of stones littering the rampart. "I want the number doubled in the next two days."

The men groaned but the sergeant saluted. "As you command."

A gust of wind beat against his face, a hint of snow in the air. The marshal pulled his wool cloak close and resumed walking.

Lothar kept pace beside him. "The wooden beast is impressive. What other surprises have you got?"

The marshal gestured to the steep sides of the valley. "Sharpened stakes run along the ridge line, to keep the enemy from scaling the cliffs. We dare not let them get above us. And we've brought wagonloads of lamp oil from Castlegard. I've ordered the oil set atop the first wall, to keep their siege engines at bay. And if the fighting breaches the first wall, I've got barrels of caltrops ready to fling into the killing field. A nasty weapon, but the spikes will wreck havoc with the enemy's horses."

Lothar shook his head. "Tricks and traps."

"Whatever it takes to win." He gave his friend a piercing stare. "If the king is right, this is one battle we dare not lose."

"My lord, a moment!"

The marshal turned to find the king's squire chasing him down. A tall skinny lad with a shock of red hair, Baldwin skidded to a stop. "The king asks for you."

"In the main tower?"

"Aye. This way."

He took his leave from Lothar, following the squire to the nearest drum tower. "Did he say why?"

"A troop arrived from Castlegard. They brought a visitor." Baldwin tugged on the ironbound door, releasing a breath of warm air.

"A visitor?" He followed the squire down the spiral stairs, grateful for the warmth. "Does the man have a name?"

"I didn't hear it, but he wears a dark blue robe."

A meddling monk, the marshal swore under his breath, an omen of dread shivering down his back. He quickened his footsteps.

Through an arched doorway, they reached the king's council chambers. A pair of guards snapped a salute. The marshal nodded. Pulling the gloves from his hands, he strode into the small round chamber. A fireplace on the far side roared with heat, while wooden shutters struggled to hold back the cold at the two windows. The room was spare and plain, a round table with ten chairs, an iron candelabra dripping tears of wax onto the oak table. The only ornament was a shield emblazoned with the octagon. Cracked and dented, it hung above the fireplace mantle, a relic from another war.

The marshal bowed toward the king. Ever a warrior, King Ursus sat at the table wearing scarred fighting leathers and a chainmail shirt, a sheaf of dispatches spread before him. Sir Abrax stood at the king's back, a sapphire-blue great sword looming over his right shoulder. As the champion of the sword, the presence of Sir Abrax told the marshal much. He nodded, approving of his king's caution.

"Osbourne, we have a visitor." The king's voice was cold, no hint of courtesy.

The monk stood on the far side of the table, his dark blue robes mud-spattered at the hem. Tall and lean, his face was fair as a nobleman's, his shoulder length hair carrying more gray than black. He smiled a greeting but his eyes were dark and sunken as if weary with strain.

The marshal stared, surprised to recognize the monk. "We've met before."

The monk nodded. "At Castlegard." He held his right arm straight out, a blue Seeing Eye tattooed across his open palm. "My name is Aeroth and I bring a message to King Ursus of Castlegard from the Grand Master of the Kiralynn Order."

The king's voice cut like a sword. "By any map the Southern Mountains are far from here. How is it you cross the kingdoms with so much ease?"

"My Order has its secrets."

"That's what bothers me." The two men locked stares, a stalemate of wills. "Your Order brings nothing but ill tidings. Are your robes blue or just another shade of black?"

The monk bore the insult well. Only a slight narrowing of the eyes betrayed his anger. "It's true we often herald dark tidings but is it not better to be warned than to fall to surprise, ambushed by the enemy?"

The king eased back in his chair, the faint creak of leather and chainmail.

The monk raised his right hand, displaying the Seeing Eye like a talisman of truth. "The Kiralynn Order has always walked in the Light. Will you hear my message?"

The king grunted assent.

"Our Order sought to avoid a perilous war, but that opportunity is lost." The monk's voice deepened, as if cloaked in prophecy. "The Mordant has crossed the Dragon Spines, reclaiming the power of the north. A dire time is upon us, a time of trials and tests, when the decisions of a few will impact many. Be warned, for the Mordant will hurl the full might of the north against the Octagon. Seeking to eclipse Erdhe with Darkness, he will risk all to succeed in this lifetime. His legions will march south wielding weapons of dark magic, weapons that time has nearly forgot. But above all, the Mordant is always the Deceiver. The Grand Master warns the King of Castlegard to beware of deceit. The Octagon is strong in war but deceit will ever be your downfall."

A grim silence settled over the chamber.

The king shook his head, his voice gruff. "Words couched in riddles. Speak plainly or leave."

"The Order fears that a harlequin lurks within the maroon, waiting for the perfect chance to betray the Octagon."

"More talk of traitors," the king's voice dropped to a dangerous growl. "My men are loyal. You slight our honor."

"Forgive my words, majesty, but it is not a matter of loyalty. Harlequins are awakened when their hosts are in their early twenties. The host has no choice in the matter, a victim crushed beneath an older soul, subsumed by a great evil. Once awakened, the harlequin can masquerade as the host knight until the time of the Dark Lord's choosing." The monk spread his hands in entreaty. "The Octagon is the shield of the southern kingdoms. If you fail, the consequences are dire. The Order fears a harlequin hides among you, waiting to turn the tide of battle." His voice dropped to a harsh whisper. "How long can you hold the walls if a traitor opens the gates?"

The king glared daggers at the monk, a storm of anger riding his face. The marshal intervened. "Grim words, but what help do you offer?"

Nodding, the monk reached within the pocket of his robe. "Once more I offer the Octagon the test of a Dahlmar crystal." He held aloft a milk-white crystalline shard, the length of a small dagger. If there was something magical about the crystal, the marshal could not see it. "Each knight need only hold this crystal in his hand. If a harlequin lurks within, the crystal will glow cherry-red."

The king stirred, his voice a low growl. "We took your test before and not one of your demon traitors was found amongst my men."

"But the test was only conducted in Castlegard. Raven Pass is guarded by men drawn from all across the Domain."

The marshal stared, hearing truth beneath the monk's words, but the king resisted, his words gruff. "The Octagon girds for war. The mere rumor of a traitor will destroy morale."

The monk nodded, his face thoughtful. "Perhaps the test can be contained. The Dark Lord is stingy with his favors. Few of his servants gain the status of harlequins. Hosts for the reborn are always chosen to give the Dark Lord the most advantage." His gaze darkened. "If a harlequin is among you, he will most likely wear the face of one of your captains, or perhaps a champion, someone of power and influence, someone who sits at your council table."

"You dare name one of my captains a traitor?" The king's voice held a dangerous edge.

"Not a traitor, a demon possessed."

"Is this a certainty or a wild accusation?"

The monk hesitated. "Nothing is certain...but it is *likely*."

"Why should I believe you?"

"Because treachery has already claimed a steep price." The monk matched stares with the king. "At Cragnoth Keep, where a traitor took your son's life."

The marshal stifled a gasp, the monk knew too much. But the argument turned the tide. He watched as anger bled from the king's face, revealing a well of grief.

The king nodded. "So be it. My captains will take your test and we will end this talk of demon cursed traitors." His face hardened and his voice rose to a shout. "Baldwin!"

The door burst open and the king's red-haired squire rushed in. "Yes, m'Lord."

"Summon my captains and the champions of the maroon. I have need of them here and now. But make no mention of our blue-robed guest. Now go and be quick about it."

Sketching a hasty bow, the squire scurried from the chamber, closing the door behind him.

"A traitor amongst my captains." The king swore. "*Likely*, you said." He drew his blue sword, Honor's Edge, and laid it across the table, a sapphire threat gleaming in the candlelight. "I'll have the head of any traitor...or the head of a fear monger." He skewered the monk with his stare.

The monk's stare dropped to the sword, his face grim. "If a harlequin is found, he must be captured, not killed. Death will only cause him to be reborn." He lifted the shard of crystal and settled it in his pocket. "And now we wait."

A grim silence settled over the chamber. The marshal stood behind his king, dreading the test, wondering if a demon hid behind the face of a friend.

12

Duncan

Unfettered by darkness, Duncan ran sure-footed through the night, reveling in his birthright. The gods had made his mother's people different, gifting them with cat-eyed vision. Even on the darkest night, his golden eye had more than enough light. In a world silvered by starlight, he saw details lost to ordinary men.

Carrying his longbow in his fist, he fell into a rhythm, running to keep a secret safe. He started with the smaller group, following a trail carved through waist-high grass, three men racing toward the northwest. Thrashed and bent, the trampled grasses screamed of panic, survivors desperate to escape the slaughter...but they carried a secret that had to be silenced. Duncan lengthened his stride, anxious to finish the task.

Stretching his senses, he tasted the wind. A northern breeze carried the sweet scent of dried grasses and the rich loam of earth but he searched for something else. Breathing deep, he caught a sour tang, the scent of fear, the scent of prey. He quickened the pace, a long loping stride.

The moon traversed the night sky, a pale glow shrouded by clouds, and still he ran, driven by the need to keep a secret safe.

Metal gleamed on the trail ahead. Duncan slowed, wary of an ambush, but it was only a discarded breastplate. Seven more strides and he found a broken gorget. A set of greaves, a gauntlet, and a dented helm followed, desperate men shedding their armor, fatigue overriding caution. Sensing weakness, he smiled, a wolf hot on the heels of prey.

The cloud-shrouded moon sank toward the western horizon, nearly set, the last dark before the dawn. He breathed deep, sensing sweat tainted with fear, the prey was close. Leaving the trail, he sought the cover of the tall grass. Crouching low, he made his way forward, an arrow nocked to his bow.

A moan of pain shivered through the night.

Duncan froze.

"Stop your belly-aching, Carlyle, or I'll stop it for you."

"It bloody well hurts. The cursed horse shattered my bleedin' shoulder. I can't feel my left arm."

The wind carried their voices, making them seem a stone's throw away. Duncan risked standing, trying to spot his prey, but they remained hidden by the tall grass. He considered loosing a volley, but he needed to see his targets to be sure. Keeping low, he crept forward, closing the distance, a black-fletched arrow nocked to his bow.

"Stop moaning, or I'll give you a taste of my sword."

Mad laughter erupted. "We're all dead men. Deserters earn the deepest level of the pit...if the damn centurions don't feed us to the bloody gore hounds first."

"We won't be going to the pit." The third voice held a note of command. "Not when they hear about the blond-haired witch."

Duncan's blood ran cold.

"They had a knight with them, but it was the witch that killed us."

"How can you be so sure?"

"The cursed Octagon never fights with magic." The voice turned to a sneer. "And they never bring women to the battlefield. Word of the witch will earn us saddlebags full of gold and a fortnight in the brothels."

"What makes you think they'll believe us?"

"The tale's too wild to be untrue. Besides, the battlefield holds the proof. Now shut your mouths and get some sleep. We've a long run to reach the nearest gate."

Duncan eased the tension on his bow, giving his prey time to sleep. The words of the soldiers clawed at his mind, confirming his worst fears. Survivors of the battle would name Kath as a witch, all the more reason they needed to die. He took a sip from his water skin and then spilled a trickle onto the ground. Working the small puddle with his dagger, he made a paste. Dabbing mud onto his face and hands, he disappeared into the darkness, a shadow of death.

Three against one, he'd need to be quick and accurate, and he'd need the element of surprise. Stretching his senses, he sought to detect movement. A chill breeze blew from the north, rustling the grasses. A cricket chirped a peaceful rhythm. But the men remained silent. He wondered if the sudden silence was an opportunity or an ambush. Either way, he was out of time.

The moon set, the deepest dark before the dawn. Selecting an arrow, he rose to a crouch. Drawing the longbow halfway, he crept forward, stepping to the rhythm of the cricket. Grasses whispered around him, just another shadow in the night.

The scent of prey intensified.

He found them in a hollow of trampled grass, three men rolled into their cloaks, lost to sleep, too tired or too careless to set a sentry.

The bowstring thrummed, the voice of death.

Quick as thought, he loosed a second arrow.

The third man rolled to his feet, his sword unsheathed. "What the..."

Duncan turned and loosed, a point-blank shot.

Thunk! At such close range, the arrow pierced armor and flesh, throwing the third man onto the ground.

He nocked a fourth, holding the bow taut, the fever of battle thrumming through him. Standing at the edge of the tall grass, he surveyed his prey, daring them to move. The first two men lay pinned to the ground, heart-shot. The third moaned, a wet gurgling sound, a feathered shaft through his lung. Duncan eased the tension on the bow, no sense in wasting a good arrow.

Drawing his dirk, he closed on the third man.

Impaled by an arrow, he lay on his back, his eyes wide with fear, blood leaking from his mouth. "W-what are you?"

Recalling the words of the soldiers, Duncan flashed a wicked grin. "The witch's assassin."

The man struggled like a stuck fish, reaching for his sword, but Duncan was quick, slashing the dirk across his throat. Just to be safe, he slit the throats of the other two and then cleaned his blade on a dead man's cloak. Sheathing his dirk, he unstrung his bow, wiping the length of yew with a soft cloth.

He stared at his handiwork. Three dead bodies, three voices silenced, but another group had survived the battle, his work was not yet done. The sun chose that moment to rise, bringing a pale blush in the east. Color returned to the world in a rush. His vision shifted, making the transition to day. His best advantage was lost.

He left the dead where they lay, food for wolves. Setting out at a lope, he ran toward the northeast, searching for a second set of survivors. If the tracks proved true, there'd be seven against one. Even for a ranger of the Deep Green the odds were grim. Duncan gripped his longbow and settled into a run, a lone hunter chasing a deadly secret.

13

Katherine

Ravens woke her, a squabble of harsh caws. Bleary from sleep and still muzzy with pain, Kath stared at a sky blackened by a thousand dark wings. Confused, she watched the ravens fly, circling and dipping, casting a black plume against the pale morning sky.

Understanding struck like a curse. Kath bolted awake. *The ravens betrayed us!* The black plume marked the battlefield, twisting their victory into a trap. Their guides had turned traitors, signaling their doom.

She threw off the blanket, wanting to scatter the ravens to the four winds...but the dark birds were everywhere, a living shroud of scavengers fighting over a field of corpses. So many dead, the stink of carrion was already rising. The grim reality of the battle hit Kath hard. Without Danya's magic they'd be lying among the dead. Without speed they'd join them. She glared at the ravens, refusing to let the dark birds steal their victory.

She pulled on her boots, provoking a blaze of aches. Her shoulder hurt, her right arm throbbed, and her left thigh burned like hellfire. Cursing the pain, she kicked the tangle of blankets away. Something silver tumbled into the grass.

Duncan's warrior ring, her heart skipped a beat. He wore it always, night and day, queen's court or forest deep. Silver embossed with Aspen leaves, she stared at the ring, terrified at its meaning. *He'd left to hunt the survivors*, a lone archer against the fleeing swords. She hadn't even asked how many. Enough swords could overwhelm even the best archer. Kath clutched the ring, desperate to believe it was his first gift and not his last.

She struggled to stand, ignoring the pain biting her left thigh. Surveying the camp, she was surprised to find Blaine sitting idle, feeding fagots to the fire.

Her voice was a goad. "The ravens set a trap."

He stared into the fire, his blue sword looming over his right shoulder, not bothering to even turn in her direction.

"If we stay here, we're dead. We have to leave."

He barked a rude laugh, his face grim. "Easier said than done. Danya won't wake, the monk's lost in a haze of pain, and we have no horses."

Anger spiked through her. "Since when does the Octagon give up?"

Growling like a baited bear, he stood and unsheathed his great sword, a flash of sapphire-blue steel. "What would you have me do?" He brandished his sword at the heavens. "Tilt at the ravens?"

"Steel is not the only way to fight." A cold anger seeped into her. "I can't carry them by myself."

He stared at her, as if slapped from a trance. "You're right. I just..." He shook his head. "When none of you woke, it seemed hopeless." He sheathed his sword. "What can I do?"

She nodded, relieved to have him back. "We'll build a pair of travois. We've got a windfall of supplies," she gestured to the battlefield. "Two spears can serve as the shafts, with blankets fastened between them. And tack from the horses can serve as a harness to ease the weight."

Blaine nodded, "I'll gather the supplies." He strode towards the battlefield, her swordmaster and her friend.

Kath unclenched her fist, staring at the Duncan's warrior ring. She missed him, yet he was barely gone. Sighing, she clutched the ring. Her hair had always been too fine to hold a ring, so she cut a leather strip from a saddlebag, threaded it through and tied it in a loop, placing it around her neck. Tucking the ring under her tunic, she let it fall between her breasts and then pressed it to her heart, praying they both survived.

Dark wings fluttered close. A raven settled on her discarded blanket. Its dark eye stared up at her. "*Caw! Caw!*"

She aimed a kick at the raven, angry at the bird's betrayal. The bird squawked and fluttered to the nearest horse bloated with death.

Pale morning light revealed a horror of corpses. Ravens squawked among the dead, a feeding frenzy of dark wings. Kath walked in the opposite direction from Blaine. Squatting behind a dead horse, she winced at the stabbing pain her thigh. Cursing the hellhounds, she made a quick toilet.

The amber pyramid called to her, a tug at the back of her mind. The compulsion pulled her through the maze of corpses. More than forty horses lay strewn across the field yet she knew the right one. Squatting, she tried the mouth but rigor had set in. The dead did not give up their secrets easily. She drew her dagger and tried prying the teeth apart, but death's bite was too strong. Anxious to regain the pyramid, she cut into the horse's jaw, a grisly task. Three cuts later and the corpse relinquished the hidden treasure. The amber pyramid nestled in her palm, a hope and a threat.

Returning to the fire, she used a full water skin desperate to wash away the stench. Kath wasn't hungry, but she forced down a fistful of dried meat. She tried to wake Danya, but the brown-haired girl remained pale and insensate. Her magic had saved them, but now it seemed she paid a steep price. Kath gripped her sword hilt in frustration, realizing magic was both a boon and a curse.

Blaine returned, dropping an armload of pilfered gear by the fire. "I tested the spears. These four seem sturdy enough."

Feeling the need to be away, they worked quickly. Laying the spears on the ground, they stretched blankets between them. Using a knife as an auger, they lashed the blankets to the spears with strips of leather. Kath doubled the knots while Blaine fashioned a harness from bits of tack.

A winged shadow passed overhead. A raven landed on the travois, dark eyes inspecting her work. Kath swiped at the bird, a squawk of feathers, wishing she could scare the whole murder away. "Time is running out."

Blaine's face tensed. "I know."

They made a last check of the bindings and then set the first travois next to Danya. Shifting the wolf-girl, Kath winced at the sharp pain lancing her thigh.

"Are you hurt?"

She shrugged. "The cursed hellhound clawed my leg."

Blaine stared at the torn strips of blanket wrapping her thigh. "Should I check that?"

"No time."

They shifted the monk onto the second travois and covered him with a blanket. Zith moaned, a sheen of sweat coating his forehead, but he did not wake. Kath hoped he survived. She wove a length of rope around his chest and under his arms, securing him to the travois while Blaine did the same for Danya.

A low growl came from behind. Kath whirled, unsheathing her sword but it was only Bryx. The wolf loped from the tall grass, snapping and snarling at the ravens.

Blaine said, "He doesn't like the ravens."

"He's not the only one." She shivered, feeling the need to be away. "We still need supplies."

"And I can't leave without my axes." She found her leather harness lying next to her shirt of chainmail, a puddle of steel links gleaming in the sunlight. The chainmail had saved her life more than once. She was reluctant to leave it but she couldn't afford the weight. Her octagonal shield would have to be left behind as well, another loss.

Shrugging the leather harness over her shoulders, Kath hurried in search of her axes. Retracing the battle, she eventually found the soldier felled by her throw. He'd seemed a towering brute, but now he was only a crumpled corpse, diminished by death, food for ravens. She whispered a prayer to Valin, knowing how close they'd come to death. Wiping her blades on the dead man's cloak, she returned to the campfire.

Blaine had loaded the monk's travois with supplies, but Danya's remained unburdened. He gave her a wary look, as if he expecting a rebuke, but Kath did not complain. Stepping between the shafts, she settled the leather harness across her shoulders and lifted. The weight seemed bearable, but the day was young.

She scanned the horizon for a gleam of black armor, but there was none...yet. She prayed to Valin for time to escape.

Blaine lifted the monk's travois. "Which way?"

The question surprised her. "Into the north."

He stared at her, as if considering her reply. For a moment, she thought he would argue, but then he shrugged. "You don't give up, do you?"

"We won a battle, not the war."

"Did we win? This doesn't feel like victory."

"We're alive. They're not."

He gave her a half-smile. "Live to fight another day."

"Just so."

The wolf chuffed, disappearing into the grass.

"The wolf has the truth of it. We'd best be away."

Blaine took the lead, breaking a trail into the north. Kath leaned into the harness, taking up her friend's weight. She lurched forward, the wound in her thigh screaming with agony. Ignoring the pain, she focused on taking one step at a time, trying to keep pace with the blond-haired knight.

Ravens circled overhead, like an omen of doom. Cursing the birds, she struggled against the traces, desperate to be away. Ten steps became twenty, a test of strength, a test of endurance. Lowering her head, she trudged forward, full of sympathy for beasts of burden. Fifty steps became sixty, a monotony of pain. She glanced back, dismayed to find the pillar of ravens alarmingly close, a beacon for the Mordant's soldiers. Staring up at the sky, she dared the gods to help, but there was no reply.

Kath chose a spot on the horizon, determined to reach it without stopping. She leaned into the traces, taking one step at a time, straining to gain some distance on the ravens.

Morning bled into late afternoon, a long haze of torment. Drenched in sweat, Kath struggled against the weight, pain ripping across her back and down her arms. Every step was a victory...or a testament to torture. Right foot and then the left, an endless shuffle forward. Pain lanced through her thigh and across her shoulders. Her left hand was rubbed raw, a mass of welts, yet she refused to loosen her grip. Sweat trickled down her face despite the chill wind. She licked her lips, a crust of salt, and kept moving.

Caught in a fog of hurt, she lost count of the number of steps. Too tired to think, she looked past Blaine, her stare fixed on the north, a golden line of grass that never seemed to end, another trick of the steppes.

The blond knight forged ahead, breaking a trail through the grass, the poles of his travois marking a path. He turned now and then to offer encouragement, waiting for her to catch up. "Let's rest for a bit."

"No, keep going." Shame flooded through her. "If I stop, I may not start again."

"You need to rest."

She shook her head. "We're not far enough."

He shot her a stubborn glare full of protest but then turned back to his own burden.

She struggled to keep pace, shamed by her weakness, knowing she put them all at risk. The travois pulled like an anchor, the harness biting into her shoulders, a dead weight tethering her to the ground. She took another step, cursing the vastness of the steppes, cursing the north, but at least the ravens had long since fallen silent.

Darkness began to claim the sky, a bloody glow in the west. Kath yearned for the night, knowing she could lay down her burden and rest. She wondered if she'd ever get up again.

Something caught at her foot. She tripped and almost fell. A half-buried skull stared up her. Picked clean by predators and weathered by age, it gave her a mocking grin. Her vision blurred, and the skull laughed, a cruel, mocking sound, an omen of death. Tightening her hold on the travois, she used the pain to cling to reality. Death was everywhere in the steppes. The golden grassland looked benign, but it was really a clever snare, an endless, relentless trap, a kind of hell.

Shivering, she bent to the traces, taking up her burden, refusing to give up.

The weight seemed to have multiplied. Kath cursed the skull, deciding it must have been one of the Mordant's men, a ghost from an ancient battle sent to plague her. Refusing to be beaten, she put one foot in front of another, trudging into the north.

A low whine brought her to a staggering stop. The wolf emerged from the grass, weaving like a rum-soaked drunk. Tongue lolling, he flopped at her feet, a dull whine of pain.

"Keep moving, Bryx." Her words were a dry croak.

The wolf whined, sprawling on the grass, blocking her way.

Sighing in frustration, she sank to her knees, every muscle aching. "What's wrong?"

The wolf rolled on his side, panting for breath.

"We're all tired." She stroked the wolf, surprised to find his dark fur wet...yet it hadn't rained. Groggy with exhaustion, she struggled to think.

Bryx whined and licked his flank. It was only then that she noticed the claw marks raking his side. Five deep cuts oozed dark pus, the festering marks of a hellhound's claws. Shame flooded through her; the wolf had fought like a warrior yet no one had thought to tend his wounds. "You need help."

The wolf chuffed and licked her hand.

All the supplies were with Blaine. Kath struggled to stand, shocked to find that the knight had lengthened his lead. Too weary to chase him, she called his name, "Blaine!" but her voice was a weak croak.

He kept walking, the fading sunlight glinting on his silver surcoat.

She had to get help for the wolf. Shrugging out of the harness, she left the travois and followed. Freed from the weight, she walked light as air, a strange floating sensation. Kath tried to run, but her legs buckled. Drenched in sweat, she sank to her knees, her voice a harsh cry. *"Blaine!"*

He turned.

"Help!" Exhaustion pulled her down. She slumped to the grass, longing to rest.

Someone called her name. Hands gripped her shoulders, shaking her back to wakefulness. She stared up at Blaine, surprised by the lines of worry on his face. He brushed the hair out of her eyes, a cool hand against her forehead. "You're on fire!"

She shook her head, trying to think. "The wolf is hurt."

"He's not the only one." Blaine held a water skin to her lips, a cool trickle soothing her throat. She grabbed the skin, greedy for more, drinking till her thirst slaked. Gasping for breath, she tried to explain. "Bryx is hurt, raked by a hellhound's claws."

"A wound from a hellhound?" He drew his dagger, worry scrawled across his face.

She nodded, confused.

He cut the blanket strips binding her thigh, releasing a sudden flair of pain.

She sat up, trying to see.

He pulled the strips away and she screamed. Clenching her jaw against the pain, she stared at her thigh. Five claw marks oozed black pus.

Her vision swam. *"No!"* She shook her head in denial. "Duncan cleaned the wound!" Kath struggled to understand, darkness nipping at her mind. She gripped Blaine's arm, a shudder of fear. *"Poison!"*

A cold shiver raced through her. She struggled to think, like swimming through molasses. And all the while the skull from the steppes kept laughing at her. "We need help." It couldn't end like this, not without meaning, lost in the god-cursed steppes, poisoned by a hellhound. Her fingers dug into Blaine's arm, desperate for an anchor. *"Duncan!"* Darkness pulled her under, a fog of poison, a dreamless haze of pain.

14

Duncan

Running by night, snatching sleep by day, Duncan followed the trail north, closing the distance on his prey. He paused to check the tracks, his haste tempered by the need to be sure the deserters did not divide. If even one escaped, then the hunt failed. The truth of the battlefield must never reach the Mordant.

A spray of stars stretched across the midnight sky. He took comfort in the familiar patterns, the Knight pointing the way north, the Great Dragon spanning the sky with his wings. But in the east, the red comet cut a bloody gash through the Big Ladle, an ugly reminder of why they'd come north.

Duncan loped along the trail, alert for details in the dark. The second group proved smarter than the first, keeping within the grasses trampled by a hundred horses. Hoof prints galloped south, footprints ran north, a mad confusion of tracks taxing his skills. But among the crisscrossing prints, his golden eye found subtle signs. Seven sets of boot prints ran north, carrying a deadly secret. The steady distance between footprints told him they kept to a ground-eating jog. One man bled, scattering fresh blood, yet he managed to keep pace with the others, proving he'd still be a threat in a fight. A discarded water flask and wrappings that smelled of salted pork littered the trail, but never any armor or weapons. Every detail added to his knowledge, but the most telling signs were the depressions in the grass where they'd slept. Five depressions for seven men, two of them always standing guard. The details told a grim tale. Disciplined in their retreat, the deserters set a fast pace into the north, keeping their armor and their weapons ready. He'd have a tough fight on his hands.

A cold wind blew across the steppes, bitter against his face. He flexed his fingers as he ran, needing to keep them nimble. Tall grasses rustled in the wind. Silvered by moonlight, they stretched in all directions, a soul-numbing sameness. He missed the shelter of the forest, the hum of the great trees, but the choice of battlefield was not his. Cursing the openness, he could do nothing but follow.

Clouds reclaimed the sky, shrouding the stars as the moon set in the west, and still he ran. He covered the leagues with a loping stride, his boots proving a boon to the long run. Fashioned from a rare swamp lizard, the boots were a Midwinter gift from Jordan. Recalling her ghost-pale face in the healery, Duncan wondered how she fared, another debt he owed the Mordant.

A blast of wind carried the faint scent of fresh urine, men waking to the dawn. Duncan scanned the trail, his golden eye catching the first glimpse of his prey. Seven soldiers clustered in a group, just out of bowshot. But beyond the soldiers, the dawn revealed a chilling sight. A great gray wall snaked across the north, only a day's run away. His stomach clenched into a knot, knowing he needed to catch them before they reached the wall...or the hunter would become the hunted. Overhead, darkness faded to dawn, stealing his best advantage. Time was against him, he could not wait for the dark. Tightening his grip on his longbow, he vowed to succeed.

Leaving the trail, he plunged into the waist-high grass, keeping the last of the darkness at his back. Racing through the grass, he threw darting glances toward the soldiers, knowing a hard stare might ruin his chance for an ambush.

The soldiers lingered, probably sharing a meal. Sunlight glinted on armor, tempting targets against the red light of dawn. Pressing for speed, he closed the distance, stopping within reach of his longbow. Setting the string to his bow, he took a steadying breath, gauging the distance to his targets. Standing at the extreme edge of his range, the accuracy of his shots would depend on luck as much as skill, but he dared not move closer till he culled their numbers; swordsmen were ever the bane of archers. He chose six of his best arrows and impaled them upright in the ground. Selecting a seventh, he nocked his bow. Taking a deep breath, he called on the full power of the great yew. Drawing the bow to its maximum curve, his muscles burned with strain. He held the draw for half a heartbeat, adjusting for the wind, and then released, a thrum of death. As the first arrow leaped skyward, he reached for the second. Moving with blistering speed, he sent six more arrows arcing into the pale morning sky. As soon as the seventh left his bow, he ran ten paces to the north and dove headfirst into the long grass.

Lying still, he waited, his heartbeat counting time.

A scream split the morning. A flurry of curses followed.

Duncan hugged the ground, hiding, letting the enemy wonder how many archers lay in ambush. Straining his senses, he listened but no sounds of attack came his way. Nocking an arrow, he knelt, peering over the tall grass.

The steppes seemed empty, golden grasses waving in the morning light.

Alerted to the threat, the hunt had become a game of cat and mouse.

Duncan stayed on his knee, studying the grassland. Sunlight gleamed on metal. At least one soldier fled north, hunched over, staying below the waist-high grass. He wondered how many survived.

Needing to be certain, he crept forward, an arrow nocked to his bow. It took forever to traverse the distance, his senses alert to ambush. The mingled scents of blood and urine grew stronger. He paused to listen but heard only the wind and the rustle of the dry grass. Drawing his bow, he stepped to the edge of the trail.

Two bodies lay sprawled in the trail. One man lay on his side, shot through the neck, his face frozen in a grimace of surprise. The other lay on his stomach, a feathered-shaft impaled in his armored back.

Duncan scanned the trail, wary of an ambush, but nothing moved.

The first man was clearly dead...but a sixth sense screamed of danger.

Keeping his bow taut, Duncan moved forward. He kicked the man's foot. No reaction. He nudged his boot under the body and rolled it over. The face was slack with death, the arrowhead protruding from the chest.

A rush of movement from the side.

Duncan whirled.

A soldier charged from the tall grass, a round shield held to the front, a short sword raised in attack.

Duncan lowered his aim, loosed the arrow, and then dodged to the right.

The soldier staggered backward, grunting in pain, an arrow protruding from his thigh. "Damn you to the nine hells!" He lowered his shield and charged.

Duncan danced away. Releasing the bowstring, he wielded the yew like a staff, poking blows at the soldier's face, trying to keep the swordsman at bay.

A gray-haired veteran, the soldier circled the archer, his shield up, his sword flashing in the morning light. His voice was a low growl. "Stand and fight."

Duncan jabbed at the soldier's eyes and backed away, desperate for some advantage.

Steel cut the air, a vicious chop at the yew wood. Duncan yanked the bow away, narrowly avoiding the blade. Sweat beaded his brow; he needed to defeat the swordsman without harming his bow.

The swordsman launched a furious attack, slashing toward the archer's face.

Duncan stayed a hair's breath away, a shifting shadow in black leathers.

"Fight, damn you." The swordsman hawked and spat, "Bloody archers are nothing but cowards." Lowering his shield, he charged. Duncan leaped aside, thrusting his bow into the soldier's feet. Entangled, the swordsman tripped and fell, sprawling face first. Duncan pounced, grappling for the sword. The two rolled across the bloody trail, knees gouging for groins, muscles straining. Slick with sweat, both men fought for the sword. An elbow slammed into Duncan's jaw, snapping his head back, but he never let go. Tasting blood, he rolled on top, wrestling for control. The soldier waged a mighty struggle, but the longbow had made Duncan strong. The sword's edge slowly turned toward the soldier's throat. Wide-eyed, he bucked and kicked, struggling to slow the blade's descent but his fate was sealed. Duncan finished the fight, burying the blade in the soldier's throat.

Rolling clear of the spurting blood, Duncan lay sprawled on the trampled grass. Every muscle ached. His head throbbed and his jaw hurt. His right arm bled, a deep gash from the sword. The fight had been close, too close. Only luck had kept a second swordsman from the ambush. He shook his head, knowing luck was a fickle mistress, but he'd trust to his bow.

His bow!

Bolting to his feet, he searched for the yew wood, finding it flung to the far side of the trail. He snatched it up, running anxious fingers along the length, checking for nicks and cracks. A single fault would ruin the bow, snapping under the strain of the draw. He sighed, relieved to find it whole and undamaged. His hands caressed the yew, giving thanks to the gods. The bowstring was lost but he had another. Bending the bow, he set the second string, once more an archer.

He swayed on his feet, hammered with weariness. Blood dripped from his right arm, and his side ached from a nasty punch, yet he had to keep going. A strip of cloth torn from a dead man's cloak served as a bandage. He bound his arm, using his teeth to tie the knot. Searching the dead, he found a flask half full of water and a single biscuit of hard bread. The biscuit went in his pouch, but he drained the flask, slaking a vicious thirst. Discarding the flask, he knew he needed rest, just an hour of sleep.

His gaze was drawn toward the north, to the long gray wall. It slashed across the horizon, dividing north from south, a chilling reminder of the Mordant's power. But it was still a day's run away. He needed to catch the remaining deserters...but he also needed the strength to prevail. Taking the dead man's sword, he moved off the trail and into the tall grass. Weary and sore, he pulled his black wool cloak close and laid down to rest.

Duncan woke with a start, dreams of ambush in his mind. Reaching for his bow, he nocked an arrow and knelt. Golden grasses stretched in every direction, no sign of the enemy...but the sky was full of threats. Dark clouds churned overhead, obscuring the midday sun. *"Darkness be damned."* He'd slept too long, giving his prey too much of a lead...but the storm clouds posed a bigger threat. Rain would negate his bow. Even the best archer could not shoot with a wet bowstring. Lady luck had turned against him.

Gambling that his prey would make a dash for the wall, he wasted no time searching for tracks. Intent on speed, he flew across the grasslands.

The wall loomed large with every passing league. He scanned the trail, praying for a glimpse of the deserters. Overhead the storm clouds thickened, a brooding menace but no rain fell. Perhaps the hunt still had a chance.

At twilight, he saw them, a gleam of armor clustered on the trail ahead, four soldiers jogging toward a break in the wall. Time had almost run out.

Deciding to attack from the east, Duncan moved into the tall grass. A final sprint put the enemy within reach of his longbow. He nocked an arrow and he paused, fighting to slow his breathing. With the wall looming close, he needed to make every arrow count. Judging the wind and the distance, he raised the longbow. His muscles strained against the mighty yew, drawing the bow to a curve. A fat raindrop slapped his face, speeding his pulse. Ignoring the threat, he focused on his prey. He loosed the bowstring, sending an arrow into the sky. As if pierced, the clouds broke, releasing a sudden downpour. Seven more arrows soared into the crying sky, defying the rain.

Cursing the weather, he unstrung the bow, putting the bowstring deep in an inner pocket, next to his heart. Wiping the length of yew with a soft cloth, he slipped a leather cover over the bow, tying the end tight, desperate to keep the wood dry.

A scream split the twilight sky; at least one arrow had found its mark.

Lightning forked the dark clouds unleashing a torrent of rain, as if the gods had turned against him.

Duncan jerked canvas covers over his quivers and reached for the captured sword, hefting its weight. The short sword felt awkward in his hand but it was the only weapon left to him. He ran toward his prey, determined to finish the hunt.

Rain beat against his face, soaking his wool cloak, muting his senses, another advantage lost. His boots squelched in puddles but they kept his feet dry. Tightening his grip on the sword, he raced through the downpour. Wary of an ambush, he slowed as he reached the edge of the trail.

Only three! The words pounded through his mind, a warning and a curse.

One man lay dead, while a second writhed in pain. A third soldier knelt to tend the second, his back to Duncan...*but where was the fourth?*

Risking ambush, Duncan lowered his bow to the ground and crept toward the third soldier, the captured sword poised to strike.

Lightning cracked the sky.

The soldier whirled as if warned, his sword rising to meet the attack.

Steel met steel, a mighty clang that competed with the thunder. The soldier glared over the crossed blades, his eyes full of hate. "I'll have your head!" He disengaged and lunged, releasing a flurry of blows.

Duncan danced away, using the captured sword as a shield, doing his best to parry the rain of blows.

"Fight, you cat-eyed bastard!" The soldier sent a slashing blow toward Duncan's face.

Duncan twisted away, narrowly avoiding the blade. Stroke and parry, slash and dodge, the archer evaded the sword but he had no attack, he was no swordsman trained to the cut and parry. Sweat trickled down his face as he strove to avoid the soldier's blade. A sword stroke whispered close to his chest, slashing at his leathers, drawing a thin trickle of blood. Duncan danced back, desperate for a way to take the soldier's skill out of the fight.

The soldier flashed a feral grin, his eyes gleaming with confidence. Brandishing his bloody blade, he leaped forward with an overhand cut. Duncan raised his sword in a two-handed grip. The two swords met in a furious clash. Like rams locked in battle, they grappled, steel straining against steel, feet churning the ground into mud.

Duncan saw his chance, a risky ploy. He dropped his own sword and wrestled for control of the other blade. Lashing out with his boot, he caught the man's shin with a wicked kick. Grunting in pain, the soldier slipped and fell. Duncan followed him to the ground, throwing his weight on top. Rolling in the mud, they fought for the blade. Slippery with blood and rain, they grappled one on top of the other. Duncan got his left hand free, reaching for the dagger at his belt. Struggling to hold the sword at bay, he positioned the point under the man's breastplate, aiming a desperate thrust deep into the belly. The soldier's eyes widened, his mouth gaping in a silent scream. Shuddering, he arched his back and lay still.

Duncan pulled the dagger free and slit the man's throat, needing to be sure. Blood filled the puddles as he staggered to his feet. Tilting his head back, he drank the cold rain, letting it run across his face like tears, thankful to be alive.

A moan of pain pulled him back to his purpose.

The second soldier writhed in the mud, a feathered shaft protruding from his chest.

Duncan knelt by the wounded man, a veteran with streaks of gray in his beard. "Where's the fourth soldier?"

The veteran fought for each breath, his face wracked with pain, but his gaze was still clear. "You won't...catch him." Triumph filled his face. "The Citadel...will hear...of the witch."

A dagger of fear sliced through Duncan's belly.

The soldier laughed, bubbles of blood foaming at his mouth.

A flash of steel silenced the laughter...but not the threat. Duncan sheathed his dagger and then retrieved his longbow. Picking up his discarded sword, he raced north, desperate to catch the last man.

15

The Knight Marshal

Silent as death, they sat in the council chamber, awaiting the captains, waiting to learn if a demon lurked inside of a friend. The marshal stared at the monk, a fierce resentment growing inside him. How easily this stranger spoke of treachery, casting suspicion on friends and comrades, men he'd fought beside in battle, men he'd trusted with his life. He clenched his fist, fighting the urge to reach for his sword.

The marshal knew his king felt the same, yet his lord hid his rage well. Stern and unwavering, King Ursus sat at the table, a chiseled look on his face, his stare fixed on the monk.

Perhaps the monk understood, for he turned away, offering his back to the room. Wrapped in robes of midnight blue, the monk drifted toward the shuttered window. Lifting the latch, he eased the shutters open, admitting a cold wind, a bitter breath of winter.

No one complained.

The sudden cold suited the chill of the room.

Candles flickered against the wind, casting an uneven light. The king's great sword gleamed upon the tabletop, a promise and a threat.

No one spoke.

Minutes seemed like hours.

A knock at the door broke the spell, a bustle of noise from the hallway. Prince Griffin was first to arrive, followed by Godfrey. Bold and confident, the two princes mimicked their father, blond-haired warriors dressed in fighting leathers, maroon cloaks at their shoulders. Griffin started to speak but one look at his father's face silenced him. The grim mood proved contagious. Wood scrapped against stone as the two princes took seats at the table.

The others came by ones and twos, the captains and the champions, big men bristling with weapons, maroon cloaks spattered with mud, answering the call of their king. Sir Dalt, the captain of Ice Tower, Sir Rannock, the champion of the morning star, Sir Odis, the champion of the lance, they tramped into the chamber, mud on their boots, the smells of sweat and horse clinging to their wool cloaks. Eighteen men answered the summons. Caught by the grim mood, they asked no questions. Veterans of many battles, they crowded into the chamber, standing behind their king, taking sides against the stranger.

The marshal knew them all, some of them friends, all of them brothers-in-arms, warrior-knights dedicated to the maroon. He studied their faces, wondering if a demon lurked among them, but the monk's accusation seemed hard to believe, a stain against their honor.

Sir Lothar flashed a questioning glance his way, but the marshal kept his face impassive, better to let the king explain.

Silence prevailed, like a lull before the battle. The fireplace snapped and crackled, spitting sparks onto the stone floor. Knights fingered their weapons, every stare locked on the monk.

Alone, on the far side of the chamber, the monk stared out the window, his dark hair ruffled by the winter wind.

The king spoke, "My council is assembled."

The monk turned, his face pale in the candlelight. "All of them?"

"All save three captains who remain at their posts along the Domain; Ulrich is at Cragnoth, Boris at Holdfast, and Clemet at Castlegard."

"So be it." The monk's gaze circled the chamber, as if searching the soul of each man. Raising his right hand, he revealed the tattoo of the Seeing Eye. "Seek knowledge, Protect knowledge, Share knowledge. My name is Aeroth, a sworn monk of the Kiralynn Order. I come to you on the brink of war, bringing warning of a dire plot by the Dark Lord, a deceit designed to defeat the Octagon."

A murmur of anger ripped through the chamber.

The monk reached into his pocket, revealing the crystalline shard. "A prophecy warns of a harlequin hidden among you, a servant of the Dark Lord wearing the face of a knight." He raised the crystal aloft, candlelight reflecting off the milk-white facets. "I ask each of you to hold this crystal in your naked hand. If it remains dormant, it proves you walk in the Light. If it glows bright red, it proves a harlequin hides beneath your face, a demon disguised as a knight."

"*Demons!*" Sir Dalt made the hand sign against evil.

A murmur of outrage rippled through the room. The captains cast uneasy glances at the monk, their hands at their weapons.

King Ursus leaned forward, stretching his open hand across the table. "I will be the first."

The monk had the grace to look embarrassed. "Majesty, it is not necessary."

The king's fist banged the tabletop, his voice a roar. "Of course it's necessary! You come here speaking of treachery. Your words stain the honor of us all." The king skewered the monk with his stare, his voice a command. "Give me the shard."

The monk moved to the table. Leaning forward, he offered the crystal to the king. Their hands met over the sapphire sword. The king took the crystal and held it aloft. The shard remained dormant. A sigh of relief rippled around the chamber.

Godfrey was the first to speak. The youngest among them, his voice burned with righteous indignation. "How dare you test our king! How dare you come here and impugn the honor of the Octagon!"

The king turned toward his third-born son, a glint of approval in his eyes. "You'll soon learn the monks dare much. But if the Octagon is to be tested, it's fitting the king be first."

But the prince was not mollified. His voice brimmed with outrage. "We spill our blood guarding the southern kingdoms!" He stabbed an accusing finger at the monk. "By what right does a weaponless monk dare judge us?"

The marshal stared at the prince, fearing he protested too much.

"Enough!" The king's roar echoed through the chamber. "By my order, each of you will take this test, but never speak of it past these walls." His stare scoured his captains, slaying any protest. He turned towards his third-born son. "We lead by example."

Godfrey glowered, but then bowed under the weight of his father's stare. He accepted the crystal, holding it aloft. The marshal held his breath, but the shard remained dormant, a dagger-length of milk-white crystal held in the prince's fist.

The king said, "And now Griffin."

Godfrey passed the crystal to his older brother. Griffin took the shard and held it aloft. "It sleeps." He turned to pass it to the next man.

The monk intervened. "Remove your glove."

Griffin shrugged. "It matters not."

"Remove your glove."

A snarl filled the prince face. "Curse your crystal." Erupting from his chair, he hurled the shard at the monk. Quick as lightning, he unsheathed a dagger and held it to his brother's throat. "Back, all of you!"

The marshal drew his sword, a stab of horror at his heart. *Not the king's son!*

Weapons sprang from scabbards, a thicket of steel surrounding the prince.

Godfrey struggled, a wild look in his eyes, but the dagger drew a line of blood at his throat. *"Father!"*

"Godfrey!" The king stood, knocking over his chair, his face a blaze of disbelief. "Don't harm my son!"

The knights growled, tightening the cage.

The demon retreated, setting its back to a wall, holding the younger brother like a shield. "Keep back, or I'll kill him."

"Do as he says." At the king's command, the knights came to a stop, their weapons raised in a ring of steel.

Only the marshal inched forward, seeking a way to save the younger son.

"All of you keep back." The demon glared at the marshal. "You too, old man." Holding the dagger to Godfrey's throat, it shuffled toward the door, its back pressed to the wall. "Drop your weapons."

The king gestured and the captains complied, a rain of steel hitting the stone floor.

Empty-handed, the marshal sidled toward the door, desperate to stop the demon.

The king took a step toward his sons, his hands spread wide in entreaty. "Griffin don't do this. Fight this monster and release your brother. I know you're strong..."

"Strong!" The thing that was Griffin snarled. Evil leached onto the prince's face, a twisted look of pure hatred. "Your son is weak, a slave crushed beneath my will. For twelve years I've worn this face and you never knew! I ate at your table, diced with you, sparred with you, listened to your petty plans, but none of you knew! *None of you knew!"* It laughed, a cruel sound full of spite. "Shall I let you speak to your precious son? To prove he's held captive to my will?" For half a heartbeat, the face went slack, and then it filled with life, a deep intelligence blazing from the eyes. *"Father, I'm sorry!"* Pleading eyes stared at the king. *"Don't let it keep me. Let me die a knight."* The words came in a rush. *"Kill me to kill it!"*

"No!" The monk screamed a warning. "You dare not kill it!"

Griffin gasped as if strangled. The gasp turned to a snarl of rage. The demon was back. "Listen to the monk! You cannot kill me." It dragged Godfrey toward the door, a hostage held at knifepoint.

The marshal stood across from the beast, his back pressed to the edge of the table, desperate for a weapon. And then it came to him. Slow and stealthy, he groped behind his back, seeking the hilt of the king's blue sword.

The demon reached the door, a look of triumph on its face. "You want a prophecy? I'll give you one." Its eyes blazed with hatred. "The

Dark Lord will crush the Octagon! He'll take your pride, then he'll take your precious honor, and then he'll crush you with defeat. The Octagon will be forgotten, while *I* live on!" It pulled Godfrey close, the dagger nicking the prince's neck. "My name is *Shmailgren! And I am the bane of the Octagon!*" Its voice rose to a shout. *"Behold, for I bring you despair!"* The dagger bit deep, slicing halfway through Godfrey's throat.

"*No!*" The king's roar echoed through the chamber.

The younger son gasped, a bloody froth at his throat.

The blue sword came to the marshal's hand. Without thought, he lunged, putting his full might behind the thrust. The sapphire blade struck true. Cleaving chainmail and leather, it struck straight through Godfrey's heart and into Griffin, driving all the way to the wooden door.

Impaled upright, the demon gasped, a look of surprise on its face. It stared at the sword hilt. "I have not failed." The demon's face twisted into a triumphant leer. "I will live...*again!*" Its eyes burned red, like twin lanterns lit from hell. And then the demon was gone, the malevolent spirit snuffed out like a candle. But the spark of life was not entirely extinguished. For half a heartbeat, the true prince stared from his eyes, his gaze seeking the king. *"Honor...always."* And then the face fell slack, the spark of life gone.

Two princes impaled on one sword.

Both dead.

Horror filled the room. Darkness had struck at the Octagon's heart.

A single tear bled down the king's face.

The marshal gaped, like watching a hairline crack ruin a fine steel sword, a death knell in the midst of battle.

"*My sons!*" Grief-struck, the king staggered to the door. He gripped the sword hilt and yanked it free, hurling the blade across the room. Blue steel clattered against stone.

Released, the bodies slumped forward. The king caught his sons and cradled them to his chest. He wept and the sound shattered the chamber.

The marshal fought despair, knowing the demon had struck a perilous blow.

One by one, the captains turned away, shaken by horror, disarmed by the king's grief, a seed of doubt in their eyes. Even the stalwart Sir Abrax turned away.

Doubt in their eyes. *The captains doubt their king.* The realization struck the marshal like a dagger in the back. Desperate to stem the rot, his gaze circled the chamber. A gleam of sapphire caught his gaze. The king's blue blade lay abandoned on the floor. As if the blade called to him, the marshal strode toward the sword. Lifting the great sword, he turned to face the captains, a flash of sapphire blue in the candlelight. "Darkness shall not defeat us." He lifted the sword like a holy talisman, his words full of conviction. "The king's sword will never fail. Like blue steel, the Octagon will never bend, never break, never grow dull. We are the sword and shield of the southern kingdoms." His gaze roamed the captains, willing the doubt away, seeking the strength within.

Pride returned with a rush of defiance. The captains reached for their weapons, a gleam of steel raised in salute. *"For Honor and the Octagon!"*

The shout broke through the king's grief. He raised his head, a smear of tears on his face, a smear of blood on his leathers. For a moment, he looked old and confused, but then his gaze settled on the monk. "You!" His finger stabbed like an accusing sword. "You knew all along! You knew and you did nothing!"

"No." The monk retreated, his face pale. "The prophecy spoke of a demon in the Octagon, nothing more. I came to warn you, to save you from a plot by the Dark Lord."

"Save us!" The king roared, his gaze fever bright. "Your words bring nothing but doom. I name you a minion of Darkness!"

"Grief blinds you. You know the Order walks in the Light." The monk's retreat came to a halt, his back to the open window. "We are allies against the Dark."

"More words. I'm weary of your warnings. You can spew your dark tidings in the dungeons!"

"No." The monk's stare flashed from the king to the marshal. "Detain me and you aid the Dark."

Gripped by a shiver of foreboding, the marshal sought to stop the madness. "Sire, he's only a messenger."

"No!" The king's anger was beyond reason. "I'll see the darkling in irons. Capture him!"

The captains obeyed, closing ranks on the monk, a ring of steel slowly tightening.

Sworn to the king, the marshal could only watch.

But the monk refused to be taken. "The Kiralynn Order serves the Light." He leaped to the windowsill, a flutter of dark blue robes. And then he jumped.

The marshal lunged, grabbing for a fistful of robes, but he caught only air. Leaning out the window, he expected to see blood and robes spattered at the tower's base...but there was nothing below. He searched for some sign of the monk but found no trace of the man. And then he saw it, a winged shadow racing across the muddy yard. A giant frost owl soared across the wall, rising toward the mountaintops. *"Magic!"* The marshal made the word a curse. He watched the frost owl disappear into the clouds, a sense of dread choking him like a hangman's noose. Feeling unsteady, he gripped the windowsill, rough stone beneath his callused hands. He was just a swordsman, a leader of knights, but the world had changed. Against demons and magic, how could swords prevail?

16

Duncan

Rain pelted his face, cold as ice. Lightning flashed overhead, slashing an ominous sky. Duncan ran into the teeth of the storm, cursing the wet weather, as if the clouds fought for the Mordant. Soaked to the skin, he ripped his cloak from his shoulders, letting the sodden wool drop to the ground, choosing speed over warmth. Released from the wet weight, he lengthened his stride, desperate to slay the seventh man.

Sword in hand, Duncan followed the trail of trampled grass. Encased in leather, his longbow beat a rhythm against his back, useless in the rain.

Lightning cracked the sky, revealing a break in the long wall. A gate of some sort lay ahead, and in front of that gate stood the silhouette of a man, the seventh soldier. His prey stood within easy reach of his longbow...saved by the dark-damned rain. Duncan cursed his ill luck. Tightening his grip on his sword, he ran harder, fighting to close the distance.

A soul-wrenching scream split the air.

Skidding to a stop, Duncan cowered to the ground. Hands over ears, he stared into the twilight sky, half-expecting demons to attack.

Howls and shrieks raged from the north, as if the very gates of hell had ripped open, disgorging the damned.

Slinking low, Duncan waited, straining his senses, but nothing attacked. The hideous screams came from the break in the long wall. Perhaps some devil guarded the way north. He gripped his sword, wondering if steel could harm a demon. Determined to finish the hunt, he advanced on the gate.

The screams of the damned beat against his ears, a torture of howls.

Lightning flared, silvering the gateway. Duncan gasped, certain his eyes played tricks. Twelve stone gargoyles reared into the sky. Thrice the height of a tall man, the gargoyles seemed cast in stone, yet...*they* moved! Like nightmares sprung to life, they writhed against the sky. Wings unfurled and fangs bared, they clawed at the heavens, howling soul-numbing screams.

Duncan shuddered, making the hand sign against evil, wondering if he faced the very gates of hell. Every instinct screamed for him to run, to disappear into the south, but for Kath's sake he had to finish the hunt.

Step by step he drew near the gateway.

The great stone beasts writhed overhead.

Gripping his sword, Duncan kept watch, expecting an attack...but the gargoyles seemed fixed to their pillars, shrieking a warning into the sky.

A warning! Perhaps the tortured screams were the gargoyles' true purpose. The ensorcelled monsters put the fear of hell into the enemy while calling an army from the north. And then he noticed the seventh man was gone. Duncan cursed the gods. If his guess was true, he did not have much time. He stared at the stone monsters, wondering if he dared to cross beneath them. Steeling his courage, he shouted a challenge, "For Kath and the Light!"

He stepped onto the stone roadway.

Lightning flashed and rain pelted down, shedding cold tears on his face...but the gargoyles did not attack. Fixed to their pedestals, the stone beasts writhed overhead, hurling screams into the sky.

Duncan took another step...and then another. Shadows reached for him, a nightmare of stone claws, but he refused to retreat. His heart thundering, he broke into a run. He sprinted beneath the gauntlet of horrors, an eternity in every stride. Six more strides...and he stumbled onto the tall grass. Falling, he dug his fingers into the earth, needing to know it was real, needing to smell the clean, wet soil.

Spattered with rain and mud, he stared back at the writhing gargoyles. He'd crossed the gates, passing into the north. Shuddering, he made the hand sign against evil, relieved to be alive.

But the screaming did not stop.

A shiver ran down his back, knowing he would not be the hunter for long.

Goaded by urgency, he got to his feet and searched the ground, looking for clues to the seventh man. A single set of tracks led north. Shivering with cold, Duncan set off at a run. He lengthened his stride, desperate to finish the hunt. The quicker he made the kill, the quicker he'd return to his wife. Thinking of Kath, he swore to find his way back...even if it meant escaping from the very gates of hell.

17

Blaine

*P*oison! The word scared Blaine more than any sword in battle. Swords he could defeat but against poison he was useless. He gripped Kath's shoulders, trying to shake her back to consciousness. "Don't leave me." Her weakness shattered him. He'd come to believe the girl was made of steel; she couldn't die like this. "Fight this, don't let the Darkness win."

Kath moaned in pain, a cold knife slashing into his guts. Always a warrior, she'd insisted on going north, pulling a travois of twelve stone without complaint...and now she lay felled by poison, so hurt, so weak, it scared him more than he could say. He wrapped his arms around her and pulled her close, willing her to heal. "Don't give up." His voice shook. "By Valin, don't abandon me." But she lay limp and unresponsive, her face pale, her blond hair sodden with sweat. Cradled against his chest, he carried her back to Danya and the wolf. Kath blazed with heat like a blacksmith's forge, as if the fever consumed her from within. His grip tightened, he'd sworn to protect her.

He laid her in the grass next to the wolf, gently easing the axe harness from her shoulders and the sword belt from her waist. She yielded her weapons without a murmur, another dagger of fear. Desperate for a glimmer of hope, he held the water skin to her lips, trying to coax her to drink, trying to draw her back, but the water just trickled down her chin. Her tunic was drenched in sweat, her face ghost pale; he was losing her.

He had to do something. Racked with worry, he struggled to think. He needed bandages and something to clean the wound...and a cure for the hellhound's poison. Where in the god-cursed steppes was he going to find a cure? Did one even exist? Balling his hands into fists, he shook his head, fighting the panic. He needed to try. And at the very least, he needed to keep them all together.

Twilight was fading to night, a thin sliver of red on the horizon; he was losing the light. He raced back to the monk and lifted the travois.

The burden seemed suddenly light, as if he carried a ghost. Gripped with fear, he stared at the monk. Hollow-cheeked and ashen, the old man looked like death but his breath made a faint rasping sound, still in the land of the living. Relieved, Blaine lifted the travois and pulled it back to the others.

He set the monk next to Danya and then dropped to his knees, ransacking their supplies. Swearing, he tore through saddlebags and pouches, looking for anything that might help, cursing himself for not bringing more. Perhaps the Mordant's soldiers carried a cure. Perhaps he'd left it on the battlefield, hidden among the dead. Spare blankets, water skins, a wine skin, a flint, a packet of salt, a sack of dried meat...and a healer's pouch. Hope shivered through him. His fingers fumbled with the leather tie, dumping the contents onto the grass. Packets of herbs tumbled from the pouch, symbols embossed on the leather wrappings...but he had no idea what they meant. Rocking back on his heels, he glared up at the darkening sky, cursing the gods and his own ignorance. A knight wielded a sword not a healer's bag of tricks. He had no knowledge of herb lore and even less of poisons.

Knowledge...perhaps the monk held the answers.

He grabbed the water skin and tried to get the monk to drink. "Zith, I need your help."

The old man groaned, his face ashen, water dribbling down his beard.

"Kath's been poisoned." He shook the monk harder than he meant to. "You have to help. She gives meaning to your dark damned prophecies. You can't just let her die."

But the monk lay still as death, a sheen of sweat glistening his forehead.

Blaine stared at the old man, trying to figure a way to break through. Perhaps the monk's wound festered, severed limbs were always dire. Blaine's fingers fumbled at the wrapping, pulling the cloth away. Branded closed, the stump was ugly and red, but the upper arm showed no taint of corruption. Then why did the monk refuse to wake? And then he noticed the old man had a second wound, strips of blanket binding his chest. Blaine gripped his dagger and cut.

"*Valin's sword!*" Reeling backwards, he made the hand sign against evil.

Five claw marks scored the old man's chest. And all of the marks oozed black pus.

Blaine staggered backwards, trapped in a nightmare. Unsheathing his sword, he pivoted, desperate for someone to fight. But the god-cursed steppes were empty...except for his companions. Four dark forms lay in the grass, helpless, still as death, as if bewitched, caught in a dark spell.

"Valin help us!" He roared his frustration at the heavens, a challenge to the gods. *"Darkness has nearly caught us, yet you do nothing?"* Furious, he stabbed his sword aloft. *"Have you less honor than a man?"*

A cold wind ripped across the thigh-high grass, the gods' only reply.

Drunk on rage, Blaine staggered in a circle, tilting at the wind. He hurled accusations at the sky...but there was never any answer. The killing rage slowly bled away, leaving a bitter emptiness. Sinking to his knees, he stared at Kath, willing her to heal. He'd risked everything for her, disobeyed his king, taken horses from the way stations, and killed knights sworn to the Octagon. There was no going back, no returning to Castlegard without a clear victory...and victory meant defeating the Mordant.

He reached for Kath's sword belt and unsheathed the crystal dagger. So many hopes balanced on a single knife-edge. He laughed, a bitter sound. So foolish to think that five could stand against the north, such a delusion. They hadn't even reached the true north, felled by the Mordant's hellhounds. *His hounds!* Blaine railed in despair, but then other thoughts intruded. Memories of the Guardian Mist assailed him, the fight with the skeleton king and his promise to the guardian. Certainty shivered through him. He wielded a hero's sword. He had a destiny, and it was more than just dying in the god-cursed steppes. Returning the crystal dagger to its sheath, he got to his feet, there had to be a way out of this trap.

Taking a deep breath, he plunged into a battle he did not understand. Starting with Kath, he cleaned their wounds, soaking up the black ooze with a wine-drenched cloth. Smearing the angry wounds with honey, he bound them with fresh wrappings cut from a blanket. The monk moaned when he cleaned the claw marks and the wolf whined but Kath never made a sound. Her silence worried him more than he dared admit.

Shivering against the chill wind, he laid the four companions close together for warmth, wrapping them in blankets. Holding a water skin to their lips, he tried to coax them to drink. Only the wolf responded, lapping at the water, a weak whine. Setting the water skin aside, Blaine knew he'd done all he could...but he doubted it would be enough. They needed a healer. They needed a cure for the hellhounds' poison.

Sitting hunched beneath his maroon cloak, he considered retracing his steps back to the battlefield. Perhaps the antidote lay hidden among the saddlebags of the dead, but he dared not leave the others to the mercy of predators. Kath had asked for Duncan. The archer knew healing lore, but Blaine would never be able to track the cat-eyed archer, let alone catch him. For all he knew, the archer might be dead, gutted on the swords of the Mordant's men. No, there was nowhere to go, nothing to do but stay and look after them as best he could, hoping at least one of them would wake.

18

Duncan

In the north, beyond the wall, far beyond the trees, Duncan shivered, feeling an unnamed doom stalking his back. All of his senses screamed in warning, yet he refused to retreat. He needed one more kill to keep the secret safe. Shivering in the rain, he tracked the last set of footprints. Empty grasslands stretched ahead, while behind him, the gargoyle gates bellowed their hellish screech. Time was running out.

At least the sun had set, giving him back the advantage of night. Storm clouds hid the moon, snuffing out the stars. Despite the dark, his golden cat-eye saw the land in silvery detail, the footprints of the seventh soldier clearly imprinted in the long grass. Duncan lengthened his stride, covering leagues with a long loping run, needing to close the distance.

Lightning cracked the sky, changing the rain to hail. Ice pellets beat against him, cold stings biting his face. The onslaught of hail rendered the land white, turning the steppes into a frozen hell. He ducked his head against the onslaught but kept running, his gaze fixed on the enemy's trail.

Screams of the gargoyles suddenly stopped, cut off in mid-screech.

As if the same power controlled the heavens, the volley of hail ended.

An eerie silence descended like a smothering pillow. The gargoyles must have served their purpose, a threat building at his back. Duncan quickened his pace, his sword gripped in one hand, his canvas-covered bow in the other. Wet and cold, he raced through the grassland, all his senses screaming of danger.

Muted thunder came from behind...the distant sound of drumming hooves.

And so it started. The hunter became the hunted.

He kept running, trusting the darkness to hide him. Leagues passed and still the hoof beats persisted...but on the horizon, Duncan caught sight of his prey. His heartbeat quickened; perhaps the gods hadn't abandoned him. Ripping the canvas sheath from his bow, he bent the yew to the string. His stock of arrows was depleted, but he'd saved the best for last. Fletched with peacock feathers, a gift from the Treespeaker, the arrows were straight and true. Iridescent eyes on their fletchings glimmered in the pale light. *Eyes of the forest, eyes of his people.* Setting an arrow to the string, he raised his longbow to the heavens. His muscles strained, demanding the maximum curve. Every sense focused on the target, adjusting for wind and distance, needing to be flawless. Half a heartbeat...and an arrow thrummed into the sky. Three more followed.

Duncan waited, willing the arrows to fly true.

Hoof beats rushed from the south...and still he waited, poised to run.

A cry split the north. His prey stumbled and fell. Experience told him all the arrows struck true. The seventh soldier died, taking the secret to his grave.

A thunder of hooves drew near, close enough to hear the jangle of armor mixed with the galloping beat...and something else, something he'd missed before...the low growl of hounds. He'd heard that sound before. *Hellhounds.* A shiver of fear raced down his spine. Duncan took off at a hard run, racing toward the northeast, praying the hounds followed the seventh soldier's scent.

Distance was his best hope. Duncan pressed for speed, dashing through the waist-high grass, and all the while his senses focused backwards, listening for pursuit.

The hounds erupted in a wild chorus of yelps, likely caused by the diverging scents. Duncan kept running, praying to all the gods that the hounds followed the original trail.

Whips cracked and men yelled commands. The hounds bayed and the horses resumed the hunt.

Duncan kept running, kept listening. The wild baying gradually receded. The hellhounds followed the seventh soldier but he'd only gained a short reprieve. He changed strides to a long, loping run, scanning the horizon, seeking for some advantage.

Running at a steady rhythm, he glided through the grasslands, but the pace began to take its toll. Sweat beaded his brow and his side began to ache, but Duncan could not afford to slow. He tightened his grip on his longbow, always listening for the sounds of pursuit.

A cold breeze blew from the north. The wind's smell changed from dry grass to the rich loam of turned soil. *Farmland...the steppes must give way to tilled farms.* And where there were farms, there were people, a way to hide, a chance to lose his scent in a tangle of humanity. He turned north, running into the wind, hope in his stride.

Behind him, the tenor of the hunt changed. The hellhounds howled, coming in his direction. The trap was finally sprung.

Ahead and to the right, something broke the flatness of the steppes. A low round structure, a hut made of stones with a sod roof. Drawn to the first sign of humanity, Duncan changed course. Breathing deep, he tasted the wind. The rich scent of loamy soil grew stronger...but he could find no trace of smoke or fire. Reaching for more speed, he ran through the waist-high grass till he burst into open farmland, the fields lying fallow for the winter.

The baying of the hounds grew louder, a relentless growl followed by an implacable gallop.

Duncan ran to the hut and put his shoulder to the oak door. The door flew inward without resistance, banging hard against the stone wall. Cold ashes and the stink of fear filled the doorway. Nocking an arrow, he stepped into the darkness.

A muffled cry came from the far wall. A man sat huddled in rags, a swaddled babe clutched tight in his arms. "Don't hurt me!"

Duncan eased the tension on his bow. "Who are you? What is this place?"

"No one." The man shook his head, his words laced with defeat. "Nothing."

Anger boiled into Duncan, he had no time for despair. "Answer me. Who are you?"

"A runner." He hugged the babe close. "My wife died in childbirth. I promised her the babe would know a better life. So I ran, stopping here for the night."

"Running to where?"

"Anywhere...away...south." The man kept his back against the wall.

Duncan pressed the question. "Are there any villages nearby?"

"A what?" His voice wavered. "Nothing here but the Citadel and the Pit."

The words struck like a death knell. No place to hide, no place to tangle his scent, no way to outrun the hellhounds...just a final battle.

The man stepped forward. "Are you from beyond the wall?" A glimmer of hope crept into his voice.

"Yes."

A wild howl ripped through the night.

"*The Mordant's hounds!*" Fear shivered through the man's words. "No one escapes those beasts."

Duncan stared at the man, knowing he'd led soldiers to his hiding place...but perhaps his bow could save two lives. "You'd best run." Duncan ushered him toward the door. "Run hard. I'll hold them off with my bow." They stepped from the hut and found the night filled with a wild clamor. The hunt drew near. The man trembled, holding the child so tight it whimpered. Duncan gripped his shoulder. "Run hard and find a better life."

"Luck be with you, stranger." The man bowed low and then sped south.

"And with you." Duncan turned and surveyed the hut. Inside was nothing but a trap...but the roof might provide a vantage point. He climbed the wall to the top, testing the sod before he stepped on it, grateful when it held his weight. He moved to the center, impaling his arrows upright in the grassy mound. Twenty-six arrows, their iridescent eyes defying the dark. He wondered if he'd ever see the Deep Green again.

He nocked an arrow and stared toward the south. The grassy rooftop provided his best view of the hunters. Six hellhounds carved furrows in the deep grass. Running straight as arrows, they howled for the kill. A troop of thirty soldiers galloped further behind, spears bristling toward the sky. *Too many*, but he'd make them pay dearly for his life. He raised his bow to the heavens, screaming his defiance. "I am Duncan Treloch, a ranger of the Deep Green, and I will not yield."

As if in answer, a bolt of lightning seared the sky.

The hounds loosed a twisted howl, a deep-throated baying.

Thinking of Kath, he whispered her words. "Make every arrow count." Focusing on the nearest hound, he drew the great bow to a deadly curve. Leading the beast by three lengths, he unleashed the longbow's power. An arrow sang into the night. Without waiting, he chose a new target. Draw and release, he sent three more arrows toward the hellhounds.

The first arrow struck true. A peal of pain erupted from the hunters. The leading hellhound yelped, rolling into a keening ball of mottled fur. Two more hellhounds dropped in their tracks...but the reaction of the rest chilled Duncan to the bone. Falling silent, the hounds scattered, abandoning their straight-arrow rush. Slinking to the ground, they disappeared into the deep grass, hard to see and harder to anticipate...as if the damn beasts knew how to thwart an archer.

Trumpets blared. Galloping horsemen drew near. The trap was nearly closed. Time was running out.

Duncan raised his bow, sending three arrows arcing toward the horsemen, hoping to slow their advance.

A low snarl came from his left.

Duncan whirled, an arrow nocked.

A hellhound broke from the grass, a tan and black fury streaking across the fallow field.

The arrow thwacked, catching the beast in the mouth. Howling in pain, it clawed at its own throat, disgorging a rush of blood.

Movement in the center, Duncan turned and released. The beast leaped to the left, showing an uncanny prescience, but the arrow found its flank. Gnashing its teeth, the hellhound lunged forward, dragging its rear leg, jaws slavering for revenge. If an animal could hate, this one did. Duncan spent another arrow, putting a shot in its right eye.

One hellhound left.

Sweat rolled down Duncan's back.

The horsemen stopped at the edge of the fallow field, watching in silence, letting the hellhound finish its task.

Duncan's muscles started to strain, keeping the great bow taut.

Lightning cracked the night.

A warning pricked at his back. Duncan whirled, his bow at the ready.

Saber-toothed jaws lunged toward his face; the beast had gained the roof.

He got the shot off and stumbled backwards.

The arrow flew straight down the beast's maw. Teeth snapped shut in a fierce snarl. The beast plowed into Duncan, pounding against his chest. Knocked backwards, he shielded his face from the jaws. Beast and archer tumbled from the roof. The ground hit hard, stealing his breath. Something snapped and a rush of hot blood soaked his leathers. The beast pinned him to the ground, a smothering weight. Holding the saber-sharp teeth at bay, Duncan lay still, staring at the beast's lifeless eyes.

Gasping for breath, he rolled the heavy body away. Smeared with hellhound blood, he struggled to stand, amazed to be alive.

A snarl of rage came from the soldiers, as if the men became their beasts.

Wakened to the danger, Duncan scrambled for his bow. The yew lay buried beneath the dead hellhound. He tugged it free and stifled a cry. *The bow was snapped in half!*

The solders advanced, their lances leveled, circling the hut.

His heart hammering, Duncan reached for the sword, his last defense.

A thicket of spears surrounded him, the final teeth of the trap.

At least he'd die a warrior's death, with his enemies slain at his feet. He beat his sword against their spears, metal clanging against metal. "Fight me, damn you. Fight me."

An officer with a plumed helmet growled, "Take him alive."

It was only then that Duncan realized the secret was not yet safe. He turned the sword to his own breast, both hands grasping the hilt. For half a heartbeat he hesitated, thinking of Kath, longing to see her one more time. Something struck the back of his head, a thunderous crack. Duncan staggered and fell. Desperate to end it, he reached for the dropped sword. A boot stepped on his hand. Had all the gods forsaken him? Another blow to the head...and darkness claimed him.

19

The Knight Marshal

Rumors spread like a plague through the maroon, slaughtering morale. The marshal prowled the walls, listening to the men, watching their faces, collecting their words. Dark tales grew with the telling, a grapevine of whispers on the ramparts, a gale of grim tidings in the great hall. Everywhere he turned, he heard tales of demons, dead princes, and treachery, proof the Octagon was cursed, fated to fall before the Mordant. Problem was, most of it was true. The god-cursed demon had done its work well. Defeat hung across the maroon like a pall yet the enemy was nowhere in sight.

The marshal balled his gauntleted hands into fists, anger in his stride. Morale was his responsibility. He had to find a way to kill the doubt or the battle would be lost ere the first sword was drawn.

A cold wind blew out of the north, bitter and harsh, suiting his mood. Reaching the central drum tower, he yanked the door open. Down the spiral steps and into the hallway, he strode towards the king's council chamber.

So much had changed in a single fortnight. Normally abuzz with dispatches and commands, the council chamber stood deserted, the hearth cold, the candles extinguished, the shutters latched shut. The stewards had done their work well. Bloodstains were long since washed from the floor, the bodies given honorable burial. But a deep cut remained on the door, a scar marking the fatal thrust of a blue steel blade. He flexed his sword hand, remembering. Two princes impaled on one sword, yet it seemed as if the demon still lived. Doubt stalked the Octagon like a hungry ghoul. Mired in worry, he paced the chamber, waging a battle of words in his mind.

The door creaked open.

He looked up, hoping to see the king, but it was just Lothar.

"Thought I'd find you here, a ghost haunting his gravestone." He eased the door shut and leaned against the wall, a grim look on his weathered face. "You've heard the talk."

"A belly full."

Lothar grunted, fingering the hilt of his battleaxe. "It grows worse by the day. Some are starting to see demons behind every face. Soon there won't be a lick of trust left among the maroon."

And then we'll have desertions. Neither man said it, but the thought hung in the room like a curse.

Lothar moved to the window, easing the wooden shutters open, letting a sliver of daylight pierce the gloom. "It doesn't help that the king stays locked in his chambers, lost in his cups."

"The king mourns his sons."

"And neglects his duty."

The truth stung, but the marshal could not disagree. "The question is, how to undo the damage? You saw his face. How do we mend a cracked blade?"

"A cracked blade is discarded, melted down for scrap. But we only have one king."

The marshal nodded. "Just so."

"And the number of heirs grows perilously short. At least the men won't be arguing about succession anymore."

But will Ulrich make a good king? Another thought left unsaid, hanging between them.

Lothar turned away. Leaning on the windowsill, he stared into a gray sky. "What did you see that day, after the monk jumped?"

He hadn't spoken of it to anyone.

Lothar sent him a piercing stare. "Your face was ghost-pale when you turned from the window...and the monk's body was never found."

His friend saw too much. "An owl. I saw a giant frost owl."

"*A changeling!*" Lothar swore, his face grim. "Bloody magic."

"Seems there are more powers at work here than we know." The marshal's voice dropped to a harsh whisper. "Sometimes I wonder if we aren't being used, just pawns in a greater game."

Lothar grunted. "Shapeshifters and magic, it's too deep for me." He sketched the hand sign against evil. "Always thought changelings were a myth." He stared at the open window. "If a simple monk wields such powers what will the Mordant hurl against us?"

"Now you know why I walk the walls so late at night."

Lothar scowled. "We need the king. Now more than ever."

The marshal nodded. "Just so."

A cold wind howled outside, banging the shutters wide open. Sunlight streamed into the chamber, a shaft of light striping the floor. The marshal pulled his maroon cloak close, a buffer against the bitter chill.

"What's this?" Lothar followed the sunlight to the fireplace grate. Something gleamed among the ashes. He knelt to work it free. Gasping, he pulled back as if snake-bit, but then he bent to pick it up. "The monk's crystal." He stood, holding the milk-white crystal aloft. "I never took the monk's test." His gaze turned to the marshal. "I guess I passed, not a demon in disguise." He set the crystal on the table.

Both men stared at it, as if it might spring to life.

Lothar broke the silence. "The bloody demon almost got away with it, wearing gloves on his hands."

The marshal shuddered at the thought, a demon-prince hiding among them, so close to the throne. In the thick of battle, the demon's orders would have been obeyed, betraying the Octagon. "The monk did us a great service...but the price was high, perhaps too high."

Lothar tugged on his mustache. "The king should not have turned on the monk."

"That was ill-done." The marshal reached for the crystal. "But this might prove a boon."

"How so?"

"Fight magic with magic. Prove to the men there are no demons among us." He fingered the crystalline shard, smooth as glass. "A wonder it didn't shatter against the hearth floor."

"A crystal tough as steel. It's not natural." Lothar's voice dropped to a low growl. "The king won't like it."

"Sometimes duty is a hard road." The marshal slipped the crystal into his pocket. "Time to rouse the king from mourning. Will you join me?"

"Me?" Lothar shrugged a bushy eyebrow. "I'll walk you to the bear's den but no farther."

"And you call yourself a knight?"

"Only a lowly captain, not the Lord Marshal."

The marshal grinned, grateful for his friend. "If you won't face the king, then go and spread some rumors, something positive to counter all the doubt."

"A tale or two told over a cup of ale? Now that's a task worthy of a true knight." Lothar flashed a rogue's grin. "What will it be? A story recounting the king's heroism, or do you fancy something new? Something about a crystalline shard?"

"Both. But don't stray too far from the truth."

"Never."

"And no talk of the owl."

Both men sobered. Shapeshifters were unfathomable evil and magic was an enemy swords couldn't fight. Both would cause doubts...doubts the Octagon could not afford.

The marshal stepped to the door. "I'll see myself to the king." He threw a pointed glare at his friend. "Keep your ear to the ramparts."

"Aye, I'll do that."

He left the council chambers, striding down the hallway and around the corner. A pair of maroon-cloaked guards snapped a half-hearted salute. Both cast wary glances at the marshal, like men uncertain of their orders. Even at the king's door he found doubt. Anger pulsed through him. "Stand straight and show some pride, for you guard our king."

Their eyes widened in surprise, but the men snapped to rigid attention, spear butts pounding the stone floor.

"Better." The marshal made his voice a command. "Let no one pass, for any reason." Taking a deep breath, he reached for the door and stepped into winter.

Every window was flung wide open and the hearth was choked with dead ashes. The king sat at the table, a cup in his hand, empty wine flagons strewn across the tabletop. Statue-still, he stared at his empty wine cup, as if someone else had put it there, perhaps Baldwin. Where was the lad anyway?

The marshal approached but the king did not stir. "My Lord, you'll catch your death of cold." He waited, but there was no reply. Frustrated, the marshal decided to play the squire. Latching the shutters, he knelt to strike a flint to the fireplace, seeking to return warmth to the king's chambers. The spark took and he added pine logs to the grate, a glow of warmth beating back the cold.

As he moved about the chamber, lighting candles to dispel the gloom, he talked as he worked, giving the king a running account of the Octagon. He spoke of morale and supplies, of catapults and horses, all in a soothing voice, like a man calming a skittish horse. Finished with the chores, he turned to study his liege. His silver hair was straggled and unkempt, his beard matted, fresh lines of grief graven deep in his face, but it was the eyes that worried him most, flat and dull, staring at nothing, lacking the spark of fire that so marked his king.

"My Lord, the men need you." He tossed the words out like a fisherman with a baited hook, desperate to lure a strike. But there was no response.

Anger mixed with desperation, the marshal's voice turned hard. Glaring at the king, he recounted the stories whispered on the ramparts. He spared no detail, repeating grim tales of demons and defeat. And all the while, he watched the king's face, hoping to rouse a reply, but there was never a flicker in those cold dead eyes. "So you see, my Lord, the men are rife with doubt. They need their king." He stared at his lord, willing a response.

The king's eyes remained dull, as if focused on some other world, but then he began to speak, his voice hoarse from disuse. "Red eyes, demon eyes, glowing in the face of my son. My son taken by a demon, cursed by the Dark, my second-born son." He shook his head, a mane of straggly silver. "Two sons pinned on one sword. Four sons dead, lost to treachery." He stared into his empty goblet. "Five true-born sons, always a surfeit of heirs, and now I have but one. *One.*" He shook his head in denial. "Red eyes, demon eyes, glowing in the face of my son."

The marshal shuddered. He'd heard it all before. A litany of repetition, the same words said over and over again, as if the king's mind was locked in a terrible loop, reliving the death of his sons, unable to move forward. It hurt him to see the king brought so low. "My Lord, you must break out of this nightmare. Don't you see? You do the demon's work for him! There are more powers at work here than we know. We dare not let the demons win."

"Red eyes, demon eyes, glowing in the face of my son..."

"Sire, this grief ill becomes you. Your son stayed true, offering his life to kill the demon. He died a knight of the Octagon. Don't dishonor his memory this way."

"Two sons pinned on one sword..." The mad mumbling continued like a chant.

Desperation pushed the marshal to anger. "We are the sword and shield of the southern kingdoms. We stand against the Dark tides." But his words made no difference. Without thought, he reached for his sword, the sword of the black knight, five feet of honest steel. Blade in hand, he stared at the king. *"Enough!"* He swept the sword across the tabletop, hurling flagons and metal goblets across the chamber. "No more!"

The mumbled litany continued. "Two sons pinned on one sword. Four sons dead, lost to treachery. Red eyes, demon eyes, glowing in the face of my son."

Frustration burned to rage. As if the demon stood before him, the marshal raised the great sword in a two-handed grip. With all of his might, he brought it down on the tabletop, a killing blow. Oak cracked in two. The table split in half, crashing to the floor.

The king staggered to his feet, his eyes blazing. "How dare you!"

Relief washed through him. "Sire, you're back."

"What?" Dazed, the king stared about the chamber, as if waking from a spell. He stared at the broken table and tugged on his disheveled beard, sniffing at the sour smell of his clothes. His lower lip curled in disgust. "How long?"

"Nigh on a fortnight, enough for rumors to run rampant."

Groaning, the king rubbed his hands across his face, lines of grief graven deep, as if he'd aged a decade. "So the men have heard the tale?"

"Heard it, re-told it, embellished it, twisted it till they see demons lurking behind every face." The marshal sheathed his sword. "It's as if the god-cursed demon still lives, wrecking havoc amongst the maroon. Morale is pushed to the breaking point. Defeat threatens before the enemy has even reached the gates."

The king moved to the fireplace, his shoulders hunched as if bracing for a blow. "Will the men still follow me? A king with a demon for a son?"

The marshal's breath caught, never having considered the question. "Sire, they'll follow you to hell and back. But they *must* see you. They need to know you still lead."

"My son a demon...yet I never knew." The king turned to face the marshal, his gaze haggard and haunted. "I never knew."

So it was not just grief that plagued his king, but doubt as well. "Sire, there was no way to know."

The king shook his head. "Four sons lost to treachery."

Fear slashed the marshal; he couldn't let the king retreat into nightmares. "Sire, you still have an heir, your first-born son."

"Yes, Ulrich, the least of my sons."

"And there's still a daughter."

The king turned from the fire, a spark of anger in his eyes. "I rule a kingdom of swords, a kingdom of steel. Of what worth is a daughter?"

The marshal did not press the point, relieved to have the king distracted from grief. "The men need to see you. We need to vanquish the legacy of the demon."

"And how am I to do that?"

The question staggered him; the king was ever in command, a master at morale. He fumbled for an answer. "By doing what you always do." His words gained conviction. "Turn a disadvantage into an advantage."

"How so?"

The marshal struggled to grasp thoughts that seemed just out of reach. "Perhaps Darkness has betrayed itself." His hand found his pocket, fondling the crystalline shard. "The demon proves we fight for more than just land and swords. The Dark Lord sent his minion against us...proving he *fears* the Octagon!" His thoughts gathered strength, like a stone rolling down a hill. "More than ever, the Octagon has a reason to fight. For we stand against pure evil."

The king straightened, as if hearing a battle call, but a nagging tic dogged his left eye, as if his reclaimed sanity was a fragile thing. "Your words ring true, Osbourne. But will it be enough to wean the men from fear?"

The marshal fingered the crystal, wondering if he dared remind the king of the monk. Deciding to risk all, he removed the shard from his pocket. "There might be a way. Fight magic with magic."

The king's eyes widened, his hand sketching the sign against evil.

"Lothar found this in the fire grate, lost in the confusion. But it might prove a boon." Holding the crystal aloft, he pressed the king with a flurry of words. "Claim the crystal as your own. Have it worked into the pommel of your sword. Let every man renew their oath by laying hands on the hilt of the king's sword. Let the men see for themselves that there are no demons among us."

"Magic worked into my sword?" Shaking his head, the king paced the chamber like a cornered bear. "I like it not."

"Dire times call for dire methods."

The king stilled, his face a snarl. "I'll think on it."

"As you wish." The marshal moved to the fireplace, setting the crystal upon the mantle, a constant reminder. "And the men?"

The king sighed. "The men need their king." He glanced down at himself, like a man waking from a long slumber. "But not like this. Where's my squire?"

"And Ulrich?" The marshal pressed the question, needing to be sure. "Shall I send for the prince, recalling him from Cragnoth Keep?"

"Only one son left." A tic worried the king's left eye like a threat. He shuddered as if throwing off a shroud. "Ulrich needs to earn his pride, to lead his own command to victory. I still believe the enemy will strike at the Crag. The Mordant dearly loves deceit." His face hardened, etched with grief, but the tic remained. "A lesson I've learned too well." His voice firmed with the ring of command. "Let Ulrich stay at Cragnoth and earn the right to wear the crown."

"As you command. Shall I summon your squire?"

"Yes." The king flicked a glance to the ruined table. "And you'd best find me a new table. Seems you've slayed this one."

The marshal could have wept with joy. His king was back. Perhaps they had a chance against the Dark.

20

Blaine

Blaine made the rounds, checking his stricken companions, praying one would wake. *Poison*, an enemy he did not know how to fight. He railed against the gods, but they offered no help. The sun's last rays succumbed, abandoning him to darkness.

Cold and desolate, he bundled Kath in blankets and dribbled water on her lips, praying for a change but he saw none. His gaze was drawn to the crystal dagger. It seemed wrong to let it lie in the grass, unprotected. Hesitating, he whispered a promise, "Only till you wake." He switched daggers, sheathing the crystal blade at his belt. Holding his breath, he listened to the night, half expecting the gods to protest...but there was no sound except the wind.

Chiding himself for silly superstitions, he unsheathed his blue steel sword and stood with his feet braced wide in a stubborn stance. He'd stand guard, keeping vigil against the predators of the night. Turning slowly, he surveyed the steppes, staring out into the darkness, hoping for friends, expecting foes.

A howl came from the south, a chorus of wolves...or hellhounds. Shivering, he tightened his grip on his sword, telling himself it was just wolves feasting on the dead.

Staring south, he tried to pierce the darkness, wishing Bryx would wake, wishing the archer would return. He kept a lonely vigil, without even the stars for company. Time seemed to crawl, a dull sameness, tempting him to sleep.

The moon traversed a cloud choked sky, a pale smudge of light. Blaine jerked awake, catching himself before he fell. Swearing, he gripped his sword, and pivoted, staring into the night, angry for drowsing. Weariness assailed him, yet he refused to succumb.

The moon disappeared, swallowed by the west, but darkness still gripped the sky. The wolves had fallen silent. Nothing moved save the tall grass rippling in the wind. The steppes seemed peaceful enough, slumbering through the night. Blaine stretched his aching muscles, waiting for the dawn.

"We see you, knight." Words whispered from the north.

Snapping his sword up, Blaine pivoted toward the voice, a chill shivering down his back. Grasses rustled around him, driven by the wind...but he saw no one.

"Whom do you serve?"

He whipped around, keeping his sword raised, the back of his neck prickling in warning.

A different voice from the left, *"Whom do you serve?"*

A shiver raced down Blaine's back. He'd heard that question before...in the Guardian Mist.

"Answer the question."

But this was a man's voice, a real voice, and it came from a different direction. Surrounded and outnumbered...but surely the Mordant's men would attack rather than talk. "I serve the Light." He kept his sword raised, pivoting, wary of an ambush.

"Then why are you here?"

The question made no sense, but he was desperate for help. "My companions need a healer."

"Everything has its price."

Anger coursed through him, he tired of their games. "Time is my enemy. Three of my companions are stricken with poison from a hellhound's claws. Do you have a cure?"

Whispers came from every direction, yet he saw no one. Icy fingers shivered down his back. Surrounded, with so many against him, he had no hope of fighting free. Blaine struggled to keep his voice calm. "Will you help?"

"Will you pay the price?"

Another voice hissed, *"Anton, they fought our enemy!"*

"I command here!"

A shiver of hope raced through Blaine.

"Will you pay the price?"

He had no idea what they wanted or why...but he had to save Kath and the others. "What do you want?"

"We value steel. Your blue sword for safe conduct to our healers."

Blaine staggered backwards. They asked for everything. A knight's weapon held his very soul. He was nothing without his blue steel sword...but then he remembered the crystal dagger.

"We trade lives for steel. Will you pay the price?"

"Can you cure them?"

"If the poison is not too far gone. You risk their lives by waiting."

He'd sworn an oath to Kath; he owed her his allegiance...even if it meant his blue steel sword. Honor was a hard taskmaster. He reversed the blade and extended the hilt. "Then take my sword and save them...or there'll be hell to pay."

Figures melted out of the grass, more than thirty. Hands on swords, they surrounded him. One drew close, moving with a lithe grace, claiming the offered sword. "The price is paid, the bargain accepted."

Blaine clenched his fists, naked without his blue blade. "Then help them." He pointed at Kath, his voice a low growl. "Help her first."

The clouds chose that moment to part, a flash of moonlight revealing his captors. Blaine gasped, retreating a step. Blue tattoos transformed their faces. Intricate designs of animals melded with human features, an eerie blending that created a wild, feral look. Fox, wolf, bear and eagle, they seemed otherworldly. Savage and fierce and illusive as legends, he stood surrounded by a pack of Painted Warriors.

Relief warred with unease. Blaine stepped forward, offering his hand. "Well met. I had not hoped to find allies of the Octagon so deep into the steppes."

The fox-faced leader barked a harsh laugh. "What allies? There's only a common enemy...or so we thought."

Warnings pricked the back of Blaine's neck. "What are you saying?"

"Tige, see to the wounded. I want to be gone before the dawn. And don't leave any of their belongings."

The fox-faced leader turned away, but Blaine grabbed his arm. "I want an answer."

"An answer!" The leader whirled, the tip of the blue steel sword poised at Blaine's throat. "Why are you here, knight? What brings you so deep into the steppes? Are you a deserter seeking the Mordant's service? Are you a spy? Or just a coward?"

"*A deserter!*" Outrage flamed through Blaine. He clenched his fists, fighting to swallow his rage. "We came to *slay* the Mordant."

"Hah! With two girls and an old man!" The leader's voice filled with scorn. "The Mordant must be trembling."

Rage erupted within Blaine, they had no idea what his companions were capable of. "You must have seen the battlefield just south of here?"

The fox-faced man gave a terse nod.

"That victory was *ours.*"

Murmurs rippled through the Painted Warriors.

The leader's face twisted to a sneer. "*Liar!*"

Blaine ducked past the raised sword and lunged, but another man stepped between them. "Stop this!"

Blaine hissed, "I do not lie."

Tattooed with a bear's face, the big man seemed unnaturally strong. "You asked for our help, do you still want it?"

Need dampened Blaine's anger. "Yes."

The fox-faced leader growled, "Let him go, Bearant. I'll spit this liar with his own sword."

The big man shook his head. "No. A bargain was made. The price was paid." He turned towards the leader, his voice dropping to a hushed whisper. "There is some riddle here, Anton. This is a matter for the Old One."

The leader snarled. "So be it." He glared at Blaine. "But if you prove false," he raised the blue sword in threat, "then your life and all of your possessions will be forfeit." He spat onto the ground as if sealing a bargain and then stalked away.

Blaine tightened his fists, staring at the leader's back, fighting his anger.

The bear-faced man leaned close, his voice a whisper. "Do not give him a reason to kill you."

Blaine struggled to sheathe his rage, watching as two of the Painted Warriors wrapped Kath into a type of carryall. "Can you heal them?"

"Our healers are skilled but we must reach the den to give them succor."

"Your den?"

"Our home."

The words held a world of pride. "Where is this den?"

"Do not get curious, knight. You'll be blindfolded long before we reach the den."

Blaine stiffened.

The man's voice held a placating tone. "It is not an insult but a matter of survival. The Mordant's forces far outnumber us. No outsider can know our secret paths." He gestured toward the northeast. "Come, we must be away. The dawn is our enemy."

The Painted Warriors gathered up his companions, including the wolf, and set off at a ground-eating pace. Silent and sure, they ran like a hunting pack, slipping through the tall grasses.

Weary and worried, Blaine struggled to keep pace. Feeling like an ox herded by wolves, he felt their dark stares tracking him, watching him, judging him, predators assessing prey. Cursing his lot, he longed for his sword, for the feel of blue steel in his hands. *A knight without a sword,* he gripped the crystal dagger at his belt. At least he'd kept that weapon safe...*so far,* but all would be for naught if the others died. Poison and hellhounds and tattooed warriors, the north was plagued with unexpected traps, worse than any nightmare. Cursing his ill fate and the indifference of the gods, Blaine ran through the tall grass, wondering if he'd bargained with friends or foes.

21

The Mordant

Darkness beckoned, a pulsing power in the dead of night. The Mordant snapped awake. Throwing off the silken sheets, he freed his arm from the concubine's embrace, ignoring her soft murmur. Drawing on a loose robe of black silk, he reached for the Staff of Pain, never far from his hand. Pulled by the summons, the Mordant strode through the palace, his bare feet silent on the cold marble floor, answering the call of his god.

The hallways were empty; the palace slumbered, but never the Dark Lord. He reached the marbled entranceway, surprising a pair of guards leaning on their spears. Snapping a salute, they scrambled to throw open the outer doors. A cold wind blew in, threatening the torchlight. He paused in the doorway, surveying the outer courtyard. Glinting with moonlight, the granite pavement shimmered like an arcane sea. Runes spiraled around the yard, black marble inlaid in granite, a ripple of spells circling the ancient boulder. Thrust up like a dark island in a sea of runes, the top of the great monolith pierced the courtyard, the bedrock of the citadel. The ancient stone throbbed with power, the summons emanating from a boulder's shadowy cleft. Drawn to Darkness, the Mordant crossed the runes till the monolith loomed overhead, a primordial darkness blotting out the stars.

Old and full of secrets, the cleft gaped with shadows, a deep gash in the side of the stone. He slipped inside, his footfalls smothered by a cold silence, as if he'd entered a tomb. Stairs spiraled down, worn with age, leading to a secret buried in the heart of the great rock. Shadows gave way to torchlight, the smell of soot hanging in the cold, damp air. Descending into the depths, the Mordant summoned the monk. *Attend me, for tonight you shall meet a god.*

Inside his mind, the monk gibbered in fear, hiding behind a litany of prayers.

You feel it, don't you monk, the call of the Dark Lord.
I walk in the Light. I walk in the Light.

Amused by the feeble defense, the Mordant laughed. His laughter echoed in the well of stone. Twisted by the depths, it became an eerie chortle, like a ghost leading him downward, a deep delving into the earth. Carved from solid rock, the steps were old and treacherous, footprints worn deep into the ancient stone. Six hundred and sixteen steps, the number of steps to power, the number of steps to hell.

The Dark summons tugged at his soul, offering the promise of power. The same song had lured him to the heart of the monolith...twelve lifetimes and over a thousand years ago. So many victories, so much dark glory, but this lifetime would exceed them all. His footsteps quickened. Infused with the vigor of youth, he returned to the source of his power.

The long descent ended in an antechamber of dancing torchlight. Two guards in black and gold armor stood at attention before the great copper Door. He stared at the guards. "Do you know your Lord, the Mordant reborn?"

They fell to the floor in prostration, a clatter of armor on stone.

The Mordant strode toward the great Door, ancient runes inscribed in the gleaming copper. He made his voice a command. *"Sion rasmathus!"*

As if drawn by invisible hands, the great Door slowly swung open. Cold air laden with the stench of sulfur flowed out, a breath of Darkness calling him forward.

The Mordant crossed the threshold, his bare feet silent on the cold floor. Ancient beyond telling, the cavernous chamber brimmed with Darkness. Red stalactites dripped from the ceiling as if the stones wept blood, a testament to so many sacrifices. Beneath the vaulted ceiling, a golden pentacle stretched across the marble floor. Five braziers glowed at the points, flames fueled by the fires of Hell, an eternal glow quenched only by the Dark God's will.

Power pulsed in the shadows, a promise and a threat. The Mordant breathed deep, reveling in the Darkness.

Bowing low, he began the ritual of opening. Slowly circling the Dark Lord's symbol, his body swayed to the arcane dance, his bare feet beating a rhythm of runes into the cold stone floor. Words of power whispered from his lips. Round and round, the tempo increased to an exultant frenzy. Infused with youth and vigor, the chant roared out of him, a herald of Darkness. His black robes rippled behind like a windblown wraith, yet there was no wind. Power crackled along his skin, aching to be unleashed. Dark magic hummed through him, an ecstasy and an agony, too much to contain. Brimming with power, the Mordant threw back his head and screamed, *"Alamat anak an!"* The braziers flared bright. Flames roared to the ceiling, releasing plumes of red sparks that fell like glowing embers. A thunderclap shook the chamber, a burnt smell hanging in the air.

Darkness roiled across the ceiling, obscuring the stalactites...the breath of a god.

Slick with sweat, the Mordant bowed low. "I have returned, Lord, eager to begin the work of this lifetime."

But every summons required a sacrifice.

He shrugged the dark robe from his shoulders, letting the silk puddle to the floor. Naked, he entered the pentacle. Falling to the floor in prostration, he struggled to still his eagerness. Turning, he lay spread-eagle, making the sign of the pentacle with his body, his arms and legs spread wide, his back pressed to the cold stone, his manhood stiff with anticipation. He stared up at the roiling Darkness, a perfect offering.

Darkness came for him. A dense cloud of inky blackness descended, pressing against his chest, bearing down with all the weight of antiquity.

The Mordant fought to breathe.

Cold and relentless, the Darkness smothered his face, seeking entrance.

Knowing total submission was the price of great power, he opened his mouth, fighting hard not to gag.

Darkness took him, pain laced with power, pouring down his open mouth.

His body convulsed, arms and legs twitching, a puppet on a string, and still the Darkness came, slamming into him, filling his mouth, roaring down his throat like a waterfall of sin. He arched his back, an empty vessel filled to the brim. Pain blurred to unbearable rapture. Visions flooded his mind, details of the great Dark design. He saw the map of Erdhe laid out before him, the winds of war sweeping across the land. Advantages became clear, plots within plots, a weft and weave of possibilities, some of the threads added centuries ago. Rivals for the Dark Lord's affection were revealed, younglings whose ambition outstripped their achievements, tools to be used and then cast aside. Chess pieces dotted a complicated board, a game long in play. A series of feints, traps, and sacrifices, all waiting to be triggered in a colossal conflict. So many pawns...and he was the only true king, the darkest power on the board. He wondered about the opposing forces, the minions of Light, but visions of the enemy were denied him...yet the blind spots spoke volumes, targets for attack. So many opportunities...and all the weapons were his to wield.

The Dark Lord's voice boomed in his mind. *This is the lifetime when old enemies will be crushed.*

Understanding shivered through him, a vision of victories long awaited.

The hidden ones have at last been revealed.

An image of the amulet stolen from the monastery filled his mind. Waves of ecstasy washed across him. He longed to claim the secrets hidden behind midnight-blue doors.

But another enemy rises in the new heart of Erdhe. A woman dares to sit upon a throne.

A tidal wave of revulsion poured across him. He felt the Dark Lord's outrage, that a single woman would dare upset the scales of prejudice. Once more he saw the map of Erdhe, a blind spot stretching over the kingdom of Lanverness, a blight of civilization, a plague of justice. He watched as the Dark Lord's wrath poured across the map, a belch of acid scorching the parchment black.

First we deceive, then we divide, then we annihilate. This woman threatens to undo the hierarchy of hatred sewn into the very fabric of Erdhe. She must be brought low, her very name defiled.

Visions flooded his mind, ways to corrupt a single thread, to turn a queen to ruin. The possibilities were delicious, full of deception, his favorite game of his past lives.

Centuries of planning culminate in this lifetime. Do not disappoint.

Power arced through him, striking like lightning, igniting every nerve in his body. He writhed in the grip of his god, torn between agony and ecstasy. His mouth stretched wide, plumbed by Darkness, too much for mortal flesh to contain. Filled with Dark power, his back arched, his manhood spewing in triumph. Once, twice, thrice, he shuddered with agony, he shuddered with delight, enduring pain and pleasure on a godly scale. Just when he thought he could bear it no longer, the Darkness withdrew.

Drenched in sweat, aching and sore, the Mordant lay gasping on the cold stone floor, flushed with triumph. The immortal touch was gone, but Darkness was forever branded on his soul, leaving him throbbing with power. Such euphoria, such sweet pain, the Mordant struggled for breath, exalted with power. Lying spread-eagle, he strained to remember every detail, so many seeds of victory, so many triumphs to come. A sound intruded. In the back of his mind, the monk wept...a shattered sob. The Mordant laughed, for none could stand in the face of the Dark Lord.

22

Duncan

Shackles bound his wrists...chains on his legs. Duncan's head throbbed...his whole body ached. A loud creaking sound split his skull, like a knife stabbing his mind. Lying face down, his cheek pressed to cold iron, he stared through squinted eyes, struggling to understand. A pair of hob-nailed boots stood in front of his face, but beyond, the world...*moved*.

The last thing he remembered was standing in a ring of spears. He should be dead instead of captured...a groan escaped his lips.

A hand gripped his hair, yanking his head up. "So it's true." A bearded soldier in black leather armor leered into his face, his breath rank with sour ale. "What the hell are you? The Pit's spawned many a freak, but never a man with a cat's eye. Do you have a tail to go with it?"

Duncan tried to swallow, his words a weak croak. "Water?"

"Water!" The soldier barked a cruel laugh. "You'll be lapping puddles of piss before the day's done." He released Duncan's hair, letting his head thump against the iron floor. A swift kick followed, a solid blow to the ribs.

Grunting in pain, Duncan rolled away but he could not go far. His back hit iron bars.

His guard laughed, but no more blows followed.

Curled on the floor, Duncan struggled to understand. Iron bars...they'd put him in a cage. But beyond the bars, the world *moved*. He shook his head, fighting for clarity. Understanding slowly dawned. The metal cage descended along a sheer cliff, hence the creaking noise. But the passing cliff face was like none he'd ever seen. Gray stone fused smooth as glass, dark planes reflecting light...almost as if the stone had been *melted*. He craned his neck for a better view, pressing his face to the bars. A gasp escaped him. Not a cliff, but a great pit. As if an angry god had punched his fist straight down into the earth, boring a hole half a league to hell.

A nameless fear gripped him. He was trussed in chains, a captive being lowered into a hellish hole. Duncan's mind shuddered, desperate for a way to escape. His gaze skittered across the pit. Like a hungry maw, it gaped wide, more than three leagues across...all the walls as slick as glass, no sign of any road or stairs...a sheer descent to the underworld. A dark brown cloud obscured the bottom...*if there was a bottom.* All his senses screamed in warning, *abomination.* Horror-struck, Duncan struggled against his chains, sensing the pit was an offense against the land, a fathomless evil.

A horn sounded from below, three short blasts, so perhaps there was a bottom.

Shackled and caged...his mind shied away from guessing what horrors might lie beneath the dark cloud. Whatever his captors had planned for him, Duncan swore to die rather than reveal the secret.

Chains clanked beyond his cage.

An arm-span away, another cage went up. Crowded with men in dirty rags, they peered through the bars, desperation etched on all their faces.

His guard chuckled, a mean-spirited sound. "Take a good look, berk. They're the lucky ones. It's always better to go up than down."

Duncan craned his neck, watching the ascent. Metal structures leered over the pit top like great praying mantises, chains dangling from their pointed heads. More cages jerked up and down the cliff walls, some of them crowded with soldiers, others with ragged prisoners.

Chains rattled and creaked overhead, marking the endless descent. His cage entered the brown cloud. A harsh tang of burnt manure and smoldering grease assaulted his nostrils. Duncan gagged. He pressed his face to his sleeve, wondering how anyone could breathe such a stench. The cloud thinned and he got his first glimpse of the bottom. A city sprawled below, a vast slum of mud huts and stone hovels, teeming with people, like beetles on a dung heap. Everything was dirt brown or stone gray, dingy and depressing, not a speck of living green. His soul shuddered. A prison modeled on hell, stocked with an army of slaves, the north proved worse than any nightmare. Kath had no idea what she faced. How could the gods let such evil exist?

The cage rattled and shook, slowly shuddering to a stop.

The guard prodded him with the toe of his boot. "On your feet, berk."

Duncan struggled to stand, clinging to the bars as the world spun, willing his vision to clear.

The door of the cage swung open. More guards waited outside, all of them wearing black leather armor.

"Out." The guard shoved Duncan, sending him staggering from the cage. His chains clanked as he struggled to keep his balance. The ground proved soft, clay trampled to mud, his boots sinking deep in the muck. He glanced up but the brown cloud hid the sky, as if he'd passed into a netherworld, beyond the sun's warming touch.

"Keep moving, berk." His guard herded him along the cliff wall, past half a dozen cages. A troop of ten soldiers piled out of one cage, smiles on their faces, trading bawdy jokes, while a line of shackled slaves waited to load. A whip cracked and the slaves shuffled forward, heads bowed. Duncan risked a glance at the taskmaster and staggered to a stop. *An ogre!* Like a nightmare sprung to life, the ogre towered over mere men. Tall and barrel-chested, it had a sloping forehead, a chinless jaw, and protruding ridges for eyebrows, a monster clad in leather armor. Duncan traced the hand sign against evil, wondering what other horrors served the Mordant.

"Hurry up, berk!"

Something hard prodded him in the back. Duncan struggled to keep pace, stepping to the limit of his shackles. He shuffled past the line of cages, eventually reaching a raised stone platform, a crude dais set high above the sea of mud. Soldiers in black armor flanked the platform while a scribe sat halfway up the stairs, scribbling on a roll of parchment. A massive stone chair carved of gray rock dominated the dais. A fleshy man in dark blue robes reclined in the chair like a king on a throne. Bald headed and smooth shaven, he caressed a cat-o-nine tails while passing judgment on a kneeling slave.

Duncan joined the line of captives, standing behind a skinny man stripped naked except for a soiled loincloth, iron shackles on his wrists and feet. The man reeked of sweat and fear, the perfume of the Mordant's subjects.

A guard at the top of the stairs pounded his iron-shod spear against the stone platform. "Next!"

The line shuffled forward. A burly guard forced an auburn-haired woman to kneel. "My Lord, a woman of the fifth tier found guilty of trying to sell her newborn child to a third tier family. The priests have condemned her to the pit brothel as penance for her sins."

"Lift her face."

The guard forced the woman's head back.

"Hmmm." Leaning forward, the bald-headed lord smiled like a cat about to eat a bird. "Too pretty a flower for the brothels. Clean her up and send her to my residence. I'll see to it she atones for her sins."

The guard saluted fist to chest, "Yes, m'Lord," and ushered the sobbing woman back down the stairs.

One at a time, the prisoners climbed the stairs to learn their fate. Duncan stood with his head bowed, stealing glances at his surroundings. The litany of crimes made little sense. He'd expected to be questioned and tortured, but it seems they'd put him with common criminals. Perhaps there was a chance he could live to escape while keeping the secret safe.

The line of prisoners shuffled forward till only two were left.

Guards dragged the skinny dark-haired man to kneel before the throne. Trembling, he bowed low, sweat glistening on his pale white skin. "A priest, m'Lord, condemned to the iron mines."

"A bloody *priest!*" The lord scowled. "What did this one do?"

The guard shook his head. "The bishop did not say, only that the man was to serve the remainder of his life in the iron mines."

"Priests and their dark damned secrets," the lord's voice dropped to a growl, "the bloody priesthood never lets anyone peek up their robes." He gestured toward the kneeling man. "Probably sent to spy on me."

The guard answered, "No, m'Lord, they took his tongue."

"His tongue, eh?" The lord leaned forward, a flicker of interest on his face. "That's one way of keeping secrets safe. I wonder what he knows." He stared at the prisoner as if considering other possibilities, but then he shook his head, resignation in his voice. "Priests are dangerous, even with their tongues cut out. Send him to the mine's deepest level. From the looks of him, he won't last long."

The condemned man wailed in protest, a guttural sound. The guard cuffed him across the side of the face, dragging him down the steps.

Duncan's guard gave him a prod. "Your turn, berk." He climbed the steps and knelt, keeping his head and his gaze lowered.

The lord spoke first. "What've you got this time, Cribb?"

"A runner. A gate patrol found him in the farmland." The guard poked Duncan in the ribs. "They say he killed a half dozen gore hounds before they captured him."

"Ha!" The lord barked a cruel laugh. "A bald-faced lie. More likely the lazy buggers are spreading rumors, trying to gain a posting to the citadel." He gestured with the cat-o-nine tails. "Let's see his markings."

Another guard grabbed Duncan's shackles, pulling his left arm straight. It was only then that he noticed his left sleeve had been slashed open, a cut running from elbow to wrist but there was no wound to match the slice. The guard peeled back the black leather, revealing his forearm. "No markings. A rune-less bastard."

One of the guards gasped in surprise.

"That ain't all." The guard from the cage gripped Duncan's hair, yanking his head back. "Take a good look at his eye."

"Spawn of the Pit!" The lord leaned forward. "Bring him closer."

Duncan began to rise, but the guard held a dagger to his throat. "On your knees, berk."

Goaded by a sword at his back, Duncan was compelled to shuffle forward, the stone dais hard beneath his knees. He reached the base of the throne and stopped, struggling to smother his rage.

The lord leaned close, his breath like bad cheese. "An eye like a cat, that's a new one for the Pit. The breeders might be interested in him. Might even be a reward for such a big healthy berk." Avarice gleamed in his dark gaze. "I'll alert the priests but in the meantime he'll serve the mine. A turn in the iron mine will take the fight out of him." He sat back, caressing the handle of the cat-o-nine tails. "See that he's branded and fitted for a collar."

His guard nodded, a grin on his face. "I'll see to it." He gave Duncan a shove. "On your feet, berk, let's go."

"Cribb, aren't you forgetting something?" The lord's voice was smooth as velvet.

His guard turned. "What?"

"His boots, Cribb. To the Master of the Pit go the spoils."

"As you say, Lord Sleghorn." He snarled at Duncan, his voice laced with frustration. "Take'em off, berk."

They treated him like cattle...but humiliation was better than torture. Duncan worked around his chains, struggling to remove his boots, struggling to control his anger. One at a time, the boots came off, a Midwinter gift from Jordan...at least he'd left his silver warrior ring with Kath. Another guard grabbed the boots and threw them in a basket overflowing with plundered trinkets...the spoils of the damned.

His guard pricked him with a sword. "On your feet, berk."

They never even asked his name. Perhaps names did not matter in hell. He got to his feet and started down the stairs.

"And Cribb," the lord's voice cut like a knife, "don't even think of trying to collect the deformity bounty on him. This one's mine."

His guard gave a curt bow. "As you wish, Lord." He gave Duncan an angry shove, nearly toppling him down the steps.

Duncan's bare feet sank deep into the mud. Cold and clammy, it felt loathsome. Everything about the pit was vile and disgusting. He strained against his chains, struggling to keep pace with his guard, trying not to fall. He'd expected torture...but instead he found himself chained and shackled to the living damned, one among a multitude of slaves, condemned to work a prison pit. Duncan stifled a laugh, wondering if it was the onset of madness. His captors had brought him to the heart of the Mordant's domain yet he was essentially invisible, lost among so much misery. Perhaps hell was as good a place as any to keep a secret safe.

23

Katherine

Horses running, manes caught by the wind, a whole herd racing across the ceiling. *Across the ceiling,* the thought jarred her awake. Groggy with sleep, Kath struggled to make sense of her surroundings. Chalk drawings covered the cavern walls, but instead of being flat and lifeless, the horses flowed with vibrancy across the walls. Contours in the rock gave the horses an added dimension, a wild gallop of ocher, umber, and charcoal. Cunningly drawn, she half expected to hear hoofbeats. But why was she in a cave and who made the drawings?

The last thing she remembered...*poison!* Bolting awake, she sat up, the sheepskin cover slipping down to reveal her nakedness. Grabbing the cover, she scanned the small cave, relieved to be alone. Stretching, she tested her leg, expecting agony. The skin of her left thigh pulled taut with only a twinge of pain. She picked at the bandage, needing to see. Five claw marks scored her left thigh, but the wounds were scabbed over, free of the poison's black taint. Shivering with relief, she stretched muscles stiff with disuse but otherwise well. Even the blisters on her left hand had healed to calluses, becoming a match for her sword hand. Naked, she touched Duncan's warrior ring, letting the ring and the small stone gargoyle dangle between her breasts, comforted by their presence, glad to be alive.

She found her clothes folded in a neat pile next to the bedroll, her green wool cloak on top of her leather jerkin...but where were her weapons? A chill shivered down her spine. Attacking the pile, she ransacked the clothes, but her sword belt and axes were missing...and so was the crystal dagger. Fear sliced through her, without the dagger she had no hope of defeating the Mordant...and the absence of weapons meant she was a prisoner. But whose? And where were the others? A flood of questions assaulted her.

A second fear stuck like lightning. She grabbed the leather jerkin, plunging her hand into the deepest pocket, relieved to find the amber pyramid. They'd taken all her weapons, including the dagger hidden in her boot, but perhaps her captors did not recognize magic, a definite advantage. Clutching the pyramid, she pulled on her clothes, surprised to find them washed and mended. A neatly stitched patch repaired her leather pants. Why would her captors mend her clothes? Another mystery.

She tried standing, slowly easing weight onto her left leg. The leg held with only a slight twinge of pain, one less worry.

Kath searched the cave, looking for weapons, looking for clues to her captors. The narrow chamber ended in a rough rock wall, the floor worn smooth by use. A clay chamber pot sat behind a boulder, but otherwise the cave was empty, except for the chalk drawings. Horses pranced along one wall and up across the ceiling, more beautiful than any castle tapestry. Rich with color and movement, the horses ran wild and free, a vibrant celebration of life. Surely whoever made these drawings could not serve the Mordant. Perhaps there was hope.

Retreating from the dead end, she walked beneath the mural, seeking a way out. It struck her that the cave was well lit; yet there were no torches or any scent of fire. Light came from the far side of a boulder, perhaps a way out. Feeling the need for a weapon, Kath hefted a fist-sized rock, a poor substitute for steel. Sticking to the shadows, she rounded the boulder...and stared slack-jawed. Light streamed from a foot-tall crystal embedded in the floor, enough radiance to light the cave. Perhaps her captors had magic after all. Extending a hand, she slowly moved toward the crystal, surprised to feel no heat. Kath wondered if she dared touch it.

Soft footfalls came from behind. "Don't touch that."

Kath whirled to confront a middle-aged woman, dark hair framing a tattooed face. *The Painted Warriors!*

"So you know of us." The woman had a disarming smile. "I came to tend your wounds but it seems you're healed."

"Who are you? Where are we?" Kath staggered under an avalanche of questions. "Where are my friends? My weapons?" She stared at the blue tattoos, a raven etched on the woman's face, giving her an eldritch look. "How did you find us?"

She laughed, a light-hearted sound. "So many questions." Flicking her dark hair behind her ears, she settled gracefully to the floor and sat cross-legged, holding a stoppered jug in her lap. "Sit, Kath of Castlegard, and I'll do my best to answer your questions."

"You know my name?"

Another laugh. "The tall blond knight, Sir Blaine, is a plague of questions, always pestering the healers for word of you."

"Then Blaine is safe." Relief washed through her. "But what of the others? Is Danya awake? And what about the monk? And Duncan..." A cold fist gripped her heart.

"Will you not sit and join me?"

Kath bridled her questions and sank to the earthen floor, studying the raven-faced woman. Except for the elaborate tattoos, she seemed ordinary enough, clad in a sheepskin jerkin with leather pants tucked into knee-high boots. But it was the dagger sheathed at the woman's belt that caught Kath's attention. Her voice dropped to a steely whisper. "Am I a prisoner?"

The woman sighed. "Will you give me a chance to explain?"

Kath nodded, hiding the rock in her fist, unsure if it was needed.

"My name is Thera, a healer, a mother of three, and a follower of the Raven." She set the clay jug aside. "And you are lucky to have escaped the poison of the gore hounds."

"*Gore* hounds?"

"Aye, for that is their true name. Abominations created by the Mordant, made with the darkest magic." The healer's voice dropped to a whisper. "It is said that the souls of men are bound within the hounds, the reason they hunt with unnatural cunning and ferocity."

Kath reeled backwards, remembering the uncanny attack, stunned by the horror behind the woman's words. "Valin's sword." Shuddering, she made the hand sign against evil, dispelling the nightmare. "But how did you find us?"

"The ravens. Their dark wings blackened the sky, too many to merely be a trap."

"A trap?"

"We value steel but cannot make it, for the Ghost Hills provide no iron ore. So our men follow the ravens, scavenging the battlefields of the steppes. Such a huge cloud of ravens signaled a rich find of steel, a tempting prize." Her voice hardened. "But the soldiers of the Mordant know of our need. Sometimes they butcher a few slaves to draw the ravens, setting a trap for our men." The healer looked away. "My husband died in just such a trap."

"My sorrow for your loss." Kath considered what she'd learned. "So if we'd stayed at the battlefield, your men would have found us?"

"The Mordant's men got there first."

Kath's heart froze.

The healer flashed a triumphant smile. "But this time it was *our* men who closed the trap. Numbers always win in the steppes."

For a heartbeat, the raven's fierceness dominated the woman's features, blue feathers and a sharp beak accenting the wild gleam in her dark eyes. Kath half expected the woman to sprout wings and caw. "Why does a healer wear the tattoos of a raven?"

"Ravens know death." She cocked her head like a bird. "Know your enemy in order to defeat him."

And these people know the Mordant, living in his very shadow. Fierce warriors, they could be the very allies she needed. Kath leaned forward, anxious to learn more, but the healer forestalled her with a question. "How do you know of my people?"

"I grew up in Castlegard, listening to tales of the north. The knights tell stories that are almost legends, about an elusive people who tattoo their faces with images of animals and dare to ambush the Mordant's forces."

"So, we are little more than legends to you?" The healer's voice held a bitter edge.

Surprised by the bitterness, Kath sought to repair the damage. "I met a Painted Warrior once, in the courtyard of Castlegard." She remembered the morning when a patrol of knights clattered into the castle's inner courtyard, two years and a lifetime ago. "Tattooed like a mountain lion, he wore a shirt of soft white leather embroidered with small blue flowers."

The healer gasped, her face turning ghost-pale.

Kath studied the woman, trying to read the emotions swirling beneath the blue tattoos.

The healer fondled a beaded leather bracelet on her left wrist, avoiding Kath's stare. "The mountain lion is rare among our people."

"And the blue flowers?"

"Maiden's Tears." Her voice was distracted, her gaze fixed on the bracelet. "It is said that Maiden's Tears only bloom on the graves of heroes."

Kath sat statue-still, watching the healer, trying to avoid pitfalls in a conversation she did not understand.

The healer glanced at Kath, dark eyes framed by raven's feathers. "What happened to this man of the mountain lions?" Her voice was deceptively calm, a subtle warning.

Kath hesitated, feeling as if she stood on the edge of a cliff...but the woman deserved an answer. "He died..."

"Stop!" The healer's hand flew to Kath's lips. "Do not speak of it!" The raven glared fierce from the woman's face. "The truth of such a death must first be told in the Great Hall, for all to hear and learn and remember."

Kath nodded, wondering why one man could matter so much.

"Promise that you will not speak of it until the appointed time."

"If you wish."

"Swear it." The words were flung like daggers.

Kath did not understand, but she nodded, her voice solemn. "I so swear."

"Good." The healer raked a hand through her long hair, her face a mixture of grief and worry, her voice cold. "Come, I will take you to your friends." She rose to her feet, turning her back on Kath.

Trying to bridge the sudden chasm, Kath gripped the healer's arm. "I did not mean to offend."

"No offense was taken." But her tone remained cold.

"Are my friends well?"

The healer hesitated. "The girl is awake but heart-sore, eating little and saying less. The old man," Thera shook her head, "the poison of the gore hounds is slow to act but terrible in its vengeance. With the loss of an arm," she shrugged, "it remains to be seen if the old man will defeat the poison."

"He *must* survive." The words hissed out of Kath.

"We do our best, but his life depends on the gods."

Thera turned to go, but Kath had one more question. "My weapons?"

The healer stopped, her face guarded. "Your throwing axes with their red hawk harness are much admired. Good steel, excellent craftsmanship."

No mention of the crystal dagger. "I need my weapons."

"They are being held in safe keeping."

The meaning behind the words hit Kath hard. "So we're prisoners."

"Not prisoners...guests who are not yet trusted."

"But we both fight the Mordant."

The raven stared back at her, eyes as cold and hard as ebony chips. "Freedom is hard won."

Her reply struck like a cold slap. Kath felt as if she teetered on the edge of a chasm, a division of history and customs, a great divide sundering potential allies. "How can I win the trust of your people?"

The raven retreated, letting the woman return. "The Ancestor will decide." She raised a hand forestalling any more questions. "When the old man's battle is either won or lost, then you will be tested." Her voice held a note of finality. "In the presence of the Ancestor, much will become known." She turned. "Now come, your friends await."

24

Duncan

"On your feet, maggots!" The harsh cry came from overhead. "Rise and serve. The Mordant needs his ore." A grated trapdoor clanged open and a wooden ladder was thrust through the hole. Three boys in ragged clothing scampered down into the chamber. Two carried large buckets while the third held a bulging sack over his shoulder.

The smell of sour gruel pierced the chamber, pulling even the sick and the feeble from their straw pallets. Only the dead did not respond, two men sprawled face down in the soiled straw.

Fifty-eight prisoners rose and stood along the rock walls, a clang of chains and a shuffle of bare feet, every pair of eyes focused on the two buckets. Like a pack of starving wolves, the men slavered to be fed. Duncan stood with the others, fighting the urge to lunge for the pail of murky water. More than food, he craved an end to his raging thirst, but he bridled his need, refusing to act like an animal.

Light blazed in the chamber's heart, a lantern lowered on a chain through the trapdoor. Grack, the one-armed turnkey followed, the ladder groaning under his massive weight. Maimed and battle-scarred, the ogre-like Taal wore cruelty like a cloak. "Get to it boys." His voice sounded like gravel. "Feed the maggots and then we'll get them into their holes. The day's a wasting."

The three boys leaped to obey, working their way around the chamber.

One at a time, the prisoners reached into the bag and grabbed a small metal bowl and a cup. The bucket boys followed, allowing each man one dip of gruel and one cup of murky water. Duncan waited his turn, watching the buckets with desperate eyes, angry if even a single drop was spilled. Any man who wasted water or gruel rarely lived to see another morning.

When his turn finally came, Duncan plunged his bowl into the grayish-brown gruel and dipped his cup into the bucket, careful not to spill a drop. Like the others, he ate standing, quickly lapping the foul-tasting gruel like a starving cat. A sour mash of barley and wheat, he licked the bowl clean. Finished, he gulped the muddy water, the taste of metal fouling his mouth. All too soon, the cup ran dry, leaving his raging thirst unslaked. One cup was never enough.

While the others slurped their morning meal, Grack prowled the chamber, swinging his spiked mace in a deadly arc. "We'll have no slackers in this cell." The fearsome weapon whistled with threat. "Only death frees a man from the mines." Moving with surprising speed, the massive Taal strode to the nearest dead man, smashing the mace into his head. Blood and brains splattered the chamber. Grack laughed. "Meat tonight, boys." Two quick strides and the mace struck the second corpse. The skull shattered with a sickening crunch. Death was never feigned in the mines.

Accustomed to cruelty, the boys continued working their way around the chamber, gathering the empty cups and bowls. Grack chose two prisoners to strip the dead, lifting their shattered bodies up through the trapdoor. Duncan used the time to stretch, knowing what lay ahead. Bare-chested, he'd cut his leather shirt to strips, wrapping his feet for protection against the rock shards. His ankles were free of chains but he still wore shackles on his wrists and an iron collar around his neck. Collared and chained like a beast, they'd even put a brand on his left forearm, a rune of some sort, marking him like cattle. The brand had long since healed, but Duncan couldn't stand the sight of it. Being 'owned' was anathema to the people of Deep Green...but he was a long way from the great forests, chained in this hell-spawned pit. His hatred ran deep; the Mordant had much to pay for.

"All right maggots, time to earn your gruel."

The prisoners shuffled into line as Grack unlocked the iron-studded door. One at a time, they shambled through. Duncan waited his turn with the others. His fellow prisoners were a strange bunch, as if a freak-show carnival had been captured and forced to work the mine. Hal was a giant of a man, with a face like a Taal and the mind of a child. Gren was a dwarf with a nasty temper. Simeon and Brent were hunchbacks. Trell had a clubfoot and Stan a cleft lip. But Nef and Bredan were by far the strangest. Nef had six fingers on each hand, making him an excellent juggler, but Bredan's deformity was downright eerie. The older man had a closed eyelid in the middle of his forehead, like some monster from a bard's nightmare. Duncan found himself staring at it, wondering if the lid truly hid a third eye. He shivered at the strangeness of the thought. Deformities were not unknown to the villages of Erdhe, but it seemed to Duncan that nature had run amok in the pit...or perhaps nature was not the cause. The Mordant's hellhounds were not natural...and neither was a third eye. Shuddering, he made the hand sign against evil, following the others toward the door.

"Hurry up, maggots." Grack growled, "The Mordant needs his iron ore. Meet the quotas or no one eats."

The prisoners quickened their pace. Duncan reached the doorway and one of the bucket lads handed him a flaming torch. Every tenth man got a torch, the only light in the depths of the mine. Twenty steps and the rocky corridor opened onto the side of a deep vertical shaft, the throat of the iron mine. A massive set of chains dangled down the center, with buckets attached every ten feet. Rumors said the chains went all the way to the surface. Duncan stared up, hoping for a glimpse of sky, but the mineshaft was too deep.

One at a time, the men swung out into the shaft, clinging to the iron ladder. Hammered into the rock wall, the ladder disappeared into the depths, a line of ragged men clinging to the rungs. Some of the rungs were missing, making for a tricky descent. Careful not to drop the torch, Duncan followed the others. Like spiders descending a single strand, they made their way down. Abandoned galleries began to appear, dark mouths gaping in the rough rock wall. More than a few side tunnels were clogged shut with rock-falls, proof of the danger of cave-ins. Duncan wondered how many men lay buried beneath the rubble, a grim way to die.

A hundred rungs of the ladder and still he descended, as if hell had no bottom. The mine grew hot and the air tasted stale with sweat and rock dust. Above him, a man slipped, his foot missing a rung. Duncan braced for the impact but it never came. Dangling by his hands, Clovis regained his footing. Relieved, Duncan kept moving, slick with sweat by the time he reached the bottom.

A deafening clatter filled the central shaft. The bucket-chain rattled to life like some ancient metal monster wakened from slumber. Running all the way to the surface, the chain slowly jerked around a wheel fixed to the bottom of the mineshaft. Clanking and clattering, the empty buckets went down one side while full buckets went up the other, an endless chain of buckets starving for ore.

Giving the bucket chain a wide berth, Duncan paused to stretch muscles aching from the long descent. Clovis joined him and the two men entered the long gallery that led to the ore face. Forty smaller tunnels branched off the main gallery, two men working each tunnel. Hammers pounded against rock, flooding the mine with a wild heartbeat. The men worked without overseers, yet they wasted no time, knowing if the quota was not made none would eat. Hunger proved a powerful force, bending the men to the will of their jailors.

Duncan walked the length of the gallery. His torch guttered and dimmed, as if struggling to breathe. The air was heavy, stale and hot and spiked with the stench of piss and sweat and fear. The dark depths reeked like hell, torturing his sense of smell.

Seating the flickering torch in an empty bracket, Duncan entered the first tunnel devoid of hammering. Forced to his knees by the low ceiling, he crawled toward the ore face, pulling a wooden sledge behind him. Clovis followed, his workmate for the tunnel.

It was Duncan's idea to pair the strong with the weak. The stronger of the two worked the ore face, while the weaker pulled the sledge from the face to the bucket-chain. He'd chosen Clovis despite his racking cough and slight build. The redheaded man had served less than half a year in the mines and already showed signs of rocklung. Despite his weakness, Duncan liked the older man, finding his tales of life in the north the only relief in an otherwise damned existence.

The tunnel narrowed, choking the light from the torches, but Duncan had no problem seeing. He reached the ore face and found his tools waiting, a pointed metal wedge and a heavy stone hammer. Hefting the hammer, he checked the ceiling for signs of telltale cracks, always wary of cave-ins.

Clovis slumped to the ground behind the wooden sledge, consumed by coughing.

Duncan waited for the fit to pass and then asked his first question. "Why are so many prisoners deformed?"

Clovis chuckled, "You never run out of questions."

Duncan shrugged. "I've a friend who says knowledge is power. Perhaps if I understand this place I'll find a way to defeat it."

"Still hoping to see the sky again?"

"When you lose hope, you die."

The older man fell silent.

Duncan studied the rock face, setting the wedge into a thick band of blood-red ore. "Why are so many malformed?" Kneeling, he hefted the stone hammer, taking aim at the wedge. Stone pounded against metal, driving the wedge a finger's width into the stubborn rock face.

Clovis began to talk, weaving his words around the hammer's cadence. "I don't know the *why* of it, only that it has always been so. The Pit is fecund with freaks. The breeders keep track of every deformity. The useless ones are sent to work the mines, while those of value are encouraged to breed, given ample access to the pit brothels. The Taals are the breeders' greatest achievement, prized for their brute strength. Even rarer are the Duegar, the stunted dwarves who can sniff magic." Clovis coughed, his voice falling to a hush. "But not all deformities can be seen."

Hairs prickled at the back of Duncan's neck. "What do you mean?"

"Some of us hide our special abilities." His voice dropped to a whisper. "A rare few are born with the third eye, the gift of prophecy."

Duncan shivered. Prophecy had brought him to the god-cursed north. He hefted the hammer, swinging it with vengeance. "What kind of prophecy?"

"Our best seers tell of a Light Bringer, one who will release our people from the Pit."

Anger pulsed through Duncan. "People always expect someone else to save them, for the gods to send a hero." He swung the hammer sideways, his gaze fixed on the metal wedge. "If you wait for the gods, you're lost. You have to save yourself." The hammer struck a mighty blow. The rock face crumbled, releasing a cloud of dust. Coughing, Duncan pressed his face against his arm. When the dust thinned, he began dumping rocks in the sledge. He flicked a glance at Clovis. "What do you believe?"

"That your golden cat-eye lets you see in the dark."

He glared at the older man. "Then we both have our secrets."

"I believe you are the Light Bringer."

"Me!" Duncan barked a rude laugh. "You're mad, old man. I'm just a god-forsaken prisoner like you." He lifted a chunk of ore, throwing it onto the sledge.

"I've watched you, Duncan Treloch. I've seen how you've changed the others with nothing but words." He pointed to himself and then at Duncan. "The weak working with the strong, helping each other to survive. You've given us back our humanity, turning animals back into men."

Duncan stared at his friend. "Yes, but will they listen? Will they dare to save themselves?"

"Ask them." His voice rang with conviction. "I believe they're ready to hear your plan."

"Is this your second sight speaking...or just the last hope of a tired old man?"

Clovis shrugged the leather harness across his bony shoulders. "Perhaps a bit of both." Coughing, he turned and leaned into the harness. "Perhaps you're not the only one who wants to see the sky." Wood scraped against stone as the sledge slowly lurched toward the tunnel's mouth.

Duncan grunted and hefted the hammer, his hands hardened with calluses. Pounding his anger against the wedge, he sent a steady beat through the tunnel. Sweat dripped into his eyes, his knees ached and his thirst raged. He worked the ore face, falling into the weary drudgery of the mine. Clovis returned with an empty sledge, but by then neither man had the strength to talk. They filled the sledge with tumbled rock, coughing on the dust. Clovis leaned into the harness and Duncan picked up the hammer, each man yoked to his task.

One stroke after another, Duncan kept beating his rage against the ore face. Better to have died in the steppes than in this hellhole. He longed for fresh air, for the smell of green on the wind, for the crystal waters of a mountain stream...and for Kath. The hammer missed the wedge, striking stone, sending chips flying. He swore, ducking the shards, but then he noticed a trickle of water. Dropping the hammer, he pressed his face to the flow. Sucking the rock like a tit, he swallowed the trickle, the tastes of rock and iron lingering on his tongue. The taste didn't matter, only the water...warm and wet, like a balm to his parched throat.

Clovis's voice came from behind. "See, the gods watch over you, Duncan Treloch, suckling you even in the depths of the earth."

The trickle ran dry before he could get enough. "It's only water trapped in stone." He gripped the hammer. "The gods care nothing for the plight of men."

"You're wrong."

The conviction in the old man's voice made Duncan turn. "Why?"

"Because I've seen pure evil." Clovis sketched a warding sign with his left hand. "I've witnessed things you wouldn't believe...for I was once a guard in the citadel." His voice dropped to a hush. "The Dark Lord is real, the true master of the north. If the Dark Lord exists, then there must be other gods, benevolent gods, else what chance does mankind have?"

For a moment, the old man's faith was contagious...but then Duncan shook his head. "If the gods exist, then they should show their faces and strike a blow against evil." He swung the hammer, driving the wedge deep in the ore face.

The earth rumbled and shook.

A mighty roar came from the tunnel's mouth. A belch of rock dust rolled towards them like a storm cloud. Duncan threw himself to the ground, his hands over his head, expecting the weight of the earth.

The rumbling stopped...and the screaming began.

Fear hung heavy in the stale air. Duncan squeezed past the sledge, pushing Clovis toward the exit. Choking on dust, they crawled on hands and knees till they reached the gallery. Other prisoners spilled out of their side tunnels, shock and fear etched in rock-dusted faces.

A wail of pain shuddered through the gallery. "My legs! I can't feel my legs!"

The cave-in was three tunnels down. Trell lay pinned beneath a tumble of stones, half-swallowed by fallen rocks.

Duncan began shifting stones while Clovis tried to calm the injured man. "We'll get you out. Lay still." Duncan set his shoulder to a large rock, but it would not budge. It was only then that he realized the others were not helping. He turned to confront their stony stares. "Help me save him."

A few men looked away, others fidgeted, but Brock met his stare. The big man shook his head. "No use, cat-man. He's already dead."

"You don't know that."

"Look at the size of those rocks." Brock's voice was hard as iron. "His legs are crushed, eaten by the mine."

Trell loosed a keening wail, the sound clawing at raw-edged nerves.

Duncan pointed to the rock-fall. "And beyond the fall? Perhaps the other man still lives."

Doubt flicked across Brock's face.

Duncan pressed the point. "I'll not leave a man buried alive." Some of the others began to nod. "We work together and live...or we stand alone and die." He extended his hand. "Don't let the mine defeat us, brother."

The big man hesitated...but then he stepped forward and clasped Duncan's forearm. "We stand together."

A ragged cheer rose from the other men.

The cheer soon turned to resolve; the men knew time was against them. Brock issued orders and the men formed a line, passing the fallen stones from hand to hand, stacking them at the far end of the gallery. Duncan worked with the others at the rock-fall, trying to clear the entrance. Smaller stones rattled and fell as the larger rocks were muscled away. Trell whimpered, a trickle of blood at his mouth. Clovis whispered, "I think we're losing him."

Duncan grabbed another rock, careful not to start a slide. "Ask him who he works with. Who wields the hammer?"

Clovis answered. "It's Bruce."

Duncan pictured the tall, blond-haired man. "A strong one." He wrestled a large rock from the pile. "I'm betting he's still alive."

Trell moaned, his eyes glazed with pain.

The men worked with grim determination, whittling away at the rock fall. An opening appeared at the top. Duncan peered inside. Dust choked the darkness, making it hard for even Duncan to see. Brock grabbed a torch and handed it up. Duncan poked it through the opening, calling for the missing man. "Bruce! Do you live?"

No response.

Duncan withdrew the torch. "It's too dusty inside, too hard to see. Keep working, he might still live."

Doubt clouded the other men's faces, but they kept at it. More stones were cleared, opening a space large enough for a man to squeeze through. Duncan stared at the hole, fearing another collapse. "My idea. I'll go."

No one argued.

He took the torch to protect his secret and climbed to the opening. Rocks shifted under his weight, a bad omen. Thrusting the torch forward, he crawled on his belly, stones scraping against his bare-chest. His shoulders just fit, like a well-measured tomb. The way ahead narrowed. He shoved a rock aside, praying the ceiling would hold. Stones tumbled forward with a disturbing clatter. Duncan waited, holding his breath...but the ceiling held. Worming his way through, he gained the other side. Dropping the torch, he pulled free of the passage, peering through the dust. "Bruce! Do you live?" Halfway back, he found the blond-haired man sprawled amongst a tumble of stones. His face was covered in rock dust...but a strong heartbeat pulsed at his neck. Duncan shook him hard, willing him to wake.

Bruce's eyes fluttered open. "W-what happened?"

"A cave-in. We need to get out. Can you move?"

His eyes widened in fear. "I'll bloody well try."

Duncan led the way, Bruce struggling to follow. Ahead, the torchlight glowed like a beacon in the dust. They reached the rock-fall and Bruce gasped. "Buried alive!" The big man began to shake.

Duncan gripped his arm. "We work together and we live."

Bruce nodded, his eyes wide and wild, his face pale.

Brock's voice came from the far side. "Any luck?"

"I found him. He lives!"

A muffled cheer rose from the far side.

Brock's voice bellowed over the others. "Then get your lazy asses back on this side before more rocks fall."

Duncan looked at Bruce. "Sound advice. You go first."

Trembling, Bruce nodded and then scrambled up the rock-fall to the hole. Duncan retrieved the torch, knowing that Grack would punish them if it was lost.

Rocks shifted under Bruce's weight, a few stones clattering to the tunnel floor, but the hole remained open. Duncan followed, worming his way back, rocks scraping against his bare skin. Hands reached for him, pulling him from the rock's embrace. The others gathered around, pounding Bruce and Duncan on the back, talking all at once, celebrating a victory over the grave. Only Brock and Clovis stood apart.

Duncan looked at Clovis. "Trell?"

The older man shook his head. "He died before we could get him out."

Duncan frowned, another life claimed by the mine, another victory for the Mordant.

Brock gripped his arm. "Bruce nearly died as well, buried alive. A terrible way to die." The big man shuddered. "You were right, cat-man."

Duncan nodded. "You see what men can do when they work together."

Bitterness flooded the big man's voice. "Yeah, we can live to die another day. We're all fodder for the mine."

"Maybe not."

A spark of interest lit the big man's eyes. "You have a plan, cat-man?"

The deafening clang of the bucket-chain rattled to a stop. The sudden silence signaled an end to their time in the depths.

A cheer rose from the men, they'd survived another day in hell, rescuing one of their own from death's embrace.

Duncan nodded at Brock. "We'll talk later."

The men moved along the gallery to the central shaft, but instead of shuffling with weary defeat, they walked with purpose, even pride. Duncan noticed the change. Perhaps the cave-in was a godsend. Tonight might be his best chance to convince them to fight.

25

The Mordant

Splendor was the decree of the day. The Mordant abandoned subtlety for the trappings of power, choosing the garb of a warrior king. A gleaming gold breastplate inscribed with a pentacle, black leather pants tucked into knee-high boots, and upon his head he wore an iron circlet studded with black diamonds, a king come to claim his throne.

A dozen guards scrambled to open the massive bronze doors.

A gong sounded, a deep-throated voice announcing his presence.

Thousands of supplicants fell prostrate, their faces pressed to the cold stone floor.

The Mordant crossed the narthex, boot heels ringing on polished marble. He stood on the threshold, backlit by the fading sunset.

Intimidation wrought into stone, the Basilica of the Dark Citadel proclaimed a thousand years of dominance. Vast enough to foster echoes, the cavernous hall wielded proportion like a war hammer. Massive pillars lined the nave, supporting a vaulted ceiling shrouded in darkness. Slender rays of sunlight speared the upper dome, but they quickly faded, consumed by the gloom. Massive candles sculpted like malformed faces provided the light, weeping waterfalls of wax tears. Mosaics glorified his past lifetimes, every detail designed to enhance his power. Built of dusky-colored stone, the Basilica portrayed all the subtle shades of Darkness from smoky-gray granites and dark-green marbles to the true black of onyx. Gold provided the only relief, a crushing display of wealth paving the steps to the throne. And upon the glittering dais, exalted above all else, sat the Ebony Throne. Carved from the heartwood of a giant tree, the massive throne was jet-black with rich swirls of green in the ebony grain, a wealth of rare wood, a triumph of Darkness over nature...and all of it, his to use, his to command.

The Mordant strode down the long aisle, his black cape flaring behind, the Staff of Pain clicking on the marble paving. Beneath his stride, he walked on names. History was written on the Basilica's floors. Names of battlefields won, cities plundered, towns burned, and villages raped. Most were long forgotten, missing from present-day maps, but in the Mordant's citadel they remained etched in stone, eternally trod beneath his boot heel.

Dark glory echoed from every aspect of the Basilica. The Mordant breathed deep, imbibing the heady rush of unrestrained power. Virile with stolen youth, he traversed the immense nave. His boot steps echoed on marble, the only sound in the vaulted hush. His stare feasted on the sea of prostrate subjects, as if the path to the throne was paved in mortal souls. Reaching the dais, he mounted the steps, a fortune of gold beneath his boots. His black cape swirled as he turned to survey the long hall. Thousands of subjects remained prone, covering the stone floor like a living tapestry. Not a single man dared to lift his head. The Mordant smiled, fear was such a beautiful thing.

He took a seat on the Ebony Throne, regal in black and gold.

The voice of the gong rumbled like thunder.

Thousands rose to their feet, a shuffle of humanity, all bowing toward his throne. Familiar faces stood the closest, the high priests and the generals, dressed in their finest, come to pay homage to his reign. He gave them a paternal smile, and then he began to speak.

"The Mordant has returned!" A trick of the architecture allowed his voice to boom through the Basilica. "The time of waiting is over. I have come to take up the Dark Lord's sword, to bring the destiny of a thousand years to fulfillment. A new age of Darkness yearns to be born. Like all births, it will be drenched in blood, the blood of the southern kingdoms, for *we* are the Masters of War." Cheers rose from the crowd but he quelled them with a raised hand. "The Basilica bears the proof of our prowess. Triumphs of the past surround us. Melted crowns gild the steps of our dais. Names of the vanquished are trod beneath our boot heels. Nothing in history has ever stopped the Dark Lord, and nothing will stop us now."

"Victory!" A single shout rose from the base of the dais. The crowd took up the chant. *"Victory! Victory!"* A rolling thunder echoed through the dark vault.

The Mordant eased back against the throne, basking in their adoration, more proof of his power. After a time, he raised his hand to still the crowd. When silence returned, he nodded to his High Priest.

Gavis climbed halfway up the dais, resplendent in robes of the blackest silk trimmed with runes of gold. "My Lord, shall we begin?"

The Mordant gestured with a flick of his hand.

Gavis snapped opened a scroll and began to read the list of names. His baritone voice summoned two hundred of the most powerful men in the citadel to swear allegiance to their god-king, a public display of fealty.

General Haith came first. Resplendent in burnished armor, the old soldier bowed low. Drawing his sword, he extended the gilded hilt toward the Mordant. He climbed the dais and he knelt to make his offering. "My sword is yours to command."

The Mordant touched the hilt in acceptance.

The general sheathed his sword and completed the oath of loyalty. "As the Dark Lord is my witness, I swear to serve my lord, the Mordant, to obey his every command, to crush his enemies, to extend his reign, to live or die for him." Falling prostrate to the golden steps, he kissed the Mordant's boot, the ultimate act of submission.

Pleased with the display, the Mordant smiled. "Your fealty is accepted. Serve well and live long."

The general retreated while other powerful men came forward to make their pledge. One at a time, they climbed the golden steps and knelt before the Mordant, swearing the oath of fealty. Generals, bishops, stewards, and assassins, they all abased themselves before the power of the Ebony Throne.

The Mordant watched them come, his face set in a benevolent mask, his malevolence hidden behind a cloak of stolen youth. He studied each soul, marking their names, gauging their worth while enjoying their abasement. He accepted them all, even the ones who carried the scent of treachery...until a certain bishop dared to climb the dais. Fat with easy living, Bishop Tynes huffed up the stairs, his multiple chins quivering with each step. Dropping to his knees, he pressed his hands together in prayerful worship, intoning the words of ritual. "As the Dark Lor..."

"Bishop Tynes."

The bishop stuttered to a stop, confusion beaming from his moon shaped face. "Yes, Lord?"

The Mordant smiled, the corpulent bishop would make a fine example. "I received your gift of brandy."

The bishop gaped liked a fish pulled from water but the sweat on his forehead ruined his performance. "Brandy, Lord? I know nothing of any gift."

"A cup of death brought by a priest in your service." The Mordant despised bad liars but he kept his voice soft and paternal. "Surely you will not lie to your Lord?"

The fat prelate shook his head, his jowls quaking like a stormy sea. "I don't know what you mean."

"Did you think I wouldn't know?"

The bishop stared, wide-eyed, his face flushed with fear.

"The truth was written on Fenthane's soul." Leaning forward, he prodded the bishop's belly with the butt of his staff. "Confess your sins."

Screaming, the bishop scuttled back down the golden steps, cowering at the foot of the dais like a crab looking for a rock to hide under. "I only obeyed! It wasn't my idea!" His voice twisted to a screech. "I've done nothing but serve the Pentacle." His stare raced around the Basilica but whatever support he sought did not come forward.

The Mordant called the Darkness. "Look at me."

Huddled at the base of the dais, the bishop raised a tentative stare.

"Treachery can be transformed...but never stupidity."

The bishop whimpered and tried to look away but his gaze was already caught. The Mordant plunged into his soul, plucking details from the fat prelate's mind. The trail of names led all the way to the royal palace, so predictable, so disappointing. In all the years he'd ruled the Ebony Throne, the conspirators never thought to send an honest man against him. Finished, the Mordant withdrew, burying his powers beneath a mask of youth.

Released, the bishop crumpled to the marble floor, gasping like a hollow reed.

Sitting back in the throne, the Mordant studied the powerful men clustered around the dais, making note of those who trembled and those who hid their guilt well. He decided to let them stew in their fear; one example should be enough. Pounding his iron staff against the golden dais, he made his voice a command. "For committing treason against the Lord of the Ebony Throne, Bishop Tynes is hereby stripped of his robes and his priestly duties. Expelled from the citadel, he is condemned to spend the rest of his life in the Pit, chained to a slave in the iron mine till his soul departs from his body."

"*Nooooo!*"

"Let my will be done."

The gong sounded, a deep thunder sealing the Mordant's command.

General Haith gestured and a pair of bare-chested Taals pushed their way to the foot of the dais. Over eight-feet tall and muscle-bound, the ogre-like Taals bowed to the Mordant and then stepped to either side of the condemned bishop. Hands the size of shovels gripped the prelate's robe. Silk ripped down the center, sundering the robe in two. The bishop fell back on his rump, dumped like a lamb from the womb, naked except for a silk loincloth. Fat and quivering, he stared at the crowd, his eyes wide with horror. The Taals gave him little time to react. Lifting the fat man between them, they carried him down the long nave. The bishop writhed in their grip, screaming as his feet wind-milled a foot above the marble floor. The great doors opened. The Taals and their burden passed from sight. The massive doors shut with a dull thud.

Minutes passed before the echoing screams fell silent.

An ominous hush settled over the cavernous hall.

No one moved.

No one dared meet his stare.

The Mordant smiled, a lesson well learned. He gestured toward his High Priest. "Continue."

Bowing, Gavis returned to the list of names.

The elite of the Citadel answered the summons, a newfound fear etched in their faces. Bowing low, they crept up the golden stairs, every man making a full obeisance.

The Mordant enjoyed the spectacle, watching their faces, reading their souls. So much abasement for a single death, the portly bishop was coin well spent.

Gavis was the last to take the oath. Holding his staff up in offering, the High Priest lay prostrate on the golden stairs, his words a hushed whisper, intended for the Mordant's ears alone. "Treachery can be transformed."

Amused, the Mordant stroked the beginnings of a beard. "Why waste a sharpened dagger, eh?"

Gavis lay still, his black silk robes draping the golden stairs like a shadow. "A dagger against your enemies."

The Mordant waited, drawing out the lesson. Beads of sweat glistened on the High Priest's forehead...but he did not beg, and he did not waver. The hand holding the staff remained rock-steady. This one had potential. Leaning down, the Mordant touched the staff in acceptance. "Serve well and live."

Remaining prostrate, Gavis completed the oath of fealty. "As the Dark Lord is my witness, I swear to serve my Lord, the Mordant, to obey his every command, to crush his enemies, to extend his reign, to live or die for him." He crept forward to kiss the Mordant's boot.

"No." The Mordant pulled his foot back, his words loud enough for the elite to hear. "I set my High Priest above all other men."

Gavis looked up, a glint of gratitude in his dark gaze. He rose from the steps and took his place halfway down the dais, his face lined with dignity, his back stiff with pride.

The Mordant smiled, a dagger turned but not blunted.

The High Priest resumed his duties, his voice echoing through the Basilica. "The oaths of fealty have been pledged and accepted. In celebration of our Lord's return, the Mordant will hear the petitions of his people. Come forward and ask a boon from your liege."

A murmur of anticipation swept through the crowd.

The elite of the citadel were the first to approach. Leading women veiled in colorful silks, the lordlings offered their daughters to serve as concubines. Fathers unveiled their nubile young daughters, displaying their curves like gifts before the dais. Most were comely enough, some were even stunningly beautiful, but he took them all, even the dowdy and the plain. Instead of influence the fathers gained obligation, bound to the Ebony Throne by their own ambition, desperate to see the Mordant succeed in the hopes that their grandsons might one day wield power. Each daughter gained him a willing vassal, chained by blood and ambition. The Mordant chuckled, so much loyalty bought for the price of sex.

When the parade of daughters ended, the rabble of the lower tiers came forward. Approaching the throne on their knees, they begged opportunities for their sons, for better wages for their craftsmen, and for more food for their tables. The lower tiers especially, begged for the largess of more bread and gruel. The Mordant played the benevolent ruler, granting a majority of requests. He'd leave it to the priesthood to renege on his promises, enforcing austerity and sacrifice, all in the name of war.

Growing weary of the petty rabble, he signaled an end to the petitioners. The hallway cleared but no one dared leave.

Gavis pounded his staff against the steps. "Summon the Sea Lords."

The Mordant sat forward, keen to renew the longstanding alliance.

The booming voice of the gong thundered a summons. The doors of the Basilica swung open. Twelve men in fish-scale armor swept in like a storm-blown gale. Their bronze armor gleamed in the torchlight, their long capes the deep blue of a bottomless sea. Tall and proud, they carried trident-tipped spears, their faces weathered by salt and sun. Marching the length of the colonnade, they strode to the foot of the golden dais and made a curt half-bow.

The Mordant kept his face still, allowing the stiff-necked sea-folk the illusion that they were more than mere vassals.

One of the twelve stepped forward, his voice a deep rumble. "The Sea Lords answer the call of the Ebony Throne." The speaker was an older man, tall with streaks of gray in his long dark hair, his beard braided into a three-forked trident that reached to his waist. "MerChanter Timoth comes to renew the alliance of sea and land."

The plans of the Dark Lord required ships, but the sea had never been the Mordant's domain. Many lifetimes ago he'd struck an alliance with the sea-folk, using them as mercenary vassals, his wolves of the ocean. "Emissaries of the Sea Lords are ever welcome in our court."

Another man from the MerChanter's party stepped forward, laying a cloth-wrapped bundle at the foot of the dais. "A gift from the Miral of the sea."

The Mordant gestured and Gavis bent toward the bundle. The outer wrapping fell away, revealing a glitter of gold on black. The High Priest stood, holding a man's cloak trimmed in sealskin, gold discs shimmering along its length.

The Mordant waved him forward. Gavis climbed the steps, laying the cloak across the Mordant's knees. The truth of the cloak lay in the details. Gold coins were cunningly bound into the sealskin like a shimmer of scales. But every coin was different. Many were worn smooth with age while others bore a coats-of-arms or a crowned visage few would recognize, tokens of kingdoms long lost to history. The Mordant fingered the cloak. None save a harlequin of many lifetimes would know the true age such coins. "A most fitting gift." A smile graced his face. "The cloak of an eternal conqueror."

The MerChanter grinned, a flash of gold in his teeth. "You see the truth of it."

He gestured to Gavis and to General Haith. The two men climbed the dais. The Mordant stood and they removed the black wool cloak, settling the cloak of many coins across his shoulders. He liked the weight of it. The cloak felt like destiny, the solid tug of inevitability. "We are pleased with your gift."

The MerChanter nodded. "Then the Miral will be pleased."

"But you have come for more than ceremony."

"Aye." The MerChanter tugged on his beard, his face stern. "Long have we hunted distant shores as per our accord with the Ebony Throne. But the sudden crossing of the great ocean has taken its tithe. The holds of our longships are empty. Our rowers grow hungry for meat and mead."

The Mordant nodded. "Your holds shall be filled and a feast laid for your people." It was part of their longstanding bargain, safe harbor below the Dark Citadel and stores to fill the holds of their ships.

"We've crossed the great ocean at your summoning, but our tridents long for blood and our Miral seeks fresh plunder."

"You shall have both." The Mordant raised his voice, his words meant for the crowd as well as the sea folk. "I have returned to lead the Pentacle to war. The southern kingdoms are fat with peace. The southern coast will provide rich pickings for the Trident, especially the seaside kingdom of Navarre."

The MerChanter grinned like a sea wolf. "Then the tides run true for us both."

"The tides of blood and plunder." The Mordant descended the dais. "Come, let us seal our alliance with a feast, for we have much to discuss." He strode down the long colonnade, the sea folk marching behind like an honor guard. The multitude fell prostrate as he passed, like wheat bent before the scythe. The Mordant smiled. Now that he had the Dark Citadel in hand, he could turn his attention to conquest. A thousand years of destiny yearned for fulfillment, calling to him like a siren, the rapture of power pulsing through his veins. Soon the southern kingdoms would cower beneath his boot heel, setting all of Erdhe beneath his dominion, an undisputed god-king ruling for all eternity.

26

Katherine

Bear and Boar stayed two steps behind, a pair of shadows Kath could not shake. Surly and taciturn, the guards followed her everywhere, speaking only when something was forbidden, refusing all conversations, not even offering their names. Kath had taken to calling them by their tattoos. If either man minded, they did not say. Undaunted by her silent shadows, Kath spent the better part of her days exploring the caves, seeking clues to the riddle of her captors, searching for a bridge across a chasm of differences.

The den proved to be a maze of chambers, galleries, and tunneled passageways, an easy place to get lost. Animal paintings dominated most chambers. A celebration of life danced on the rough rock walls, raced across the vaulted ceilings, and peered from the faces of young and old. Bears, foxes, badgers, owls, boars, and at least one eagle, stared back at her, etched with blue ink on the faces of men and women alike. A melding of human and animal that suggested a feral power. And all of them carried a weapon of some sort, a dagger, a sword, a mace, a battle-axe, more proof they lived in the Mordant's shadow.

The tattooed people seemed as strange and daunting as the caves in which they lived, but Kath knew they'd make valuable allies against the Mordant. The Painted Warriors were a riddle waiting to be solved...if only she could find the key to their trust. She shivered, missing the monk's wisdom and Duncan's instincts. Somehow she'd have to find a way to turn her captors into allies. Feeling their hostile stares, she wondered if it could be done.

Kath persisted in exploring the caves. Her wanderings had yielded at least one secret. The caves were best traversed by following a single animal. Today she followed the white-tailed deer, eager to discover where they might lead. Ocher deer pranced across the rough rock walls, leading her through a series of twists and turns. Bold strokes of color gave the deer a sense of motion, as if they might leap off the walls and race down the rocky corridors. The artistry never failed to amaze her. Startling in their intensity, the chalk drawings transformed the caves into a cathedral, evoking a reverence for life, a vibrant celebration of freedom. If the drawings mirrored their makers, then the Painted Warriors would make stout allies of the Light...if only she could win their trust.

The corridor twisted left and then forked into three separate passageways, including one that was little more than a three-foot wide crack. Curiosity drew her to the narrow cleft. Saber-toothed lions lurked in the shadows, slinking across the rocks, teeth bared in a snarl of rage, as if they protected the narrow entranceway. A shiver of anticipation raced down her spine. She'd been searching for lions, trying to understand the importance of the Painted Warrior who'd died in Castlegard, but so far she'd had little luck. Lions seemed to be rare in the caves...perhaps this narrow passage held the insights she so desperately needed. Kath stepped towards the cleft.

"Not that way." Bear's gravelly voice tugged like a leash.

Hating to be caged, she dared another step.

"Not that way."

She whirled, confronting her shadows. "Why not?" Boar spoke even less than Bear, so she turned her anger on the blond giant. "What's down there? What are you hiding? What's so special about the lions?"

"Not that way."

Anger boiled within her. "Give me a reason."

But the bear of a man just stared at her, his face impassive, his hand on his sword hilt.

It was like talking to a rock, a *pair* of rocks. Tall, barrel-chested, and blond, Bear had the flattened nose of a brawler. In contrast, Boar was dark and stocky, with an ugly scar that ran along his tattooed tusk, as if the boar had ripped through the man's face trying to break free. She wondered which came first, the scar or the tattoo. "Tell me about your tattoos. Why do you wear them? What do they mean?"

Neither man offered any response; they just stared, their hands on their weapons.

Grinding her teeth, Kath considered sprinting for the narrow passage, certain she could outrun her guards, but trespassing on forbidden ground was not the best way to win friends. Swallowing her frustration, she decided to try a different tactic. "You won't return my weapons. You won't show me the way out. You won't tell me about the caves. You won't talk about this so-called Ancestor. And you won't even give me your names." She dropped her voice to a whisper. "Then tell me about the Mordant."

Boar's dark eyes widened, his gaze flicking to Bear...but neither man answered.

Encouraged, Kath pressed the attack "Tell me about the Dark Citadel. What weaknesses does it have? There must be a secret way out, an escape route that could be used for an attack? And what about the gates that guard the long wall? How do you get past the magic?" Hands on her hips, she glared at the two men, daring them to answer.

Bear met her gaze, while Boar fingered his mace, staring at the ground.

"You're both warriors. You know the enemy." She stepped close, invading their space. "My companions and I came north to fight the Mordant." Her words stabbed like a sword. "Don't send us into battle blind."

Boar gasped and retreated a step, but Bear just stared.

Seeking to keep them off-balance, Kath pivoted and started to walk away...but Boar's gruff voice raised a stubborn challenge. "Women don't fight."

She'd found a chink in their armor. Slowly turning, she fought to keep her face neutral. "Why not? Every woman in the den carries a weapon, so why don't they fight?"

"To defend the den, yes, but not in the open steppes."

She drilled Boar with her stare, demanding an answer. "Why not in the steppes?"

"Because..." he stammered, "men can endure." Blood rushed to his face. "Far better for a woman to die than to be taken prisoner."

"Why?"

"Because..." Boar's face flushed red.

Kath's stare intensified. "I need to know."

His voice dropped to a strangled rasp. "Because captured women are sent to the breeding pens."

A chill gripped Kath. "The *breeding* pens?"

Boar nodded. "In the Pit."

The more she learned about the Mordant's domain, the more she hated it...but she needed to understand the enemy. "So you've been in the Dark Citadel?"

"A slave of the ninth tier."

Bear scowled, his voice like a thunderclap. *"Enough!"*

Boar looked away, his face flaming red, his fist gripping his mace.

But the words were said...explaining much. Kath waited, hoping for more, but the stony silence returned. Pivoting, she strode down the widest passage, setting a fast pace, forcing her guards to rush to catch up. Boar's words shivered in her mind, *breeding pens,* such a revolting thought, another reason to defeat the Mordant. She wondered how many of the Painted Warriors had once lived within the Dark Citadel. Their knowledge would be invaluable, if only they'd help, but their frosty silence was proving hard to crack. Whoever ruled the tattooed people did so with an iron fist.

Kath followed the deer, lost in thought, hoping Blaine was having better luck. They'd split up, trying to cover more of the caves; perhaps the knight would discover the meaning behind the lions.

The passage widened, spilling into one of the many long galleries. Half a dozen passageways emptied into the chamber, white-tailed deer mingling with aurochs, horses, and wolves across the vaulted ceiling. A crowd filled the gallery, young and old standing in a circle, straining to see, as if watching a juggler or a mummer. Men cheered and women made a strange humming sound. Surprised, Kath drew close. She'd seen large galleries where the tattooed people gathered to card wool, weave cloth, cook meals, or repair chainmail, but she'd yet to see any form of merriment or revelry. Curious, she joined the crowd, threading her way to the front. Gaining a clear view, she gasped in surprise.

Blaine's blue steel sword!

A fox-faced man gave an exhibition of sword work, blue steel slicing through imaginary foes. Pivoting and leaping, he slashed and hacked, fighting a mock battle. The man proved agile and quick but the sword strokes were crude and clumsy, a self-taught brawler wielding a hero's sword. The coarse display sickened her, a waste of blue steel. The great sword deserved better, yet the painted people did not seem to know it.

Kath studied the crowd, tattooed faces eagerly following the sapphire sword, cheering with appreciation. If they only knew what an Octagon knight could do with such a blade.

Blaine! As if conjured from thought, the blond-haired knight stood on the far side of the crowd...but one glimpse of his face warned her of trouble. Like a starving lion, the knight's hungry stare followed the blue sword. His hands were balled into fists, his mouth curled into an ugly smile, his eyes burning with a devil-may-care attitude, all the telltale signs of a berserker on the brink of battle...yet he had no weapon. Kath feared that he might get hurt, feared that he might ruin any chance for an alliance.

Desperate to stop him, she pushed through the crowd. A smother of people blocked the way. Dodging the press, she fought her way forward, straining to reach him in time. She lunged, grabbing his sleeve. *"Blaine!"*

He whirled, his eyes smoldering with rage, his face on the verge of a berserker's madness, no recognition in his stare.

Pounding his chest, she tried to get through to him. "Stop it, Blaine."

Snarling, he batted her away, turning back toward the sword.

She grabbed his arm, but he shook her off.

Thwarted by his strength, she reached for her father's voice, a battle leader using the voice of command. "Sir Blaine, attend me!"

He staggered back a step, his gaze snapping toward her.

She seized the chance. Laying a hand against the stubble of his cheek, she held his gaze, appealing to the man instead of the battle-crazed warrior. "I can't lose you."

He swayed on his feet, his gaze uncertain.

Kath persisted, her voice a hushed command. "By the Octagon, do not risk our victory."

He came back to her then, the anger in his eyes dampened to a sullen bitterness. "I need my sword." The battle madness left him in a rush, his shoulders slumping forward, a defeated, hangdog look souring his face.

A hard stare drilled into her back. Whirling, she locked eyes with the raven-faced healer. So, they were being watched, judged by standards she didn't understand, all the more reason to get Blaine away.

Kath gripped his arm, drawing him away from the tattooed stares. "Come." Blaine kept pace, his face sullen, but at least he did not argue. Four guards followed, Bear and Boar and the two that shadowed Blaine. Irritated by the nagging shadows, Kath tried to ignore them. Retracing her steps, she followed the chalk horses, leading Blaine back to the privacy of their sleeping chamber.

Ducking low, she entered the small side cave, thankful the guards remained outside, stationed at the only entrance. Their sleeping chamber was L-shaped, more horses cantering across the low vaulted ceiling. A large glow crystal sat on a central boulder, casting a soft white light. Bedrolls lay spread across the floor, the rear of the chamber reserved for the chamber pot. Danya sat on her bedroll, hugging the wolf, her face buried in his thick black ruff, but at least the wolf-girl had stopped her muffled crying. Bryx chuffed a greeting but the girl did not stir.

Blaine sprawled on his bedroll, his voice sullen. "Prisoners returned to their cage."

Kath did not like his tone, especially after the incident in the gallery. "They've given us the freedom to explore the caves, a chance to change our fate."

He shook his head. "We're still prisoners."

Kath's anger snapped. "That's the trick," she glared down at him, "turning captors into allies."

He glowered, looking away.

"You were supposed to befriend them, explore the caves and try to win their trust, *not* start a fight and get yourself killed." She stubbed her boot hard against the sole of his foot. "What were you going to do? Fight him with your bare hands?"

He sprang to his feet, a coil of anger. "*Allies* shouldn't demand payment for help."

"Exactly."

"What?" He stared at her, confusion muting his anger.

"We need these people for allies." She drilled him with her stare. "They live in the very shadow of the Mordant. They know his ways. They know the Dark Citadel." She lowered her voice to a whisper. "And they have the *crystal dagger*."

Blaine glowered. "I tried to keep it from them...but they took it with the rest of our weapons."

She willed him to understand. "Win their trust and we'll regain our weapons."

"I want my sword back."

"To get it, you must first understand them."

His gaze burned into her.

"Trade stories with their warriors. Find out how they fight the enemy, discover how they make decisions, how they divide the spoils of war. Learn about them and find a way to regain your sword without raising their ire."

Blaine scowled. "Just that simple."

"There's nothing simple about it." She had to make him understand. "It's up to us to find the common ground, to forge an alliance. We're being watched. Every move we make is being judged. Don't you see that?"

"What I see is my sword in another's hands." His voice dropped to a growl. "A knight is nothing without his sword."

Her anger boiled over. "*No!* A knight is *honor*." She jabbed the maroon octagon emblazoned on his surcoat. "*You* are *honor*, never forget that." She glared up at him. "And you are sworn to me. I'll not have you risk your life needlessly."

He stared at her, wide-eyed, caught in an ambush of words.

"But you still want your sword."

"Yes." His mouth hardened to a stubborn slash.

"Then go and talk to them. Time is running out." She waved him toward the exit. "See what you can learn...but *don't* pick a fight."

He grabbed his maroon cloak, twirled it around his shoulders and then left, ducking through the exit without looking back.

Weary from arguing, she threw herself on her bedroll. Her frustration gradually subsided and she found herself running her hand through the bedroll's thick fleece. Sheep seemed to be the main staple of the painted people. The evidence was everywhere, from sheepskin bedrolls, jerkins, and cloaks, to haunches of lamb for supper, and chunks of mutton in the midday stew. The painted people depended on sheep. It was the one obvious truth about their captors...while so much else remained a riddle.

Closing her eyes, Kath sank back into the fleece, weary of so many problems. Reaching beneath her jerkin, she gripped the silver warrior ring and thought about Duncan, praying for Valin to keep him safe. She missed him so much, she ached.

A wet rasp licked her face.

Startled, Kath sat up.

Green eyes stared back at her, a soft whine.

"What do you want, Bryx?" Sometimes the wolf seemed half human.

He chuffed and whined and slunk back to Danya, his tail between his legs. Settling next to the brown-haired girl, he stared back at Kath, reproach in his gaze.

Kath sighed, another problem. She'd tried talking with Danya, tried pulling the wolf-girl out of her grief, but words seemed to have little effect. The brown-haired girl remained listless, eating little and saying less, clutching the wolf as she rocked back and forth, locked within her own remorse. Still, the wolf was right, Kath could not give up.

Her bedroll was too far away. She moved it closer, sitting across from Danya with the wolf lying between them. Reaching out, she stroked the thick, dark fur. The wolf rumbled in pleasure, rolling onto his side.

"Danya, talk with me." Kath kept her voice soft, cajoling, inviting a response. "You grieve too much." She shook her head, recalling the horrors of the battlefield. "You saved us all. If not for you, we'd all be dead, or worse, prisoners of the Mordant."

But the brown-haired girl made no reply. She sat hugging the wolf, her face buried in the black fur.

Kath leaned forward, trying to shatter the wall of silence. "Battle is simple, kill or be killed. The Mordant's soldiers would have taken our heads. You waste your grief on them."

"No." The word was little more than a moan.

Kath held her breath, hoping for more.

"You don't understand." Danya raised her head, her face streaked with tears. "It's not the soldiers...but the horses."

Kath rocked backwards, struck with understanding.

Danya sat up, her gaze haunted, her voice a harsh whisper. "I *tortured* those horses."

Kath scrambled for a reply. "You commanded them to attack. You saved our lives."

"I did far worse than that." Tears spilled down her face. "I know wolves." Her voice dropped to a guilty whisper. "I put wolves in their minds."

The terrible carnage finally made sense, horses screaming, stomping their riders into puddles of gore. Kath shook her head, dispelling the horror. Somehow she had to save Danya from an abyss of guilt. She gripped the wolf-girl's hands, conviction in her voice. "We need you, Danya." The girl tried to pull away but Kath held tight. "Some larger destiny is at work here. We all have a role to play. Can't you feel it?"

"What I did was unforgivable! And you want me to do more? Use my god-cursed magic to torture more animals?" Her voice flooded with scorn. "Animals feel too. They love life. They know pain and death." Danya pulled away, her face full of outrage. Ripping her shirtsleeve, she revealed the silver cuff. "This *thing* is a curse...yet I cannot bring myself to be rid of it!"

"Not a curse." Kath shook her head, there had to be a way to use the magic and still walk in the Light. "Perhaps there is another way."

"What do you mean?"

Kath stared at Bryx, struggling to put her thoughts into words. "The wolf helps...he's a true companion, one of us."

"So?"

"So...instead of commanding, ask."

Danya shook her head. "I don't understand."

"You've seen what the Mordant does to horses, riding them till they drop, leaving them for dead without even removing the saddles."

Danya nodded, her face pale.

"And the gore hounds, a twisted abomination of man and animal."

The wolf bared his teeth, a menacing growl.

"The Mordant has no compassion for men or animals, an ancient evil that must be stopped.

"Yes."

"Then show the animals what we fight against and *ask* them for help. Ask them to fight on our side."

"Ask?" Danya hugged the wolf. "And if they say no?"

Kath hesitated, but no matter the risks, there could be only one reply. "Then the answer is no." She saw the hesitation in the other girl's eyes. "I swear by my sword."

Danya hugged the wolf, her face thoughtful. "It might work." She wiped her eyes, a look of reason replacing her grief. "I could ask."

Relief washed through Kath. She gripped Danya's arm. "We truly need you."

The wolf-girl blushed and looked away.

"Come, you must be hungry." She pulled the other girl to her feet, refusing to let her pine alone in the cave. "Let's see if there's any supper left in the cook pots."

The wolf chuffed.

"I'll wager a gold, it's lamb again."

Danya ruffled the wolf's fur. "Bryx likes lamb."

Kath turned, shocked to find a woman standing in the shadows of the entranceway.

"May I enter?"

Kath nodded, wondering how much she'd overheard.

Thera stepped from the shadows, the tattooed raven staring from her face like a dark omen. The healer smiled, dispelling the grim illusion. "I bring word of your companion. The fever has broken, the old man will live."

Kath sighed in relief. "Thank Valin."

"I bring other news as well. The Ancestor will meet with you in three days time. She's called for a conclave in the Great Hall." A raven peered from the healer's face, keen eyes surrounded by dark feathers. "At conclave we will learn the fate of the man who walked among the lions, the man who died in Castlegard." Her dark gaze drilled into Kath. "You'll tell his tale and then much will be decided." She turned, her back stiff with silence. "Come, I will take you to your companion."

*A conclave...*the words had the ring of a trial, or a judgment. Kath followed the healer, needing to speak to Zith. Perhaps the monk knew the key to the painted people...or perhaps the answer lay in Castlegard, with a tattooed man two years dead. Either way, she still had a riddle to solve...the sands of time were running out.

27

Duncan

Duncan waited with the others for a turn at the ladder. Bruce went first, scrambling up the rungs as if death tugged at his heels. One at a time, they scaled the mineshaft, white-knuckles grasping the rungs, refusing to look down. Duncan waited till last. He was accustomed to heights, having climbed the great trees as a child, but this was different. The climb seemed to stretch to forever, testing muscles already weary with strain. Relief washed through him when he finally reached the top.

Grack waited at the door to the sleeping chamber, thumbing a string of knots as each prisoner passed. Duncan wondered if the big Taal even knew how to count, but he kept his thoughts to himself. A boy accepted his torch, snuffing it in a bucket of sand. Duncan followed the others into the cell. The men shuffled forward, keeping their backs to the rough-hewn walls. Hungry and parched, their stares fixed on the two buckets waiting beneath the trapdoor. One held a slop of brown-colored stew, while the other brimmed with murky water, their second meal of a long hard day. Duncan breathed deep, hoping to catch the stew's scent, but the combined reek of sweat and piss overpowered the stale air. Anger thrummed through him, how he hated the mine.

The iron door clanged shut.

The men kept their heads lowered.

Grack strode into the torchlight, his sheer bulk enforcing a brooding menace. "One's missing." His voice was a low growl, his stare full of suspicion. He poked a thick finger at Brock. "You, explain."

"A cave-in." Brock kept his head bowed. "Trell died in a cave-in."

"One less maggot to tend." Grack prowled the chamber. "One less maggot to feed," his spiked mace whistled though the air, "one less maggot to work." The mace swung close to Martin's head, but the skinny man knew to keep still. Grack scowled, "One less man to work but the quota stays the same." The big Taal came to a stop next to the bucket of stew, his booted foot poised to kick.

The men gasped, a strangled sound.

Grack laughed. "Meet the quota or go hungry." He kicked the bucket, just a light tap, but the stew slopped over the side, forming a small puddle.

A few men, the skinniest ones, whined and trembled, leaning toward the spill...but discipline held.

Grack scowled, disappointment in his voice. "All right, feed the maggots."

The boys leaped to obey, circling the chamber with the two buckets.

Grack pulled Clovis from the line. "You get to eat the spill. Nothing's ever wasted in the Pit." The Taal laughed like a crush of boulders. "On your knees, maggot. I want to see you use your tongue."

Clovis knelt. Keeping his gaze on Grack, be bent forward, lapping the spilled stew from the floor. Duncan glowered, hating to see his friend debased, but there was nothing he could do.

The boys made the rounds, doling one bowl of stew and one cup of water to each man. Clovis finished the spill, scrambling to his feet in time to get the last serving. Grack scowled but said nothing. Ravenous, the men ate standing, slurping down their supper. Duncan got lucky, two greasy lumps floating in his stew. Tough and stringy, the meaty lumps tasted like salted pork. Duncan ate them, despite his suspicions. He licked the bowl clean and then gulped his one cup of water, thirsty for more.

Empty cups and bowls clattered into the leather sack. With the meal over, the three boys scampered back up the ladder. Grack prowled the chamber, swinging his mace in a deadly arc. "Sleep well, maggots, for tomorrow's another day in hell." Laughing, he hooked the mace on his belt and then struggled one-handed up the ladder.

The ladder disappeared, yanked from above. A heavy metal grate clanged shut. A key turned in the lock and the shadow of the big Taal moved away. Lantern light bled through the grate, casting a checkered pattern on the rock floor, the only light in the chamber.

Three men lunged forward, fighting to lick the floor where the stew had spilt, desperate for anything Clovis might have missed.

Duncan looked away.

The rest of the men claimed their lumps of straw for the night. The choicest spots were farthest from the piss-buckets. Duncan sat halfway along one wall, staring up at the grate, watching for shadows. A few men talked in quiet murmurs, but most succumbed to exhaustion, snoring on their pallets.

Brock rose from his pallet and stood over Duncan. "Seth, take my place."

Seth grunted. "What's a matter? You don't like yer own lice?" A few men sniggered, but Seth moved to Brock's pallet at the far end of the chamber.

Brock settled to the floor, sitting with his back against the wall. "You had something to say, cat-man?"

Duncan kept his voice a low whisper. "Fifty-seven against one."

Brock shook his head. "Yeah, but that one's a vicious mother-of-a-Taal."

"A *one*-handed Taal."

Brock just stared.

"We could take a one-handed Taal." Duncan lowered his voice. "Wouldn't you like to see him dead?"

Brock grunted, his fists clenched.

"We take him when he's halfway up the ladder."

"And then what?"

"We release the other prisoners, take the mine and then the pit."

"Just like that?" Brock shook his head. "You're a crazy bastard."

"You'd rather die in the mines?" When Brock did not reply, Duncan pressed his argument. "From what I saw of the pit, I figure we have the numbers all the way...but only if we work together. It'll take all of us to succeed."

"It will never work."

"If we don't try, then we all die."

Brock shook his head. "We'd have a better chance of finding a tit on a bull."

"But it's a chance, no matter how slim. I'll take a chance over certain death any day."

Brock grinned. "I like you, cat-man. I like the way you think." He nudged the man next to him. "Wake the others, pass the word." Men snorted awake, nudged by their neighbors. Brock got to his feet, his voice a command. "Hal and Feldon, check the grate."

Hal grumbled and complained, but he knelt below the grate while Feldon climbed on top. The giant stood with the skinny man perched on his shoulders. Feldon grasped the grate and peered through the bars. "No one above."

"Good, keep watch." Brock raised his voice, claiming the men's attention. "The cat-man has something to say."

Duncan rose and stood in the checkered torchlight, letting the men see his face. He turned slowly, surveying each man, and then he stopped and spoke, putting steel in his voice. "Fifty-seven against one."

A few men swore. Some looked away while others grumbled. "Not a chance."

"Certain death."

"No chance in hell."

Duncan spoke over them. "And when Grack kicks the bucket so there's no food for any of us...what then?"

Anger rippled through the men.

"This morning there were fifty-eight of us. Now we're fifty-seven." Duncan's stare circled the chamber. "Death stalks us all." Raising his left forearm, he pointed at the hated brand. "We're like cattle marked for slaughter. Death brands our skin. If we don't fight, the mine will slay us all." His voice hardened. "How will you die?" He turned and pointed at Bredan. "Crushed in a rock fall?" He pointed at Seth, "A fall from the ladder? Bashed by Grack's mace? Death by hunger?" Someone coughed and his finger pointed in their direction, "Death by rocklung." Duncan turned and pointed at Bruce, "Or buried alive."

A harsh silence settled over the chamber.

"We can wait for death to claim us...or we can fight and take a chance at life."

Most swore and muttered "no", but a few said, "How? Tell us how?"

"It starts after the evening meal. We swarm Grack when he tries to climb the ladder. Grab the mace from his belt and give the bastard a taste of his own weapon."

A few men grinned. "The bloody Taal deserves it. Shove his head in the bloody piss bucket and let him choke on it."

Duncan hissed. "Listen to me!"

An uneasy silence held sway.

He met their stares. "This isn't about revenge, it's about *escape!*" More than a few nodded. "We kill the Taal and then climb the ladder and release the others. Rumors say there are five other cells, as many as three hundred prisoners." He let the numbers sink in. "Three hundred is an army. Enough to take the mine."

"Yeah, but then what?"

"Then we take the pit." He filled his voice with confidence, trying to stem the avalanche of doubt. "We rouse the people. If the people fight with us, then we'll have the numbers to win. It's all about the numbers."

A grim silence choked the chamber.

Bruce spoke, voicing the fears of the others. "What about the soldiers? The Mordant has a whole army in the citadel. We can't fight trained soldiers. We'll be crushed like glass beneath a blacksmith's hammer."

"We'll have the element of surprise." Voices started to protest, but Duncan talked over them. "The brown cloud hides the pit from above. We take the pit and then wait till nightfall. We fill the cages with our own men and capture the cranes. Once we win the pit top, then we ferry up the rest."

"But the Mordant's army?"

"We don't fight the army. We get out of the pit and run. We head south, seeking a better life."

Some men shook their heads in disbelief; others gaped. Simeon, one of the hunchbacks said, "You're preaching doom, a death wish for us all."

"Aye, you'll get us all killed."

"Or worse, tortured and then beheaded."

Clovis raised his voice above the others. "We're already dead." He stared at the others. "The cat-man is offering us a chance at life."

A grim silence choked all argument, like a hand snuffing a candle flame.

Duncan stared at the men, his voice a whisper. "Like you, I want to live...but I'd rather die fighting than let the mine have me." He circled the chamber, pointing to the weak and the vulnerable. "Feldon, you're nothing but skin and bones, how much longer can you live without a decent meal? Gren, how many times have you slipped on the ladder? And Seth, you're already coughing up blood, how much longer till you succumb to rocklung?" He turned and stared at Bruce. "And Bruce, you're a strong one yet you should already be dead, buried alive, the worst fate of all."

More than a few men made the hand sign against evil.

"So instead of dying like slaves...let's live like men. Take a chance and fight. Who's with me?"

Brock stood. "I am."

Clovis was next. "I am." Seth followed Clovis. A few became many, swaying the reluctant, pulling them to their feet. Bruce was the last to stand. "I guess I owe you my life." A cheer rippled through the men, a pulse of pride in their voices.

Duncan raised his hands, drawing their attention. "And so it's decided. We'll fight as men."

Brock stepped forward. "When?"

"Not tomorrow, but the day after. Save your strength, working just hard enough to make the quota. We need to eat in order to fight." He stared at the men. "In two days, we fight for our lives, for our freedom."

The men murmured assent, all talking at once.

Brock silenced them. "We'd best get some sleep. And act like nothing is planned. Don't let Grack suspect anything."

The men returned to their pallets, but it took a while before the snoring started.

Duncan lay on his back, running the plans through his mind. The odds were long, nigh on impossible, but he refused to die a slow death in the mines. He'd find his way to freedom or die fighting, taking his secret to the grave. Rolling on his side, he tried to still his mind. Weariness claimed him. For the first time since his capture, he dreamt of green trees, and crystal waterfalls...and Kath.

28

The Knight Marshal

R ed eyes stared back at him, demon eyes, full of hate, taunting him with visions of defeat. The marshal bolted awake. Soaked in sweat, he shivered. *Another nightmare,* he wondered if it was a warning or a threat. Either way, those red eyes mocked him, as if the fate of the Octagon rested on his shoulders alone. Groaning, he banished the thought, a disloyalty to his king. "Enough of sleep." Wiping the sweat from his face, he threw off the wool blanket and climbed from his cot. Still dressed in fighting leathers, ready for any summons, he pulled on his boots.

Ice rimed the water bucket. He used a dagger to break through, splashing cold water on his face. Grimacing against the chill, he fingered the stubble on his face. Too cold to shave but he did it anyway, a matter of pride, setting an example for the men. Shrugging a chainmail shirt over his head, he fastened his wool cloak with a pin and then reached for his sword. The harness felt right across his shoulders. Another man's sword had become his own. Good steel should never be wasted.

Guards saluted as he strode the length of the hallway. He climbed the stairs to the tower top, stepping out into the bitter wind. Leaning on the rampart, he watched a bloody sun rise on the steppes, another cold day of waiting. He'd learned long ago that battles were mostly about waiting, long stretches of boredom punctuated by frenzied periods of killing. Judging by the empty grasslands it'd be another day of boredom but he dare not let the men grow complacent. So he made the rounds, inspecting arms and armor, adjusting duty rosters, bolstering morale, but all the while the red demon eyes haunted his mind. How could men defeat demons? How could swords defeat magic? Questions nagged him like a plague of worries. He dare not burden the king with his premonitions and Lothar had little patience for nightmares. A pity the king had turned against the monk. He bet there was much the blue-robed monk could have told them, but that chance was gone, flown south like a frost owl on the wing. He shook his head in chagrin; he shouldn't even think such thoughts. Morale was fragile enough without rumors of magic and shapeshifters.

Finished in the yard, he found his footsteps turning toward the eastern tower. With so many men drawn from across the Domain, the towers of Raven Pass were jammed to the hilt, men billeted in every nook and cranny. But one floor remained eerily empty, a pity it wouldn't stay that way.

The sharp smell of lye soap mingled with the scents of dried herbs, proof he'd reached the healery. The outer ward was deserted; rows of cots waiting for the wounded, but a crack of light beneath the far door betrayed the healer's presence. The marshal crossed the ward and rapped on the door.

"Come."

It was a small room, made smaller by a jumble of crates and bottles. Rows of dried herbs hung from the beamed ceiling, releasing a medicinal scent. A single window stood wide open. Admitting the morning light and a breath of cold air, the wind competed with a blazing hearth, a tug-of-war between heat and cold. The master healer sat with his back to the door, fiddling with a flask boiling over a lit brazier.

"Yes?" Quintus threw a glance over his shoulder, his eyes widening at the sight of the marshal. "Something I can do for you?"

"I've come to see how you've settled in." The marshal closed the door and turned the latch. "Do you have everything you need?"

"I brought two wagonloads of supplies with me from Castlegard." Short and pudgy, with a mop of unruly black hair, the healer set the flask aside and banked the brazier. Turning, he gave his full attention to the marshal. "But only the gods can say if it will be enough."

"Just so." The marshal circled the chamber, pretending an interest in the odd assortment of bottles, instruments, and scrolls that littered the crates. "How was the ride from Castlegard?"

"Long and bumpy, why?"

The marshal guessed the healer was in his early forties, relatively young for such a learned position. A modest man, he wore a dark brown robe, the color of peat, cinched at his waist, a dollop of paunch overshadowing his thick leather belt. His face was disarmingly pudgy and jovial, but the marshal knew a keen mind dwelt beneath the amiable appearance, a perfect combination for a healer. "I heard a visitor shared a ride on your wagon."

"Aye, you mean the monk, Aeroth." The healer shrugged. "He preferred the bump of the wagon to the bounce of a saddle."

No doubt. Horses can't abide a changeling, or perhaps that's just superstition. The marshal pulled a scroll from a bundle and found a list of ingredients for an ointment. "A long trip from Castlegard, you had plenty of time to talk."

"So you've come about the monk." Something dark flashed in the healer's eyes. "I've heard the rumors. Did the prince's eyes really glow red?"

"Aye, red like the fiery pits of hell."

"Then the monk did the Octagon a great service. A demon hiding beneath the face of a prince could have destroyed the maroon."

"True enough. But such a discovery is not without shock, or pain."

"So you blamed the messenger?" A sharp-edged question, flung like a dagger. The healer's eyes bored into him, as if passing judgment.

The marshal bristled under the scrutiny, but then he sighed, realizing it was no more than the truth. "The king was grief-struck. His treatment of the monk was ill done."

The words hung between them, as if weighed on a scale. "And what about the monk's crystal, how did it end up in the king's hands?"

"The demon hurled it across the room." The marshal shrugged. "Lothar found it abandoned in the fire grate. Amazing it didn't break."

"Lucky for the Octagon." Quintus gave him a searching stare. "Mounting the crystal on the king's sword was well done. With one stroke, you counter the foul rumors, proving there are no more demons among us."

"One was too many," the marshal scowled, "and a prince at that."

"True enough." The healer's glaze softened and it seemed as if some tension leached out of the chamber. "But you're here for more than just rumors."

Suspicion rose like a tide in the marshal. "Why so prickly about the monk?"

Anger flashed in the healer's dark eyes. "Because day after day we sit here on this bloody wall, without a lick of help from any ally, waiting for the Mordant's hordes to attack, and finally someone comes to help. A monk warns us of treachery and when that treachery proves true, the king seeks to lock him in the dungeon. That's not the Octagon *I* serve."

The marshal crossed stares with the healer. "Have a care, healer." He brooked no disloyalty to the king...but the words were true enough, so he bridled his temper. "As I said, the king was grief-struck. A debt of thanks is owed to the monk."

Anger bled from the healer's face. "Sorry." He turned toward his workbench, his shoulders hunched, a hint of weariness in his voice. "It is hard to sit here, waiting for cartloads of wounded to arrive." Quintus shrugged, fiddling with a mortar and pestle. "You wanted to ask me something?"

"Aye." Now that it came to the asking, the marshal found it hard to explain. He paced the chamber, frustration riding his shoulders like a harness. "The monk said a lot, but he also said too little." He shrugged. "There was never any chance for questions." The marshal raked a hand through his hair. "Swords I know. But demons and dark magic?" He shrugged, forcing the words out. "Whatever comes from the north won't just be swords and spears. I need to know how to fight magic."

Quintus stared at him. "You should have asked the monk."

"Yes, but that chance is lost. So I'm asking you."

"I'm just a healer." Turning his back to the marshal, Quintus swirled a flask filled with a pea-green potion, a puff of smoke rising from the brazier.

The marshal refused to be defeated. "You're the most learned man among us. I've even heard tales that you once studied in the queen's great library in Pellanor. Surely with all that learning you've read something of magic?"

Quintus sighed. Setting the flask aside, he turned. "It's true I've been to the queen's library and in all those thousands of scrolls you won't find a single mention of magic except in the bards' tales. The War of Wizards was a long, *long* time ago."

"But you must know something?" The marshal's stare drilled into the healer, desperate for answers.

"It's strange that you ask. Aeroth spoke of it on the ride from Castlegard."

The marshal waited.

"You have to understand that magic is nearly gone from the lands of Erdhe. Most people don't believe in it. So if they're suddenly confronted with magic, people either feel mind-numbing fear or worshipful awe. I suspect either will get you killed on the battlefield."

"So how do I counter it?"

"You keep your wits about you."

"That's it? That's your advice?" He would have laughed except those demon-red eyes kept haunting him.

Quintus shrugged. "What I mean is, consider magic like a sword, like a weapon, albeit a very dangerous weapon, but like most swords it can only cut one way."

"Explain."

Quintus sighed. "If the legends are to be believed, then most surviving magic is dependent on an artifact, a focus, leftover from the War of Wizards. And each artifact has a single purpose, a single magic, like being able to sculpt stone with just your mind, or summoning a fireball. But most magic wielders can only do *one* thing, one single magic. So once you know what that one thing is, you keep your wits about you and you find a way to block that skill so it doesn't turn the tide of battle."

It made a strange kind of sense, like dealing with the first trebuchet. "And if the magic wielder is killed?"

"Then the skill will be lost to the enemy."

So wizards can be killed, the marshal took comfort from the answer. "So what kind of magic will they have?"

Quintus barked a laugh. "Only the gods know."

"You must have some idea?"

"Legends are full of stories about magic. Any or all of them could be true."

The marshal studied the healer through hooded eyes. "And the monk didn't say anything about what we might face?"

Quintus sighed. "There was one thing Aeroth kept harping on, something troubling. He said the Mordant collects power, and the one power he covets above all others is soul magic."

"*Soul* magic?" A shiver raced down the marshal's back. "What in the nine hells does that mean?"

"It means the Mordant can twist flesh as well as spirit. It means his army may contain more than just men."

"I don't understand."

The healer's face turned grim. "The Mordant won't be bound by the Laws of Light. By wielding soul magic he can sculpt abominations. Beasts and humans melded together creating creatures of horror. Legends are rife with them. You've heard the tales and you know their names. Ogres, goblins, hellhounds, fearsome creatures twisted by the Dark, abominations loosed against mankind."

Something big at the window, gliding like a ghost. The marshal drew his sword, a scrape of steel on leather.

"Put up your sword." The healer stood. "It's just Snowman, my frost owl."

Wings spread wide, a white frost owl soared through the window, landing on a crate. Ruffling its feathers, the owl stared at the marshal, a blink of golden eyes. "*Whoooo?*"

"Just an owl?" The marshal stared at the bird.

"He hunts the mountains late at night or early in the morning. It's why I leave the window open."

Was *this* the owl he'd seen? It would explain why there were no rumors of shapeshifters...but then what happened to the monk? "I'd forgotten you kept an owl." He sheathed his sword. "You've given me much to think about. I thank you." He stepped toward the door and lifted the latch.

"Lord Marshal."

He turned back to face the healer.

"If it's true the Mordant is coming, expect nightmares."

The marshal gave a weary nod, for his dreams already brimmed with nightmares.

29

The Mordant

A line of maroon cloaks fluttered in the stiff winter wind. Thirty knights bearing the Octagon blazon stood at the heart of the Dark Citadel, a maroon slash marring the great circular courtyard. Such a sight would have been a blasphemy were it not of the Mordant's own making.

Amused by the irony, he walked among them, studying each man with a critical eye. His brief time at Cragnoth Keep had proved fruitful. By understanding his enemies he found ways to defeat them. Stealing the garb of the knights was a small thing yet it would serve him well.

Craftsmen of the citadel mimicked his cast-off garments, transforming elite soldiers of the Pentacle into knights of the enemy. Trickery appealed to the Mordant. He'd worn many guises across many lifetimes, but the Deceiver always suited him best, the role that most profited the Dark Lord.

A swagger of footsteps followed. The Mordant turned to study Sir Raymond, another spoil of treachery. Clad in black chainmail over dark leather, the unmade knight had turned his colors, serving as a captain in the Mordant's elite guard. Cloak colors were easily changed, but it was the darkness of a man's soul that truly mattered. In Raymond's case, the truth lay exposed on his face. Stubborn eyes, a square jaw, and a nose made crooked by too many brawls...but the darkest truth was branded deep into his skin. Each cheek bore the scar of a broken octagon, marking him as an unmade knight of Castlegard. The Mordant kept him close, for the fallen knight had his part to play in the great dark design. "What do you think of my loyal knights?"

Raymond studied the men. "The silver surcoats are well done. And the maroon cloaks are near perfect."

"Near perfect?"

"Near enough. Even at Castlegard the dye is not always consistent. But it takes more than a maroon cloak to pass for a knight. Let me see how they move."

The Mordant gestured and the maroon-cloaked captain barked an order. "Search the courtyard for enemies."

Thirty knights unsheathed their weapons, a whisper of steel on leather. Moving in pairs, they patrolled the courtyard, swords held at the ready.

Raymond took the time to study each pair. "They move well enough, like men bred to their weapons, confident in their ability to kill. Elite soldiers carry a certain swagger, like lions on the prowl," he cocked his head, "but something's not right."

Annoyed, the Mordant studied the knights, knowing the smallest imperfection could foil the ruse.

"It's their boots."

And then he saw it. Craftsmen of the Octagon used tanned leather, subtle shades of natural brown for belts, scabbards and boots, while the Pentacle used leather dyed to an unrelenting black. Their black boots betrayed them, such a small detail to ruin his dark deceit. "I ordered an *exact* copy. Have the quartermaster killed, and make it painful."

Sir Raymond flashed a feral grin. "I'll do it myself."

"Now call them to attention."

Orders echoed through the courtyard.

A cold wind blew out of the west, a tang of salt in the air.

The Mordant turned, his black cape billowing in the wind. Darkness rose within him, making his voice more than mortal. *"First we deceive, then we divide, then we conquer."* He studied the line of battle-hardened soldiers. More than a few bore scars on their faces, proof of their battle prowess. "A glorious task awaits you, for you are my knights of deception. Cragnoth Keep is held by traitors to the maroon. You'll cross the Dragon Spines at the keep and then fall on the southern kingdoms, raping and pillaging wherever you ride. Wearing the Octagon blazon, you are ordered to sate your every desire." His gaze bore into them, *"your every desire."* More than few men smirked hungry smiles. "Rape, torture, and murder, your every atrocity will tear at the knights' precious honor. Betrayal is the weapon that breaks men's heart and melts their resolve. Your actions will shatter the Octagon before our army ever marches south." His voice rose to a command. "Now finish your preparations and make all haste, for Darkness yearns to claim the whole of Erdhe."

The line of knights saluted, fists thumping their silver surcoats. "Honor and the Octagon!"

The Mordant laughed, his false knights would serve their purpose well. He turned, a swirl of black, and strode toward the palace. Six guards rushed to open the massive doors. He entered the palace, embraced by heat, a haven from the bitter wind.

A black-robed bishop and two priests scurried toward him, an ambush of boredom. The sallow-faced bishop waved a thick scroll. "My lord, the citadel has need of your decisions."

The Mordant did not break stride. Bishop Siff was a sycophant of the High Priest, a mere administrator bloated with self importance. Like a terrier, he dogged the Mordant's heels, reading details from a lengthy scroll. "The longships of the Sea Lords have been provisioned as per your orders, but the grain of the city's third silo has been sorely depleted. The Quartermaster begs leave to order new shipments." The bishop droned like a bee in his ear. "The third ward of the ninth tier is rioting for more food. Two guards were killed, trampled by the rabble. Captain Lornid seeks permission to retaliate against the mob. And the blacksmiths require more iron ore if they are to meet the increased quota of swords, they..."

Anger flared through the Mordant, he'd nearly forgotten the mundane drudgery of ruling. He whirled on the bishop, his voice a cold whisper. "Enough."

The bishop froze, his mouth sagging open. Scuttling back two steps, he held the scroll aloft like an offering.

The Mordant struck the scroll, sending it skittering across the marble floor. "A flood of petty details." He snarled at the bishop. "I know what it is you do, for I have ruled longer than your petty mind can imagine." The bishop gaped like a fish out of water. The sight of the simpering fool only stoked the Mordant's anger. "Your face displeases me. In the future, Lord Gavis will make the reports himself. Let the priesthood drown in the details of the mundane," his voice dripped with menace, "for that is your true purpose." He turned, a whirl of black, his boot heels ringing on the marble hallways.

A slow anger burned in the Mordant; perhaps he'd been too lenient with the priesthood. Perhaps more examples needed to be made.

"My lord, a word." A man's voice echoed from a side hallway. General Haith approached, a glitter of gold on black.

The Mordant slowed his steps, annoyance buried beneath a mask of calm.

The general matched his stride, a parchment clutched in his left fist. "I've just received a dispatch from the fourth border squad. There's been a battle in the steppes."

The Mordant came to a sudden stop. "A battle?"

"Our scouts detected an immense flock of ravens, a sure sign of a battle. When they reached the site, they found more than a hundred dead. All the dead bore the tattoos of the citadel."

"Where?"

"Deep in the steppes. Three days ride beyond the third gargoyle gate."

He'd entered the north through the third gate; perhaps there was more to this than met the eye. "And the enemy?"

"Most of the bodies were trampled to gore, leaving little to identify. But scouts report the battlefield was stripped of steel and leather, every dead horse butchered for meat. Only one enemy scavenges the steppes like that. The painted slaves have grown bold in your absence."

The Mordant resumed walking. "Bold indeed. Any signs of movement from the Octagon?"

"None reported." The general matched his stride, a shadow at his left shoulder. "My lord, it is well known that the painted men hide within the Ghost Hills. Riddled with caves, the hills are a haven for runaway slaves and other vermin." He clasped the hilt of his sword. "Lord, give the order. Let me eliminate this thorn from your side."

"How much threat is a thorn?"

"But the slaughter of a hundred soldiers cannot be ignored?"

"Butcher them in the steppes, but leave the Ghost Hills alone."

The general persisted. "But why? A troop of soldiers could easily rout the hills, putting an end to..."

The Mordant turned on his general, his words like a lash. "You exist to *serve*, not to *question*." General Haith retreated a step, his face pale. The Mordant bridled his anger, knowing the general had his uses. "For the sake of past loyalties, I will explain just this once. The Octagon knights cower behind their walls, rarely seeking battle, but the painted men dare the steppes, offering a skirmish to our soldiers. The escaped slaves keep our soldiers sharp between wars." He leaned toward the general. "Every army needs a whetstone."

Understanding dawned on the general's face. "A whetstone, not a true threat, and so you allow them to survive for as long as they serve."

"Serve to live, the eternal lesson of the citadel." The Mordant resumed walking, his black cape flaring at his back. "The painted people are nothing more than a thorn, easily trod beneath our boot heel. Our true foes lie in the south. In this lifetime, old scores will be settled." The Mordant smiled. "Summon my battle commanders. It is time the Pentacle prepared for war."

30

Duncan

A loud clang came from the trapdoor above. Duncan watched the others wake, trying to gauge their resolve. A few gave him confident nods as they shuffled into place, but too many looked away, their heads bowed, their hands shaking. Duncan tried to meet their stares, to bolster their courage, but it was too late for words.

The trapdoor clanged open and Grack descended the ladder. "On your feet, maggots!" Awkward with just one hand, the big Taal lurched down the rungs, but once he reached the bottom his awkwardness vanished, replaced by a cruel menace. Prowling the chamber, he twirled his spiked mace. "Time to earn your gruel, maggots. Serve to live!"

The bucket boys doled out the morning slop, a sour mash of oats and barley mixed with something foul that Duncan did not have a name for. Starving like the others, he gulped his portion down despite the taste.

An odd choking sound filled the chamber. Gren bent double, spewing his meal onto the floor.

Grack was on him in a heartbeat. "Not good enough for you, maggot?" His massive fist lashed out, smashing the dwarf to his knees. Grasping the small man by his hair, Grack pressed Gren's face into the stinking vomit. "Lap it up, maggot. For you'll get no more."

Gren squirmed, desperate to breathe.

Across the chamber, Brock's stare drilled into Duncan. His fists flexed, poised to fight, a burning question in his gaze.

Duncan shook his head no, willing Brock to stand down. They had to wait, or they'd all die for nothing.

Grack kicked Gren, a vicious blow to the ribs, but the small man just moaned, curling into a ball. Grack soon lost interest, his voice a snarl. "Get him on his feet!"

Seth and Clovis rushed to help. Gren tottered on shaking legs, bruises blooming on his face.

A sour smell hung in the chamber...the rancid reek of fear.

Grack scowled, "Into the hole, maggots. The Mordant needs his iron ore."

They lined up and shuffled towards the door. Duncan's stare circled the chamber, willing the others to remain calm. A handful met his gaze, Brock, Clovis, Thomas and Seth, but too many of the others looked skittish. Pale and shaken, fear etched their faces, yet none of them spoke. Perhaps Grack's cruelty had pushed them to silence. Either way, Duncan was relieved when he finally reached the ladder. He swung out and followed the others down, careful to avoid the missing rungs.

Strung out in a line, they descended into the mine.

And then the screaming started.

A piteous wail came from above.

Twisted by distance, the wail held no words...only fear.

Duncan clung to the ladder, trying to protect his head, expecting a body to come tumbling from above...but the corpse never fell. Silence followed the screams, leaving a mystery hanging in the stale air.

From below, Brock bellowed, "What's happening?" but no one answered.

Duncan yelled, "Keep moving!"

Someone whimpered, but they started moving again, shuffling down the ladder. No one spoke, but the pace increased, as if they all yearned to stand on solid ground. Duncan finally reached the bottom and found the others milling in the central shaft, a mixture of confusion and fear on their faces. Duncan took a risk and singled out Gren. "Do you still want to fight?"

The others stilled, their stares spearing the dwarf.

Bruised and battered, Gren met Duncan's stare, a glint of anger riding his eyes. "I want to *kill* the bloody Taal."

Duncan nodded. "And so you shall." He looked at the others. "It's easy to die in the mines. That's why we need to fight, but not until the appointed hour. First we work to meet the quota, then we eat...*then* we fight."

A few flashed wolfish grins.

Duncan said, "Now get to work. We need to make the quota so Grack doesn't suspect."

Stragglers descended the ladder.

Duncan longed to question them, but instead he turned for the gallery, needing to set an example. Passing close to Clovis, he whispered, "Find out what happened." Without pause, he strode down the gallery to an empty tunnel. Kneeling, he crawled to the ore face, taking up the hammer and spike.

Iron pounded against stone in a relentless heartbeat. Duncan drove the wedge deep, wondering if they'd been betrayed. Shackles on his wrists clanged with each stroke, echoing his rage. Swing and strike, he attacked the ore face, releasing a shower of blood-red rock. Coughing on the dust, he studied the rock face, desperate for a trickle of water, for a chance to slake his thrust, but the rock did not oblige. Unwilling to weep, the dark-cursed rock proved as cruel as the gods.

Behind him, wood scraped against rock. Clovis pulled the empty sledge toward the ore face. Duncan leaned on the hammer, taking the weight off his knees. "Who was it?"

Despite the dim darkness, Duncan saw a flicker of fear in the older man's eyes. "Bruce."

Bruce, the name ambushed Duncan with a spike of fear.

"Seth was the last man down. He claimed Bruce balked at the ladder, refusing the climb."

"Did Seth see what happened?"

Clovis shook his head. "Seth scrambled down the ladder, keen to get beyond Grack's reach." A racking cough shook the older man. When it finally subsided, he wiped his sleeve across his mouth. "Bruce was unmanned by the cave-in. I've seen it before. A cave-in preys on a man's mind till he can't take another day in the depths. Choked on madness, such men seek other deaths."

"But did he seek death or something darker?"

Clovis stared, "You saved his life. Bruce wouldn't..."

A cold anger burned in Duncan. "And now he seeks to save his own skin." He tossed lumps of ore into the sledge. "If Bruce sought death he could have waited another day."

Clovis had no answer.

"If he turned traitor, then death lies in wait for us all." His hands balled into fists. "I'd rather die fighting than go meekly to the executioner's axe."

Clovis gave him a wistful smile. "I'd like to see the sky again."

"And what about your gift of prophecy, your second sight? Will we succeed?"

The older man's face clouded. "Dreams are often fickle, full of fears and wishes instead of prophecy."

Clovis turned away but Duncan sensed something troubled him. "What did you see?"

Sighing, Clovis tugged on his beard. "Since you've come, I've seen many things in my dreams, fighting, blood, and pain. But last night I saw something different. Light streamed from a boulder, reflected in the faces of the people."

Duncan barked a laugh. "Light from a boulder?" He should have known not to ask. Prophecies never made sense. "Did you see the sky in this vision?"

"The sky?" A slow smile spread across the older man's face. "I stood beneath a blue sky and it was beautiful."

"A blue sky, I'll take it as an omen of victory." He gripped his friend's arm. "We rise tonight and damn the traitor." He dropped the hammer, keeping the iron wedge, a crude weapon but better than nothing. "Come, we have plans to discuss." They crawled back to the gallery and then entered the fifth tunnel. Brock worked the ore face, sweat glistening on his broad back. Stilling the hammer in mid-swing, he turned to stare at Duncan. "Cat-man."

Duncan nodded. "You've heard about Bruce?"

The big man hawked and spat. "Either a bloody corpse or a filthy traitor."

"Aye, that's the question. But either way, I say we fight."

"You said we needed surprise to win."

"Just so."

"How?"

"By rising tonight instead of tomorrow."

Brock's gaze narrowed. "You bloody schemer. You planned this all along...fishing for a traitor among us."

Duncan met the other man's gaze. "There was always a chance one of the weaker men might break...but I did not expect it from the strong ones." His voice dropped to a hoarse rasp. "I did not expect it from Bruce."

A grim silence settled over the tunnel.

Brock's voice was a low growl. "You shouldn't have saved that one."

Clovis murmured, "Perhaps he's dead, killed by Grack," but his words held no conviction.

Brock flexed his arms, cracking his knuckles. "If I find him alive, I'll break his bones for bread."

Duncan nodded. "Let justice be served. Either way, tonight we rise."

The big man grinned. "We'll take Grack as he climbs the ladder, smashing his thick skull with his own mace."

"But don't tarry. The sooner you release the other prisoners, the better chance you'll have. Numbers are key."

Brock scowled. "You talk as if you won't be with us."

"I won't. I've thought of another surprise for our jailors."

"What?" Suspicion laced the big man's voice.

"I'll ride the bucket-chain to the surface and attack from there."

Brock stared, *The bucket chain!*

Clovis hissed. "You're mad! You don't even know what's up there!"

"He's right, cat-man," Brock glared, "You'll die before ever reaching the top."

Duncan said, "Has anyone ever tried?"

Brock looked at Clovis, but neither had an answer.

"Just as I thought. I'll take the risk."

Brock drilled him with his stare. "Why?"

"Because I know a young woman who'd counsel that surprise can turn the tide of any battle."

"A woman, eh?" Brock grinned. "Now I know why you're so stubborn to survive. Is she worth fighting for, cat-man?"

Duncan thought of Kath, his voice fervent. "More than worth it."

The big man barked a laugh. "Then we'd best get you free of this hellhole."

Duncan lifted his hands, iron chains dangling from his wrists. "First the shackles."

A somber mood settled over the men. They all knew the price. Broken shackles ensured a cruel death at the hands of the torturers. Brock met his gaze. "Once your chains are struck there's no turning back."

Duncan shrugged. "Tell Grack I died in a cave-in."

"You're certain?"

Duncan nodded. "I'll need both hands to climb the bucket-chain." He knelt and stretched the shackles across a boulder. "Strike true."

The big man grunted, hefting the hammer while Clovis held the wedge between two links. It took five swings to break the iron.

The chain snapped, the sound echoing in the tunnel.

Duncan stretched his arms wide, savoring the freedom.

Clovis tore strips from his tunic and bound the loose chains to the outside of Duncan's forearms. "Clanking chains would betray you."

"Just so." He flexed his arms, adjusting the knots. "The shackles can serve as bracers. An armor of chains against our enemies." He grinned at the two men. "And so it begins. Strike hard and fast. Kill Grack and free the others. Time is our enemy and numbers our best hope." He offered his hand to each man. "We'll meet with our jailors crushed between us."

Brock thumped his shoulder. "Fight hard, cat-man."

Clovis gripped his arm. "The gods go with you."

"Keep your gods, I'll settle for luck." He took his leave of the two men and crawled back out the tunnel. Torchlight flickered along the main gallery, like fires lighting the halls of hell. Hammer-blows pounded a rhythm of drudgery from the side tunnels, the others working to meet the quota. Duncan tucked the metal wedge in his belt, his only weapon, and moved along the gallery. The fearsome clatter and clang of the bucket-chain soon eclipsed the hammer blows. Duncan flashed a feral grin. His shackles were sundered; the die was cast. He was done being a slave.

31

Katherine

Raven-faced healers fluttered around Zith like birds to a cornfield, but Kath finally got a moment alone with the monk. Leaving her guards at the entrance, she sat cross-legged next to his pallet. Light from the glow crystal fell across his face. She stifled a gasp. Pale and wan, he looked one step away from the grave. His eyes were sunken pits, his cheeks hollow, his skin gray, the stump of his left arm swathed in bandages.

His eyes flashed open. "Not dead yet."

Startled, Kath jerked backward, but then she gave him a rueful grin. "I'm glad."

"Help me sit up."

Taking his arm, she helped him up, easing a rolled blanket between his back and the rough rock wall.

"Better."

His left arm was bandaged, just a stump, severed below the elbow. He looked lopsided, like a wounded bird, broken and unable to fly. "Are you well enough to talk?"

He quirked a grin, "It's all they'll let me do." His face sobered. He looked down at his lap, his right hand worrying the frayed edge of his blanket, his voice dropping to a hush. "I failed you."

"Failed how?"

"I wasn't fast enough, too old to wield a quarterstaff. And now I'm a cripple, a burden."

"No!" Kath shook her head, willing him to understand. "It was never your sword arm we needed." But he would not meet her gaze. She reached for his right hand, slowly turning his palm up to the light. The Seeing Eye glared back at them. "This is why we need you, now more than ever."

"Even a cripple?" His gaze burned into her, as if seeking the truth.

She met his stare. "More than ever."

His right hand grabbed her wrist, a surprisingly strong grip. "Swear you won't leave me behind." His stare drilled into her.

"By Valin, I swear."

Releasing her, he slumped back against the wall, a wash of relief flooding across his face. "For my son, you see." He stared at her through hooded eyes. "I can't let him down, can't let him be kept as a slave to a harlequin."

Another reason to stop the Mordant, she'd almost forgotten.

His gaze turned shrewd, a hint of color returning to his face. "Something troubles you. More than just an old man's missing arm." He studied her face. "Duncan?"

She gasped in surprise, a worry she'd kept locked in her heart. It was her turn to look away. "After the battle, he left to track down the survivors, making sure no word would reach the Mordant. I keep hoping he'll catch up to us." She shrugged. "The painted people have seen no sign of him."

"He's a fierce warrior. If anyone can survive the steppes, Duncan will."

Kath nodded, storing his words away like hope.

"And the others?"

"Blaine smolders over the loss of his sword." Puzzlement filled his face, so she hurried to explain. "The Painted Warriors found us in the steppes, laid low by the poison of the hell hounds. They demanded Blaine's blue sword as the price of their aid."

The monk nodded. "So they value steel."

"And now Blaine resents the loss."

"And Danya?"

Kath chose her words with care. "The horror of the battlefield struck her hard. I don't think she ever expected it would be like that."

"So much power," his words held a touch of awe, "a Beastmaster unleashed." He flashed a wolfish grin. "The Mordant will not expect a Beastmaster on his doorstep."

"If she dares the power again."

"But she must! Every advantage is needed against the Mordant."

Kath shook her head, weariness hitting her like a club. "So many *musts*, we are all burdened by them."

Zith reached out but this time there was sympathy in his touch. "Forgive me for prattling. You came with questions and I have not answered a single one."

"Time is running short. I need your help." She struggled to explain. "In three days the painted people will hold some type of conclave. I fear much will be decided at this conclave yet their ways remain a mystery." Kath shook her head, trying to explain. "We're not treated as enemies, yet we're not trusted. We're permitted to roam the den, yet our weapons are not returned and guards shadow our every move." She lowered her voice to a whisper. "And we're always watched, always being judged. It's as if we must pass some test yet I don't know the rules." She stared at Zith, desperate for answers. "We need the painted people as allies. Yet I'm stymied how to do it."

He nodded, his face thoughtful. "Living in the shadow of the Mordant, they'd make formidable allies. And their desire for steel proves they're warriors."

"But how do we gain their trust? What do you know of them?"

"Little enough. They're an ancient people, forgotten by most of Erdhe. If the Kiralynn Order had anything to do with them, it was long ago." He tugged on his beard, a straggle of silver. "But I've gleaned a bit from their healers. They're a society of escaped slaves and runaway soldiers, so they know the cruelty of the Mordant more than most. And their freedom is hard won." His gaze sharpened. "Prickly with pride, you must tread lightly. You dare not break their customs or cross their taboos."

"Easier said than done." She stared at the floor, fingering the top of her boot, getting up the courage to tell him the rest. "They took all our weapons...including the crystal dagger."

"*Nooo!*" The word was a groan. "You must get it back or we have no chance of freeing my son."

"I know." She gave him a sideways glance, keeping her voice to a whisper. "A crystal dagger is a rare thing. Will they recognize it?"

He sagged back against the rock wall. "They might. The dagger has a lore of its own. But the gods meant it for your hand."

"But how do I get it back?" Her voice betrayed her desperation. "Should I ask for it, or just pretend it's another weapon?"

"If they learn what it is, then they might keep it for themselves. The Mordant is a fearsome enemy." His breath hissed in warning. "The amber pyramid?"

"I have it. And my gargoyle. They only took our weapons." She reached into her pocket, making sure the pyramid was safe. "Why do you fear for it so?"

He sighed. "There's so much you need to know." He shook his head. "So much you should have learned before ever leaving the monastery."

"That's why we have you."

Gratitude flashed across this face. "Thank you. I just hope I know enough." Zith settled back against the wall, his voice falling into the pedantic rhythm she'd come to expect in the monastery. "The pyramid is a Quickner, very rare and very powerful. It creates and strengthens the bonds between a focus and the wielder. In essence, it quickens magic. But what makes it a higher power, is the way it spans all types of magic."

"Types of magic?"

He nodded. "The power of each focus follows a single element. Your gargoyle allows you to walk through stone, so your gargoyle is keyed to the element of earth. Since magic depends on a connection between the focus and the wielder, something in the earth calls to you, connects with your inner spirit, allowing you to awaken the magic of your gargoyle. So if you found other focuses, you'd most likely be able to wield the ones keyed to the element of earth. But with a Quickner, you should be able to wield *any* focus, keyed to *any* element."

Her breath caught.

"With a Quickner you might achieve the powers of the wizards of old."

Kath stared at the amber pyramid cupped in her palm, so much power in such a small thing.

"Never let the pyramid fall into the hands of the Mordant...or any other harlequin."

Kath nodded, clenching her fist. "So what are the other elements of magic? Fire, water, and air?"

Zith nodded. "Those and one more. The fifth and most powerful element."

"What?"

"Soul magic."

"*Soul magic!*" Kath hissed, making the hand sign against evil.

"You do well to fear it." Zith nodded, his face grim. "In the hands of the Dark it is the most fearsome of magics, allowing men and beasts to be twisted together, creating abominations like those dread hell hounds." He shook his head, "Corrupted by the Dark, soul magic is a most foul curse, a bane against the world. Great wars were once fought over it."

"But how can the gods allow such a thing to exist? The mere thought is loathsome."

"Oh, it is not always evil. Wielded by Darkness, it becomes a terrible blight, the worst nightmare visited upon mankind, but used by the Light it becomes a true blessing. Souls are the gods' own element, their most wondrous creation. The wellspring of love and courage, the source of hope and compassion, the essence of an indomitable spirit, souls hold a power beyond all other elements. The best healers make use of soul magic. By coaxing and guiding the soul, they enable the sick and injured to heal themselves. As a Beastmaster, Danya wields soul magic, communicating with the spirits of animals. Soul magic is the most powerful of all the elements, for it embodies the power to create and the power to destroy, the best and the worst of us."

Kath shook her head. "I can't imagine wielding such a power."

"Oh but you do."

Startled, she stared at him, almost dreading the answer.

"Do you know what the crystal dagger truly does?"

She held his gaze, waiting.

"It slays *souls*."

Stunned, Kath gaped at the revelation.

"The crystal dagger is the only soul magic ever crafted into a weapon of the Light." His gaze pierced her, "And it is yours to wield."

"By the gods."

Zith nodded. "Just so." He leaned back against the rock wall, a stern look on his face. "And if we are to reach the Dark Citadel, there is one other type of soul magic you must face and defeat."

"What?"

"The gargoyle gates."

Memories of childhood tales reared like nightmares in Kath's mind. She shuddered at the thought.

"So you've heard of them?"

"Some of the veteran knights told tales of the north...but I did not believe them."

"Such tales often hold a kernel of truth." He tugged on his beard. "I'd like to hear these tales. I suspect the north holds more nightmares than any of us know." Zith fell silent, his face locked in thought.

"But what of the gargoyle gates?"

"Oh, yes." He nodded, his gaze refocusing on her. "From what I've gleaned, the gargoyle gates are a true horror. Souls of men and beasts forever locked in stone, they act as sentinels, coming to life if anyone dares to cross the gates. The painted people fear them, and rightly so."

Kath made the hand sign against evil. "But how is such a thing defeated?"

Zith shook his head. "I do not know. But if we are to follow the Mordant, we must cross the gates."

A mountain of worries fell on her shoulders.

Zith leaned forward, gripping her arm, his voice a whisper. "And above all else, you must regain the crystal dagger, or all is lost."

"Pardon me," a raven-faced healer intruded. "There's been enough talk for one day. Rest is the key to healing."

Kath clenched her fist, hiding the pyramid.

A raven-faced healer stared back at her, a stranger, another watcher passing judgment. Kath wondered how much she'd overheard. Slipping the amber pyramid into her pocket, she took her leave of the monk. "I'll see you tomorrow." She left the chamber, her two guards dogging her heels. Trailing a hand along the rough rock wall, she walked through the corridors blind, her mind a whirlwind of thoughts, a storm of worries. But above all else, one thought rang through the chaos. *I must regain the crystal dagger...or all is lost.*

32

Duncan

Duncan reached the central mineshaft, the fearsome clatter assaulting his ears. Like a metal monster ravenous for ore, the massive chain rattled up and down the central shaft, enormous metal scoops spaced along its length. Never in his life had Duncan seen such a thing. It seemed almost evil, a strange metal beast, yet he'd made up his mind to ride it to the surface. Desperate to glimpse the top, he stared aloft, but even his golden cat-eye saw only gloom.

One of the hunchbacks emerged from the gallery, struggling to pull a sledge loaded with ore. Covered in red dust and bent to his burden, Simeon looked like a gargoyle sprung from the underworld. Duncan joined the hunchback, pushing the sledge from behind. Simeon threw a questioning glance his way, clearly surprised by the aid, but he did not protest. They muscled the sledge toward the bucket-chain. The great chain rounded a wheel fixed to the bottom of the shaft, massive metal buckets gaping for ore. Three buckets passed before the chain rattled to a sudden halt.

Simeon said, "Hurry."

They grabbed lumps of ore and heaved them into the bucket.

Simeon stared wide-eyed at Duncan's sundered shackles. "You're marked for death."

Duncan flashed a grin and spread his arms wide. "No, for freedom."

"It's today then."

The bent-back man was not stupid. Duncan nodded, "Spread the word, we rise tonight, attacking Grack as he climbs the ladder."

"But not you," Simeon heaved a lump into the bucket. "If you climb the ladder like that, Grack will kill you."

They worked to fill the bucket. "I'll not be climbing the ladder. I'm riding the bucket-chain aloft."

Simeon gaped. "You're mad!"

Duncan grinned. "A surprise for our jailors."

The bucket jerked and the two men jumped back. The great chain rattled to life like a metal monster suddenly wakened, hauling the ore aloft. Other buckets descended, waiting to be fed.

Simeon stared at Duncan. "It's madness to ride the chain."

"I have to try."

"You're a dead man." The hunchback made a strange warding sign with his left hand and then shrugged into the harness affixed to the sledge. Turning without a word, he trudged back into the gallery, dragging the empty sledge behind him.

Duncan remained in the throat of the mine. He waited for the chain to come to a stop and then climbed into the massive bucket. Rock dust covered the bottom, the dented sides rising to his waist. Spreading his feet wide, he gripped the chain, his heart thundering.

The chain clattered to life, lifting him as easily as a load of ore. He clung to the sides, enduring the jerking motion. Thirty feet up, the chain shuddered to a sudden halt. From below, he heard loud thumps as ore was dumped into a bucket. Two hundred heartbeats later, the chain lurched upwards again.

Lift and stop, he rode the bucket up through the mineshaft. It was a strange sensation, moving without effort, like riding the back of a giant metal beast. He watched the ladder rungs as they passed, a measure of his passage up the shaft. Abandoned galleries began to appear, dark mouths gaping in the rough rock wall. For the first time, he noticed subtle colors striping the mineshaft, bands of ocher, rust, and umber, proving the deep depths had their own strange beauty. Duncan shivered, longing for leaf and bark and honest sky, hoping the bucket-chain reached all the way to the surface. He stared aloft but saw only gloom. Once he looked down, but the view made him queasy, a sheer drop into hell. He'd always been callous to heights, but somehow this was different.

The slow ascent gave him time to ponder his chances. He yearned for his longbow. With a single quiver he'd cut a swath through the guards but his only weapon was a crude iron wedge. He barked a laugh at the folly of his plan. Surprise was his only advantage, a slender hope. He'd have to find a way to distract the guards. Wielding chaos like a sword, he'd look for the chance to free other prisoners. With luck he might even live to glimpse the sky again.

The chain quaked and shuddered, nearing the ladder top. Duncan crouched, hiding in the bucket, hoping Grack did not wait for the prisoners below. His luck held, for the threshold stood empty. Just to be safe, he stayed crouched till he was a good twenty feet past the ladder top. Standing, he peered up through the gloom, but even his cat-eye was of no help. Only the gods knew what waited above.

Rattle and groan, the bucket-chain slowly strained upwards. Just when he thought there was no end to the shaft, details began to appear. A wooden platform with holes cut for the bucket-chain covered the mineshaft. Yellow torchlight flickered through the holes, a bitter disappointment. Either it was night above or the platform was still below ground. Sounds filtered from overhead, the crack of whips and the creak of wood. Duncan leaned out of the bucket, needing to find another way up. Wooden beams angled out from the mineshaft, supporting the underside of the platform, but it seemed a risky jump. He scanned the darkness, but he found no other way.

The chain jerked upwards like a fisherman's line, pulling him ever closer to the platform. Only one bucket remained above him, time had run out. His heart racing, he gripped the chain and balanced on the lip of the bucket. Refusing to look down, he launched himself across the void. Arms stretched to their limits, he seemed to leap forever. His fingernails scraped against wood. One hand found a hold. He fell hard, dangling from the beam. The iron wedge slipped from his belt, tumbling into the void. Cursing his ill luck, he struggled for purchase. He gained a second handhold and pulled up. Breathing hard, he straddled the beam. He listened for the falling wedge, but heard nothing. Hugging the wood beam, he stared down into the murky depths, shuddering at the fall.

The chain rattled to life and his bucket passed beyond the platform. Footsteps shuffled overhead but there was no cry of alarm. He hugged the beam, waiting for a chance at surprise. Full buckets continued to rise, empty buckets descending. Lulled by the dull repetition, Duncan lost count, every third or fourth bucket filled with ore. His legs cramped and still he waited.

The bucket-chain clattered to a stop...and this time it remained still.

Spiked alert, Duncan held his breath and listened. The sounds from above slowly dimmed, signaling the end to the toil in the depths. By now, the others would be making the long climb back up the ladder. He wondered who would die tonight, Grack or his friends. If the gods cared for justice, then the one-armed Taal was doomed to die. Either way, Duncan would find a way to bleed the enemy.

He stretched his muscles, needing to be limber, and then crawled along the angled beam till his head touched the underside of the platform. Leaning out, he stretched for the opening but it was beyond his reach. Coiling into a crouch, he leaped for the opening. He caught the edge, dangling below the platform. His hold was awkward, but his strength prevailed. Slowly pulling up, he raised his head through the hole.

Torchlight glinted on rough rock walls. A massive winch loomed overhead like a wooden dragon, but he saw no guards. He swung up through the opening and rolled towards the shadows. Crouching low, he breathed deep. The air was cooler than the mines but it held the same cloying stench of sweat and fear and oppression, proving he'd find allies on this level. Duncan grinned; oppression was such a fertile ground for revolt.

His gaze swept the cavern, searching for a weapon. Torches lined the walls, the only source of light. On the far side, a mound of ore rose like a pyramid, a monument to slavery. Overhead, the winch was built of massive timbers. Old and dry, the wood was desiccated by the mine's stale air. *Old and dry*...a grin spread across his face. If not a weapon, at least he could wreck havoc. Chaos might compensate for numbers.

He collected five torches. Thrusting them deep into the winch, he prayed for the wood to catch. As if the gods approved, the fire embraced the old timbers. A belch of black smoke billowed to the ceiling. Duncan grinned, a distraction for the guards...and a stop to the Mordant's iron ore.

Knowing time was against him, he raced to the exit. The cavern narrowed to a long corridor, the floor worn smooth by countless footsteps. Torches lined the walls, casting islands of light in the dim gloom. Duncan stretched his senses, alert to danger, but the corridor proved empty.

A short run brought him to a three-way fork. Pausing at each opening, he breathed deep, questing for clues. The air to the left seemed less stale, as if the mine's stench was diluted. Perhaps the left led to the surface, an alluring choice...but he'd promised Brock and the others. He chose the right, satisfied when the floor began to angle downward.

Footsteps ahead! But there was nowhere to hide. Duncan retreated to the darkness between two torches, crouched to flee or fight.

The footsteps came closer, only one set, but the tread was soft, not the tramp of hobnailed boots. Puzzled, he waited, a lump of iron ore clenched in his fist. A figure rounded the bend, a young woman, blond-haired and slender, with a basket perched on her head. *A woman*, Duncan took a chance and stepped into the light. "Greetings."

She startled but she did not scream. Wide-eyed, her gaze traveled the length of him, from his leather-wrapped feet, to the broken shackles lashed to his forearms, to his naked chest, finally fixing on his mismatched stare. "You bear the mark of the Pit. If it's escape you seek, you've run the wrong way."

Duncan had to smile; for once his cat-eye gained him an ally instead of enmity. "I've come to set the prisoners free."

Her eyes widened while her left hand sketched a strange sign. "Do you have a name?"

"Mara." She gestured to the basket perched on her head. "I bring supper to the winch guards every night." Something dark flitted behind her pale green eyes.

"How many guards?"

"Six including Mardak, the Taal." She gestured back up the corridor. "First door on the right. They were eating when I left."

"And the prisoners?"

"Two doors beyond but you'll need the keys. Mardak keeps them on his belt."

A bloody Taal. "I need weapons."

She stared at him, as if peering into his very soul, but then she nodded, her voice firm. "My brothers died in the mine. I'll help you. Come." She took his hand, and led him back up the corridor to the fork. A faint whiff of smoke rode the air, confirming the fire still burned but he heard no cry of alarm. Mara took the central passage, leading him to an iron-studded door. "In here."

He pressed his ear to the door...and heard nothing, yet he hesitated, without weapons, a room full of guards would be a deathtrap.

The tramp of boots echoed up the corridor.

Out of time, Duncan shouldered the door open. He plunged into darkness, pulling the girl with him. Easing the door shut, he held his breath, listening. The tramp of boots passed them by. Duncan leaned against the door and took a deep breath.

Light slivered beneath the door, more than enough for his golden eye. Weapons lined the walls, racks of spears and bundles of short swords, enough for a hundred men. He moved to the wall and reached for a scabbard, buckling a sword around his waist, a warrior once more.

"How can you see?"

He'd almost forgotten the girl. "I see well enough."

"Oh." She stayed by the door, setting her basket on the floor.

He found a cache of daggers and stuck two through his belt. Circling the room, he prayed for a bow, but the gods were not that generous. Axes and whips lined another wall, but then he found a rack of crossbows. Duncan grinned; not as elegant as a longbow, but it would serve. Beneath the crossbows, he found a pile of small canvas sacks bulging with quarrels. Tying two to his belt, he took down a crossbow. Setting his foot in the stirrup, he cocked the bowstring, loading an armor-piercing quarrel. One shot was all he'd get, but it might be enough to bring down a Taal. He stared at the other crossbows, wondering if he could wield two of the cumbersome weapons.

"I can help."

"What?"

The girl had come halfway across the room, lifting a dagger from a shelf. "If you're going to kill the guards, I can help."

"You're no warrior." He picked up a second crossbow and cocked the string.

"If you load it, I can shoot it."

"And once you've shot it, you're dead." He shook his head at her folly. "Six against one, the odds are grim."

"Six against two would be better." She lifted her chin and stared at him. "You don't understand, I want them dead." Her voice held a hard edge.

She reminded him a bit of Kath...just a bit. And another crossbow would help, a chance to improve the odds. "Can you hold this?" He handed her a crossbow. "Careful, it's loaded." The weapon looked awkward in her hands, but she held it steady enough. "You loose the quarrel by lifting the tickler here." He pointed to the mechanism. "Aim low because most crossbows kick high. Aim for the groin and you'll likely hit the chest."

"And if I want to hit the groin?"

So that was the way of it. "The chest makes a better target. But if all goes well, I'll do the shooting." He loaded a fourth crossbow. "I'll kick open the door and loose the first two and then drop them. You hand me the other crossbows and then run. I don't want your blood on my hands."

She nodded, a bitter smile on her face.

Duncan shook his head, another stubborn woman...but he did not have time to argue. He looped the strap of the crossbow over her shoulder. "Can you carry two?" She nodded and he gave her the second. "Careful, they're armed." He picked up the other two and moved to the door. Easing the door open, he checked the corridor, relieved to find it empty. "Come." Holding a crossbow in each hand, he retraced his steps to the place where he'd first found her. "How much further?"

"Just around the bend."

"Remember, hand me the crossbows and then run." He did not wait for an answer. Rounding the bend, he heard voices, men laughing at a ribald joke. The door to the guardroom gaped open. He crept toward the door and then stared at the girl. She eased the bows off her shoulders and nodded, her face set in stone. He gripped his crossbows, his thumbs near the ticklers. Taking a deep breath, he raised both bows and stepped into the doorway.

Five men and a Taal sat at a table...the big Taal had his back to the door.

Surprise lit their faces.

Duncan eased the tickler, sending the first bolt at the Taal's broad back. *Thunk!* The second crossbow kicked high, taking a man in the throat. A gurgled scream filled the room. Empty crossbows clattered to the floor. Shouts erupted from the guards as they pushed back from the table, scrambling for their swords. Mara was ready, handing him another crossbow. *Thunk,* he got the shot off and grabbed the last bow. Three guards rushed the doorway, their swords glinting in the torchlight. The crossbow bucked, taking the closest man in the face. *Thunk,* the force of the blow flung the body backwards into the remaining two guards. Brains and blood splattered the room. Duncan hurled the empty crossbow at the guards and unsheathed his sword, charging the tangle of men. He hacked at an arm, releasing a fountain of blood...but his sword stuck in bone, refusing to move.

A blade slashed towards his face.

Unarmed, Duncan ducked sideways, but the sword chased his face. Raising his arm to block the blow, he braced for pain but the sword clanged against iron; *the chain of the shackle saved his life.* Twisting away, he reached for a dropped sword, aiming a slashing cut at his opponent's legs, but the guard was too quick, parrying the blow. Steel clashed against steel. The guard drove him back into a corner. Hack and slash, Duncan retreated, taking cuts to his arm and across his chest, paying for his lack of skill. The guard laughed like a berserker, wielding his sword with brutal strength. Duncan parried a stroke to his face...but the sword twisted out of his hands, clattering across the floor.

Disarmed, he scrambled backwards, drawing a dagger from his belt.

Laughing, the guard pressed the attack, poised for the killing stroke...but then he staggered to a stop, his eyes wide with shock. Roaring in pain, he turned away, as if seeking a different threat. Duncan lunged forward, skewering the guard under his left armpit.

The dagger bit deep, thrust all the way to the hilt. Shuddering, the guard groaned and slid to the floor.

Mara stood over him, holding a bloody dagger. She fell on the guard, hacking and slashing. Blood coated her hands like gloves, her face contorted in a fit of rage.

Duncan gripped her arm, taking the dagger from her hand. "He's dead."

She shuddered, her eyes glazed with hatred. "He deserves more than death."

He wiped the blood from her face, wishing he could ease the hatred in her eyes. "He's dead, you've killed him...and you saved my life."

Mara gazed up at him, her face solemn.

Just for a moment, she looked like Kath. "There's strength behind your eyes...like another woman I know." He helped her to her feet, brushing a strand of hair from her face. "Like a hidden dagger poised at the Mordant's back, you women find a way to tip the balance." He reversed the dagger and handed it back to her. "Keep your blade sharp."

She accepted the dagger and smiled, a mixture of pride and determination.

"We've won a small victory but we dare not tarry. Close the door and bring the crossbows to me." She sprang to life, rushing to the door. The room was awash in carnage, the smell of blood thick in the air. Duncan sheathed his sword and reached for the nearest crossbow. He cocked the string and loaded a quarrel, arming all four bows. Handing two to Mara, he crossed the room to the table. The big Taal lay slumped in a pool of blood, a fist-sized hole punched through his back. Even a Taal could not survive such a wound. He rolled the body from the chair and took the ring of keys from the belt. Holding the keys aloft, he flashed a smile at Mara. "Time to gain some allies."

Mara returned his smile, her left hand sketching a strange sign.

Armed with two crossbows, he eased the door open. The corridor stood empty, but a loud clamor echoed from the direction of the winch chamber. Perhaps the guards fought the fire. He flicked a glance at Mara. "Hurry." They raced down the corridor, passing one door and stopping at the next. He kicked the door open, holding a crossbow in each fist. A single guard sat on a stool. *Thunk,* the quarrel took him the chest, a look of surprise frozen on his face.

A terrible reek rose from two iron grates set in the floor, the stench of unwashed bodies and overflowing piss-buckets. Duncan gagged. He shuddered, wondering how he'd ever grown accustomed to the stench of captivity.

Dropping the crossbows, he knelt by the first grate, trying the keys from the ring. The third key worked. Ripping the grate open, he yelled into the hold, "Rise up and fight, you're free men!" He thrust a ladder down and then raced to the next grate. By the time the second grate clanged open, men were staggering up out of the first hold. Filthy and bedraggled, they milled around the chamber as if dazed. Most looked defeated, lash-marks striping their backs, but a few still had the spark of anger in their eyes.

Duncan leaped onto a wooden stool and raised his voice to a shout. *"Hear me!"* A hundred faces turned his way. He raised his arms, displaying his broken shackles like trophies of war. "Chains can be broken. Guards can be killed. The men of the mines are rising! This is your chance. Find weapons, kill the guards, and release every prisoner. We take the mine and then the Pit."

A few men cheered but most gawked as if he'd grown a second head.

Unsheathing his sword, he raised it high, the steel blade glittering in the torchlight. "This is your chance. Claim a sword and be men once more!"

A dozen roared their approval, pumping their fists in agreement, but the others just stared, cowed by captivity.

Duncan pointed to a big man in front, a giant with a wild shock of flaming-red hair. The mark of the Pit dominated his face, a third eye in the middle of his forehead. "You, what's your name?"

"Krell Three-eye."

"Will you fight with me, Krell?"

"Aye, with my bare hands if needs be!"

Others began to shout, "I'll fight! Give me a sword!"

Duncan kept his gaze on Krell. "Pick a dozen of the best fighters." As the big man began choosing, Duncan tried once more to rouse the others, raising his voice above the murmur of talk. "Time is against us. We have this one chance to escape the doom of the mine. The choice is simple. Fight to live or cower and die." Too many hung their heads like whipped curs, their souls shriveled by slavery, but Duncan had no more patience for the timid and the meek.

Turning his back on the others, he joined Krell and his men. The big man grinned a gap-toothed smile. "I've got your dozen." Raising fists as big as hammers, Krell cracked his knuckles, a ruthless grin on his freckled face. "We're ready to break heads."

Duncan grinned, liking the big man's bravado. "I've friends rising in the depths of the mine. I need men willing to go deep, to take the guards from behind and crush them between us." He stared at the men, noting the anger smoldering behind their eyes. "Are you with me?"

A chorus of 'ayes' answered his question. Krell had chosen well.

"First we get weapons, then we fight." Duncan handed a crossbow to one of the men. "Follow me."

Mara waited by the door, her back to the wall, clutching a crossbow as if she wasn't sure whom to trust.

Duncan gripped her arm, flashing a reassuring smile. "We've gained allies." He eased the extra crossbow from her shoulder and gave it to one of the men. "Come."

The corridor rang with distant shouts. Duncan's senses pricked with warning. Gripping the crossbow, he set off at a run, leading the men back to the guardroom. Shouldering the door open, he was relieved to find the bloody carnage undisturbed. "Choose your weapons." The men poured into the room, pillaging the dead for swords, daggers, and whips. A few struggled to strip boots and leather jerkins from the corpses. Krell wrestled the boots from the Taal, grinning when they fit.

Duncan kept watch at the door, anxious to be gone. "Krell, which of these men do you trust with your life?"

Krell pointed to a dark-skinned man with scars crisscrossing his face. "Naga is a good man. I'd trust my back to him."

Duncan nodded. "Naga, to me."

The dark-skinned man belted a sword to his waist and then joined Duncan, bowing his head in deference. "M'Lord."

"I'm not a lord."

Naga gave him a broad smile. "A man who frees other men from the heart of evil must truly be a lord."

Duncan shook his head, impatient with the banter. He gestured to Mara. "This is Mara. Every man here owes his freedom to her. Guard her close and see that she escapes unharmed."

Naga grinned, thumping his chest with his fist.

Mara gasped. "You're leaving me?"

He gave her a soft smile. "You've already saved my life once. I won't have your blood on my hands."

"But I can help..."

"...by leaving the mine." He met her gaze. "If we take the mine then we must also take the Pit. It's all or nothing, victory or death." Her face paled but her stare never wavered. "If you want to help, then seek out the leaders of the Pit and tell them what we do here. If we win the mine, we'll need their help."

"Spread the Light." She nodded, her face solemn. "I can do that."

"Then hurry, before the jaws of death snap shut around us." He stared at Naga. "Go."

They burst out of the guardroom, swords at the ready. The clangor of fighting echoed down the hallway, but the corridor remained empty. Naga shepherded the girl away, setting off at a run. Duncan watched till they rounded the bend, "The luck of the gods go with you," then he turned and led his men into the depths of the mine.

33

Bryce

Bryce crouched in the gray void of his prison, peering through the keyhole of light. He watched as the Mordant took the woman. A tumble of long blond hair framed a heart-shaped face, so achingly beautiful. His gaze roved across her, feasting on every detail. Her blue eyes looked eager, her curves tantalizing beneath diaphanous silk. She leaned forward, her silken shoulder straps giving way. The woman laughed, her nipples swelling to his touch. *His touch!* Yet Bryce felt nothing, locked within his prison, reduced to a voyeur of his own body.

"Come, my Lord." She tugged at the Mordant's hand, pulling him toward a massive bed. "Let me please you."

Her words came to Bryce like an echo through a tunnel.

A sheath of pale silk slipped from her hips. Naked in the candlelight, she offered a beguiling glimpse of ecstasy. "Come to bed, my Lord, and together we shall make a son."

The Mordant laughed, a throaty rumble. "Is that what you think I want?"

She rubbed against him like a cat, marking him with her scent, pulling him down onto a sea of pillows. "Of course, my Lord, for a son is a man's immortality."

He rolled on top, pinning her beneath his weight. "Children are the weakness of mortals."

She gave him a playful pout. "But all kings need a son."

"I need no sons." He caught her wrists, pinning them to the bed. "But I'll take your pleasures." And then he took her, hard and triumphant, reveling in each thrust. "*I* am my own legacy." He pounded each phrase home. "*My* own past...*my* own present...*my* own future."

Shuddering, Bryce pulled away, tortured by an intimacy he could only watch. Writhing within his prison, he felt both repelled and attracted to the keyhole. The narrow glimpse of life let him eavesdrop on the Mordant, but it was a sterile view, without taste or smell, or touch. How he longed for a single touch, a single caress. The keyhole kept him sane, a gift from the gods, yet sometimes it seemed a cruel curse, leaving him parched for life. Nights were the worst, a torture to endure. The Mordant kept a harem of lovers, a bevy of concubines, taking a different one every night, yet Bryce had never known a woman. Closing the keyhole, he succumbed to the gray void, a ball of misery locked away from the world.

Later, much later, he felt the Mordant stir. He'd grown attuned to the moods of his jailor. Sensing a keen interest, something much more than sexual, Bryce dared a glimpse of the world.

Night cloaked the royal bedchamber, the candles melted to stubs. Naked, the woman lay sprawled across the bed, lost to sleep, her blond hair tousled across the pillow. The Mordant shrugged a black robe over his shoulders. Barefoot, he prowled the marble corridors.

Bryce kept vigil, spying through the keyhole. There had to be a reason the gods gifted him with this view, some way he could make a difference. Perhaps the Mordant hid a weakness, a key to unlock the harlequin's ruin. Bryce clung to the hope, desperate to give meaning to his cruel existence.

Monsters filled the keyhole.

Bryce stifled a gasp and then took another look. Candlelight revealed a torment of fangs and claws...but the monsters were all frozen in stone. So lifelike, Bryce shuddered, wondering if they were more than carved rock. After the gargoyle gates he'd learned to distrust stone.

Demons of every description leered from the walls. Winged harpies flew across the ceiling, while snarling balrogs and horned devils cavorted along the hallway. Shifting shadows gave the illusion of life. A seamless nightmare carved into the walls, every inch riddled with details.

Bryce craned for a better view. He'd never seen this hallway before, never seen anything like it. He kept watch, desperate to understand.

The Mordant claimed a candle from a wall sconce and knelt to inspect a devil's grin. Sculpted of gray marble, the carving bore a long pointed face with curved horns, the face frozen in a perpetual wink, as if the imp kept a secret. Covering the devil's left horn with his thumb, the Mordant pushed. *The horn slid into the wall*, a soft grating sound.

The Mordant chuckled, his voice a soft whisper, "The devil's in the details."

Startled, Bryce froze, expecting pain...but his jailor seemed preoccupied with the carvings.

Moving through the hallway, the Mordant stopped at specific demons...and all the while, Bryce watched.

Eye of varg and claw of balrog, tongue of ghoul and skull of lich, a code of details slid into the wall, a rhyme of monsters carved in stone. A hidden doorway eased open. A lich king glared from the darkness, ruby eyes glinting in the candlelight. The Mordant stepped into the narrow passage. He pressed the lich king's left eye and the outer door swung shut.

Cobwebs choked the inner passage, decades of dust on the stairs, proving the passage was long forgotten. The single candle guttered, casting a feeble light. The Mordant made his way down a short spiral staircase. A profound darkness lurked at the bottom, a crypt carved from solid rock. He paused at the entrance and turned a tap protruding from the wall. A dark liquid gushed into stone runnels. The Mordant set the candle flame to the liquid.

Light leaped to the oil. Flames rushed along the runnels, drawing a line of light along the walls. Fire spewed from the mouths of demons filling basins carved from stone. Braziers erupted with flames, belching sparks to the ceiling. The walls of the crypt glowed bright, revealing a glittering treasure.

Bryce gasped, dazzled by the glow. Gold gleamed along the back wall, chests brimming with emeralds and rubies the size of a large man's fist. Jewels and coins spilled careless from caskets, the fortune of many kingdoms strewn across the floor. Bryce gaped at the unimaginable wealth. Other treasures sat nestled amongst the gold, stacks of cedar chests and baskets brimming with scrolls. Amongst faded battle banners, a suit of armor stood proud upon a rack. The armor trapped Bryce's gaze. Fearsome to behold, the breastplate showed the ribs of a skeleton etched in silver, the helmet fashioned into a grinning skull, a legend thought lost to time. Even coated with dust, the armor radiated fear, evil annealed into steel. Bryce trembled, knowing he beheld the ancient armor of the Skeleton King. The monks had thought the armor long lost, succumbed to legend, yet here it was, hidden amongst the Mordant's treasures, a powerful relic of war. Bryce pulled his gaze from the horror.

Everywhere he looked, treasure lay strewn across the floor, a king's crown tumbled next to a silver goblet, a hoard of wealth mingled with history, but one thing did not belong. An elegant throne sat in the center. Sculpted into silver wings, encrusted with sapphires and yellow diamonds, it glowed like captured starlight, like hope chained in the darkness. A feast for the soul, Bryce fixed his gaze on the throne.

Coins scattered underfoot. The Mordant moved through the chamber, touching his treasures. He caressed a faded battle banner and then lingered over a stone reliquary. For the longest time, he stood in front of the Skeleton armor, but then he turned to face the throne. The details became clear. An eight-pointed star adorned the winged seat, a legend proved true. Bryce wept when he saw it, how could the gods be so cruel?

Come, monk, attend me.

Terror rushed through him. Bryce slammed the keyhole shut just as a relentless force snatched him up. The hand of his jailor drew Bryce into the eyes of the Mordant. The unfettered view struck him like a hammer blow, treasure in every direction.

A triumph of spoils, the Mordant spread his arms wide, his gaze circling the crypt. *A thousand years of pillage gathered from across the ages. Wealth and weapons, magic and spell lore, treasures that time has forgot. Like the Dark Lord, I take the long view, waiting for the right lifetime.* He crossed the chamber and pulled a shroud from an altar stone, revealing a great sword. Black as sin, the folded steel rippled with evil, dragons forged into the crossguard. *A triumph of my fifth lifetime. A sapphire blue sword corrupted to black, made stronger for its dedication to the Dark Lord, a surprise for the Octagon Knights.* He moved to a small cedar chest and opened the clasps. Three dull-iron statues shaped into the form of crude fists sat nestled in black velvet. *And these rare beauties, three Wizard's Knocks, the last of an ancient magic. Power enough to topple the strongest walls.* He caressed the iron fists, like a miser counting his treasure. *Behold the treasures of my past! Enough secrets to fell all my enemies...even your precious monks.* His gaze came to rest on the silver throne. *But one secret still eludes me.* His tone darkened. *Do you know it, monk?*

Bryce shuddered, held in the grip of his jailor. *I've heard legends.*

And you despair to find it here. The Mordant chuckled. "Despair is good, you please me monk," he stepped toward the throne, *but do you know its purpose?*

He felt the Mordant hover close, like a raptor keen to strike. Bryce chose his words with care, never straying from the truth. *Only an acolyte, never a full-sworn monk. I've heard legends, nothing more.*

And?

And the legends speak of a winged throne of the Star Knights. A throne dedicated to the Light and endowed with a greater magic, lost long ago.

The legends lie. It was never lost, but captured by my legions, a spoil of treachery. The Mordant paced a slow circle around the throne, frustration coiling like a whip. *It reeks of magic, yet in all my lifetimes it has never served me.*

And it never will.

The Mordant hissed in anger. *What?*

Bryce cowered in his prison. *I don't know!* He hid behind a thin shield of truth, desperate to keep his secret safe.

Darkness loomed like a fist. *Tell me.*

Soul magic! He did not know where the words came from, yet they seemed true. *The throne is keyed to the Light of the soul and the depth of the need.*

And mine is full of Darkness. The Mordant stared at the throne, a coil of cold calculating anger. *Yet in all my lifetimes, I have never before worn the face of a monk,* he circled the silver seat, *or held a monk's soul locked within my own.* He came to rest in front of the throne, the silver wings gleaming in the torchlight. *Perhaps the time has come for old magic to awaken. Will it serve you monk?*

Me? Bryce quailed in his prison.

After all, the monks are kin to the Star Knights.

But I'm not a monk, only an acolyte! Bryce clung to the slender truth, terrified that Mordant might somehow use him to betray the Light.

Come, monk, let's test the strength of your soul. The Mordant dared to sit on the throne.

Bryce huddled in his prison, expecting a thunderbolt.

Nothing happened. The Mordant settled on the throne, his back pressed against the silver wings, his hands gripping the armrests.

Bryce prayed for the throne to strike, for the silver wings to incinerate the Darkness. Take my life, me for him! Strike now while you have the chance!

The Mordant chuckled. *Yes, pray for my demise. But in all my lifetimes, the throne has never struck against me.* The Mordant caressed the silver seat. *Perhaps together we can claim the magic.*

Flames danced along the crypt walls but the throne remained dormant.

It will never serve you.

The Mordant chuckled, a mocking sound tinged with cruelty.

Bryce felt something change within his prison, like a lock slipped from the chain, or a key turned in the cell door. Gray walls receded, disappearing like mist in the sunlight. He felt himself unfold, expanding outward, claiming his body, a man once more. He took a deep breath and stale air filled his lungs. *His lungs!* He gasped, giddy with life. His hands clutched the silver armrests, his bare feet pressed against the cold stone of the crypt. *Cold,* he could feel cold! Hope raged through him like a river in flood. He dared to flex his fingers, but it was hard, harder than he ever remembered; like being encased in rusted armor, yet his fingers began to move.

Call the magic! The Mordant's command thundered through his mind.

"I don't know how." Bryce said the words, *real* words. His voice echoed in the hollowed chamber.

The Mordant roiled through his mind, a malignant darkness, tentacles spreading everywhere. Darkness found a hidden doorway, a shadowy place buried deep within the monk's ancestral memory. Assaulted by the Mordant's will, the doorway burst open. Knowledge poured out, releasing a sixth sense attuned to magic, a gift he never knew he had. Guided by the Mordant, tendrils of thought yearned towards the throne. *Serve me!*

"No!"

Together we can be great, the knowledge of the monks serving the Dark Lord. Submit your soul to me, for it is your destiny.

"Never!" Bryce fought the command, his scream echoing against the rock walls. He yearned for a way to end this evil, to end his life. The black sword was too far to reach, the mere sight of the blade making him queasy. Frantic, his gaze roamed the chamber, desperate for a weapon. A jeweled dagger gleamed near the throne, a trinket of conquest tossed aside, but perhaps it would buy his freedom. Bryce strained against his bonds, concentrating on his right hand. Like swimming in molasses, the hand lifted from the throne, reaching toward the dagger. He leaned forward, his body slow and sluggish, slumped across the throne like a drunk, straining to reach the dagger. Fingertips brushed the hilt, just a little further.

He felt the Mordant connect with the throne, a flush of triumph.

Light flared like an exploding star.

Bryce was hurled through the air, flung from the throne like a rag doll. He landed on a heap of gold coins, gasping and flailing, desperate to master his body.

The Mordant reached for him. Gray walls slammed down. *No!* Pain lanced through him, the thrust of a thousand spear tips. Ripped from his body, he was hammered into a small ball of consciousness and forced back into his prison. Bryce railed against his bonds, but he had no form, no substance, just a wisp of thought beating against steel walls.

A malevolent presence surrounded him.

The Mordant lashed out. *You failed me, monk. The throne rejected both our souls.*

Pain ripped through him, like a scourge of acid, but in a corner of his mind he stayed connected to his jailor.

Enraged, the Mordant stood, sending a shower of gold coins clattering across the floor. Ripe with vengeance, he strode across the crypt and took up the black sword. Darkness rippled along the five-foot blade, drinking in the light. Armed with the fearsome weapon, he turned to face the throne.

No! Bryce screamed, desperate to save the last relic of the Star Knights.

Oppose me at your peril. The Mordant raised the sword in a two-handed grip...but then he stopped. The sword hovered above the winged throne like an executioner's axe. Flames in the braziers guttered, casting strange shadows across the crypt. The Mordant's rage slowly annealed to a cold anger. He lowered the weapon. *Another time, another lifetime. Like the Dark Lord, I take the long view.* Gripping the sword, he turned and strode toward the staircase.

Bryce huddled in his prison, locked in misery, but in the depths of his heart he nurtured a thin hope. He'd learned his prison had a key. Perhaps in time he'd find a way to unlock the door...to reclaim his body. And then he'd rid the world of a thousand-year-old evil.

34

Duncan

Twelve men. He'd freed a hundred yet he'd gained only twelve warriors, a grim start to the rebellion. Duncan hadn't reckoned on the soul-eating nature of slavery...or the help of a young woman. The Mordant used the mine to crush men's spirits but perhaps the gods lent a hand. Either way, the die was already cast, victory or death the only possible outcomes.

Clutching a loaded crossbow, he led his small band through narrow corridors and vaulted caverns, always choosing the deepest route...but with every step his senses screamed that he ran the wrong way. To control the mine, he needed to control the entrance, but first he had to find Brock and the others. Together they'd sweep upwards, killing the guards and releasing the prisoners. A simple plan, but the mine was proving a labyrinth, a kicked anthill swarming with armed guards.

Rounding a bend, he heard a subtle snick. *"Crossbow!"* Duncan screamed a warning as he lurched left. A quarrel rushed past his right ear, a deadly hum. The man behind shrieked, clutching at his face.

Shadows crowded the corridor but Duncan saw every detail. Twenty guards with swords drawn, but the immediate threat was the single crossbowman. While the other bowman struggled to reload, Duncan raised his own crossbow. He loosed the tickler. The weapon bucked, spitting a feathered quarrel. The crossbowman screamed, crumpling to the floor. Duncan followed the bolt with a bloodthirsty yell, wielding the crossbow like a club. The wooden stock smashed against a guard's face, felling him with a sickening crunch. Dropping the crossbow, Duncan drew his sword. Chaos erupted around him. Howling like banshees, his ragged band attacked. Fighting with scavenged weapons and bare fists, they rushed the guards. Some fought with their shackles, clasping their hands together and wielding the chains in a deadly arc, cracking the skulls of their jailors. Ferocity proved their best weapon, driving a wedge into the guards.

Duncan rode the tidal wave of hate, fighting at the spear point. Hack and slash, he wielded his sword, twisting away to avoid a low thrust. Beside him, Krell laughed like a berserker. The big redhead picked up the felled body of a guard. Wielding the corpse like a battering ram, Krell charged. Shocked by the barbarity, the lead guards pulled back, seeking to retreat, but the passage was clogged by other guards. Confusion reigned and the battle became a rout. Duncan's men swarmed forward, releasing a frenzy of hate. Blood slicked the floor and screams filled the corridor. Showing no quarter, they hacked at their jailors, prying weapons from their dead hands. The remaining guards retreated into a tight knot, presenting a hedgehog of swords. Laughing, Krell heaved a corpse at them. Another prisoner threw a severed head. Other body parts followed, a bloody bombardment.

Barbarity turned the tide of battle. The guards broke and ran.

The prisoners howled in victory, giving chase like wolves hot on the scent of prey.

Duncan tried to stop them, fearing the mad rush would end in an ambush. His roar cut through their howls. *"Hold your ground!"*

Krell staggered to a stop, the glaze of battle leaving his eyes. He grabbed the nearest man and dragged him to a stop. "The cat-man's right. *Stand your ground.*" His voice boomed through the corridor, tugging at the men like a leash.

They stumbled to a halt. Battle lust slowly bled from their faces. Some leaned against the wall, clutching their weapons and gasping for breath, while others winced in pain, feeling wounds for the first time. One man lay dead and two badly wounded, a steep price for victory but the alternative was death.

Duncan strode amongst them, offering words of encouragement. "We've proved the guards can be defeated." The spark of pride lit their eyes, transforming ragtag prisoners into fighting men. "But we must stay together and make the most of our numbers. We've had our first taste of victory but there are more battles to be won, and more prisoners awaiting release. Bind your wounds and loot the fallen. We can't afford to tarry." Duncan joined the search, surprised to find a half-full wineskin hanging from a belt. Sniffing the stopper, he took a long pull. His mind knew it was swill, but his mouth savored the sudden taste of grape.

"Share the spoils, cat-man." Grabbing the skin, Krell spouted a red stream into his open mouth. "Ambrosia of the gods! Now that's worth fighting for." The wineskin made the rounds, each man gaining a mouthful.

Krell grinned, slapping Duncan on the back. "The men fought well, cat-man."

"Ferocity won the first battle but that mad dash could have been our undoing. We need to stay together and not rush into a trap. One defeat and we're all dead."

Krell growled. "You worry too much, cat-man."

"Someone has to." Duncan retrieved his crossbow, making sure the mechanism still worked. Putting his foot in the stirrup, he reset the tickler. The crossbow suited him so much better than a sword, but in the heat of battle it was only worth one death. He searched the dead bowman, scavenging another handful of quarrels. The looting proved a boon. The dead guards gave up a score of swords and half as many daggers. His band of freed men bristled with weapons, some wielding a sword in each hand. Duncan called the men back to their purpose. "We've gained the teeth of war; now let's show the guards how freed men fight!"

The men growled their assent, a pack of hungry wolves at his back. Duncan led them into the depths, running at a lope. Despite the danger, he set a hard pace, feeling as if a trap closed around them. Always taking the downward path, he stretched his senses, alert to ambush. Breathing deep, he tasted the air. The corridor stank of blood and death yet he heard no clash of steel. He readied his crossbow, his thumb near the tickler. Rounding a bend, he found a corridor awash in blood. Corpses lined the hallway, a dozen prisoners hacked to death. A few still gripped swords, at least they'd died as warriors. Duncan stared at their faces, relieved to find them strangers. "The rebellion spreads. We need to find our brothers-in-arms."

Torches flickered in the hallway. They came to a three-way fork and he paused to listen, testing the scents at each passage. The middle fork rang with the faint clash of steel. "This way." The sounds of battle drew them on.

Figures appeared ahead, blocking the corridor, black leather armor, fighting with swords and spears. A host of guards...*all showing their backs!* They'd come up behind the guards, the clamor of battle covering their approach.

Beside him, Krell flashed a feral grin. "The gods favor the bold!"

Whispered words passed between his men.

They approached from behind, cold and silent, the perfect ambush. Two strides from the guards, Duncan loosed a quarrel. *Thunk!* The bolt punched a fist-sized hole through the first man and skewered the second. Duncan swung the crossbow like a club. Slash and hack, they fell on the guards, blooding their swords without opposition. They cleaved a swath deep into enemy ranks before the guards began to turn. The murderous ambush turned into a desperate fight. Trapped between two bands of prisoners, the guards fought like rabid dogs. No quarter was asked for and none was given, a bitter struggle to the death.

Krell led the advance. Bellowing a fearsome laugh, the redhead wielded a sword in each fist. Wrecking havoc with each blow, the big man scythed through the enemy like a god of war reaping a bloody harvest. Duncan followed in his wake. Reloading the crossbow, he killed two men with one quarrel, smashing a third with the heavy wooden stock. Parry and strike, the battle became a blur...till Krell staggered to a stop.

The swords fell silent...corpses strewn across the floor.

From across the corridor, a ragged band of prisoners stared back at them, an odd jumble of weapons gripped in their fists.

For a moment, both sides stared in disbelief...but then one man cheered, and the cheer became a roar. The two sides rushed together, pounding each other on the back, talking at once, brothers-in-arms.

Duncan looked for his friends. Familiar faces crowded the corridor, Seth, and six-fingered Nef, and Simeon the hunchback, but there were two he wanted to see more than the others. He finally found Brock and Clovis together. The big man grinned, brandishing a spiked mace like a rare trophy.

Duncan answered his grin. "So Grack gave up his mace."

"We took the one-armed bastard on the ladder, just as you said." Brock twirled the blood-soaked weapon, beaming like a man in love. "This spiked beauty cracked the Taal's skull like an eggshell. You should have seen the look on the bastard's face when we charged the ladder." Grinning, he thumped Duncan's back hard enough to rattle his teeth. "Your plan worked, cat-man! But I never thought to see your mismatched stare again."

Duncan gave the big man a wry smile. "Cats have nine lives."

"Ha! I hope you saved some for the fight ahead. The tunnels teem with guards."

"All the more reason why we can't tarry." He felt the press of time, like a hand strangling his throat. "Get the men ready. Bind their wounds and strip the dead of weapons. We have a mine to take." Brock grinned and began issuing orders. Duncan turned to Clovis, relieved to find the older man unharmed.

"The gods watch over you, Duncan Treloch." Clovis smiled, rock dust coating his straggly beard.

Duncan clasped his friend's arm. "I'd rather they lent a hand."

Torchlight glinted in the older man's eyes. "Perhaps they do."

Duncan shook his head, but there was laughter in his voice. "You and your gods. Better to put your trust in steel, or a good bow."

Clovis lifted his sword, an odd smile on his face. "Seems I haven't forgotten the way of the sword...but I long for the color of the sky."

"We'll see it again, my friend, but first we must take the mine." He turned away and lifted his crossbow, raising his voice above the clamor. "We've clawed our way out of hell...but I've a yearning for the sky. Are you with me?"

The men cheered a roar that shook the corridor.

"Then let's show the guards how freed men fight." Setting off at a run, Duncan led them through rock-carved passageways, but this time they traveled up. Left and then right, he threaded a path through the rabbit warren of stone, always heading toward the surface. Wary of ambush, he strained his senses, trying to detect the first clank of steel.

Ambushing guards from behind, they fought a running battle. With scavenged weapons and bare hands, they clawed their way toward the surface.

Needing more men, Duncan breathed deep, always searching for the rotting stench of prison holds. Twice they stopped to release men from bitter hellholes. Shackled and chained, the prisoners climbed out of the depths, astonished by the sudden chance for freedom. Some cowered and slunk away, too broken to fight, but most joined the struggle, their courage bolstered by the sight of so many freed men wielding swords. Their numbers swelled to over two hundred, half of them armed, all of them desperate, a mob running at his back.

Guards blocked their way, setting a thin picket of swords and spears, but the mob would not be denied. Howling like the damned, his men overwhelmed the guards, carving a swath of death through their ranks like justice on a rampage.

One battle at a time, they fought their way up through the twisting passageways, leaving a trail of carnage in their wake. The narrow corridors proved a boon, the perfect funnel for their ferocity. Swarming the enemy, they never lost a battle, but the fighting took its toll, leaching their stamina and culling their numbers to half. Caught in a labyrinth of stone, it seemed they waged an endless struggle...till the air began to freshen, and the men caught the first hint of the surface.

It smelled like victory.

A sense of triumph pulsed through the men, lifting their spirits and renewing their strength. Gripping their weapons, they pounded through the rocky corridors like a force of nature that could not be denied.

They rounded a bend and found a clog of guards blocking the corridor. Duncan loosed a quarrel as Krell led the charge. Screaming like banshees, they fell on the guards. Slash and hack, they smashed the blockade, ferocity overwhelming discipline. The guards broke and ran.

Baying like hounds, the men gave chase, their blood hot for battle.

The corridor widened into an enormous cavern. Howling for vengeance, the men spread out, chasing their prey across the broad expanse, hungry for blood.

Duncan ran with the pack, wielding his crossbow like a club. Halfway across, a warning thundered through his mind. He slowed to a stop and stared at the cavern...and then he knew. *"Stop! Fall back! It's a trap!"* He screamed at the top of his lungs, grabbing the men around him, knowing that discipline would defeat ferocity in such a large space. *"Krell, stop them!"* But the big man was lost to the battle-fury. Leading the wild charge across the cavern floor, Krell laughed like a berserker, his flaming-red hair waving like a banner. Caught in the rush of war, the men streamed past Duncan, brandishing their weapons, their eyes glazed with the heat of battle, giving full throat to their blood lust. Sensing disaster, Duncan tried to stop the rush, but he was one lone man straining against a blood fury.

And then the drumming started. Like a heartbeat of war, the sound thundered through the mine with the force of doom. Ranks of soldiers appeared blocking the far end of the cavern. Not guards, but disciplined soldiers. A solid line of rectangular black shields embossed with golden pentacles, they formed a wall across both ends of the cavern, deadly barriers bristling with spears.

Trapped! Duncan struggled to reform his men. "To me! To me!"

Krell slowed to a stop...and the wild dash veered to a sudden halt. Turning away from the barrier, the men milled in confusion, caught between two shield walls.

A centurion stepped from the ranks, his voice echoing through the cavern. "Put down your weapons! Serve to live!"

Krell gave the answer. Plucking a fallen spear from the ground, he hurled it at the centurion. "Live free or die!" The spear took the centurion in the throat. Roaring, Krell chased after the spear, charging the wall of shields like a magnificent lion...and the men followed.

Heartened by Krell's audacity, Duncan laughed, embracing the madness of battle. Bellowing a challenge, he charged with the rest. He loosed a quarrel and then swung his crossbow like a club. A hundred strong, they raced toward the shield wall, a ragtag army wielding a motley of stolen weapons, courage and purpose their only armor. As if sanctioned by the gods, a wild hope surged through Duncan, a feeling of desperate invincibility.

Their roar shook the cavern, a righteous wave bearing down on the shield wall.

But the Mordant's soldiers did not fight fair.

Handlers stepped from the shield wall. Like spurts of black venom, they launched nets into the air. Falling like spider webs, they trapped the rabble army, pinning them to the ground. A net caught Duncan in the face, binding him with sticky strands. Thrashing against the tangle, he tripped and fell. Weighted with leads, the sticky nets tangled arms and weapons in a stranglehold, pulling men to their knees. Across the cavern, men thrashed and hacked but the struggle only deepened the web's embrace. Swathed in sticky cocoons, they writhed on the floor like flies awaiting the bite of a spider.

One man broke free.

Somehow Krell broke the sticky bonds, rising like a god of vengeance, a sword in each fist. Roaring in defiance, he charged the shield wall like a maddened lion. *"Fight me, damn you, fight me!"*

A deadly hum of crossbows filled the air.

Krell stumbled, quarrels piercing his arms and legs...but he did not fall. Bleeding from a half-dozen wounds, he lurched toward the shield wall. Roaring like a fiery-maned lion, he beat his sword against the line of spears. *"Fight me in single combat! Come out from behind your shields and fight!"*

Trapped in a cocoon of nets, Duncan thrashed against his bonds, desperate to fight by the big man's side.

Krell staggered along the shield wall, bellowing his challenge...but no champion ever emerged. Instead, the soldiers thrust their spears at the big man, aiming to wound not to kill. Like a pack of jackals, they harassed the last lion.

"No!" Duncan struggled to his knees, clawing at the nets.

As if Krell wearied of the game, he beat the spears away and rushed the shields. A single spear took him in the chest. Even then, Krell did not stop. Impaled on the shaft, he lunged forward, reaching for the soldier who'd killed him. Halfway up the shaft, the big man staggered to a stop. The swords fell from his hands, clattering to the stone floor. Groaning, Krell slowly toppled sideways, felled like a mighty oak.

"No!" Duncan's scream split the cavern. He struggled to stand, his arms bound by sticky webs.

The shield wall opened, disgorging a score of leather-clad handlers. Wielding heavy clubs, the burly handlers moved among the cocooned men, beating them into submission, forcing shackles onto their hands and legs, making them prisoners once more.

Wild with anger, Duncan bucked against his bonds. His arms remained pinned to his sides, but his right hand reached his dagger. Pulling it free, he struggled to a crouch.

Mocking laughter beat against him. "Where do you think you're going?" A big brute of a handler sneered at Duncan, thumping a club in his left hand.

Gripping the dagger, Duncan struggled to stand. "Fight me!"

"Why bother?"

Snarling, Duncan lunged at the handler, seeking a warrior's death...but the smothering web tangled his legs, making a mockery of his charge. He tripped and fell hard, the dagger skittering across the floor.

The handler barked a crude laugh, aiming a kick at Duncan's groin.

Twisting away, Duncan glared up at the brute, hawking a wad of spit at his face. "Kill me and be done with it!"

Wiping the spit from his cheek, the handler snarled. "Your life is not your own." He brought the club down with expert blows, hitting flesh instead of bone. "Even maggots live to serve."

Duncan writhed in pain, longing for death. The club thumped against the side of his head, the taste of blood flooding his mouth. The world began to fade...cruel laughter chasing him into the darkness.

35

Katherine

Kath dreamt of Duncan, of their wedding night in the Shield Forest. Moonlight filtered through the branches, silvering their bower like a blessing from the gods. Naked, they lay entwined beneath the great oak tree. She kissed him, reveling in his touch, in his taste, in his warmth. Tenderness burned to a deep-seated need. She ached for him. He rolled on top, his mismatched gaze full of love...but something changed. Bruises appeared on his face, his gaze full of pain. *No!* Kath fought the nightmare, struggling to scream.

"*Shhhhh!*"

Kath woke, reaching for a sword that was not there.

"*Shhhhh!*" A raven-faced woman hovered overhead, ebony eyes demanding silence.

Recognizing the healer, Kath shucked the nightmare, struggling to wake.

"*Come,*" a whispered command. Thera handed Kath her boots, gesturing for her to follow.

Her companions slept, wrapped in their bedrolls, the glow crystal dimmed to a pale light. Even the wolf slept, huddled close to Danya...so perhaps there was no cause for alarm. Rubbing her eyes, Kath crept from her warm blankets, wondering at the late night summons.

The healer moved toward the chamber opening, her footfalls soft on the earthen floor. It was only then that Kath noticed she carried a candle, the first she'd seen in the caves. Why a candle instead of a glow crystal? Another riddle of the night, yet she followed without comment.

A pair of grim-faced guards waited outside the sleeping chamber, but these were strangers, not Bear and Boar. The smaller of the two men wore the tattoo of a badger...but the larger guard bore the snarling tattoo of a mountain lion. Kath stifled a gasp. "What's this about?" She turned to confront the healer.

"You seek to learn our ways?" Sharp eyes stared back at her, full of judgment.

"Yes."

"Then come."

"But the others?"

"Just you."

Kath sensed Thera's words were chiseled in stone, leaving no room for debate. She looked at the lion-faced guard and then back to the healer, but their faces held no answers. Swallowing her questions, she gave a terse nod.

The healer whirled, setting a brisk pace, a single candle clutched in her fist.

Kath rushed to keep up. The corridors were empty, the light dimmed for sleep. Shadows hovered close, obscuring the drawings. Kath peered through the gloom, searching for landmarks. Horses galloped across a vaulted ceiling, marking a familiar cavern. Three passageways later, the horses gave way to a pack of wolves baying at an ocher moon, but the healer did not tarry. More twists and turns followed, as if Thera deliberately sought to confuse her in a tangle of stone.

Kath kept pace, struggling to memorize the progression of paintings. Horses, wolves, badgers, snow geese, the narrow passage opened to a long gallery, a place she'd never been before. Charcoal ravens took flight across a rocky sky. The long cavern tightened to a narrow chokehold, the low ceiling almost touching her head. Ducking low, Kath shuddered at the suffocating closeness. The den seemed an endless warren of rock. No sky, no stars, no moon, a place forgotten by time. Kath wondered how the painted people could go so long without feeling the sun's kiss or the wind's breath.

Left and then right, the passage widened and then narrowed. Strange glyphs appeared on the walls. The crude drawings seemed older, more simplistic. Kath felt as if they walked backwards in time. Handprints filled an entire wall, a primitive accounting. Done in a dark reddish stain, Kath wondered if they were marked in blood. One of the hands held a sword, the first weapon she'd seen in the drawings. She wanted a closer look, but the healer forged ahead, walking deeper into the caves. Kath hurried to keep up, not wanting to be lost in the stone labyrinth.

Light from the glow crystals disappeared, leaving only Thera's candle.

The smothering darkness drew near. Kath rushed to stay close to Thera, nearly treading on her heels.

Thera's footsteps slowed, the candlelight flickering against rough rock walls. The passage opened to a chamber that seemed a dead end…till Kath glimpsed the jagged crack running the height of the far wall. Like a bolt of darkness, a lightning-shaped crack split the rock, creating a narrow passage. A great stag protected the opening, magnificent antlers spread wide above a noble neck. Drawn in bold lines of charcoal and umber, the stag's dark eyes seemed to bore into her soul, full of primal power.

Kath approached the jagged opening, acknowledging the stag with a nod. "Lightning in the depths of the earth." Awe prickled the back of her neck, feeling the breath of the gods. "What is this place?"

"A sacred trust." The healer stared at her, the tattooed raven supplanting the woman. "A bolt of knowledge split the earth. Do you have the courage to follow it into the depths?"

"A test?"

Thera nodded, the barest hint of approval in her smile. "One rarely given to outsiders." The raven peered from the healer's face, dark eyes surrounded by tattooed feathers. "What god do you pray to?"

"Valin, the god of warriors."

"Can your god see into the earth?"

Kath had never considered the question yet she staunchly defended Valin. "He sees into the heart of every warrior."

"Then pray to him now." Reaching into her pocket, Thera removed a fresh candle. "To each soul the gods give a single Light against the Dark." Her face solemn with ritual, she slowly waved the two candles in an intricate pattern, as if scribing a great rune in the air. "Light conquers the Dark." She touched the two wicks together. The second candle flared bright. She offered the slender taper to Kath. "Guard it well."

Accepting the candle, Kath stared at the lightning bolt cracking the wall. "Alone?"

"Yes." Thera's voice held a solemn tone. "To the very Womb of the World."

A feather of foreboding shivered down Kath's back. "What will I find there?"

"That depends on what you take." The healer's gaze narrowed. "Your candle is lit, don't squander the Light."

The words held a note of finality. Shielding the candle, Kath stepped toward the lightning bolt. Cold air seeped out. Nodding to the great stag, she slipped through the crack.

Darkness rushed to surround her. Her single candle cast a feeble glow. The rock walls pressed close. Musty and cold, they crowded her shoulders, a smother of rock too close for comfort. Shielding the candle, she walked forward, studying the walls, searching for animal guides but the rock proved barren.

The earthen floor dipped away.

Kath stumbled and nearly fell, almost dropping the candle. Clutching the taper, she regained her footing. Shaken, she leaned against the cold rock wall, her heart hammering. Without flint, the candle flame was her sole shield against the dark. She stared back toward the lightning bolt opening...but only darkness lurked behind. Taking a deep breath, she pressed on, caution in her steps.

The steep descent continued, twisting and turning like a serpent delving into the earth. Rounding a corner, she stifled a scream. A skull stared back at her, yellowed with age. It sat in a niche, no bones, no coffin, just a hollow-eyed stare, perhaps a guardian of the cave...or a warning of things to come. Sending a prayer to Valin, she ducked past the watcher.

Deeper...darker...colder...she followed the narrow passage into the depths...till she came to a choice. The passageway split in two, both branches equally narrow, both slanting down. Holding the candle to the rock walls, she searched for a clue, a hint about one path or the other...but she found no markings. Why give her a choice with no way to choose? Hot wax dripped like tears on her hand, goading her forward. On impulse, she took the right-hand passage.

Kath searched the walls as she walked, hoping for a sign that she'd made the right choice...but saw nothing to mark the way. Down and around, the darkness grew more oppressive. Doubt gnawed at her mind, dragging her footsteps to a crawl. Her breathing sounded loud in her ears. What if she'd taken the wrong turn, forever lost in a labyrinth of stone? Icy fingers slid down her back. Feeling a cold stare, she whirled, holding the candle out...but it was just another skull, staring with vacant eyes, death keeping watch.

Taking a deep breath, she struggled to bridle her fears.

Candle wax dripped on her hand, more than a quarter gone.

Kath turned a corner and the passage branched again. A sob threatened the back of her throat but she forced it down. Making a choice, she moved forward, wondering if she made a mistake.

The passageway brought more branches, a maze of choices. Her doubts multiplied with every twist and turn. Molten wax dripped on her hand, a measure of the time lost. She stared at the candle, surprised to find it three-quarters melted. Panic threatened, crowding the darkness. Kath stifled the urge to turn and run. Darkness tightened around her, as if the weight of the world pressed down. She longed for a sword but her belt was empty. Feeling naked, she gripped Duncan's warrior ring, a comfort in the dark. Fighting the urge to run, she forced herself to think. They'd come to the north to defeat the Mordant, but to do that, they needed allies. And that meant gaining the trust of the painted people. In order to gain their trust, she would have to trust in return. The insight stiffened her resolve. Facing the darkness, Kath clutched the slender taper of wax like a sword. *"A warrior does not run."* Her whispered words formed a shield against the dark. Gripping Duncan's warrior ring, she descended into the depths.

A row of skulls sat on a rocky shelf at eye level, a long line of disembodied sentinels. Yellowed with age, some were half-crumbled to dust. She met their ancient stares, wondering if she walked to her own grave.

Beyond the skulls, the passage twisted and turned, a torturous meander of stone. Her candle melted to a nub. Chased by darkness, Kath rushed through the passageway, desperate for an end. Just when she thought it was hopeless, she turned and saw the light.

Light, warm and welcoming, a distant glow that beckoned.

Tempted to run, Kath slowed to a crawl, wondering if it was trap. Breathing deep, she caught the musky aroma of peat, proof the light was no illusion. She crept forward, peering around the corner.

The passage opened into a round chamber with a domed ceiling. The near half glowed golden with light, a thousand candles perched on rocky shelves...but the far half was pitch black, as dark and forbidding as a sealed tomb. A great crack, three feet wide, split the chamber asunder, like a bolt of divine lightning separating light from dark.

Drawn towards the divide, Kath entered the chamber, stepping to the jagged edge. The great crack split the ceiling and the floor, creating a jagged gaping darkness, as if an angry god had sundered the world in two. Cold seeped up out of the depths, laden with mystery and a feeling of great age, like the first breath of the world. Kath stared into the depths, wondering what lurked below. Gripped by curiosity, she nudged a small rock over the edge. The stone disappeared, swallowed by darkness. She waited, poised on the edge, but there was never a sound, as if the great crack had no bottom.

"Few are so brazen at the boundary of the gods."

Startled, Kath spun. Putting her back to the dark half, she searched for the speaker. Glowing candles filled every niche and cranny of the domed wall, tears of wax dripping down. A peat fire burned in a circle of stones, providing warmth and the loamy smells of grass and roots. A mound of blankets and sheepskins sat on the far side of the blaze. A face peered out of the mound, so wrinkled and worn that the blue tattoos were muddled to a blur.

"Come and sit by my fire."

A woman's voice, frail with age. Kath stepped away from the crack, taking a seat near the blaze.

"Blow the candle out, dear, before it burns you."

She'd forgotten the candle clutched in her hand, a mere nubbin of wax. She blew it out, sending a curl of smoke to the ceiling, and then stared across the flames at the woman. So old, her face was a mass of wrinkles, only a few wisps of long white hair on her head. She sat huddled under the sheepskins as if a breath of wind would blow her away...but then Kath looked into her eyes. Dark brown eyes stared back at her, impossibly deep, wells of memory, full of power, as if they held the wisdom of the ages. "Who are you?"

A soft cackle of laughter, "Always the first question." The old woman smiled, a toothless grin yet full of mirth. "The oldest one, the guardian of truth, the keeper of memories, the Ancestor."

"Keeper of memories?"

"The mind is full of doorways. Memories leak past the doors, around them, beneath them, images of other places, other lifetimes. And sometimes those doors open wide, revealing much that was lost."

Kath held her breath, thinking of her visions in the broken tower. "Why am I here?"

"To confront the Dark, a test all leaders must take." The woman reached into a pouch, throwing a scattering of herbs into the fire. The herbs sparkled and cracked, releasing a blue smoke, a faint scent of sage...and something else, something Kath could not name.

The old woman gestured to the domed ceiling and the great dark divide. "Light balanced against the Dark, we are all drawn into the battle immortal...but some bear more of the burden than others."

Kath shuddered, having heard those words before, *the battle immortal.*

The old woman's voice dropped to a hushed whisper. "Deep in the bowels of Mother Earth, a warrior can feel the weight of the world." Dark eyes bored into Kath. "You felt it, didn't you, child, the weight of the world on your shoulders?"

Shivering, Kath nodded, caught by the old woman's stare.

"You wished for something when the earth settled on your shoulders...what was it?"

The words whispered out of her. "A sword."

"And something else?"

"Duncan."

"War and love, an unlikely pairing." The old woman rocked back and forth, eyes closed, humming a wordless tune.

Lulled by the scents of sage and burning sod, Kath leaned toward the fire's warmth, listening to the old woman's wordless song, thoughts of Duncan tumbling through her mind.

Dark eyes snapped open, a piercing gaze. "Why did you come north?"

"To fight the Mordant."

The old woman reached beneath her blankets...unsheathing a dagger. "With this?"

Kath gasped, *the crystal dagger*.

A hand as frail as a bird's claw held the dagger aloft, firelight dancing along the milk-white crystal. "An ancient weapon, a dagger of Light, formed by the powers of earth and magic...a weapon that evokes the oldest of memories." The old one blinked, slow like an owl, her eyes pools of mystery. "The tall knight carried it...but it is not his to wield."

"No."

"How did it come to your hand?"

Kath yearned to hold the dagger, a burning need that welled inside of her. "I found it in a ruined tower, deep in the heart of Wyeth."

"And its purpose?"

"To slay the Mordant, so he can never be reborn."

The old woman nodded. "A soul-slayer, a powerful weapon of the Light...borne by an unexpected champion." More herbs were thrown on the fire, creating a blaze of sparks. "Only an old soul can wield such a blade." The old woman pointed the dagger at Kath. "Tell me, youngling, what memories do you harbor in your soul?"

Kath shivered, remembering the Star Tower. "A broken tower, deep in the forests of Wyeth...I saw it whole and at the peak of its glory. I wore armor, a great sword belted to my side...and there was a man, another knight, his face more familiar than my own..." Kath shook her head. "A fragment of a dream...I don't understand."

"I think you do. Some destinies are stamped on our very souls."

A rush of cold air belched out of the great crack. The fire guttered against the Dark assault, but the flames held. A snap of red sparks danced across the domed ceiling, like fireflies trapped within the earth.

Kath made the hand sign against evil, moving closer to the fire, her voice a hushed whisper. "So you're saying my vision was true?"

"A memory from another life, seeping beneath a closed door."

Kath struggled to understand. "So we're destined to repeat the past?"

"*No.*" The old woman made a cutting gesture with the dagger. "Not repeat, never that, repetition breeds stagnation. We learn from the past, always driven by a greater destiny." A handful of herbs renewed the fire, sparks of red and blue dancing among the golden flames. "The dagger of Light appears only when it is most needed." The old woman leaned forward, her eyes pools of ancient wisdom. "Are you the one to wield it? Are you the queen of swords?"

Memories shivered within Kath. Her voice dropped to a hushed whisper. "Only a pawn can become a queen."

The old woman chuckled. "A pawn is the least expected piece. Easily overlooked, it slips past the other players, strength hidden beneath weakness, an irony of the gods." Another handful of herbs ignited in the fire. "But who taught you the purpose of the crystal blade?"

Kath hesitated, but she saw no reason not to answer. "The Kiralynn monks."

"The Eye in the Hand."

She nodded, surprised by the old woman's knowledge.

"Long have they remained hidden...since the time of the sundering."

Dizzy from the strange blue smoke, Kath shook her head, trying to think. "The sundering of the world?"

"No, the sundering of civilization, broken by the War of Wizards, when magic was lost and women became chattel."

Kath held her breath. "How old *are* you?"

"My memories are beyond age." The old woman fingered the crystal dagger, her expression hidden by a mass of wrinkles. "My great granddaughter tells me that you met a lost son of the painted people, one who wore the face of a mountain lion."

A mountain lion again, Kath tried to concentrate. "Yes, in Castlegard, over two years ago."

Dark eyes stared back at her like fathomless wells. "It seems many destinies are entwined in you." The old woman hefted the crystal dagger. "The gods make their choices known." Leaning forward, she held the dagger over the flames, extending the hilt toward Kath. "Use it well."

Kath reached for the dagger...but the old woman held on. Bathed in smoke and the heat of the flames, their stares locked across the fire, their hands joined by the dagger. Light leaped along the crystal, creating a bridge of magic. Kath felt a relentless pull in the depths of her soul. She fell into the old one's stare, plummeting through the ages, tossed and turned by thousand questions: *Who are you? Will you be true? Why are you here?* Questions beat against her mind like the wings of ravens...till a single word was spoken. *Remember!* Like the pure note of a gong, the command shivered through her mind. Kath gasped, feeling as if a forgotten doorway suddenly burst open.

The old woman released the dagger.

Kath rocked backwards, clutching the blade. Coughing on a lungful of smoke, she shook her head, a tumult of thoughts. "I don't understand."

"A consequence of youth."

Anger pulsed through Kath. "Will you help us against the Mordant?"

"Help is here...if you know where to look." The fire snapped and crackled, sending curls of blue smoke wafting to the ceiling. "Mother Earth has the longest memories. In such a place, it is difficult to lie...even to yourself." She smiled, a mass of wrinkles, amusement glinting in her dark eyes. "Memories of the past, visions of the future, the Womb of the World holds them all, waiting to be born. Breathe deep and open the doors of your mind." The old one leaned toward the blaze, gently fanning the smoke toward Kath.

A cloud of blue wafted her way. Kath coughed, but the coughing only made her swallow more. Smoke surrounded her. The domed chamber seemed to spin. A distant chime sounded...and then her mind exploded in visions. She knew things she never could have known. Images of the past, of that shining time before the War of Wizards, when knowledge and honor held sway. She wore a sword belted to her side, and on her shield, an eight-pointed star. *A Star Knight!* The great sword felt right in her hands, as if it was meant to be. But all too soon, the scene shifted and she saw the Star Tower betrayed, the knights murdered in their sleep, the tower desecrated, the great library burnt...even the stones were pulled down, as if the dark ones sought to destroy the very memory of the Star Knights. But a few who lived remembered. In the darkest of times, the shield was re-drawn. Lines connected the eight points of the star...to create an *Octagon!* The symbol blazed in her mind...but then the world was spinning, and she knew time skipped forward, leaping by centuries. She saw her father, King Ursus, standing on a rampart, his blue sword drawn for battle. The scene shifted and she glimpsed his foe. Her soul quailed, shaken by the multitude. A sea of enemies stretched to the horizon, as if the very gates of hell had disgorged all the armies of the past. And above the vast horde flew the Darkflamme, the war banner of the Mordant. She quailed at the sight, fearing for the Octagon. Once more, the scene shifted, this time to a cavern deep in the earth, red stalactites dripping like blood from the ceiling. A foul taste filled her mouth, reeking of evil. She wanted to flee but there was something here she needed to see.

Beneath the stalactites, Darkness clutched a man, chained to the symbol of the pentagram like a dark offering...and then she saw his face...*Duncan!*

"*No!*" Kath stood, the crystal dagger clutched in her fist, poised to strike. Reality returned in a rush. She lurched forward, gasping for breath. Seeking an anchor, her stare roamed the chamber, from the dark to the light, coming to rest on the old woman's face. "What did I see?"

"In the Womb of the World...old souls are gifted with images of the past." Dark eyes glittered beneath the mound of sheepskins.

"It wasn't just the past."

Her face was hard to read, a mass of wrinkles, a muddle of blue tattoos, but her voice held no surprise. "Tell me."

Kath explained about the dark horde...and about the man trapped in a cavern of weeping stone...but she did not yield his name.

"Mother Earth knows of this cavern, a place of the foulest magic...it lies at the heart of the Mordant's kingdom...beneath the Dark Citadel."

Kath shuddered. "But is it the future? Or can it be changed?"

"Nothing is written in stone. Everyone has the chance to write his own destiny. And a rare few have the chance to change the course of the world."

Kath gripped the crystal dagger. "Then I have the chance to change my vision?"

"Perhaps." The old woman nodded. "Or perhaps you are given a choice, to take the crystal blade south to the Octagon or to go north to the Dark Citadel."

Kath shuddered, the taste of ashes in her mouth.

The old woman stirred beneath her sheepskins. "There is a thing you should know. Our scouts keep watch on the Mordant's domain. The Dark Citadel prepares for war."

"The horde of my dream."

The old woman nodded. "Your dreams are powerful, they rush to be born." She clapped her hands and a man stepped from a side passage. Tall and brawny, clad in pale white leathers, he bore a snarling mountain lion on his face. He nodded to the old woman and then gathered her into his arms, carrying her as easily as a small child.

Cradled in sheepskins, the Old One lost none of her dignity. "Come, child, the painted people are already gathered. It is time to hear the truth of my great grandson." She gave Kath a piercing stare. "Time for destinies to collide."

36

The Knight Marshal

A horn sounded in the courtyard, a trill of notes full of triumph. The marshal strode to the battlement and gazed down into the muddy courtyard.

Thirty knights galloped into the yard, maroon battle banners fluttering from lances, arms and armor gleaming in the sunlight. They rode with their heads held high, as if fresh from victory.

King Ursus joined him at the battlement. "Ulrich returns from Cragnoth Keep."

The marshal saw that the king had the truth of it. The lead rider had the same bearish build, golden hair beneath a burnished half helm, a blue sword strapped to his back. Perhaps the prince was just the tonic the king needed.

Turning from the battlement, the king called for his squire. "Baldwin, summon the other captains. I'll meet the prince in my council chambers."

A lanky red-haired lad snapped a salute and then sped away.

The king strode the length of the battlement, the marshal at his side. They reached the drum tower and clattered down the stairs. A pair of guards saluted as they entered the king's chambers.

"Ulrich's return can only mean one thing." The king stood in front of the cold hearth. Ever the warrior, the hilt of his great blue sword loomed over his right shoulder, the monk's crystal glinting in the pommel. "The Mordant must have struck at Cragnoth Keep, hoping to claim treachery's wages. Rebuffed at the Crag he'll soon come calling at Raven Pass. I'll wager we'll see his army before winter ends."

"He'll dare the steppes in winter?"

The king nodded. "A goad to his army."

"A cruel ploy, befitting a foul lord." The marshal set a lit taper to the kindling. Fire erupted in the hearth, a welcome blaze of heat.

The king paced in front of the fire. "A doom stalks us, Osbourne. I can feel it in my bones. The Mordant will send a slavering horde against us, the likes of which none has ever seen."

The marshal had long ago learned to trust the king's battle sense. "We're as ready as we can be. We've pulled men from all across the Domain, leaving skeletal forces in the other towers. There are none left to answer the summons." He did not raise the specter of magic; that nightmare he kept to himself. "In times past, allies would have marched from the southern kingdoms, to stand shoulder to shoulder with the Octagon, fighting to hold back the Dark."

"Peace has blunted the swords of the south. They've forgotten what lurks on their northern borders. We'll have no help from the south," the king scowled, "and we have not done enough to prepare."

"What more can we do?"

"Catapults. We need catapults or trebuchets mounted on every tower of Raven Pass."

"A long haul from Castlegard."

"Then build them. There's plenty of trees further down the pass. I believe Sir Hunter has the plans. And get the healer involved, he's a scrollish man."

"The healer building catapults?"

The king glared. "We need to find advantages, Osbourne, for we shall not have the numbers."

The words fell like a sword stroke. The marshal stared at his king.

"Come, let us hear what Ulrich has to report." The king swept out of the solar, the marshal a half step behind. A pair of guards snapped a salute as they entered the council chamber. A dozen captains sat waiting at the round table. They stood at the king's entrance, big men in leather and chainmail, the smells of sweat and horse clinging to their maroon cloaks. The king greeted them by name, making his way to the high-backed chair. The king took his chair and the council began. Captains made their reports on men, weapons, and stores, the steady preparation for war.

The marshal listened to their tone as much as their words. Circling the table, he stood with his back to the roaring fire. Confidence ran high among the captains, perhaps bolstered by the king's presence, yet it was in this very room that two princes had died, impaled on a single sword. The others seemed to have forgotten, or perhaps they hid it better. Red eyes of the demon still haunted the marshal, a threat and a warning. He wondered if swords alone would be enough to win the coming battle.

Lothar sent him a questioning glance.

The marshal stilled his face and gave his friend the smallest of nods.

The door opened and Ulrich and two of his captains clattered into the room, mud and sweat staining their riding cloaks. A big bear of a man, with his father's broad shoulders and deep voice, the prince seemed to crowd the chamber. "I've come as you commanded, father. Cragnoth Keep remains safe in the hands of the Octagon."

A cheer filled the chamber.

The king rose and greeted his heir, clasping him close.

The marshal watched from the warmth of the fireplace. Ulrich seemed a younger version of the king, a big-boned man, a fierce warrior, yet there was something unfinished about the prince, something lacking, a pale imitation of the king. Perhaps the prince would grow into his role, given time.

The prince took a seat opposite the king, accepting a goblet of mead.

"Yours is the first true battle of this war." The king gestured to his son. "I would hear your report."

Ulrich nodded. "I bring word of victory...and treachery."

His words sobered the room.

"More treachery!" The outburst came from Sir Dalt. "The Crag is truly cursed."

"*Enough!*" The king made a cutting gesture with his sword hand. "I'll have no more rumors started at this table. Let the prince make his report."

Ulrich fingered his beard, his face troubled. "They came at sunset, thirty knights returning from a northern patrol. Sentries spotted them long before they reached the keep, a long maroon line riding up the switchbacks. Their horses were hard ridden, streaked with sweat. Their captain's name was Sir Lavor. He claimed they'd spied the vanguard of a vast army marching south across the steppes."

Surprised by the mistake, the marshal flicked a glance to the king.

The king's face hardened to stone, yet the prince did not seem to notice.

The marshal asked the question. "How did you learn his name?"

"I questioned him myself. He claimed Lionel sent them on patrol."

The twitch in the king's eye quickened. "So how did you spot their treachery?"

The prince paled but he did not balk at the question. "A small thing, really. They did not stable their own horses."

"Betrayed by arrogance," the marshal nodded. "And then?"

"I pressed them with questions and they answered with steel. The battle was bitter but we outnumbered them." Ulrich nodded to the king. "Treachery came to Cragnoth, just as you foretold."

"Yet you let them in." Anger rode the king's words.

The prince glared at his father. "They spoke of Lionel and other knights of the Crag." He reached behind to one of his captains. "And their cloaks and surcoats were without fault." From a saddlebag he pulled a maroon cloak and a silver surcoat, tossing both onto the table. Blood stained, the surcoat was pierced by many sword strokes.

Sir Dalt hissed, fingering the wool cloak. "So now the enemy wears our own colors."

Lothar scowled. "Another way to divide us."

Ulrich leaned forward, his fist on the table. "Yes, but now we're forewarned."

The king's gaze narrowed. "What of the survivors?"

Rebuffed, the prince scowled. "They fought like demons, refusing to surrender. But two of the wounded talked before they died." His gaze circled the table. "It seems they expected traitors to man the gates. Barring that, they planned to slit our throats in the dead of the night."

"And after that?"

"They did not say."

The king's face was rife with displeasure. "Then you bring but half a warning."

Anger stormed across Ulrich's face but the marshal intervened. "Did you check their left arms?"

"Yes. Later. After the fighting."

"And?"

Ulrich blanched. "They all bore the marks, black runes tattooed on their left forearms."

A ripple of nods circled the table.

Sir Rannock broke the silence. "The Mordant marks his own, like brands on cattle."

Sir Dalt nodded. "Making the enemy easily identified, no matter the color of their cloaks."

The king turned his gaze to the marshal. "Send a message across the Domain under my seal. Warn the others of this ploy, though I doubt it will be repeated." The king studied his captains. "We've had our warning. Now the Mordant will come in force."

Ulrich looked indignant. "That's it? You make light of the attack."

"I make *light* of nothing." The king's words struck like a slap. "The council is dismissed. Remind your men of the lesson of Cragnoth, especially the sentries. See that they remember the runes. Now go, for I would speak with my son."

The king's anger rippled through the chamber. The captains rose from their seats and left without speaking. The marshal moved to follow but the king raised his hand. "Not you, Osbourne."

The marshal resumed his post, his back to the blazing fire.

The chamber emptied and the door closed. Pine logs snapped and crackled in the hearth. The king glared at his only remaining son, but he did not speak. The prince broke first, words erupting in anger. "I did what you ordered. I held the Crag and defeated the enemy. The men celebrate my victory."

"You opened the gates for the enemy." The king's voice simmered with rage. "You were warned of treachery yet you never looked past their cloaks."

The prince flamed red. "They're dead, what does it matter?"

"Did you even remember the runes?"

Ulrich looked away.

"No." The word fell like an axe. "I'll wager a veteran told you after the battle."

The truth was writ large across the prince's face, yet he tried to cover his shame with bluster. "I gained a victory for the Octagon. What else matters?"

The king's voice dropped to a deadly hiss. "The *crown* matters. A king needs to know his enemies, to always out-think them." Disdain filled his voice, "Yet you did neither."

Outrage claimed the prince. "I slew more enemies than any of my men!"

"It's not your sword that's in question." The king glared at his son. "Strategy is stronger than steel. It is the first and best weapon of any king." His voice dropped to a deadly growl. "Lionel would never have made your mistake."

Ulrich's head snapped back as if slapped...but then his eyes hardened to chips of flint. "Lionel's dead, isn't he? Clever enough to get himself killed...and now *I'm* your only remaining son."

The marshal caught his breath.

The king stared, his face stone hard...but the tic in his left eye had returned with a vengeance, an ominous sign.

Ulrich glared. "You never see *my* worth."

"I've seen more than enough." Disgust filled the king's voice. "Get out of my sight."

Ulrich stood, his face a deadly grimace. "You wrong me, father. I'm not just a sword looking for a fight."

"Then prove it."

Stares clashed across the table, but it was the prince who flinched first. "As you command." The prince strode from the chamber.

The door slammed shut but the king remained seated. He leaned back in the chair, his face creased with worry. "The gods mock me, Osbourne. First Tristan, then Lionel, then Godfrey and Griffin. They steal the best of my sons and leave me a hollow sword. Ulrich should have remembered the runes. My squire would have known better." He shook his head, a mane of silver. "I fear for the Octagon." The tic at the king's left eye beat a fierce rhythm.

The marshal worried for his lord. "Perhaps the prince will grow into his role. Give him time."

"Time is already late." He shook his head like an angry bear. "How many good men died because Ulrich opened the gate to the enemy?"

The marshal had no answer.

"The Octagon cannot afford such mistakes. We fight with our wits as well as our swords."

"Given the right advisor, Ulrich may learn to avoid such mistakes."

The king sighed. "Then you'd best outlive me, Osbourne."

The words shivered like a doom, scrapping against the marshal's nerves. He shook his head in defiance. "We'll defeat the Mordant together and then worry about the throne."

The king's face turned hard as stone. "Yes, the Mordant. I've a fearsome blood debt to collect." Grim as death, the king strode from the chamber. The marshal followed, but he could not shake the feeling of dread. He wondered how much time they had left.

37

Duncan

Chains on his ankles, shackles on his wrists, Duncan knelt on the cavern floor. Pain blazed in every part of his body, a prisoner once more.

Whips cracked and handlers yelled, moving up and down the ragged line. One of a hundred, he knelt in a long line of rebels, all of them shackled and chained. Most bore wounds, bloody badges of honor; but all of them wore nasty red welts crosshatched on their skin, badges of defeat. The sticky webs were gone, and so were their weapons, stacked in a mound like an offering to a god. Fresh air wafted through the chamber like a taunt, so close to victory it hurt. Krell's body lay crumpled near the entrance, a spear rampant in his chest. A fallen hero, Duncan envied the big man his fate.

A whip cracked close to Duncan's face. "Don't wish for death, maggot." A leather-clad handler sneered down at him. "Your life is not your own."

Duncan lowered his gaze, smoldering with hate.

A flourish of drumbeats came from the entrance, accompanied by the rhythmic tramp of hobnailed boots. Soldiers marched into the cavern, a disciplined gleam of gold and black. *Soldiers*...not mine guards, they formed a line opposite the prisoners, presenting a solid wall of shields.

A trumpet echoed through the cavern, a haughty blare. The shield wall parted to reveal eight slaves struggling to carry a gilded chair perched atop a raised platform. A single man sprawled in the sedan. Big and bald headed, with muscles gone to fat, he wore robes of green wool, gold rings on his fingers, a cat-o-nine tails in his hands. The slaves lowered the chair. An entourage of guards and scribes hovered around like flies buzzing to carrion.

The handlers bowed deep and the soldiers snapped to attention.

The lordling rose from his gilded chair, using the height of the sedan to survey the prisoners. Flexing the cat-o-nine tails between his hands, his voice filled the cavern. "Nothing in the Mordant's domain is ever wasted. *Nothing*. Not even your pitiful lives. But punishment is owed...and the debt will be paid." The lord flashed a sleepy smile. "Your leaders will serve by example...while the rest return to work in the mine. Lest you think to rebel again, each of you will be marked with a special brand. If the iron ore does not flow within a day, then every tenth man will pay a tithe to the Mordant. The tithe will be nothing important, nothing to hinder your work in the mine, just a small payment of useless flesh...*just your manhood*."

A shudder passed through the prisoners.

Duncan's mouth went dry.

"But first I'll have your leaders." The lord gestured and a blond-haired courtier emerged from his entourage.

Something familiar snagged Duncan's stare. And then he saw it, the distinctive gleam of polished gray leather. *The courtier wore his boots,* his Midwinter gift from Jordan. Like a bauble tossed to a fawning servant, this courtier dared wear his boots! Outrage flooded all reason. Duncan surged to his feet, his hands balled into fists.

A whip cracked.

Fire lashed across his back. Duncan staggered forward.

A handler appeared, pressing a dagger to his throat. "On your knees, maggot."

Duncan snarled but he had no choice. His chains clanked as he knelt, but his stare never left the courtier. Tall and clean-shaven, with close-cropped blond hair, the man strode toward the kneeling prisoners. One at a time, he moved down the line, studying each rebel. He paused before Seth and gestured. "This one." A pair of handlers dragged Seth to his feet. The courtier continued down the line.

Something about the blond-haired dandy scratched at the back of Duncan's mind, but it was not until he drew near that understanding struck. *Bruce!* The man he'd saved from the cave-in...the filthy, god-rotting *traitor*. Rage boiled through Duncan, but the dagger at his throat held him in check.

Duncan watched as Clovis was chosen, then Brock...and then Marcus, and then the traitor stood before him. Their stares locked like crossed swords...till a smug smile appeared on the traitor's face. "This one, definitely this one."

"We saved your life!" Hands gripped Duncan's arms, dragging him to his feet, but he kept his gaze fixed on the traitor.

Bruce shrugged, "Your mistake," and moved to the next prisoner.

Duncan lunged but the handlers held him firm. He hawked a wad of spit at Bruce's back. "There's a special hell for traitors."

Quick as an adder, a handler buried his fist in Duncan's groin. Doubled with pain, he gasped for breath. Hanging between two handlers, he speared Bruce with his stare, but the traitor seemed impervious as stone.

Six men were chosen. Two of them were only followers, not leaders, but their desperate pleas went unheeded. Lord Sleghorn gestured and the six were herded together without question or trial, condemned by a traitor's word. "Bring them."

A drum roll filled the cavern and the slaves hoisted the sedan chair onto their shoulders. Leather-clad handlers closed in on the six. Duncan and the other five were driven behind the lord's chair, prodded with clubs, herded like cattle to the slaughter. The cavern narrowed to a long corridor. Duncan sidled next to Clovis, trying to catch his friend's gaze. Chains clanked with each step, accompanied by the tramp of hobnailed boots. The handlers moved close, gripping Duncan's arms as if he might bolt...and then he noticed the floor slanted *up*. The tunnel opened to daylight.

Duncan shuffled from the mine, blinded by sunlight. He stumbled and almost fell, tears crowding his eyes. Taking a deep breath, he nearly swooned. After the stench of the mine, the air smelled fresh. Teeming with scents, the first breath swamped him with the mingled smells of dung fires, pan baked bread, roasting grease, and the crowded stink of too many people. Duncan gulped the air like a drowning man, drunk on scent.

The handlers kept him moving. Poked and prodded, he shuffled forward. With each step his senses adjusted to the deluge. Reason returned like a slap. Duncan strained against his shackles, desperate to escape. Chained and surrounded by guards, he struggled to bide his time.

The lord and his entourage led the procession. Borne aloft on the shoulders of slaves, the gilded sedan gleamed like a beacon, at odds with the muddy lane. Dirty faces peered from a slum of mud huts and thatched hovels. A gaggle of raggedy children capered alongside, grinning as if they watched a troupe of mummers, but the adults were stone-faced and wary. A crowd swelled behind, chirping like birds following a trail of breadcrumbs.

Duncan slipped and almost fell. A handler caught him, shoving him forward. The pit seemed an endless sea of mud huts and bedraggled people, a vast city of slaves. So many people, enough for an army, he wondered if any of them still had the will to fight.

The long walk became a difficult trudge. Dread began to dog his steps. Duncan stared up, hoping for a glimpse of the sky, but the brown cloud hovered close, sealing the pit like a lid on a cauldron. At least he'd gotten out of the depths. Out of the mine and into the cauldron...just another layer of hell.

Trumpets blared and the muddy lane widened into a common area, like the spoke of a wheel joining a central hub, but even here there was no grass, no speck of green, just a cluster of enormous boulders. Thrice the height of a tall man, the boulders formed a crude circle, as if frozen in a strange dance. Tall and majestic, the gray stones cast an aura of strength and serenity...till he saw how they'd been defaced. Meat hooks protruded from their tops, rust stains marring the stones like open sores. Duncan looked away, shuddering at the obscenity.

Slaves settled the lord's sedan chair in the heart of the boulders. The prisoners were herded to the side, surrounded by handlers. A pair of Taals emerged to stand at the base of each boulder. Around the stones, a crush of people crowded close, an army of witnesses come to view the pageant.

Lord Sleghorn rose from his chair. Standing atop the sedan's gilded platform, he addressed the crowd. "The Stones of Agony serve their purpose." The lord flashed a serpent's smile. "Gather close and witness the price of rebellion."

Duncan scanned the crowd, desperate for a weapon or a way out...but he found neither, just a sea of faces staring back at him. Time tightened like a noose around his neck. Luck and the gods had both deserted him. Taking a deep breath, he sidled close to Clovis, his words a hushed whisper. "I'm sorry. I never thought it would end like this."

The older man met his gaze, but instead of recrimination his eyes held a strange sense of peace. "Some endings are but beginnings."

Duncan stared at his friend, wondering if he'd slipped the bonds of reason.

Clovis gave him a soft smile. "I'm glad to have met you, Duncan Treloch. You brought Light to the depths of darkness."

Brock leaned close. "It was a good fight, cat-man. At least we're free of the god-cursed mine"

Such friends, Duncan shook his head, their words proving a balm to his soul. "Then let's show them how brave men die." Duncan gripped each man's forearm, fiercely wishing for a different ending...but time had run out. Silence tightened around them. The lord's speech was over...and the Taals came for them.

They took Marcus first.

"No! I didn't do anything." He squirmed in the Taals' grip, digging his heels in the mud, but the Taals were not deterred. They carried him

like a broken doll to the largest boulder. Using a hook on a long spear, they hoisted Marcus into the air by his shackles. The small man screamed and writhed like a fish on a line but it made no difference. The chains of his shackles slid onto the meat hook atop the boulder. Marcus sobbed as iron weights were hung from his feet, stretching him along the boulder's face, a slab of meat dangling from a hook.

Duncan shuddered and looked away, knowing it would be a slow and painful death. The Stones of Agony were aptly named.

The Taals returned, claiming another victim.

Brock was next. The big man remained silent as they hoisted him onto the hook. One at a time, Duncan watched as the others met their fate with stoic courage. Clovis was the hardest to watch; the older man deserved a better end. And then it was his turn.

Part of him wanted to fight, to grab a weapon and claim a warrior's death, but he could not degrade the courage of his friends. Shaking off the Taals, he walked to an empty boulder between Clovis and Brock. "This will do." He fixed his stare on the lord, contempt on his face as the Taals hooked the spear through his shackles. "Better men than you die this day." And then he was dangling in air, leveraged onto the hook. Weights were hung from his feet, heavy as lead. He felt the stretch along his spine, the tightening of his chest muscles and the harsh strain in his shoulders. Duncan shuddered, gulping for air.

Lord Sleghorn glared up at him. "Mock all you want, but you'll soon be begging for release." His face twisted into a cruel smile, his voice a command. "Let the rebels hang till they're carrion, nothing but spoiled meat rotting on the hook." Making a curt gesture, he leaned back in the gilded chair. Slaves struggled to lift the sedan. The lord and his entourage slowly marched from the circle. Most of the soldiers followed...but the people remained.

Duncan smeared his bare feet against the stone, looking for purchase. His left foot found a slight bulge, taking some strain from his shoulders. Even now, he could not give up.

Seeking distraction from the aching pain, he studied the crowd, wondering if they stayed out of cruelty or mere curiosity, but their faces proved hard to read. Cold and wary, they kept watch, as if the stage was set for some larger drama.

Marcus whimpered and moaned, pleading for mercy, but the others bore their pain in silence. A dozen soldiers patrolled the inner circle, spears gripped in their hands, their faces closed. Duncan licked his lips, fighting a raging thirst, desperate to keep his footing. Twice he slipped, sending a rush of pain through his chest and shoulders.

Regaining his perch, he kept still, wondering if he could somehow climb the boulder and win free of the hook.

A lazy sun crawled across the shrouded sky, marking a slow agony of time. Nothing changed except the shadows. The guards made their rounds, the people kept vigil, and the prisoners suffered in silence...a stalemate waiting for death.

And then Clovis began to speak. His words were hushed at first, but then his voice gathered strength. *"You have the numbers! A handful of guards against a thousand. The numbers are the same everywhere in the Pit!"*

Duncan stared at Clovis, startled to hear the echo of his own argument.

"Look around you. Your numbers give you strength, a chance for freedom; but you must work together. Dare to be free! Rise up and take the Pit!"

The guards gripped their spears, darting nervous glances at the crowd.

Duncan watched the people, wondering if they'd listen.

"Hear me! For I am Clovis Farsight, born of the Pit, gifted with the third eye, the inner sight of prophecy. I have seen the victories that can be yours!" Clovis coughed, struggling for breath, but he would not stop. "You have the numbers! Sleghorn can only rule if you let him. You sin against the Light by doing nothing, by wallowing in slavery. Freedom is worth fighting for, worth dying for! A sign will fall from the sky, written in stone. Do not miss your chance! Heed the words of the gods. Walk in the Light and dare to be free!"

His words evoked a shiver in Duncan's mind. So this was the meaning of the older man's prophecy, *"Light from a stone reflected in the faces of the people."* A wild hope surged through him; perhaps all was not lost.

A soldier threatened Clovis with his spear. "Shut up, old man."

But Clovis would not stop. Hanging from the boulder, struggling for breath, he spoke with the eloquence of a preacher and the conviction of a prophet. First cajoling and then haranguing, he strove to rouse a crowd of thousands. Defying the agony of the boulder...he talked till his voice failed. Falling silent, he hung limp in his chains, his chin sunk to his chest, as if his words had consumed the last of his strength.

The crowd stirred but Clovis did not move.

Duncan studied his friend, anxious for some sign of life. "Clovis, are you with us?" But there was no reply. *"Clovis!"* Duncan's foot slipped, the lead weights pulling him down. Pain tightened like steel bands around his chest. Gasping for breath, he fought the weights, struggling to regain his footing. Drenched in sweat, he balanced on his perch, staring at the crowd. *"Will you let your prophet die?"* His voice shook with rage...but the crowd did not move. Desperate to save Clovis, he willed the crowd to action but they just looked away.

Silence hung like a shroud over the boulders...till Brock took up the argument.

Slow and steady, the big man used simple words, but he spoke with the voice of a warrior, a leader of men. Like a blacksmith forging a sword, Brock spoke a steady hammer-fall of words, pounding the same message over and over. "You have the numbers. You've heard the prophet. Dare to rise and win." He talked till the sun began to set, quenching the pit in shadow. As the last rays pierced the brown cloud, his voice fell silent, like a heavy hammer laid to rest.

The crowd stirred. A line of torches carved a path toward the boulders. Duncan watched with interest, till he realized it was merely soldiers come to replace the guards.

Twilight gave way to darkness, and the crowd began to leave, trickling away in twos and threes. Duncan hung from his chains, drenched in bitterness and despair. So many people complacent in their bondage, how could men become such sheep? He sent an accusing stare to the heavens, but the pit was covered in a vault of darkness. Not a single star shone through the murk, as if the gods had turned their backs on his plight. Rage and resentment boiled inside of him. *"Why?"* He shook his chains, his voice a raging bellow. *"Why should good men die for you?"* His shout rang across the pit, as much a question for the gods as for the retreating crowd...but there was no answer. Disgusted, he clung to his perch, a purgatory on the edge of pain.

The night proved a torment.

Every part of his body ached, his shoulders worst of all. Shackles cut into his wrists, heavy weights dragging on his feet, a grim tug-of-war. And then there was his raging thirst. He bit his lip and sucked the blood, desperate for moisture. Exhausted, he sank into a haze of pain. Three times he dozed. Three times his foot slipped from his perch, yanking him back to wakefulness in a blaze of agony.

Morning came but there was no relief.

Sunrise revealed the suffering of the others. Clovis hung like a waxen corpse, his head sunk on his chest, no sign of life. Duncan mourned his friend, but at least he'd passed beyond the agony of the stones. Death was an escape of sorts. Brock still struggled for breath and so did Seth but the others hung like carrion from their chains, locked in shrouds of pain.

Daylight brought the return of the crowds. They sat in widening circles around the boulders, like vultures drawn to the spectacle of death. Their morbid fascination sickened him. He wanted to scream at the crowd, but his mouth was too parched to shout. Instead, he glared, picking out individual faces and compelling them to leave. A bearded man with the shoulders of a blacksmith, a woman with a babe in arms, an old hunchback with a third eye...and then he saw a familiar face. Startled, he stared. Short and slender, blond hair framing a serious face...he was sure it was Mara...so the girl had escaped the mine. He grinned, flushed with an irrational spark of triumph. Not everything had been in vain.

She gave him a soft smile, and he nodded in reply, but then he forced his gaze away lest he entangle her with his own doom.

The day passed in a dull haze of misery. Twilight came and the crowd grew restless, perhaps disappointed by the lack of drama. Duncan looked for Mara, surprised to find her moving closer. Puzzled, he looked away, but a sixth sense told him when she reached the base of his boulder.

"*Clovis was a respected prophet.*" Her voice reached him, a soft whisper. "*His words were heard by the elders. Some see the strength of numbers. A few work to convince many.*"

Hope struck like a lightning bolt, but he made no movement, watching the guards through hooded eyes.

Mara slipped away, mingling with the departing crowd, but the hope stayed with him, an inner strength that got him through the long night.

Something spattered against his face. Cold and wet, he opened his mouth to the rain. Duncan drank the drops, a sweet relief for his parched throat. The storm lasted long enough to quench his thirst. Perhaps the gods had not forsaken him.

For six days he hung on the boulder, nurtured by rain and a persistent hope. Seth died on the third day and Brock on the fourth. On the fifth, Duncan slipped from his perch, no longer able to resist the lead weights. Pain racked every part of his body, a deadly stretch pulling him apart. Every breath a tortured struggle, he thought he saw Mara weaving her way through the crowd, or maybe it was Kath. Everything blurred in a haze of pain.

A woman's soft voice whispered at the base of his boulder. "*The elders cannot agree...I tried...I'm so sorry.*"

Her words cut through his pain like a knife, killing his last shred of hope. He'd fought death for nothing. The taste of ashes filled his mouth. *"Tell them,"* his voice was a harsh rasp, *"those who will not fight for their own lives...are not worth saving."*

It was over. All he had left was death. Duncan shut his eyes and surrendered his body to the agony of the boulder, while his mind fled to better memories. Green, he longed for the smell of crisp pine needles, the heady scent of a spring forest. And water, swimming beneath a crystal clear waterfall, drinking his fill, the luxury of so much water. ...And Kath, taking his wife's hand, leading her to a hidden glen, to lie entwined among the ferns, slow and sure, all the time in the world.

38

The Mordant

The Mordant entered the map room. His battle commanders snapped to attention, fists thumping against breastplates. More than a few gasped when they saw his armor. Golden ribs etched on burnished metal, like death come to life, the ancient armor glittered in the torchlight. Clad in the breastplate of the Skeleton King, the Mordant reveled in the legendary power. Fear annealed into metal, the armor evoked a primal sense of dread few mortals could withstand.

Cowed by the armor, his generals backed away. Confronted with a legend, they kept their distance, hands gripping their sword hilts, fear flickering across their faces.

"*So it's true!*" General Haith dared to speak.

The Mordant smiled, enjoying their unease. "Yes, the Dark Furies ride to war. There will be no half measures in this lifetime."

He strode to the iron railing, drawn to the gods-eye view. Built to his design, the map room was like a silver jewel box. Balconies lined the four walls, overlooking the windowless chamber. Light from a hundred torches cast a bright glow along the walls. Sheets of beaten silver mirrored the glow, illuminating the room's treasure. Spread across the sunken floor, the map was exquisite, the chessboard of the Mordant.

Silk rustled at the doorway. Gavis and a pair of black-robed bishops glided onto the balcony. "You summoned me, my Lord?"

"You're late." The Mordant turned to face his high priest.

Gavis stared at the armor. His face remained impassive, but his left hand clutched his staff with a white-knuckled grip, the only betrayal of his fear. "I beg your pardon, Lord." Elegant in robes of black embroidered with gold runes, Gavis made a curt bow and then moved along the balcony. He claimed a spot opposite the battle commanders, the priesthood balanced against the army, competing rivals overlooking the map of Erdhe.

The Mordant studied his high priest. Gavis had courage, but his insolence was one step away from a corpse. Still, now was not the time to deal with his high priest. "You all have your roles to play." He turned, a swirl of black and silver, and descended the stairs to the narrow walkway. Like a god, he loomed over the knee high map.

Carved from six massive tabletops, the map showed every mountain, hillock, valley, and river of Erdhe. A century in the making, it drew on details from a thousand sources. A legion of thieves had spent a lifetime scouring the southern kingdoms, procuring a host of maps. Master craftsmen sculpted the maps into mountains and valleys, creating an eagle-eye view of Erdhe. Color brought the board to life, shades of amber for the steppes, deep greens for the forests, frothing blues for the rivers, and a dusting of ground quartz crystals for the snowy mountaintops. Paint froze the landscape in summer, the season of war, but not everything on the map was fixed. Elaborate chess pieces sat upon the tabletop. Castles carved from ebony, ivory and emerald, man-made landmarks carved from gemstones, easy enough for the Mordant to tumble their walls or change their colors.

He stood at the north, at the source of his power.

A massive onyx castle marked the position of the Dark Citadel, fixed on the shores of the Western Ocean, surrounded by a sea of grasslands. Granite walls cut the steppes in half, ten rearing gargoyles marking the ten gates. Beyond the steppes, the mighty Dragon Spine Mountains reared like a wall, a snowcapped barrier to the south. Castles, walls and keeps carved from maroon garnets studded the mountain passes like clots of blood, marking the strongholds of his enemies. The Octagon knights blocked the mountain passes, the gatekeepers to the south. Beyond the Dragon Spines, the rest of Erdhe waited. Verdant farmlands and rolling hills dotted by gemstone keeps and ivory castles. A rich land, besotted with peace and ripe for plunder, awaiting the hand of Darkness. And in the far south, in the corner opposite the Dark Citadel, a vast jumble of mountains crowded the edge of the tabletop, the impenetrable Southern Ranges. The Mordant smiled, his words a whisper. "Your secrets are safe no longer."

The Mordant followed the walkway, moving along the perimeter of the map, east along the steppes and then south toward the Dragon Spine Mountains. Like a lover coveting the curves of a woman his fingertips caressed the map's contours. He paused to hover over Castlegard, the great garnet castle dominating a saddle-shaped valley, always a thorn in his side. So tempting to reach out and obliterate the ancient stronghold yet Castlegard was one place he needed to avoid. He'd squandered a lifetime trying to break those cursed mage-stone walls. Memories of the battle assailed his mind, the smell of blood, the ring of steel, as if it were yesterday.

He felt the stares of his generals, calling him back to the present. They lined the iron railing, waiting to hear the details of war.

"Yes, you've come for war, for battle plans and destruction." Darkness rose within him, a tidal wave of power. A thousand years of history coursed through his mind. Immortality was nearly his, close enough to taste. Flush with dark power, his voice rang with certainty. "We stand on the brink of a great Dark destiny. In this lifetime, old scores will finally be settled." He stood over the map like a god. "The first to fall will be the Octagon knights. But their fall will be no ordinary victory. Killing is easy. Taking life pleases the Dark Lord, but it garners the least of his favors. Our god favors those who have a long reach, those who affect the ripples of time, changing the very nature of history. In this war, we seek more than just victory. The defeat must be a rout, a total humiliation, so that the very name of the Octagon knights will be forever ground into oblivion."

"Victory to the Dark Lord!" The shout echoed through the chamber. His generals howled like a pack of hungry wolves eager to be released.

The Mordant raised his hand, stilling the tumult. "I will empty the north in order to win the south. Every Taal shall be called to battle. Half the guards of the Pit and the citadel will be summoned to join the army. I shall unleash a mighty force, an unstoppable horde, the likes of which the south has never seen."

Reaching back, he unsheathed his great sword. Darkness rippled the length of the five-foot blade, evil annealed into steel. "And where will they strike?"

He looked at his generals, but none dared to speak. "I will send the full might of the north against Raven Pass." His blade pointed toward a steep-sided valley cutting through the Dragon Spine Mountains. Three walls carved of blood-red garnet blocked the valley, three choke points held by the Octagon. "We will swarm the walls, opening a road to the south." With a flick of the sword, he knocked the walls over, one by one.

Triumphant, he stared up at his generals. His commanders struggled to hide their doubt but he saw through their mortal masks. "I know what you think. You fear a siege in winter."

A wave of nods passed through his commanders, their faces grim. Only General Haith dared to speak. "The Octagon wrought well at Raven Pass. The walls are not mage-stone but they are built tall and stout. It will take siege engines to defeat the walls," his voice dropped a notch, "and while we batter away at their gates, winter will lay siege to our army. Ice and snow respect no battle banner. The steppes are cruel in winter."

"There will be no siege."

"But my Lord, numbers alone cannot defeat such walls."

The Mordant thrust his sword aloft. "Behold the sword of the Mordant." Darkness rippled along its length like a slash in the fabric of the world. Most of his commanders looked away, unable to endure the Dark malice radiating from the blade. "This was once the sapphire sword of an Octagon knight, made stronger by its dedication to the Dark Lord. Look upon this sword and wonder how many other Dark Furies serve at my command."

A murmur of awe rippled through the chamber.

"Power begets power," he lowered the sword. "I will gift my army with three Wizard Knocks. Mounted on the tips of battering rams, and carried by a gang of Taals, the magic of the Knocks will sunder any wall save mage-stone. Knock thrice and Raven Pass shall fall before you."

General Haith stood at the center of the battle commanders, a look of confidence on his face. "And once the pass is taken, what are your commands?"

"Then old scores will finally be settled." The Mordant used the sword to point toward the map. "Once the Octagon is defeated, the army will split in two. A small force of elite cavalry will ride to the east, heading for the great southern road. General Haith will take command of this force, making all haste for the Southern Mountains." The Mordant circled the map, removing a carved gemstone from his pocket. "Long have the Kiralynn monks eluded me, but in this lifetime their secret is at last revealed." He held aloft a small monastery carved of sapphire. "Behold the missing chess piece, the last bastion of the monks." Tracing a path down the southern road and into the mountains, he settled the monastery on the side of a snow-capped peak. "At long last, the map of Erdhe is finally complete." A sense of triumph rushed through him, knowing his destiny was at hand. He stared up at General Haith. "I give you the task of taking the monastery and killing the last of the monks. You'll find it full of bearded old men and young pups in training. They'll fight with quarterstaffs, if they fight at all."

General Haith grinned. "Sticks against steel. Hardly a fitting contest."

Memories of his brief time in the monastery flashed through the Mordant's mind. Walls painted with illuminated script, forbidden secrets hidden behind midnight-blue doors. "The monks fight with sticks but you should expect trickery. There's no telling how much magic they still possess." He stared down at the sapphire monastery, a lone flash of blue in a jumble of white peaks. "Capture the monastery and kill the monks, but do not attempt the midnight-blue doors. The secrets locked behind those doors are *mine* alone." His stare drilled into his best general. "Spoil them at your peril."

General Haith saluted, his fist thumping against his gold breastplate. "As you command."

The Mordant paced the map's perimeter. Rounding the Southern Mountains, he headed west, toward the shores of the Western Ocean. "While General Haith rides south, the rest of the army will swing down through Navarre, plunging like a dagger for the heart of Lanverness. The Rose Court must be destroyed." Anger pulsed through him. "A woman dares to sit alone on a throne, ruling the most prosperous kingdom in Erdhe," his voice shook with revulsion, "The bitch queen is an abomination in the eyes of the Dark Lord." He tightened his grip on the sword. "We fight for the present as well as the future. This queen of Lanverness is a history that must be undone, a legend that must be fouled. It is not sufficient to defeat Lanverness with swords."

He stared up at his battle commanders, seeking out the slender form shrouded in shadows. "I grant my assassins a special task."

Like fluid darkness, a figure emerged from the shadows. Short and spare, the man had the stunted frame of a fifteen-year-old boy, yet he moved with a feral grace. Muscles rippled beneath black leather, a baldric of nine throwing knives slung across his chest. Black as sin, the nine knives gave testament to his prowess, a master assassin of the ninth rank. Making a curt bow, Dolf stood poised by the railing.

The Mordant smiled, for his best assassins were ever spare with words. "A MerChanter longship waits to take you and your brethren south. To my assassins, I give the task of laying the groundwork for the fall of Lanverness. A troop of the best Duegar will be assigned to serve you. I suspect the meddling monks will attempt to save the Rose Queen. The magic sniffing dwarves will help thwart their plans." He pulled a sealed scroll from his belt and tossed it to his master assassin. "Now go and prepare for your voyage. We will speak again before you sail."

Dolf caught the scroll and bowed low. Easing backwards, he disappeared into the shadows.

"Each of you has your appointed tasks." The Mordant slashed the dark sword across the map, cutting through a triangle of enemies. "First the Octagon, then the monks, and then the bitch-queen of

Lanverness. Topple these three and all of Erdhe belongs to the Dark Lord."

"But what of Castlegard?" The question came from General Marris, a tall thin man with iron-gray hair.

The Mordant nodded, allowing the question. "The heart of the Octagon will be shattered at Raven Pass. Once the rest of Erdhe is secured, then the army can lay siege to the great castle. Huddled behind their mage-stone walls, the last of the knights will die of starvation, a fitting end for the vaunted maroon." He studied his battle commanders, peering into each man's soul. Satisfied, he turned his stare toward his high priest. As he expected, Gavis wore the sour look of a man forced to sup on bitter wine. "And upon my priests I bestow the task of inspiring the army with omens of victory." He sheathed his sword and began to climb the narrow steps to the balcony.

"What say you, Gavis?"

"I don't know what to say, my Lord."

"What, my high priest struck dumb?" The Mordant reached the balcony and stared across the map at Gavis.

"I fear for the safety of the Dark Citadel."

"But the citadel is kept safe by my priesthood."

Gavis shook his head. "You risk too much on war. Take the guards from the Pit if you must, but leave the citadel at full strength."

"Are you saying the priesthood cannot control the mob?"

Gavis blanched, his eyes like daggers.

More than one general smirked.

The Mordant caught their mood. Like a pack of jackals, they yearned to see the priesthood cast low, but Gavis still had a role to play. He turned on his generals, barking a command. "You have your orders. Within a fortnight, the army marches to war." He strode toward the double doors. "Lord Gavis attend me. I will sup with you tonight."

A pair of guards rushed to open the doors. The Mordant left the map room, striding through the marble corridors. Braziers lit the long hallways, dispelling the winter chill. Gavis kept two paces behind, a silent shadow at his back.

Golden doors marked the entrance to the royal chambers. A pair of blond beauties rushed to attend him. He stood with his arms spread wide as they worked to divest him of his armor. The Mordant kept his gaze fixed on his high priest. "Why do you object?"

Gavis avoided his gaze, watching the women instead. "My only concern is for the safety of your citadel."

"Yes, *my* citadel." Freed from the armor, he waved the women away. "And it is the priesthood's duty to keep the rabble in check." The

Mordant strode to an adjoining chamber. A round table was set for two, a pair of silver plates and goblets hewn from chunks of crystal, the scent of roast pork teasing the air. He waved his high priest toward the table. "Join me."

Gavis took a seat as a servant hastened to pour goblets of fine red wine.

The Mordant swirled the goblet, his stare piercing his high priest. "I am not pleased."

"But my Lord, the lower tiers already riot for more food. The guards are needed to keep order in the citadel."

"*Fear* keeps order in the citadel." His voice dropped to a dangerous hiss. "For nigh on a thousand years, the people of the citadel have submitted to the rule of tiers. Trapped within the station of their birth, they are trained only to serve, expecting nothing more than what they are born to. It is their lot in life, like oxen forever yoked to the plow. And now you dare tell me the priesthood cannot control the citadel?"

"No my Lord, that is not what I'm saying." Gavis reached for a goblet, the tremble of his hand betraying the steadiness of his voice. "I am merely preaching caution. Take the guards from the Pit but leave the citadel untouched."

"Has decadence eroded the power of my priesthood?"

"Not while I hold the staff."

"Good, else I would need to look elsewhere for a new high priest." The Mordant clapped his hands. "Perhaps a hearty meal will strengthen your convictions.

Rich scents of cinnamon apples and roast pork swirled through the chamber. A pair of servants presented a silver domed platter. Candlelight reflected against the dome, casting a distorted view, a pair of misshapen monsters sitting at the table.

"Replenish the wine and then leave us."

Servants rushed to obey.

The Mordant eased back in his chair, studying his high priest. "Those who serve the Dark Lord are continually tested. Fail and damnation is assured. Succeed and the rewards are beyond measure." He fingered the crystal goblet, swirling the wine like blood in a chalice. "The time of testing is upon you, Gavis. This war is a holy calling, a dictate of the Dark Lord. The whole of the citadel must make sacrifices for the sake of victory, including the priesthood." He lifted the goblet, tasting the wine. "The pulpit is yours to use, the power of the priesthood at your command. Curse the people, bless the people, damn them to hell. Do whatever you must, but keep them in their place." He set the goblet down, a drop of wine running down the side, like a stain of blood on the tabletop. "Hold the citadel and it will be yours to rule at the war's end."

Gavis gasped, sitting forward in his chair. "Mine to rule?"

The Mordant chuckled. "Yes, I told you, rewards beyond measure."

"But the citadel has ever belonged to the Mordant, the high priest nothing more than a steward?"

"And so shall it ever be. Succeed and you shall rule as my vassal, a king in everything but name."

"And all this will be mine?" His gaze wandered the luxuries of the royal chamber, a cautious look on his face. "And where will you reside, my Lord?"

"In the heart of Erdhe. I will claim the queen's castle, making Lanverness the new seat of my power."

Gavis nodded, a gleam of avarice in his dark eyes. "The citadel is too far from the south."

"Exactly." The Mordant lifted his goblet in salute. "Do we have an understanding?"

"Yes, my Lord, we do."

"Then serve the meal and let us sup together to seal our agreement."

Gavis rose from his chair, tall and elegant in his robes of silk. Rounding the table, he lifted the domed lid, releasing the scent of roast pork. Gavis gagged, a hand pressed to his face. He staggered backward, the silver dome clattering to the floor. Bishop Siff's head stared from the platter, an apple stuffed in his mouth, surrounded by a garnish of greens.

The Mordant chuckled. "A reminder of the cost of failure."

Gavis dropped to his knees, his face pale. "I swear I will not fail you."

"Succeed or be damned." The Mordant hardened his voice. "Now be gone, before I have you made into the second course."

Gavis scurried from the chamber, his face ash-white.

The Mordant sipped his wine. It was good to rule, to make other men fear. Power was a heady elixir, better than the finest wine, a dish fit for a king. And soon, very soon, all of Erdhe would be his to rule, a dish of a different sort. Gifted with immortality, he would crown himself the first and last Emperor of Erdhe, and every mortal would tremble beneath his boot heel.

39

Duncan

Surrendering his body to death's sure grip, Duncan's thoughts fled to Kath. Moonlight shimmered through the trees as he lifted her in his arms, carrying her to their marriage bower. Naked in the silvery light, she quivered beneath his touch. Bud-tight breasts and a slender waist, his lips and hands played across her, exploring all the tender places, slowly rousing her passion. A blazing heat built between them till the wanting became unbearable. Moist and open, she waited beneath him. *Beloved!* He entered her with a rush of ecstasy.

Rough hands on his body...they grasped his arms, pulling him down. A thunderous pain roared through him, racking his back and arms, a terrible torture...but then the weights were gone. No weights, no chains, no endless pull, was this death? Was this heaven? Confused, his mind hung in a daze. Water at his lips...but he wanted to stay in the silvery forest, to stay with Kath. He reached for her, struggling to find his way back.

Rough hands held his face, prying his eyelids open. Light spiked his eyes. Duncan tried to flinch away, but they held him fast. A centurion's face leaned close, staring down. A man's harsh voice beat against him, slaying the silvery dream. "A golden cat-eye, just as they said. You're lucky he still lives."

No!!! Duncan howled in his mind...so close to heaven...one more step and he'd be there...but instead, they snatched him back, pulling him down into hell.

"Clean him up. This one's for the Mordant."

40

Katherine

Like spirits escaping the netherworld, they climbed from the depths, leaving the Womb of the World. The lion-faced man carried the Old One, while Kath walked a step behind, clutching a lighted candle. Smoke clung to her hair and clothes, a cloud of scent evoking half-formed memories. So many twists and turns, yet the lion-faced man took them in stride, never hesitating. Kath walked behind in a daze, her mind a tumult of thoughts. Her right hand clutched the crystal dagger sheathed at her belt, making sure it was more than a dream.

The candle guttered and nearly went out, a slender light against the labyrinth of darkness. Shielding the flame, she rushed to keep up, relieved when they finally passed through the lightning-bolt crack.

Crude handprints gave way to galloping horses. They returned to the occupied caverns, the clean smell of rock giving way to the jumbled scents of habitation. Kath began to recognize the drawings, a splendor of ocher, umber, and charcoal decorating familiar ceilings. Painted people emerged from the side passages. Thera was the first, the raven-faced healer falling into step behind Kath. The Old One gained a following as they made their way through the cave dwellings. Men in jerkins of pale white leather embroidered with fine beadwork and women in sheepskin cloaks carrying wooden staves adorned with small brass bells. All of them bore the tattoo of the raven or the snarling mountain lion. A soft chime of bells marked their steps, like a secret sect summoned to ritual.

Kath walked among them, keeping a step behind the Old One, caught up in something she did not understand. A shiver ran down her back. She gripped the crystal dagger, knowing the ordeal of the depths was not yet over.

A murmur of voices filled the passage. Like the rush of a mighty river, the voices pulled the procession forward. The passageway spilled into an enormous cavern, unlike anything Kath had ever seen. Glow crystals lined the walls, revealing magnificent drawings. Three beasts of mythical proportion rampaged along the far wall, huge curved tusks and flared ears raised in warning, like mighty war beasts drawn from legend. A vast migration of animals galloped across the vaulted ceiling, a wild celebration of life so lifelike Kath could almost hear the thunder of their hooves. The magnificent murals transformed the cavern into a stone cathedral. Beneath the drawings sat a river of people. A great host crowded together, men and women, young and old, all of them marked with blue tattoos.

Startled, Kath stared at the assembly, ambushed by the numbers.

Thousands of tattooed faces turned to stare. The river of voices stilled to a reverent hush. Like a pebble dropped in a pond, a path opened for the procession. The lion-faced man led the way, holding the Old One cradled in his arms, his pale leather jerkin startlingly white against the dull browns of the crowd. A rain of soft chimes marked each step like a blessing. Kath stayed close to the lion-faced man, held in the grip of the procession. Solemn and slow, they walked the length of the cavern, through a crush of tattooed faces. Buffeted by an avalanche of stares, Kath endured a gauntlet of hostility, struggling to make sense of the gathering.

At the cavern's heart they reached a raised platform, a natural dais of rust-red rock, a raised island of stone in a sea of faces. The lion-faced man climbed the steps and settled the Old One on a mound of sheepskins. One at a time, the members of the procession mounted the dais and nodded to the Ancestor. *They nodded but they did not bow*...that told Kath a lot. The Old One was respected, even revered, but she did not rule, not like a queen. The painted people displayed a fierce pride, jealously guarding their freedom. They'd make fine allies if she could just win their trust. Wary of making a mistake, she watched as the others sat cross-legged in a solemn circle around the dais, a ring of ravens and snarling mountain lions staring back at her.

Kath was the last one standing. Clutching the lighted candle, she waited at the edge of the dais, unsure what was expected of her.

The Old One gestured. "Come, child, set your candle on the pillar."

A single pillar of rust colored rock thrust up from the heart of the dais. Five feet tall, the pillar was sheathed in a thick shroud of white wax, as if thousands of candles had wept upon the rock. Approaching the pillar, Kath tilted her candle, letting droplets of warm wax puddle before crowning the stone with her lighted candle.

An angry murmur swept through the crowd.

A shiver of foreboding raced down Kath's back. She needed to gain the trust of the painted people but a chasm of differences gaped between them.

One of the lion-faced men strode to her side. A tall man with dark hair, he faced the crowd, his voice echoing across the cavern. "Strangers have come among us. Without runes, without brands...without any marks of enslavement...without proof they understand the cost of freedom. They bear no tattoos yet they seek our help. *Our help*, when so for so long none have come to *our aid*."

The crowd stirred.

"I say, they are not worthy."

Kath remained statue-still, swallowing her unease.

The lion-faced man resumed his seat and Thera rose to take his place. The raven-faced healer turned toward the crowd, her voice rising to fill the cavern. "A handful of barefaced strangers have come where armies fear to tread. They claim to oppose the Mordant, and they ask for our aid, but they also bring word of one of our own. Over two long years ago, Valdur, a Taishan of the mountain lions, was lost on a vision quest. Lost but never forgotten. Now a barefaced stranger comes to bring us word of his fate." She gestured to Kath, her voice dropping to a whisper. "Turn and face the people."

Kath slowly turned, impaled by a thousand stares. So many tattooed faces, most filled with smoldering outrage, as if she'd defiled a sacred ritual. Bears, boars, badgers and wolves, hawks, eagles, and owls, a press of predators stared back at her, studying their prey, waiting to pounce at the first sign of weakness. Kath fought the urge to flee, and then she saw them. Her companions sat at the base of the dais. Blaine in his silver surcoat, looking lost without his sword. Zith in his robes of midnight blue, his face haggard from his ordeal, his ruined arm held in a sling. And Danya, looking strangely confident, her right hand buried in the wolf's dark fur. A rush of gratitude filled her; she was not alone.

Another lion-faced man strode to the heart of the dais. A wild mane of auburn hair gave him a feral look. His voice boomed through the cavern, pulling Kath back to the proceedings. "We meet in the Great Hall to bear witness to the fate of every Taishan. Listen and hear the fate of Valdur, a Taishan of the mountain lions." He sketched a strange sign with his hand, as if drawing a rune in the air. "May the gods grant us the wisdom to defeat the Dark."

"Show us the Light." The words rippled like ritual through the crowd.

He gestured for Kath to step forward. "Tell us what you know." He sent her a piercing glare and then took a seat with the others.

Kath stood alone at the heart of the dais, surrounded by thousands of hostile stares.

A chime of bells shivered through the cavern.

Kath shuddered, feeling the crushing weight of destiny. Somehow this lost man of the mountain lions was of great importance...but it was an importance she did not understand, a riddle mired in the mysticism of a fiercely proud people. Yet instinctively she knew her fate was bound to his, tied by destiny to a dead man she did not even know. Kath felt as if she walked along a cliff edge, where a single wrong word would send her plummeting to the depths.

Taking a deep breath, she tried to still her mind...but each breath was laced with smoke from the Womb of the World. It clung to her clothes, a rich earthy scent of sage and peat and something else, something mysterious. Memories flooded her mind, as vivid as if they'd happened yesterday. Kath closed her eyes, shutting out the hostile stares. "It happened on a crisp spring morning, the first rays of sunlight hitting the castle ramparts. Late for the healery, I took a shortcut through the great yard. A cavalcade of mounted knights returned to the castle, their armor gleaming bright, maroon octagons emblazoned on their shields, a proud sight...till I saw the horses lathered with sweat. Something was wrong. The patrol leader called for the healer. Trapped by curiosity, I had to see for myself. No one noticed as I drew near. And then I saw him." Shivers feathered down her spine, as if a ghost reached out to touch her. "He was slumped on the back of a horse. Pale white leather embroidered with delicate blue flowers marked him as a stranger. And then I saw his face. Whirls of blue ink transformed him into a snarling mountain lion. For the first time, I saw a *Painted Warrior.*" She gripped the crystal dagger, struggling to hold her voice steady. "But beneath the blue tattoos, he'd turned ashen, one step away from death's door. I ran for a water skin. Most of it dribbled down his chin...but then his eyes flew open, a sky-blue stare filled with desperate need. His bloody hand gripped my tunic." Kath's eyes flew open, fleeing the past...but the present crowded close, trapping her in the grip of a thousand anxious stares. Strangled by a truth she dared not say, her voice fell to a harsh whisper. "He died in my arms...in the heart of Castlegard. No one even knew his name."

The stares of the crowd impaled her.

"Tell us how he died." It was the voice of the Old One...prodding her toward the cliff edge.

Trapped, Kath teetered on the edge of destiny. Everything she'd learned of the painted people screamed of a warrior's pride. And this man of the mountain lions was somehow special, even revered. How could she tell them the truth? How could she speak of arrows protruding from his back? That he'd died running...taken by a coward's death.

"*Tell us.*" The whisper came from every direction, a cold chant pelting her like hailstones, pushing her toward the precipice.

Forced to speak, Kath reached for a sliver of truth, hoping it would be enough. "He was wounded, slain by soldiers of the Mordant."

The crowd stirred, anger and disbelief warring across their faces.

Kath dared a glance to the Old One, desperate for guidance, but the wrinkled face remained impassive, her voice a persistent goad. "How did he die?"

The truth was so hurtful, even damning...but she could not bring herself to lie. If she wanted the painted people's trust, she would have to trust in return. Kath nodded to the Old One and then turned to face the crowd, braced for the backlash. "The truth is...he died from his wounds...two black and gold fletched arrows skewering his back. He died fleeing the soldiers of the Mordant."

A gasp rippled through the cavern.

Kath remained statue-still, struggling to understand.

"Did he speak before he died?"

The question carried the weight of destiny.

Kath nodded. As if it had happened yesterday, the dead man's words rang through her mind. "*Be prepared! The gods give warning! A great Evil returns!*" Kath rocked back on her heels, stunned by the strength of her memories.

The Old One prodded. "What else?"

"He grabbed my tunic and pulled me close...and with his dying breath he said, *Claim the war helm...yours to use.*"

The cavern erupted in chaos. Shouts rang from every quarter.

"*She lies!*"

"*The War Helm cannot be claimed by a woman!*"

"*Women don't fight in the steppes!*"

"*We'll not follow a barefaced intruder!*"

Confused, Kath stared at the Old One, but it was Royce, the lion-faced man who came to her rescue.

"*Enough!*" His roar cut through the clamor. "Where is your pride? Where is your honor?" He gestured to Kath. "This one was tested by the ancient rites of our people. She braved the depths, facing the trial of souls, her memories weighed by the Ancestor." He pointed to the single candle glowing atop the pillar. "Out of the depths, a Light is brought to us, proof she is worthy to stand among our leaders."

A ripple of protest raced through the crowd.

A tall man with iron-gray hair climbed the steps of the dais, his eagle face set in a defiant scowl. "The test of the depths earns her a seat at the leader's council...but she has no right to wear the War Helm. The eagles have that honor."

Thera answered, "Will you defy the voice of the gods?"

The eagle-faced man flinched but he did not retreat. "Valdur is two years dead. His words are lost to the wind."

"The gods found a way to bring his words back to us."

"There's no proof!"

"The proof is in the manner of his death." Thera shook with outrage. "A true son of the mountain lions, Valdur proved himself worthy of the gods. He kept his oath, running instead of fighting, forswearing violence while on a vision quest. And despite his wounds, he found a way to preserve the words of the gods." She raised her voice to the crowd. "The Taishan succeeded, sacrificing his life for his vision. His words come to us from beyond the grave. It is our duty to heed their wisdom."

The eagle-faced man scowled. "I'll not listen to lies."

Royce shook his head, his words a low growl, "Shagrith, you speak blasphemy."

"No, I demand proof. The War Helm will not be won by the lies of a barefaced girl." He pointed an accusing finger at Kath. "As leader of the eagle den, I demand proof." His face curled into a sneer. "I demand a trial by combat!"

The cavern erupted in argument.

Kath stared at the Old One, ambushed by the turn of events. "What does this mean?" But her words were lost in the uproar.

Brass bells jangled against the noise of the crowd. Royce paced the length of the dais, calling for quiet. The chaos subsided to a dull murmur. He confronted the eagle, his voice full of anger. "You dispute the words of a Taishan?"

"I do."

"Such a challenge has not been issued in many lifetimes."

Shagrith grinned. "Then perhaps it's past time. I demand trial by combat, a fight to the death, here and now, in front of this assembly." He threw a look of disdain at Kath. "The liar has the choice of weapons." His smile turned into a sneer. "And the choice of champions. Let the gods decide the truth of her words."

Thera protested, appealing to the lion-faced man. "Royce, this is not right. The council..."

He raised his hand. "As the leader of the eagles, Shagrith has the right to challenge." He turned to Kath, his face solemn. "Will you fight, or will you rescind your words?"

Kath stared at Royce, trying to read the message behind his eyes. "I spoke the truth."

He nodded, and it seemed a weight was lifted from his shoulders. "Then you must fight."

"But I..."

Shagrith interrupted. "Choose your weapon!"

Blaine vaulted onto the dais, his voice bellowing through the cavern. "I will be her champion!" Tall and proud, shimmering in his silver surcoat, he looked like an avenging hero. "And the weapon will be swords!"

Shagrith flashed a scathing grin. "So the girl hides behind the knight."

"Hold!" It was Thera, her dark eyes glittering. She flew across the dais to stand at Kath's side. "It's not the knight's decision...it's Kath's. And she does not understand our ways." She leaned close to Kath, her voice dropping to a whisper. "Think before you choose."

Kath felt as if she'd stepped into a quagmire, trapped by politics, egos, and fate. Her gaze roamed the dais, searching for allies, for a way out of the trap. Her stare settled on the Old One. "I would speak with the Ancestor."

Shagrith protested but Royce cut him off. "It is allowed."

The Old One nodded, bird-bright eyes huddled beneath sheepskin robes.

Kath crossed to the Old One. Kneeling on the cold stone floor, she leaned close to the old woman, keeping her voice to a whisper. "You know I spoke the truth, about his death, about the War Helm."

The Old One nodded. "Valdur was true to his oath and you were true to his memory. Even death cannot keep the words of the gods from finding their way back to the people."

The old woman's words brimmed with certainty, setting a spark in Kath's mind. "You knew this would happen! Yet you did not warn me?"

"It is all part of the test, to see if you would choose the hard truth...or a convenient lie. Integrity is easy to claim but hard to live by."

Anger boiled inside Kath. "And this is another test?"

"A choice."

"But since you know the truth, why should I fight?"

"Because a people divided are a blunted weapon. It takes fire to forge a strong sword." The old woman's gaze burned into her. "Remember your visions of the future. You will need a strong sword to face the Mordant."

Kath shivered, knowing one wrong step would shatter the future.

The old woman grinned, a gap-toothed smile...and Kath realized she was missing something, another piece to the puzzle, another layer to the challenge. She leaned back, replaying the last few moments in her mind, considering the words of Royce, and Shagrith...and Thera. She glanced at Blaine, certain the knight could defeat any champion, yet it seemed too easy. She stared at the Old One. "I have the right to choose a champion?"

"The right is yours but the fight is for the fate of the War Helm. Whoever wears the War Helm leads the people into battle. And to lead, you must eliminate doubt." She laid a gnarled hand on Kath's cheek. "The Womb of the World opened the doors to your past. Those doors have not yet closed." Her voice dropped to a hoarse whisper. "The old ways are strong in you, like undercurrents of destiny they flow through your mind, lending strength to your convictions. Remember the past and find the strength to change the future."

Kath knew what she must do. She bowed to the Old One and then stood, weariness settling on her shoulders like a cloak. Gripping the crystal dagger, she turned to face the others, her words ringing with certainty. "I spoke the truth of his death, and I spoke the truth of the War Helm. The challenge is accepted."

A roar ripped through the people.

Royce raised his fist, demanding silence.

Shagrith shouted over the din. "And the weapon?"

"I choose the sword."

Blaine stepped forward. "And I will be her champion."

The pride in his voice almost choked Kath to silence...almost. Nothing was ever simple...and every choice had its price. Why did the gods make it so hard? She met his stare, willing him to understand. "For the fate of the War Helm...I must fight my own battles."

Blaine gaped, floundering in disbelief.

But Shagrith grinned, more like a wolf than an eagle. "And for the sake of truth, I name Anton of the fox den as the gods' champion."

Shocked murmurs rippled through the cavern.

A tall red-haired man strode toward the dais. A grin split his face, the wily leer of a fox...and in his hands he bore Blaine's blue steel sword.

41

Duncan

D uncan lingered on the edge of sleep, a pillow beneath his head. *A pillow!* The thought pierced him like an arrow yet he remained still as a possum. Alert to danger, he took slow and shallow breaths, his eyes closed, his face relaxed, while his senses probed his surroundings. Naked, he lay on a soft pallet, a wool blanket providing a comfortable warmth. Beneath the blanket he flexed his right hand, testing his body. Gone were the weights, and the chains, and the endless pull. The fierce agony of the hanging stones was banished, replaced by a dull ache. His raging thirst was slaked as well, a mere memory. Puzzled, he breathed deep, tasting the air. A hint of rosewater and the smell of soap but the stench of the Pit was absent. Perhaps he'd been rescued. Against all odds, perhaps Kath had found a way.

He dared a glance through hooded eyes.

Tapestries adorned the stone wall; the glimpse of luxury deepened his puzzlement. Beeswax candles littered the bedside table, a copper basin filled with water, but he detected no sign of movement or sound; perhaps he was alone. He lay in a four-posted bed in a small round chamber, sunlight striping the coverlet. *Stripes in the sunlight*, a nasty suspicion spiked him. Discarding caution, he turned and stared at the window. *Bars on the window*, hope sank like a stone in his stomach. So he was still a prisoner, but why the opulence? He racked his mind for answers but all his memories were mired in pain.

Throwing the covers aside, he rose from the bed and tested his body. Muscles ached with disuse but the raging pain was gone. His lice-ridden beard was shaved clean, smooth as a courtier's cheek. A healing salve coated his wrists and his back, the raw marks of shackles and lashes fading to a dull sore. Someone bothered to heal him, but why?

He strode to the window set high in the wall. Grabbing the bars, he pulled himself up. The view took his breath away. High in a tower, he looked down on a tiered citadel of black stone. A dizzying height, he counted nine tiers of walls, a stone beehive rising from the steppes. So this was the Dark Citadel, the stronghold of the Mordant. He could have wept. The god-cursed monks had sent the six of them against *this?* The monks were barking mad, naïve beyond belief. He vented his anger against the bars but the iron was sunk deep, impossible to bend.

Dropping down from the window, he prowled the chamber, searching for a weapon...or a way out. A stout oak door barred the only exit, locked from the other side. Twitching the tapestry aside, he found bare stone beneath. Candles, a copper basin, a chamber pot, nothing he could use as a weapon, not even a stitch of clothing. Trapped in a silken prison, but why the royal treatment? They'd cleaned him up and fed him...like a nobleman held for ransom...or a lamb fattened before the slaughter. A premonition of fear shivered down his back.

A key rattled in the door.

Fight or spy? He leaped for the bed and pulled the covers close, spying through hooded eyes.

The door eased open and a dark-haired beauty slipped inside. She carried a tray, the rich scent of lamb stew swamping his senses. *Lamb stewed with vegetables,* the mouth-watering smells nearly drove him mad with hunger yet he feigned sleep, his gaze fixed on the woman.

Balancing the tray on one hand, she moved toward the bed, a gown of diaphanous silk revealing every detail. And every detail proved enticing. After the depths of the Pit, she seemed an illusion. The grace of a dancer and the curves of a courtesan; not what he expected in a jailor.

She set the tray on the table and perched on the edge of the bed. Leaning forward, she tugged the covers away from his chest.

His hand snaked out, catching her wrist. "*Why am I here?*"

Brown eyes flared wide, startled as a deer.

"*Why am I healed?*" He pulled her close, his grip like steel. "*I mean you no harm but I need answers.*"

She shook her head, her eyes wide in panic, but she did not speak.

"*Answer me!*"

She made an odd gurgling sound and then opened her mouth wide.

No tongue! She had no tongue! "Who did this to you?" Horrified, he let her go.

Suddenly free, she lurched backwards, knocking the tray from the table, a clatter of dishes across the floor.

He rose from the bed, never mind his nakedness. "Who did this to you?"

The door crashed open and guards rushed in. Six spears thrust toward him, poised at his throat. Naked and without a weapon, Duncan was forced to yield. Hard-faced guards pushed him against the wall. Sobbing, the girl fled the chamber. A leather-clad man appeared at the door. Small and slight, dressed all in black, he lounged against the doorframe, his arms crossed, a baldric of nine throwing knives strung across his chest like a banner. "So you're finally awake."

Duncan kept still, his back pressed to the wall, his throat a hair's breadth from the spear points. "Six against one is hardly fair."

The small man grinned. "Nathan, go tell the priests he's finally ready."

One of the guards snapped a salute and then rushed from the chamber.

So the small man held sway despite his slight stature. "Why the priests?"

"All in due time."

Duncan studied his captors. Five guards with spears but the one that worried him the most was slight man leaning against the doorframe. Short and wiry, he had the stunted body of a fifteen year-old boy, yet years of struggle were writ across his face. Cloaked in black, he carried an intensity about him that reeked of coiled danger. "Who are you?"

"They say you killed three gore hounds. Not an easy feat."

So they knew he wasn't from the Pit. Duncan hardened his resolve, knowing he still had a secret to protect.

"What do you see with your golden cat eye?"

Perhaps the luxury was all about his eye, a better topic than the gore hounds. "I see a silken prison with too many guards."

"I'm betting your golden eye gives you an advantage, an aid in hunting the gore hounds."

Interest laced the man's words, or perhaps it was jealousy. "Why? Do you need an advantage to kill one?"

The man flashed a mocking smile. "Deformities of the Pit often carry a purpose." He eased away from the door, moving with a feral grace. "The Taals have obscene strength, the stunted Duegars can sniff magic, and rumors say some of the Pit-born have the gift of prophecy. So I'll ask you again, what do you see with that golden eye?"

"Not the future."

The dark man paused, as if weighing the answer, and then he flashed a devilish grin. "No, you don't see the future," the grin turned nasty, "else you'd reek of fear."

"Who are you?"

His grin widened. "The Mordant's assassin."

A clatter of footsteps approached the doorway. A dozen guards crowded into the chamber. A tall man in a long black robe followed. He carried himself with an air of authority, studying Duncan like a bug stuck on a pin. "So the rumors are true." Nodding, he made an imperious gesture. "Take him. The Mordant awaits."

Spear points dropped. A dozen hands reached for him.

Duncan seized his chance. His right fist snaked out, connecting with a jaw. Bone crunched and a guard fell screaming. Instinct took over, a cornered animal desperate to escape. He whirled, throwing elbows at faces, knees to groins, dealing a whirlwind of pain. Twisting and turning, he fought like a rabid animal, nothing to lose. A gap opened between two guards. Duncan lunged for the doorway, but the small man was suddenly there, a blur of shadows. Something solid struck the side of Duncan's head. He staggered to his knees. A dozen hands grabbed his arms and legs. A strangler's noose was slipped around this throat. It pulled tight and Duncan gasped for air. Ignoring the pain, he fought to win free, but the guards were too many. Ropes lashed his arms, and still he fought, trying to bite his captors.

"Follow me." The priest turned, a whirl of dark robes, and strode from the chamber.

The soldiers hoisted him onto their shoulders, borne like a felled deer fresh from the slaughter.

Naked, Duncan writhed against his bonds, but he could not win free. They carried him through a maze of marble corridors, a palace of some sort. A pair of massive doors opened, admitting a rush of cold air. They bore him out into the bitter wind. A flock of sea gulls wheeled overhead, their mournful cries filling the air. Across a rune covered courtyard, they carried him toward a massive boulder. "Where are you taking me?" But there was no answer.

A dark crack creased the boulder, like a doorway to hell. Spiral stairs cut into solid rock, a steep descent. Duncan breathed deep, tasting the air. Stale smells filled the stairway, scents of stone and blood and pain laced together, a lingering nightmare. Duncan struggled, but the guards kept their hold.

Torches lit the stairwell, so many steps, like descending into hell. Rough rock walls carried a feeling of age and menace, a place that time forgot. The stairs leveled out and he caught a glimpse of a great copper door.

Cold brushed against his skin like dead fingers. Naked, he writhed against his bonds, but the soldiers did not stop. They carried him through the doorway and into a massive chamber. Red stalactites hung from the ceiling as if the stone wept blood. Raw scents of blood and fear intensified, a tortured reek suffocating him. Every aspect of the cavern was carved from nightmares. Duncan's stare skittered around the chamber, desperate to win free.

"Put him here."

They carried him to the heart of the chamber. Five braziers glowed with flames. Someone yanked the strangler's noose taut and he gasped for breath. Soldiers lowered him to the ground, his naked back pressed against cold, hard stone. His arms and legs were pulled tight, put in a spread-eagle position. Iron clamped around his wrists and ankles, binding him to the floor like a sacrifice.

One of the soldiers removed the noose.

Duncan gasped for air, desperate to keep the panic from his voice. "What is this place? What do you want from me?"

The priest smirked. "Only your soul." He made a sharp gesture and the soldiers followed him toward the round doorway.

"You're leaving me?" Duncan bucked against his chains, but he was held tight, only able to lift his head. "Don't leave me!" His cry echoed against the stalactites, a pitiful wail. Straining against his chains, he watched his captors leave, till their footsteps died to echoes. He fought the chains, desperate to win free, but the cruel iron could not be defeated. Exhausted, he slumped against the cold stone, chained in a god-forsaken place.

Movement at the edge of his vision, a dark figure stepped from the shadows. Gliding like a shade, the assassin moved to stare down at him, a hint of regret on his face. "You would have made a worthy opponent."

"Then fight me, here and now, man against man!"

The assassin shook his head. "Orders." He cocked his head as if listening to a hidden voice. "But I'll give you a piece of advice. If ever you have the chance, fall on the spears. A much better death than this." And then he was gone, striding toward the doorway.

The great copper door shuddered closed and Duncan was alone. Chained to the floor, splayed like a sacrifice, he watched the shadows cavort among the stalactites, struggling to keep his sanity.

42

Blaine

"**M**y sword!*" Blaine stared at the blue steel sword, desperate to reclaim it. Hands balled into fists, he strode towards the fox-faced man, but Kath was suddenly in the way.
"No."

He towered over her, his voice a low growl. *"I'll have my sword."*

Kath stood her ground, keeping a hand on his chest, her voice a hushed whisper. "You'll get your sword back." She turned, appealing to the wrinkled crone huddled beneath sheepskins. "We're allies of the painted people, sworn to fight the Mordant. Our weapons should be returned to us."

The crone nodded. "As you say."

Blaine waited, keeping a leash on his anger.

Three lads, all of them tattooed with badger faces, scurried up the steps to the dais. They brought Kath her sword in its leather scabbard, the dagger for her boot, and her throwing axes in their hawk-harness...and they brought Blaine a dagger. *A dagger.* His anger erupted. *"The blue steel sword is mine!"*

Grinning like a thief, the fox-faced man raised the sapphire sword with both hands. Blue steel gleamed as keen as when it was first forged, death crafted into steel. The fox sneered, "The sword is mine, given as payment for your rescue. The price for our aid." Twirling the blue blade, he glared at Blaine, his every gesture a taunt.

Blaine's rage boiled over. "Are you a merchant or a warrior? Where's your honor?"

Anger rippled through the crowd.

Kath stepped between them, her gaze fixed on the old woman. "The matter of the blue sword must be decided. Allies should not require payment."

Blaine hissed, "Just let me fight for it!"

Kath gave him a barbed stare, her voice a hissed whisper. "We need allies not enemies."

"Tell that to him!"

The old woman gestured to Blaine, her hand as frail as a bird's claw. "Come closer, knight of the Octagon."

Scowling, Blaine sidestepped Kath and strode to the old woman. A wizen sack of bones swathed in sheepskins, she looked so frail he could snap her neck with a single hand. He wondered how such a shriveled old thing could hold sway over a warrior people...but then he looked into her eyes, dark brown flecked with gold, bottomless pools of memory, tugging at his soul, pulling him into an abyss of obligation. A question whispered in his mind, *Will you be true?*

A witch! He tired to pull away, but she held him with her stare.

Will you be steadfast or will you reach for glory?

His mind reeled, why couldn't he have both? Honor *and* glory, *I'll have both!*

Beware the choice, knight of the Octagon.

Something snapped in his mind. Blaine staggered backwards...and the link severed. Shaking his head, he studied the crone through hooded eyes...but she was just a shriveled old woman, harmless beneath a sheepskin cloak.

But there was nothing frail about her voice. She pointed a bony finger at him. "Is it true you bartered the sword for aid?"

"Yes, but..."

"And was the aid given?"

His anger simmered, ready to over boil. "Yes, but..."

"Then the bargain was kept."

His rage exploded. "But there never should have been a bargain! Not among allies."

She nodded like a sage. "Two sides of the truth. Both claims have merit." She gave him a small smile shrouded with meaning. "Let the gods decide the sword's fate."

"What?"

"Let the blue sword belong to the winner of the challenge."

A fight, he could live with that...but only if *he* fought the challenge. Turning on his heel, he strode towards Kath. "Name me as your champion!"

Kath gave him the smallest shake of her head. "I cannot."

"But I'll win."

"I know."

"*You know!* Then let me fight!" He stared at her, struggling to understand. "There's no loss of honor in naming a champion."

"It's not about honor."

"It's a fight to the death!" but she just gave him an obstinate stare. He wanted to shake her, to slap some sense into her, but he used words instead. "*Look at him!* He has the advantage of reach and strength, and he has a *blue steel sword!* You dare not fight him! One mistake and he'll gut you like a spring lamb."

"Then I best make no mistakes." Her face was ghost-pale but her voice was steady.

"You're mad! There's too much at stake. You can't afford to lose."

"I know." A shadow of fear touched her eyes. She handed him the harness with her throwing axes, "Hold these for me?" and buckled on her sword.

The girl was stubborn beyond reason. "Tell me why?"

Around them, the dais was being cleared.

Kath pulled the crystal dagger from her belt, "Because of this." She gestured with the blade toward the tattooed crowd, "and because of them. We need allies...and they need proof."

"Proof?"

"Proof enough to follow a woman into battle." She gave him a weary smile. "The gods gave me the crystal dagger, mine to wield against the Darkness, but they did not make me tall, or strong, or male...so I must always find more proof." She reversed the crystal dagger, extending the hilt toward Blaine. "If I fail, then this is yours to wield."

The crystal dagger, her trust staggered him. He took the blade but it felt awkward in his hand. He was meant to wield a sword not a dagger. "You best not fail."

She nodded, her face solemn, and then she did something that totally ambushed him. Standing on tiptoes, she brushed a quick kiss across his cheek. "For believing in me."

His face flamed red. Unsure what to say, unsure how to feel, he just stared at her...but she'd already turned away, studying her opponent, preparing for battle.

A voice at his back said, "You must leave."

It was the lion-faced man, gesturing toward the stairs. Blaine shook his head, realizing he'd wasted precious time; he should have been counseling her on the fight instead of arguing, but it was too late for that. He tucked the crystal dagger in his belt and followed the lion-faced man down the stairs, into the crush of spectators. Frustrated and angry, Blaine shouldered his way through hostile faces till he reached the monk and Danya.

Zith stared at him, his face haggard. "She does what she must."

Blaine glared at the old man. "She'll get herself killed, and then where will we be?"

An expectant hush settled over the crowd.

"Challenge has been given and accepted." Royce extinguished the single candle burning on the central pillar. "The champions are named. Swords are chosen. The War Helm is in the hands of the gods. Let the swords decide." Bowing to Kath and the fox-faced man, he descended the stairs.

The dais stood empty except for the two combatants. The fox-faced warrior stood to the right, six-feet tall, broad shoulders, a nimbus of bright red hair surrounding an insolent face. He wore a patched chainmail shirt over a leather tunic, a seasoned warrior ready to fight. Bristling with bravado, he twirled the blue steel blade, slashing the air with sweeping strokes. The blue sword was mesmerizing, a thing of beauty, so keen it whistled as it cut the air. The great blade scribed five-foot arcs, a deadly swath unmatched by any other weapon. To Blaine's eyes, the strokes were wild and undisciplined...but every cut held the promise of death. Even in the hands of an unskilled warrior, a blue steel sword was a weapon to be reckoned with.

On the opposite side, Kath stood alone. Long blond hair tied at the nape of her neck, clad in brown fighting leathers, no shield, no greaves, no armor, nothing but a simple short sword. She stood flat-footed, the sword hanging listless in her right hand, the point dangling toward the ground, looking vulnerable and unprepared, but Blaine knew better. He recognized the flinty look on her face. She was thinking, trying to outsmart her opponent, and that was good, because everything else was stacked against her. Blaine ground his teeth, knowing she should have named him as her champion. A trial sanctioned by the gods should be fair. Not leather against chainmail, not a short two-foot sword against a five foot blade, and certainly not ordinary steel against a *blue steel blade*...but then the gods weren't known for their fairness. Blaine balled his hands into fists, praying for Valin to intervene, knowing Kath would need more than luck to survive.

A murmur rippled through the crowd and he realized the fight had begun.

The fox-faced warrior circled the dais, slashing the air with his sword, as if intimidation alone would win the fight.

Kath stayed still, letting him come to her.

The warrior barked a laugh. "Aren't you going to fight?" His voice changed from a taunt to a sneer. "A barefaced woman pitted against a painted warrior. Of course you're scared stiff, turned to stone."

Kath remained statue-still, watching through narrow eyes.

"Soon your fear will turn to water, running down your leg." Laughing, he drew close, the blue sword whistling with menace. "Beg for mercy and you'll live." He sprang forward, aiming a viscous slash at Kath's head...but the girl was already gone. Dancing backwards, she kept one step away from the great sword.

Snarling, he gave chase, "Stand and fight!" but Kath did not listen. Round and round the dais, she led him on an intricate dance, flirting with death, always staying a handbreadth away from the blue blade. Her timing was uncanny, always dodging at the last moment, goading her opponent to a fit of wild rage.

Blaine leaned forward, his fists clenched, knowing the girl played a dangerous game. It took skill and nerves to dance so close to death...but she couldn't afford a single mistake...and sooner or later she'd have to attack.

Kath dodged left...and *slipped!*

The crowd gasped as she fell, sprawled beneath the blade of her opponent.

The fox grinned, struggling to change a horizontal swing into a downward slash.

Blue steel struck stone, sending up a shower of chips...but Kath was already gone. Springing to her feet, she lunged forward with a lightning strike, her sword slashing toward his face. *"Yield!"*

Steel met flesh with a sickening crunch.

Kath danced away.

Blood blossomed on the fox's face. He staggered backward, his nose smashed flat...but he did not die! Blaine groaned; she'd attacked with the flat of her sword! The girl was going to get herself killed!

Kath backed away, her sword raised, her voice loud enough to echo through the cavern. *"Yield! We aid the Mordant by fighting amongst ourselves!"*

Enraged, the fox was beyond reason. Wiping the blood from his face, he charged like a bull.

Kath dodged away, narrowly evading the sapphire sword.

The fox swung wide. Slash and hack, he fought like a demon enraged, wild swings seeking Kath's head, attacking with a flurry of blows.

Kath sidestepped, dodging the blue sword by a mere whisker.

Blaine bit his lip, drawing blood, bitterly aware of Kath's deadly dilemma. Against blue steel, she couldn't engage and she couldn't parry, speed and grace her only weapons. A small woman fighting against a tall man, like pitting a deer against a lion, the outcome seemed inevitable. Blaine couldn't watch, yet he couldn't look away, knowing a single mistake would cost her life.

Drenched with sweat, both combatants slowed but neither gave up. Locked together like ill-fated lovers, the macabre dance moved to the center of the dais. Kath retreated, almost in a straight line, her footsteps dragging, her blond hair streaked with sweat, her eyes glazed.

The crowd stood, sensing the end was near.

Blaine edged towards the dais, his hand on his dagger, but Zith grabbed his arm. "*No.*"

Time had nearly caught Kath. Exhausted, she staggered backwards, her sword a frail weapon against blue steel.

The fox rushed in for the kill. He loosed the blue steel blade in a mighty shoulder-high swing, a killing blow aimed at her neck.

Kath stared as if transfixed.

Blaine screamed. "*No!*"

At the last moment, Kath stepped sideways...and the sword struck stone! Sparks flared. Blue steel cleaved into the stone pillar, shattering the wax sheath, biting deep into the red rock pillar...and then it stopped, the sapphire blade held fast. The sword *stuck* in the stone.

The crowd gasped in disbelief.

Kath raised her sword to the warrior's throat. "Yield."

The fox strained to pull the sword free, corded muscles bulging at his neck.

Kath forced his head back, the tip of her sword drawing blood. "*Yield!*"

Shagrith, the leader of the eagles, leaped onto the dais. "*Kill him!*"

Blaine gaped, ambushed by the eagle's betrayal of the fox.

"I said *kill him!*" Shagrith raged at Kath. "The fight is to the death! You *dare* to claim the War Helm yet you're *afraid* to kill!"

Kath's voice shook with rage. "I kill *enemies* not *allies*. Are the lives of your men worth so little?"

Anger ripped through the crowd.

Kath kept her sword pressed to the warrior's throat, drawing a bead of blood. "For the last time, will you yield?"

Confusion played across the fox's face. He looked from the eagle to the sword and then slowly raised his empty hands, his voice distorted by his smashed nose. "I yield."

Kath lowered her sword, weariness crashing across her face. She stared out at the crowd. "Now do you believe? Do you have the proof you need?" Striding to the front of the dais, she raised her voice to a shout. "*We are allies!* Our swords are joined with yours. Together we're destined to defeat the Mordant."

The crowd stirred but they did not cheer.

Blaine kept his gaze fixed on Kath.

Movement on the dais, Shagrith raced towards Kath, a dagger poised to strike at her back.

The crowd gasped.

Blaine screamed, *"Behind you!"*

Kath whirled. Swift as lightning, she parried the blow and then lunged forward. *Strike of the dragon,* so fluid it was like nothing he'd ever seen. Her sword struck deep, taking the assassin in the chest, a killing blow straight to the heart.

Impaled, the eagle sagged dead on her sword, surprise scrawled across his face.

Kath shook her head and pulled her sword loose, blood dripping from the blade.

Blaine vaulted onto the dais and stood at her back, his fists clenched, his voice a hoarse whisper. "I've got your back."

She nodded, her sword held in a warrior's stance.

A chime of bells filled the cavern, like the sound of soft rain.

The Old One was carried onto the dais, followed by a procession of lion-faced men in pale white jerkins and raven-faced women in sheepskin cloaks. They stepped around the slain eagle and nodded to Kath, taking positions around the dais.

Royce, the big man with the wild mane of auburn hair, the one Blaine thought of as the leader of the lions, was the last to climb the steps. Solemn with dignity, he carried a swath of sheepskin. Nestled on the sheepskin sat a helmet, a simple conical half-helm with a cruciform nose guard. Made of ordinary steel, the helm was burnished bright. Despite the polish, it had an ancient look about it, a relic of the past. Blaine was tempted to dismiss it, till he saw the detail on the nose guard. Cunningly wrought in gold, a pantheon of predators decorated the helm: wolves, badgers, foxes, and owls, too many to count, and on the crest reared a roaring lion, a single paw outstretched in victory. Something about the helm stirred Blaine's blood, a call to battle. *"The War Helm!"* The words whispered out of him, a touch of envy in his voice.

Royce turned towards the crowd, his voice echoing to the far reaches of the cavern. "The gods have spoken. The War Helm is fairly won!"

The crowd sat stunned, thousands of faces staring at the dais.

Royce carried the helm to the Old One, leaning down for her approval.

The Old One raised her arms, gnarled hands hovering above the gleaming helm like a benediction. "The will of the gods has prevailed. May the Light lead us to victory."

The crowd remained silent, the weight of judgment hanging in the air.

Blaine stood behind Kath, his hands balled into fists.

Royce walked towards Kath, offering her the helm. "Great change is upon us. Never before has a woman, let alone a barefaced stranger, won the War Helm. Yet the gods have spoken. Your claim is proven in front of all the people. Predicted by the vision of a Taishan and sealed by the test of combat, it is yours by right. Lead us well."

Blaine whispered, "Take it."

Kath hesitated.

Royce smiled, his voice dropping to a whisper. "By tradition, the war leader places the helm upon his...*her* head...in front of all the people."

Still Kath hesitated. "And there are no words to speak? No oath of fealty?"

His smile deepened. "Your deeds speak louder than any words." He proffered the helm toward her, his voice dropping to a whisper. "The Old One had it lined with sheepskin to ensure a better fit."

Blaine glared at the old woman. So the wrinkled witch had foreseen the outcome, yet she'd made Kath risk her life. The painted people were hard to understand and harder to trust.

Royce said, "Will you accept the War Helm?"

Kath reached out with both hands, gently lifting the helm. Turning to face the people, she raised the helm into the air. "By the Light, I swear to value every sword among you." She slowly settled the helm on her head, burnished steel set over long blond hair. "By the Light, I'll find a way to victory!"

Blaine's vision blurred...and for a heartbeat he saw a crown upon her head.

A chime of bells shimmered through the cavern.

"Victory!" The people erupted in a jubilant shout, the single word echoing against the cavern. The yell became a chant, breaking across the dais like a wave.

The crowd converged on Kath, smiling faces full of congratulations, sweeping her away in a rush of words.

Blaine watched, bemused by the sudden change in fortune...but in the pit of his stomach he felt left behind, like flotsam spurned by the tide of fate.

As if Kath read his mind, she turned and fought her way back to his side. "Your sword."

His sword! The words shivered through his mind. *What was a knight without his sword!* He strode to the rock pillar. An awesome sight awaited him. The sword had cleaved halfway through the stone pillar, a prodigious feat even for blue steel, a feat worthy of legends. The sight deepened his hunger for the sapphire blade. Blaine stepped to the pillar and gripped the hilt, a hilt made especially for his hands. Taking a deep breath, he pulled...but the sword did not move. He twisted, he shoved, and he strained with all his might ...but the sword remained locked in stone. *"By Valin!"* Sweat beaded his brow; he refused to abandon his sword to the pillar.

"Let me." Kath stood behind him, holding her gargoyle in the palm of her hand.

A crowd formed around them, watching.

Reluctantly, Blaine stepped aside.

Kath gripped the gargoyle in her left and reached for the sword with her right. With the barest of tugs, she eased the sword from the stone, as easy as butter.

An awed hush rippled through the crowd, their faces full of wonder.

Like a vision from legend, Kath held the sword aloft. Light gleamed along the sapphire steel, the War Helm on her head. For half a heartbeat, Blaine feared he'd lost his sword. But then she turned, and offered the sapphire blade to him, a soft smile on her face. "The sword of a knight."

His hands closed over the hilt, hungry for the great blade.

Cheering, the crowd bore Kath away, carried on the shoulders of lion-faced men.

Blaine watched them go, gripping his sword, overcome by a tidal wave of emotions. She'd won the challenge. She'd regained his sword...and an army of allies. He should have been elated...but in the depths of his heart a shadow of resentment grew. Blaine wondered if she'd leave any glory for him.

43

Duncan

Shadows skittered among the stalactites, too many to count. Duncan watched through hooded eyes, trying to tell if they were real or imagined. Sometimes the shadows took forms, horns, and tails, and ebony eyes staring back at him, full of malice. Duncan rattled his chains, bound too tight to move. Naked, he lay sprawled across the cold stone floor like an offering, nothing for company but shadows. Smells assaulted his senses. The lingering stench of blood and pain mingled with the raw stink of sulphur, the residue of other men's nightmares. Writhing against his chains, Duncan yelled in defiance, needing to hear a human voice. *"My name is Duncan Treloch and I still live!"*

"live...live...live," the words echoed back at him like a mockery.

Five braziers erupted in flame, bathing him in light. Sometimes bright, sometimes dim, the flames moved to a pulse he did not understand. Time had no measure in the cavern, but the waiting proved hard, time enough for nightmares to take hold. Horrors stalked his thoughts, a promise of things to come. Taunted by shadows, his imagination ran wild. Duncan closed his eyes, forcing his mind to recall the rich scent of a cedar tree, the lush green of a summer forest, the hint of a smile on Kath's face. But when he opened his eyes again, he was still chained to the floor, a god-forsaken prisoner bound in this infernal place.

If evil had a smell, the cavern reeked of it. Duncan had never really believed in the gods, but if the Dark God was real then the Lords of Light had to exist, else mankind was doomed to eternal Darkness. Faced with the truth, he prayed like he'd never prayed before.

Footsteps echoed against the cavern walls. He raised his head, surprised to find it wasn't an illusion. A black-robed priest strode toward him, red runes embroidered on the hem of his robe. A soldier walked two paces behind, carrying a small ironbound chest.

Perhaps the waiting was finally over. Duncan's mouth went dry, parched as a desert, suddenly desperate for more time.

The priest stared down at him, a pinched look on his narrow face. "Put it there, just beyond the sacrifice."

Anger blazed in Duncan. "I'm no sacrifice. What do you want?" But the priest ignored him.

The soldier set the ironbound chest on the floor, just beyond Duncan's left hand. Retreating a pace, he darted nervous glances at the ceiling, his right hand on his sword hilt.

The priest knelt, holding the tip of a wineskin to Duncan's lips. "Drink."

Duncan jerked away. "What is it?"

"The only drink you'll get."

He was tempted to refuse but thirst won out. The priest shoved the tip deep, a sudden gush of tepid liquid. Duncan almost gagged, but then he swallowed rather than drown, a flood of watered wine and a hint of something else, something bitter. He struggled to keep pace, a gush of liquid down his throat. The flood came to a sudden stop. The priest yanked the wineskin away, leaving Duncan gasping for breath, a trickle of wine on the side of his mouth.

The priest stood, disdain on his face, and turned and walked away, the soldier staying two paces behind.

Duncan watched them go. "That's it? You're leaving me?" But his only answer was a mocking echo, "*me...me...me?*"

The copper door shuddered closed.

Silence descended like a pall. They'd left him alone to stew on his torture. Curiosity preyed on his mind. His stare kept returning to the ironbound chest, wondering what horrors lurked within. He should have died on the steppes, a warrior's death, anything but this. Something broke inside his mind. Raging against his chains, he strained with all his might, but he was bound tight, held spread-eagle against the cold stone floor. Defeated, his head lulled back, his eyes closed. He felt like a soul trapped in a bottle. Condemned to a nightmare he'd never dreamed, he dared not guess how it would end.

He must have dozed. Perhaps it was the wine, but when he woke, he found he was not alone. A tall man, dressed all in black, stood statue-still, staring down at him, like a crow studying carrion. A nobleman's face, young and fair, with blond shoulder length hair and a neatly trimmed beard, but it was the eyes that captured Duncan's attention. Ice blue and piercing, full of patient malice.

"Who are you?" Duncan's voice sounded hoarse in his ears.

The tall man smiled. "Can't you guess? I'm the Lord of the citadel."

The Mordant! It took all of his control not to shudder. Balling his hands into fists, Duncan forced himself to meet the ice-blue stare.

The Mordant leaned forward. "That's it, meet my stare."

Something slammed into him, something dark and oily, trying to worm its way inside. Clawing at the edge of his mind, it pried at the hinges of Duncan's soul. But Duncan fought back, refusing entry. Like a knight in a beleaguered castle, he locked the doors of his mind and stood his ground, refusing to yield. The assault turned ugly, a black battering ram at the gates, the weight of centuries pounding against him. His walls crumbled under the onslaught. Battered and bruised, Duncan retreated inward, curling into a ball. Darkness followed, a relentless, smothering wave of corruption. Thick and oily, it pressed against him, seeking entrance, searching for any crack or crevice. Just when he thought he would succumb, he found a light blazing deep within his soul. Bright as a torch at midnight, it held the best of him. Radiating confidence, the light echoed his own words back to him, words he'd spoken in the depths of the Mordant's iron mine. *Instead of dying like slaves...live like men. Take a chance and fight.* Buoyed by the light, Duncan fought back, pushing outward, wielding memories like a sword. He thought of the Deep Green, mighty redwoods towering overhead, the soul-soaring beauty of a leaf-green cathedral. He thought of the Treespeaker, and the endless wisdom in her golden eyes. And then he thought of Kath. Suddenly, the darkness retreated, routed by a blazing light.

The Mordant jerked back as if burnt. "So, an honest soul," his face twisted into a sneer, "a soldier of the Light." He circled like a hungry wolf, boot heels clicking on stone, an angry swirl of his black cape. "I cannot touch your soul...not...yet...but your pain will serve. Believe me, your pain will serve."

Duncan struggled against his chains. "Kill me and be done with it."

The Mordant smiled. "Not so hasty." He stopped pacing and stood, staring down at Duncan, as if studying a bug beneath his boot. "Tell me about your eye."

It was always about his eye, a man could never escape his heritage. "It sees."

"A stubborn one, but you'll soon tell me everything." The Mordant cocked his head as if listening to another voice. "I know about the Deep Green."

Duncan remembered the fire, blackened trees and murdered clansmen, a cowardly attack against his homeland, another reason the Mordant had to die.

"I breed abominations, a specialty of the Pit. Yet I've never seen a man with a golden cat eye." The Mordant began to pace a slow circle, his face thoughtful. "With most abominations, the form tends to follow the purpose. A golden cat eye, the eye of a cat." He stopped in mid-stride, a shrewd smile on his face. "You can see in the dark."

It was the most obvious advantage of his heritage. Better to admit one and keep the others hidden. Duncan made his voice reluctant. "Yes."

"A strong advantage for any warrior. You've just saved the lives of your kinswomen. When my army conquers Erdhe, I'll have them spare the young women of your forest. They'll make good breeders. Imagine an army of Taals that can see in the dark, a formidable force for an emperor."

Rage claimed Duncan. "*No!*" He bucked against his chains. "The Light...strike...you...dead!"

"*...dead...dead...dead...*" his words echoed back like a mockery.

The Mordant grinned. "Plenty of fight left in you, that's good. Now tell me why a half breed of the Deep Green comes north?"

Duncan felt the Mordant's stare dissecting his face for answers.

"No need to be stubborn." The Mordant's voice sounded so reasonable. "I know about the crystal dagger."

Chilled to the core, Duncan willed his face to stone, desperate to hide his secret.

"The blue-robed monks sent a party of champions chasing after me. Sent on a fool's errand, sent to their deaths, but that never bothers the monks, a gaggle of old men hiding safe behind their mage-stone walls." The Mordant stopped pacing and stared down at him. "Are you one of their champions?"

Afraid to give anything away, Duncan kept silent, watching the Mordant through hooded eyes. Breathing deep, he tasted the air. Beneath the lingering stench of blood and pain, he caught the Mordant's scent, so elusive it was hard to read, but then he understood. The Mordant reeked of the subtle stink of half-truths. "You know nothing."

Anger sparked in the Mordant's ice-blue eyes. "Oppose me at your peril." He turned, a swirl of black, and strode to the ironbound chest. Kneeling beside it, he trailed a hand across the top, almost a lover's caress.

Sickened, Duncan tried to look away but he couldn't.

The Mordant turned toward Duncan, his face congenial once more. "Perhaps you've wondered at your fate?"

A shiver of dread ran down Duncan's back.

Pale hands flicked open the latches of the chest. The Mordant reached inside and withdrew a slender dagger cast in silver, runes etched along the blade. "There's a hundred more just like this one." Long and slender like a silver thorn, it gleamed wicked keen in the flickering light. "A thousand years is not nearly long enough, but it's given me time to master many things. Time enough to learn how to sculpt flesh and twist souls, but first, one must master the way of blood and sinew and bone, the things that bind a man to the mortal coil." He lifted the dagger up to the light. "These knives were crafted to my own design. They'll make a man suffer unspeakable pain without dying, teetering on the very brink of hell." The Mordant smiled. "You'll beg for death long before I'm done."

Sweat erupted from Duncan's skin, betraying a rush of fear. He strained against his bonds, desperate to escape, but his voice was full of bravado. "I'll tell you nothing."

"You'll tell me everything." The Mordant eased to the floor. Stretching out his long legs, he lay beside Duncan, his head cocked at an angle, his right hand toying with the silver dagger...close enough to be a lover.

Repulsed, Duncan flinched away, but the chains held him fast.

The Mordant smiled. "Torture is a very intimate act."

Duncan's stomach roiled. He stared at the Mordant, his mouth desert dry.

The dagger point traced a trail down his chest, the metal as cold as sin. His skin seemed to shrink away, desperate to retreat. The dagger paused at his manhood. Duncan stared at the knife-edge, taking short shallow breaths, afraid to move.

"Aren't you going to plead for your manhood?"

Duncan clamped his mouth shut, a scream growing in the pit of his stomach.

"Torture is a rare art. It takes a master to evoke pain without killing." The Mordant chuckled, moving the knife-edge back up toward Duncan's throat. "So many points of pain, it took me a lifetime to find them all, to perfect the craft. Take this point for example," the dagger moved along his left arm, "so easy to slip the dagger between muscle and bone."

Pain stabbed into his left arm. The Mordant pressed down, forcing the point all the way through. The tip emerged on the other side, skewering his arm with silver. Duncan bit his lip, stifling a groan.

"No need to be stoic. I'll enjoy your screams."

Duncan stared at his tormentor, seeing him with fresh eyes. The Mordant was a monster. Little wonder the monks sought to destroy him. "Just kill me and be done with it."

"Oh there will be no killing, but the pain will be exquisite." The Mordant reached for another dagger. "You see, the Dark God requires an offering before granting a boon. But one of the many advantages of serving Darkness is that the sacrifice need not be my own." The Mordant flashed a malicious smile. "Your pain will provide a bridge to the Dark Lord, a continual feast of agony, the perfect offering. A single drop of your blood in a scrying bowl and I'll be able to reach the Dark Lord no matter how far I travel. As long as you live, I'll have my link to the Dark God...and all his power." The dagger traced a line along Duncan's left forearm, pausing at a point near his wrist. "Your pain is my offering."

Silver stabbed into his wrist, a blaze of agony. Duncan turned his head away, biting his lip, but the scream broke free.

"That's it, embrace the pain. Let the suffering roll out of you."

"I won't...serve you."

The Mordant chuckled. "You already do." He held a glass vial to Duncan's wrist, catching drops of blood. When the vial was full, he reached for another dagger. "Now tell me, who wields the crystal dagger?"

"I don't know."

A dagger plunged into his side. Duncan shrieked in pain.

"Some spots hurt more than others. I can be merciful in my choices." The Mordant smiled, his voice a whisper. "Beg me to be merciful." A dagger pricked his left thigh. "But first I need know about the wielder of the crystal dagger."

"I don't know!"

"I think you do."

The dagger plunged deep. So painful, Duncan nearly swooned.

"Tell me." The Mordant whispered in his ear like a lover.

Duncan flinched away. Swallowing his pain, he struggled to think. A quick death was his only hope. He needed to goad the Mordant to a killing rage. Turning towards his tormentor, he breathed deep, tasting the air for weakness, searching for a scent masked by his own fear. So much fear, so much pain, the scents were tangled, too muddled to read, yet he found his answer in the Mordant's cocky smile. Duncan forced himself to laugh, a low chuckle. "You didn't expect me."

"What?" The Mordant paused, another dagger in his hand.

"For all your vaunted powers, you didn't see a cat-eyed man sneaking into the north."

"But I have you now."

"Yes, but what else have you missed? You're weaker than you think." He forced contempt into his voice, striving to hide his own fear. "A thousand years of evil and you're still playing with knives?"

The Mordant reared up like an angry cobra. "Mock me at your peril."

"Or what, you'll kill me?"

The Mordant stood, his face a swirl of anger. "Mortal, you've no idea whom you deal with." He threw his head back and shouted a command, his hands reaching toward the vaulted ceiling. "*Sabilanth Tarant Har!*"

A clap of thunder shook the cavern. Darkness boiled overhead, a swirling cauldron of shadows.

"*Imlanth Tahra!*"

Duncan stared wide-eyed, trying to disbelieve his eyes.

Shadows coalesced, thickening to pure black. A swirling storm cloud descended from the stalactites like a suffocating hand.

The Mordant dropped to the stone floor, lying next to Duncan.

Above, the shadows kept coming, a roiling cloud pressing down, a mere hand's width above the Mordant's head.

Duncan tried to shrink into the cold stone floor. Drenched in sweat, he stank of his own fear. A primal terror gripped him, the age-old fear of the Dark. Wide-eyed, he turned his head, taking short sharp breaths, afraid the evil would get inside him.

"Witness the power of Darkness." The Mordant's voice dripped with malice. He reached upward, extending a silver blade into the dark cloud. Twirling the blade, he drew it down. "Now you'll pay." A thread of inky darkness bound the blade to the hovering cloud like a tentacle of evil. "Now you'll scream."

The blade plunged into Duncan's side, a flaming agony. A scream roared out of him. He convulsed against his bonds, skewered by agony.

"Yes, the Darkness burns like acid in your blood." The Mordant raised another knife, gathering another thread of shadow. "Now tell me about the crystal dagger."

"*I don't know!*" Pain exploded in his shoulder. He screamed a babble of words. Chained to the floor, his mind fled, his world dissolving into a nightmare of screams.

44

Katherine

Kath squinted against the blinding sun. After so long in the caves, the dazzling brightness hurt yet she yearned to feel warm sunlight on her face. She followed Bear through the narrow crevice, squeezing past a thorny bush to stand on a rocky outcrop. A cold wind beat against her face but it was the view that took her breath away. "So these are the Ghost Hills."

Bear nodded, a man of little words.

As a child, Kath had heard tales of the Ghost Hills, how the spirits of slain warriors were forever imprisoned in stone, waiting to be summoned for a final battle. Intrigued, she'd pestered the knights for details but none had ever seen the hills. Most considered them nothing more than a minstrel's fable, but no minstrel's ballad had ever captured the wild strangeness spread before her. Staring at the land, she drank in the sights, as if imbibing pure myth.

Smooth and sculptured, the wind-hewed hills took fantastic shapes. Giant beehives of yellowish-orange rock dominated the land, like the dream of a drunken god obsessed with honey mead. Amongst the beehives sat massive cones and twisted towers, each more astonishing than the last. Majestic curves and towering beehives carved in sun-burnt colors, a stunning display of ocher, oranges, and reds. Jumbled together the sculpted hills formed an ancient and mystical landscape. Strangely spiritual, the hills evoked a sense of wonder...and peril, as if the gods drew near. Kath shivered, feeling a sense of awe.

Bear broke the spell. "This way."

Halfway up the side of a massive beehive, they followed a narrow track, little more than a goat path. Bear led the way, his hand on his sword, with Boar following close behind Kath. The two men had gained great status by her victory, becoming sworn bodyguards of the new War Lord. Vigilant and stubborn, they took their oaths seriously, staying close by her side, a pair of brooding shadows bristling with weapons.

The track spiraled upward, around the steep-sided beehive. Hungry for fresh air, Kath breathed deep, savoring the clean scent of sage. After winning the War Helm she'd met with the council of leaders. For three days and three nights she'd listened to arguments and petitions, mired in the politics of competing factions. The lions wanted war while the boars counseled caution and the eagles acted like vultures, waiting to pick apart any plan. In the end, they'd all turned to her, expecting a decision, but Kath sensed it was another test, another trap. Too many faces were filled with hostility, waiting for her to fail. So she'd delayed, saying she needed a chance to plan, she needed fresh air to think and the council demurred to her wishes. Having gained a short reprieve, she escaped to the outdoors. She took Bear and Boar with her because they seemed loyal and quietly competent and she liked them. Solid soldiers, dependable as steel, they served as guides and bodyguards, but more importantly, they gave her answers that weren't mired in politics. "Tell me again about the warriors of the painted people."

Bear answered as he picked his way up the narrow path, his voice deep and gruff. "The men number thirty-six hundred at last count. About half are armed with good quality swords and axes, taken from our enemies' hands. Steel is revered, handed down from one generation to the next, but there is never enough. Swords become brittle with age or are ruined in battle, so we must always seek more." He shrugged. "The rest of the men carry slings and daggers, fighting with whatever they can."

"What about the women? I've seen armed women in the caves."

"The last defense. Women protect the hills and the caves, rarely venturing into the steppes." He shrugged. "But for you, they might fight. Women warriors would add another six hundred to the total, mostly armed with long knives and slings."

Too few and too poorly armed, she'd gained a ragtag army, yet somehow the gods expected her to defeat the Mordant. It seemed a hopeless task. "What about archers?" Her mind skittered to Duncan but she forced that worry away.

Bear gestured to the barren hills. "Wood is dearer than steel. Without trees we can't make bows or even arrows." He shook his head, a tangled mass of shaggy blond hair. "Slings are much better, plenty of stones around. Every child grows up wielding one. Good enough for killing scrag cats and deterring hungry wolves. Good enough to keep the sheep safe."

She'd never considered the sling as a serious weapon. Stones against steel, the gods must be laughing, but she couldn't afford to scoff at any weapon. "Do you carry a sling?"

"Always."

"Show me."

He came to an abrupt halt. Kath almost ran into him. She watched as he removed a four-foot length of braided rope from his belt-pouch. The rope had a loop at one end and a large knot at the other, with a leather cradle in the center.

"Pick a target."

The hills were truly barren; nothing but sculptured rock, thorny brush, clumps of sage...and sheep. Now that she looked, there were sheep everywhere, white and shaggy with small curved horns, scrambling up sheer cliffs, hunting for morsels of scrub. "How many sheep are there?"

Bear shrugged. "Too many to count. It's the children's task to keep the predators away so the sheep flourish. Without sheep we could not survive."

Kath nodded, pulling her borrowed sheepskin close against the bitter cold, grateful for the added warmth.

Bear stared at her, the sling hanging from his right hand. "A target?"

"But I don't know its range."

He pointed up the path. "See that small head-sized stone perched on the edge?"

Kath judged it to be about a hundred yards away, half the range of a longbow. "It will do."

Bear stepped a few paces away. Grasping both ends of the sling, he fitted the pouch with a small stone. Standing at an angle to the target, he whirled the sling overhead, putting his entire body into the motion. It happened faster than Kath expected. A single lightning-fast revolution and he released one end of the sling. A loud crack echoed through the hills. The head-sized stone toppled backwards, clattering down the side of the beehive. It took forever to fall.

Bear turned and stared at her, his face impassive.

"Impressive, but it won't stop a man in armor."

"It might. One stone in the head will kill a sheep, a scrag cat...or a soldier. It's one of the reasons the Mordant's men never follow us into the hills. From the cliffs, a rain of sling-stones is deadly."

"Will any stone work?"

"Smooth pebbles fly the farthest." He gave her one from his pouch.

She weighed it in her hand. "There's something carved on this one."

Bear cracked a smile. "A message for the enemy."

She stared at the symbol but it meant nothing to her. "What does it say?"

Laughter tugged at the side of his mouth. "In polite words, *ouch*."

She laughed, suspecting it meant something else entirely. Tucking the stone in her belt-pouch for luck, she gestured for Bear to keep walking, glad she'd asked for the demonstration. The sling had its advantages, a simple but effective weapon...very much like the painted people. But it still didn't solve the problem of numbers.

The trail steepened to a climb. Single file, they spiraled up the great stone beehive, scrambling over rugged terrain. Two thirds of the way up, Bear stopped and turned, his eyes glittering. "Listen."

At first she heard nothing, but then the wind picked up. A frigid blast from the north howled through the sculpted rock. An eerie wailing keened through the hills, like the spirits of slain warriors roused to a wordless fury. Kath shivered, making the hand sign against evil. The Ghost Hills were aptly named, worthy of a bard's ballad.

They climbed to the beehive's leeward side, protected from the worst of the wind. Bear led them to a smooth flat perch overlooking a deep gorge. The view was amazing. Every direction revealed a jumble of wind-sculpted rock, each formation more beautiful than the last.

"Will this serve?"

She'd asked for a high place with a good view, a place where she could sit and think. "Better than I could have imagined."

Bear gave her a rare smile while Boar swept his sheepskin cloak from his shoulders, spreading it across the rocky ledge with a gallant flourish. The unexpected chivalry ambushed Kath, her face flaming bright red. Flustered, she stole a glance at the two men but they turned away, their faces stony and their fists clenched...as if they feared she might refuse. Such big, rough men, their faces etched with fierce tattoos, yet they'd shown her more courtesy than most knights in her father's service. Their gallantry could not be ignored. She settled on the sheepskin, her words heartfelt. "Thank you."

Bear grinned and Boar flushed beet-red. They set a water skin and a small packet of dried meat on the ledge. "In case you get hungry."

Kath hadn't thought about bringing food. She hadn't considered how long it might take.

Bear gestured back down the path. "We'll keep watch. No one will disturb you."

Boar nodded. "May the gods grant you a true vision." And then they were gone, retreating down the path, far enough away to be unobtrusive but close enough to keep watch.

May the gods grant you a true vision. The words rang in her mind like a bell. Perhaps Boar had the truth of it. She needed a vision, a solution to an impossible problem. If the gods cared about Erdhe it was past time they showed their hand. Her fingers wove through the sheepskin, absently tugging on soft tufts. *Or perhaps the gods already had.* Surely the War Helm was a gift from the gods, an unforeseen boon, but what was she supposed to do with it? She'd gained a ragtag army, proud and fierce, but their numbers were too few. In the north, numbers always held sway. The god-cursed steppes negated the elements of surprise and strategy. Any battle always came down to the harsh reality of numbers, crush or be crushed. Against the hordes of the Mordant, the painted people would be slaughtered to a man...and she couldn't let that happen, she couldn't betray their trust. The gods had set her an impossible task.

Kath closed her eyes, and stared inward. Visions from the Womb of the World filled her mind. Once more she saw the Mordant's army, a vast horde marching south, an endless sea of enemies stretching to the horizon. How could the Octagon hope to hold against so many? Who would come to their aid? She could lead her small army south and attack from the rear, but the problem of the steppes remained. Her army would be crushed, swatted like an annoying flea, their deaths making no difference to the Octagon's fate. The taste of ashes filled her mouth. Why had the gods shown her such a vile vision if there was nothing she could do about it?

And then there was Duncan. With every passing day, a fear grew in her heart. She'd badgered the scouts but none had seen any sign of the leather-clad archer. He must have been captured...*or worse.* Her mind shied away from the thought. In depths of her heart, she believed he still lived, waiting for her to come...but how?

Shivering, she took a deep breath, trying to quell her rising panic. Sitting cross-legged, her chin in her hands, she huddled under her sheepskin cloak, seeking refuge in the wild beauty of the wind-swept hills. Sunlight played across the sculpted stone, accentuating the giant beehives. She wondered how long it had taken the wind to shape the stone. Surely the gods took the long view.

The thought spurred something in her mind. *The gods take the long view.* Perhaps the solution lay in the past. The gods had sent the Taishan of the mountain lions to Castlegard more than two years ago, before she'd even found the crystal dagger. Perhaps it was all connected. She'd needed to journey south before she could come north. But what had she learned? She'd gained the crystal dagger and learned to master her gargoyle; surely both were needed in the north. And then there was the monastery. Master Rizel had said she'd find help in unexpected places. His words had surely come to pass. She'd found an army hiding in the Ghost Hills...but a ragtag army was not enough. What else did she have? *A Beastmaster always fights alongside the Star Knights.* Danya was a newly awakened Beastmaster, full of potent magic, clearly an important part of the puzzle. The wolf-girl had already saved their lives once, but the trick with the horses would not be repeated. There must be something else Danya could do, something subtle...something that would make a great difference.

Thunder rumbled on the horizon, a flash of lightning cracking the distant sky.

The lightning served as a goad to her thoughts. There had to be something else, something Master Rizel had said. She pictured the blue-robed master in the garden of contemplation; warm sunlight shining through the glass ceiling, the lush smell of green...and then the words came back to her. *You must understand the true nature of evil in order to be victorious.* Perhaps she was meant to turn the enemy's tactics back against him. But how did the Mordant wage war? There hadn't been any major battles fought in her lifetime, only a series of tricks and traps. That got her thinking. They'd followed the Mordant north, but what had they learned from their prey? In Wyeth they'd been chased by frightened peasants and bloodthirsty mercenaries...all because of Zith's tattooed hand. In the Deep Green they'd endured suspicion and hatred because of the burnt forest. And in Cragnoth Keep they'd discovered a bitter betrayal. They followed a trail of evil, a series of tricks and traps...but what was the underlying principle? And then she saw it, as clear as a lighting flash. *First he deceives, then he divides, and then he conquers.* She shivered with understanding, so simple yet so effective.

Small stones tumbled down the beehive. Alarmed, Kath reached for her sword...but it was only a sheep, scrambling along the beehive's crest. So many sheep, if only the painted people were half as numerous.

Kath stretched, staring up at the sky. She watched the distant storm dissolve to nothing, leaving a clear horizon. The sun sank toward the west, a great orb of red. Snuggled beneath her sheepskin, Kath watched the landscape change, the stone beehives deepening from burnt orange to a deep crimson. A bloody sunset, an ominous sky painting the land red, the steppes would run with blood if she didn't find a solution.

Pieces of the puzzle tumbled through her mind, but they made no sense. Try as she might, she couldn't find an underlying pattern. She knew the Mordant's army had already marched south, the citadel's great gates thrown open, disgorging a horde of soldiers. But had the Mordant marched with them, or had he stayed in the citadel...or had he gone elsewhere? *First deceive and then divide.*

Like a bolt of lightning it hit her. The Mordant had divided his forces, emptying the citadel. Her best opportunity lay in the north...but she still did not have the numbers, not enough to take a fortress...and she had no time for a siege.

The sun sank toward the horizon in a blaze of reds and golds. Shadows cast by the beehives undulated across the land like great sea serpents, creating a compelling illusion, simple but deceptive. And then she saw it, an elegant solution. She needed a deceit of swords, a way to make the rule of numbers work in her favor. Kath studied the hills, seeing everything they held. A smile lit her face, a plan inspired by the gods. The plan would require every element from her past, her gargoyle, the crystal dagger, the magic of a Beastmaster, a knight with a blue steel sword, and a small army of fierce warriors. Together they'd deceive, they'd divide, and then they'd conquer, dealing the Darkness a crippling blow.

45

The Knight Marshal

Drums thundered in the dead of night. The marshal bolted awake. Boom...boom, boom, the sound shuddered through the walls, loud enough to wake the dead. His heartbeat quickened, answering the drums...so the enemy had finally come. Dressing with haste, he strapped his great sword to his back and grabbed his shield.

The marshal took the steps two at a time, climbing to the rampart. A cold wind buffeted his face, tugging at his maroon cloak. Beneath the night sky, unmuffled by stone, the drums sounded twice as ominous. Clouds hid the moon, too little light to see by, yet he was drawn to the battlement, staring down into the inky darkness. Knights lined the wall, summoned by the drums, straining for the first glimpse of the enemy.

Despite the dark, Lothar found him, a gruff voice at his shoulder. "How many?"

The marshal shook his head. "Too dark to tell. But judging from the sound, they've brought a battalion of drummers."

Lothar growled, "Leave it to the Mordant to come calling in the dead of night, ruining a man's sleep."

The marshal grinned, appreciating his friend's levity, yet there was truth beneath his words. "I'm sure it was planned. The drums will fray nerves before the battle ever begins." His gaze was drawn to the other men crowding the battlement. "We should double the night watch and get the others to rest. I doubt they'll attack before first light."

Lothar nodded. "I'll see to the watch."

The marshal roamed the wall, speaking words of courage to those on duty while urging the others to return to their pallets. The young ones were too riled to leave but the veterans nodded, knowing the value of sleep. Five times he traversed the wall and all the while the drums boomed, a deep, spellbinding throb, shouting the promise of war.

His gaze was drawn to the north. Curiosity warred with dread, fueling a need to see their numbers. Hours passed and the weight of sleep dragged at him, but he could not leave the wall. He found a niche shielded from the wind and sat wrapped in his maroon cloak. Perhaps he dozed; a veteran knight could sleep anywhere.

Dawn broke across a cloud-shrouded sky, red as blood. The marshal woke and stared in shock, staggered by the truth. Morning's first light revealed the enemy's numbers, too many to count.

Lothar stood at his shoulder, *"By the gods!"*

The enemy swarmed the grasslands like a kicked anthill.

Lothar shook his head. "Where in the nine hells did he get them all?"

The marshal agreed, but the words stuck in his throat. In his wildest nightmare he'd never imagined the north held such an army.

Lothar leaned on the battlement, caressing the mitered stone like a grateful lover. "Thank Valin for strong walls, else we'd be overrun in less than a day."

"Mind your tongue!"

Lothar bristled. "You're thinking the same."

The marshal could not disagree. Instead, he stared at the enemy, searching for a weakness in their ranks. Their numbers filled the steppes, an ugly roil of black armor, a grim bristle of spears and battle banners. And then he saw it. *"No siege engines!"* Disbelief warred with hope. He searched their ranks for trebuchets and siege towers but found none.

Lothar grinned, "Trees are scarce in the north."

"True enough...but to hurl an army against fortified walls without siege engines is pure folly." A deep dread settled in his stomach. "And the Mordant is never a fool."

Lothar stirred beside him, squinting into the north. "And there's not much cavalry either. He brings an army south without siege engines and cavalry?" Lothar shook his head. "An odd way to wage war."

A terrible foreboding gripped the marshal. "It's as if he's only brought half his forces."

Lothar shuddered. *"This* is *half?"*

The marshal had no answer. He stared at the horde, silently giving thanks for the stout walls of Raven Pass.

Trumpets blared along the wall, competing with the drums. Knights, archers, and soldiers answered the call. A surge of maroon cloaks took up their positions. Most gaped at the horde, shocked by the numbers. One man retched and another stank of urine. The marshal strode among them, offering words of courage, working to bolster morale.

The king appeared on the battlement, a bold gleam of gold. The men raised a mighty cheer, swords drumming against shields. Girded for war, King Ursus wore a crowned helm and a burnished breastplate, an octagonal shield on his left arm. His great blue sword loomed over his right shoulder, the perfect image of a warrior king. Baldwin carried the king's battle standard, a maroon pennant emblazoned with a gold crown.

The marshal moved to join his liege.

Standing atop the drum tower, the king surveyed the enemy. "So the Mordant has finally come."

The marshal nodded. "Their numbers are daunting but there's no sign of siege engines or cavalry."

The king scowled. "Another trick. What's the devil up to?"

But the marshal had no answer.

As if in reply, the drumbeat changed to a faster tempo. The enemy swarmed forward, marching toward the walls. Details became clear. Officers in plumed helms strode the front lines, pentacles inscribed on their breastplates. Bearded faces howled a war cry. Rows of spears bristled in a deadly thicket. Swords pounded against black shields, keeping time to the drums. The thin strip of open grassland shrank to fifty yards, a narrow killing field.

"Sound the alert." The trumpets obeyed, a trill of notes.

From the height of the second wall, the marshal watched as knights on the first wall readied for battle. Dubbed Shieldbreaker by the men, the thirty-foot outer wall suddenly seemed a meager barrier against the surging horde.

A shout rose from the enemy. Spears launched into the morning sky. So many, they rose in a thick arc, a wave of darkness blocking the sun. Uttering an unearthly wail, ten thousand spears screamed a shrill whistle as they fell. "*Raise shields!*" Shields snapped skyward all along the first wall, a maroon bulwark raised in defense. The timing was perfect. Spearheads thudded into thick oak. A few men screamed but most roared their defiance.

"Give them our answer." The king spoke and the trumpets sounded.

Archers on the first wall raised their bows, releasing a rain of arrows.

Trebuchets on the second wall creaked and groaned, hurling massive boulders into the sky. As if lobbed by giant hands, the boulders tumbled upward, rising over the first wall and sailing out over the horde. An impossible weight of stone, the marshal watched them fall, clouds of blood and gore marking each strike.

Beside him, a squire yelled. "Twenty men with one stone!"

It seemed a mighty feat, yet it was like dropping a pebble in the ocean. The enemy ranks closed and the bloody holes disappeared.

Archers loosed another volley. A wave of spears answered. The sun climbed the sky and still the rain of missiles fell. Raised shields caught most of the spears but there were always a few shrieks of pain. Healers raced along the wall, removing the dead and the dying, a slow winnowing of the maroon.

Once more the drums changed their beat.

The marshal tensed, knowing what was to come.

Archers appeared in the enemy's front lines. Black fletched arrows soared skyward. A wave of darkness sailed over the first wall, reaching for the second.

The marshal stood his ground, watching the deadly arc. "Wait for it!" The first wave was always the hardest. He summoned his courage, refusing to flinch. The faint whistle grew louder, the sound of death's herald.

"*Shields!*" He screamed the command. Braced for impact, he lifted his oaken shield. Beside him, the king leaped forward, raising his own shield over a fear-frozen squire. "*Sire!*" He yelled a warning but death was upon them. A hail of steel tipped arrows plummeted down. Feathered shafts thudded around him, biting deep. Two struck the marshal's shield, a third just missing his foot. Someone screamed a howl of pain. A few frantic heartbeats later, the rain of arrows stopped.

Lowering his shield, the marshal sprang towards the king. Miraculously, the king and squire stood unscathed, but others were not so lucky. All along the wall, men screamed while others lay dead, felled where they stood. "Sire, you dare not take such risks."

The king replied with a frosty glare. "Young Emmett here has learned a lesson." The king gave the squire a conspirator's smile. "Next time, you'll keep your shield raised."

Hero-worship beamed from the lad's face. "Yes, Sire."

"Now get to the armory and tell Steward Malt we'll be needing more arrows."

The lad sped away, the north wind tugging at his gray cloak.

A faint whistle warned of another assault.

"*Shields!*" The marshal screamed the order, but this time he stayed close to his king. Arrows thumped into oaken shields while others clattered harmless against stone walls. But some found their mark. Beside him, a squire screamed in pain, an arrow piercing his shoulder.

The marshal bellowed, "Get him to the healers!" Two soldiers leaped to obey. Further down the wall, someone shrieked in pain.

"Ware the arrows!"

The marshal raised his shield. Between each wave, the Octagon replied in kind. Trebuchets groaned with effort. Boulders and arrows hurled upward, answered by arrows and spears. The deadly war of attrition lasted for the better part of the day. The marshal figured they killed more than they lost, but the size of the horde remained staggering.

Late in the afternoon, the enemy changed tactics.

Their drums beat a wild rhythm as their front lines parted with a roar. Twenty men emerged, carrying a massive battering ram.

"On the ram!" The king shouted the order and the trumpets gave a complicated trill.

A flight of arrows launched towards the ram like a swarm of angry hornets.

A few of the enemy staggered and fell, but the others ran on, bearing the ram toward the outer gate.

Prince Ulrich had the honor of holding the outer wall. His men swarmed the barbican above the iron-shod gate, a gleam of silver surcoats and maroon shields.

Another flight of arrows and still the ram came.

"Get them." The marshal's gaze followed each flight, willing the arrows to strike true. The gods must have heard. Feathered shafts pricked the men like quills of a porcupine. Skewered, they dropped their burden, falling twenty yards short of the gate.

A cheer rang from the walls, but the victory was short lived.

Another twenty men emerged from the horde. Holding shields overhead, they raced for the ram. Taking up the fallen burden, they lumbered toward the gate. A thicket of arrows flew from both sides, yet the ram drew near.

Boom! Like a massive fist, the ram came calling. But the maroon cloaked defenders knew their craft. Men scurried across the barbican dousing the attackers with oil. Fire arrows followed. Flames roared to life just beyond the gate. Men screamed and flailed, black smoke belching into the sky. Capering like fire demons, they fled from the gate, abandoning the ram.

Cheers erupted from both walls, but the king and the marshal remained silent.

Three times the enemy rammed the gate and three times they failed.

The king watched from the second wall, the marshal by his side. "Ulrich and his men fought well this day." He spoke loud enough for those around him to hear. The marshal knew the king's praise would be repeated till it reached the prince's ear.

The sun sank toward the horizon, calling an end to the bloody day. The drums pounded and the enemy withdrew, leaving their dead littered across the trampled grass like flotsam on the shores of hell. The horde retreated beyond reach of the trebuchets. Massive boulders studded the trampled grassland, blood spatters giving proof to their kills. A grim silence drenched the steppes, a sodden lull before the next storm.

Struck by weariness, the marshal leaned against the rampart plucking arrows from his shield. "The fighting seems done for the day. Shall we retire, my lord?"

"Not yet."

Beyond the killing ground, tents mushroomed across the steppes, too many to count. Twilight faded and the sky deepened to purple. The marshal kept vigil with the king. "Do you see, Osbourne?"

And then the marshal understood. Tents sprawled below but there were few campfires. "Just as you foretold, they have no wood for campfires."

The king nodded. "The Mordant uses winter as a goad."

"Yet we won the day." The words sounded hollow to his own ears. The first day in any war was always a test, two armies trading blows, gauging the strength of the other.

The king seemed to hear his thoughts. "They held back."

Truth rode the king's words, truth and a hint of doom. The marshal put steel in his voice. "Arrows and spears will never win the wall."

The king gave him a piercing stare. "The Mordant does not ride to war with numbers alone." The king gazed down upon the steppes. "We have not yet seen their worst."

A cold wind gusted out of the north like an evil portent, tugging on their maroon cloaks.

"Come," the king turned away from the rampart, "I've seen enough for one day."

He followed his king to the stairs. "And what do you expect on the morrow."

"I cannot say." The king flashed him a grim look. "But if the gods owe you any favors, pray for snow. Winter's likely to be our only ally."

46

Katherine

They did not believe her. It was written upon their faces. Kath balled her hands into fists, wondering what it would take to win their trust. Thirty-six council leaders sat cross-legged on the floor of the small oval cavern, glow crystals casting shadows against the rough rock walls. Tattooed faces stared back at her. Eagle, bear, boar, fox, owl, mountain lion, a pantheon of predators listened to her plan for war. The Ancestor sat on the far side of the cavern, a mass of wrinkles peering from a mound of sheepskins. The Old One's face proved hard to read but it was the others Kath needed to convince. Her stare circled the chamber, willing the council to believe. "It's a rare chance to strike a dire blow at the Mordant. But the opportunity is fleeting. Are you with me?"

Her words collided with dead silence.

The quiet proved unsettling. Half the council stared at her with faces grim as stone, while the other half sneered in open disbelief.

Hands on hips, she met their stares, a brazen show of confidence. She wore the War Helm, a not-so-subtle reminder of her status, but even that did not seem to help.

An eagle-faced warrior broke the silence. "You call *that* a *plan*?" He snorted, his face full of loathing. "Sounds more like the ravings of a drunken bard."

A storm of protests followed. "You'll get us all killed."

"It will never work."

"This is what comes from letting a woman wear the War Helm."

"Never trust a barefaced stranger."

Kath shouted over their insults, desperate to make them believe. "Don't you see? You dare not fight a conventional war. You're out-numbered; you're out-trained; you're under-armed. In a straight attack, you'll lose every time." Hostile faces glared at her, insulted by the truth, yet it needed to be said. Taking a deep breath, Kath plunged on. "Deception, guile, and daring, these are your best weapons! This plan gives you, gives *us*, the best chance to strike at the Mordant."

A fox-faced man leaned forward, a sneer riding his face. "Perhaps you seek your missing archer. Risking us all in a bid to get him back?"

Duncan. For half a heartbeat, Kath swayed on her feet. *Where was he? Did he still live?* Her nightmares were getting worse. Desperate to see him again, she longed to prove he still lived, but this was about more than one man. She took a steadying breath, her voice as hard as stone. "We fight to defeat the Mordant, to strike a blow at the Dark."

The fox leader scowled. "So you say, but words are cheap."

The Old One intervened. "A Taishan of the painted people foresaw her coming. She bears the crystal dagger and sees the world differently. Her words are worth considering."

A few of the leaders nodded, the Old One's words held sway.

Kath seized the advantage, pressing her argument. "Your scouts report a great war host marched south. The Mordant empties the north in a bid to conquer Erdhe. This is our chance to strike at the citadel, to cripple the Dark. The odds will never be better."

"But the steppes are cruel in winter."

Kath nodded. "The Mordant chooses the time for battle. *Now* is the time to strike no matter the weather."

Royce, the lion-faced leader with a mane of auburn hair, nodded encouragement. "Tell us more."

She gave him a grateful smile. "Timing is critical. We attack the citadel at the dark of the moon. Danya's deception will draw their forces to the south gate, while we attack the north gate. We strike hard and fast under the cloak of confusion."

The fox-faced leader barked a rude laugh. "You'll never take the gates. And when morning comes, the truth of your deception will be revealed, fading away with the dawn light." His stare circled the chamber. "We'll all die, paying for *her* folly."

Kath stood her ground, drilling him with her stare. "It's not a folly. I'll open the gates myself."

"*You!*" His voice roared with ridicule. "By yourself? Now that makes all the difference. This slip of a girl will open the gates of the citadel? Might as well claim she can open the gates of *hell!*"

More than a few smirked in agreement.

So they didn't believe her. Words were never enough. They needed proof, they needed a miracle. "Watch and I'll prove it." Reaching beneath her leather jerkin, she gripped her gargoyle. Nodding to the Ancestor, she strode to the wall and put her back to the rough rock. For half a heartbeat, she hesitated. Walls were easy but a mountain of stone was something else, something to fear. "Watch and believe." Taking a deep breath, she called the magic, and stepped back into the rock wall.

Stone embraced her. Strong and permanent, the mountain called to her. Whispering promises of forever, the stone invited her to become one with the ancient rock, locked in an eternal embrace. Kath resisted the call, thinking of sunlight and green leaves and Duncan. *Duncan!* Her concentration faltered. Gripping her gargoyle, she stilled her mind and stepped forward, praying she hadn't lost her bearings.

Sound and light returned in a rush. Kath stepped back into the cavern.

A chorus of gasps echoed the chamber.

A few made the hand sign against evil.

She gave the council a small smile. "Stone walls will not stop me."

Nods of agreement met her words. Kath did a quick count. She'd gained half their number. But half was not enough. Kath met the stares of the doubters and filled her voice with confidence. "The plan is bold and daring, and decidedly different, I'll grant you that, but it *will* work." She gripped the hilt of the crystal dagger. "My friends and I make better allies than you know."

The Old One chuckled, dark eyes twinkling in a map of wrinkles. Few besides Kath seemed to notice.

Brant, the leader of the boars, shook his head, his face stubborn. "But even if we gain the citadel, we're still out-numbered. We'll never hold it."

She'd thought of that. "The citadel teems with slaves and servants. Given a chance, won't they rise against their captors?"

The boar leader looked troubled. "They might, and then again they might not. Slavery is bred into their bones. Few ever escape to gain the tattoos of free people."

Royce intervened. "They might rise, if they knew we were coming."

The fox-faced man barked a laugh. "What? Now we're sending heralds. So much for surprise."

Kath paced the chamber, her mind chewing the problem. Frustrated, she pushed her hands deep into her pockets, and found the answer lurking at the bottom. "There might be a way." She held the small pebble aloft, the sling stone given to her by Bear. "We could send them a message carried by ravens." She tossed the stone to the fox-faced man.

He glared at the markings carved on the pebble. "*Ouch!* That's your message?"

A few council leaders chuckled, while others looked annoyed.

"No. We'll send a simple message writ in the symbols of slaves. Something cryptic like fight at the dark moon."

Brant nodded, his face thoughtful. "In the right hands, such a message might lend courage to a few."

"Or lead to betrayal."

Kath ignored the fox and seized the boar's words. "A few can become many. Even a small rebellion will bring confusion to the enemy."

Royce nodded. "It might work." Others echoed his agreement.

Kath figured she'd won two-thirds of the council. She began to hope they'd agree.

An owl-faced woman blinked up at her. "But your plan requires stealth and surprise. How will you sneak an army through the gargoyle gates?"

The question struck like an ambushing dagger. Kath struggled to keep her face still. It was the one problem she hadn't solved. The gargoyle gates scared her. Even Zith described them as an abomination. She forced herself to meet the owl woman's stare. "I need to see them before I'll know how to defeat them."

"*Defeat them!*" The fox-faced man spat the words in her face. "The gargoyle gates have stood for a thousand years and you're just going to walk up and *defeat* them?"

Kath was beginning to hate the narrow-faced man, but she kept her voice level. "I'll lead a small scouting party to the gates. If I can't find a way for an army to pass then the plan is defeated before it ever begins."

"*You'll* lead them?" The question came from Brant, the boar-faced man. "And if you can't defeat the gargoyles then the army does not march?"

She made her words a promise. "Just so."

Brant nodded, his grin twisting the blue tusks tattooed on his face. "That's good enough for me."

Others shouted their agreement. "Let the gargoyles prove her worth."

"The gargoyle gates will be her true trial."

More proof, Kath wondered if a woman's word was ever enough.

Royce, the leader of the lions, stood, "It is time to decide. A show of hands for peace, and the army stays at home. A show of daggers for war, and we follow the War Leader's plan." Royce went first. Pulling a dagger from his belt, he lifted it high.

Around the chamber, the leaders declared their choice. A few hesitated until the Old One pulled a dagger from beneath her sheepskins. In the end, even the fox lifted his dagger for war, a grudging look on his face.

Royce came towards her, beaming a smile. "The victory is yours. The painted people prepare for war."

A victory of words, Kath smiled, but it felt hollow. The real fighting had not even begun, yet she already felt tired, as if she'd run for leagues. She gave Royce a small smile. "There's much to be done before the dark of the moon."

Royce seemed to understand, his face turning solemn. "We're a proud people and we love a good argument, but once a thing is decided, you'll find us swift to act." He leaned towards her, his voice dropping to a whisper. "But can you truly defeat the gargoyle gates?"

The question pierced her to the core. She didn't know the answer but she put on a brave face. "I'll do my best." In truth, it was the only thing she could say. She prayed to Valin it would be good enough.

47

The Knight Marshal

The battle for Raven Pass became a weary blur. The marshal lost count of the number of assaults they'd repulsed. Tide lines of corpses littered the steppes, marking the waves of attack, but the walls held strong and defiant. Corpses piled like cordwood near the gate, many of them blackened and burned, raising a horrible stench, yet the horde never dwindled. The Octagon remained triumphant, vigilant atop their walls, yet the marshal could not shake the impending sense of doom.

A cold wind blew out of the north, a harbinger of snow. From the height of the second wall, the one dubbed Swordbreaker, the marshal had a clear view of the enemy. *A pity the living so outnumber the slain.*

Lothar joined him, a shield on his left arm, his battleaxe strapped to his side. "What are they waiting for?"

The marshal shrugged, "Perhaps they're conjuring a nightmare."

"I like it not." Lothar shot him a grim look.

A flight of black-fletched arrows leaped from the enemy lines. Soaring over the thirty-foot outer wall, they arced skyward, reaching for the second.

The marshal watched them come. *"Shields!"* He swung his own shield up, bracing for impact. Arrows thudded down, striking oak, and stone, and flesh. A single arrow thunked deep into his shield while another clipped his maroon cloak, tearing a jagged hole. "Damn." He rubbed his shoulder, thankful for his chainmail, and plucked the offending arrow from his shield. The marshal surveyed the wall. Only two wounded, Valin's luck favored them this time. "Get the wounded to the healery!" A detail of soldiers scurried to obey.

He'd ordered a rotation on the walls, keeping the archers on the battlements while the knights waited below, easily summoned by a trumpet's call. For the thousandth time, he gave thanks for the stout walls of Raven Pass. The builders had wrought well.

A trebuchet shuddered and groaned, hurling another boulder skyward. The monstrous wooden beasts worked day and night, heaving stones against the horde. The massive boulder tumbled out over the enemy. Sailing deep behind enemy lines, it fell with a bone-crushing thud, raising a cloud of dirt and blood.

"Thirty with one stone!" Lothar shook his head in amazement. "An ugly way to kill but I wish we had twice as many of the wooden beasts."

"Aye, but even then they'd make little difference." The marshal leaned against the rampart, staring out at the enemy. So many, they eclipsed the steppes with their black armor, like a shadow cursing the land. "How many do you think we've killed?"

"I'd wager nigh on two thousand."

"Yet it changes nothing. We're still outnumbered twenty to one."

Lothar grunted, "Or more."

"Yet their tactics trouble me more than their numbers." A squire drew near, a wicker basket slung over his right shoulder. The lad stooped to collect the enemy's spent arrows, inspecting the shaft before adding it to his basket. Their own stores were running dangerously low.

The marshal forestalled his friend with a glance, waiting till the lad was well out of earshot. "We need no ill rumors."

Lothar grunted. "So what troubles you about their tactics?"

"What doesn't?" He shrugged, fingering a dagger at his belt. "After the monk's warning, I half expected monsters and magic, yet we've seen neither."

"Perhaps we haven't looked hard enough."

"Or perhaps they're waiting for something." The marshal shook his head, trying to dispel the feeling of dread. "Their tactics make no sense. I keep expecting grappling hooks in the dead of the night, or a thicket of ladders raised against the outer wall, but they seem content to fight with spears, and arrows, and battering rams." He tightened his grip on his shield. "Something's not right."

Lothar shrugged. "Thank Valin for small favors."

But the marshal did not think it was the war god's doing.

"Lord Marshal!"

A gray-cloaked squire ran toward him. "I've a message from Prince Ulrich."

He recognized the lad, a pug nose and a tousle of curly black locks, the personal squire to the prince. "What is it, Brock?"

"The prince says to tell you that he's down to just three urns of oil."

The marshal flicked a warning glance to Lothar. "Tell him to be sparing with the oil, for there's none left in the stores. Have him dump a barrel of caltrops in front of the gates. If we can't stop them with fire, we might at least slow them down with spikes."

"Yes, Sir!" The squire saluted, fist to his chest, and sped away.

Someone yelled, "*Shields!*"

The marshal spun and lifted his shield. Arrows rained down, but this time they missed him entirely. Lowering his shield, he gave the nearest archer a wry grin. "Their aim's getting worse."

Laughter rippled along the wall, part unease, part relief, but laughter nonetheless. Pride rushed through him. Despite the odds there'd not been a single desertion. "Loose a volley and show them how it's done."

Archers raised their bows. Bowstrings thrummed and three hundred feathered shafts took flight. Like a cloud of angry hornets they fell on the enemy. Screams rose from the steppes but it was never enough.

Back and forth the arrows passed, a slow war of attrition, yet the Octagon held the high ground, secure atop the walls, killing more than they lost.

"How long can they keep this up?" Lothar growled the question but the marshal had no reply.

The answer came near sunset. Lothar saw them first. "Look to the north." He stabbed a finger toward the dark host. A cavalcade thundered south, their armor tinted red by the setting sun, black battle banners flying overhead. "Must be nigh on five thousand, curse the lot of them." But then Lothar flashed a deadly grin. "Do you see it? They bring no siege engines! By Valin, our walls will hold!"

The marshal watched them come, a cold dread growing in the pit of his stomach. "No siege engines but they bring something far worse."

"What?"

"Do you see the battle banner flying at the front?" A long snake of black silk ending in two tails of bright red flecked with gold, the forked banner snapped like a serpent's tongue, creating the illusion of darkness on fire.

Lothar shrugged but his voice was uneasy. "What of it?"

"It's called the Darkflamme, the battle standard of the Mordant. Now we know what they've been waiting for." The marshal turned to summon a squire. "You there, alert the king. For the true battle is upon us."

48

Danya

Danya sat cross-legged on the steppes, stretching her feelings like a whisper borne on the wind. Gripping the silver cuff on her left arm, she drew on the magic. Tentative at first, but once summoned the ancient power coursed through her veins like liquid fire. Questing outward, she sent her power hurtling across the steppes. *Horse, I am horse, swift and beautiful and proud.* Manes streaming in the wind, hooves churning the steppes, the smell of trampled grass in their nostrils, she sought the proud swiftness that defined the pure essence of wild *horse*. Stretched thin, she leaned forward, reaching, hoping, questing, but she found...nothing.

Danya gasped with effort, her spirit snapping like a bowstring. Back within her own body, she shivered beneath the sheepskin cloak, cold and bone-tired. Magic took its toll, yet she could not afford to fail.

Bryx chuffed in agreement. Stretched beside her, the great mountain wolf yawned, revealing a mouth full of sharp teeth.

Danya sighed in frustration. "I know. I'm trying." She wasn't even sure she was doing it right. Three days and she'd had no luck. Perhaps she needed to go further into the steppes, but time was running thin. She shivered against the cold, sitting huddled beneath the thick sheepskins.

So much had changed since they'd come north. The magic was with her all the time now, singing through the silver cuff, demanding to be released. Her fingers absently traced the outlines of incised animals, wolf and eagle, horse and lion. But magic was not the only thing that had changed.

She flicked a glance over her right shoulder. Ten painted warriors sat at her back, keeping watch a discreet distance away, swords and slings at the ready. She'd grown accustomed to their blue tattooed faces...especially the one. *Neven,* his name whispered through her mind, evoking a smile. She'd known he was the one as soon as she saw him. His smile caught her heart, yet it was more than that. She'd found a deep recognition in his dark brown eyes, as if it was always meant to be. Their first kiss had proven the promise in his eyes. She loved everything about him, the rough stubble on his chin, his dark hair cascading in waves to his shoulders, and especially his tattoo, the blue wolf staring back at her with the eyes of a man.

Danya pulled up her right sleeve, needing to know it was real. A blue tattoo graced her right arm, the paw print of a wolf, her first step toward joining the painted people. A thrill of pride rushed through her. She'd finally found a place she belonged, where her magic and her love for animals was respected, even revered, instead of being cursed.

Bryx chuffed in agreement.

Smiling, she hugged the wolf, her fingers running through his thick black fur, loving his musky scent. "We finally found a home."

The wolf licked her face.

But she hadn't come to the steppes to daydream. She owed Kath and Duncan a great debt, and the monks too. A cold wind whistled across the grasslands, the promise of snow hanging in the clouds. The steppes looked peaceful enough but she knew it was a lie. The painted people lived in the very shadow of the Mordant. They'd never be safe unless the Darkness was defeated. Danya took a deep breath. For the past and the future, she needed to succeed.

The ravens would be easy enough to persuade. A bribe of fresh entrails and the greedy birds would agree to carry the message carved in sling stones. Intelligent and curious, the ravens would see her request as a game, but the mountain sheep were another matter, a stubborn breed. And then there were the horses.

Nightmares crowded her mind. Danya shuddered, remembering the battle in the steppes. *Never again,* she'd sworn it over and over, half a thousand times. She would not use her magic to compel; yet magic was her only weapon.

Hunched beneath the sheepskin, she took a deep breath and tried again. Closing her eyes, she dreamt of horses. In her mind she galloped across the steppes, the wind tugging on her mane, her hooves churning the soil, pounding a wild beat of freedom. Danya reveled in the glory of *horse.* Over and over again, she dreamt the dream. And then she felt them, answering her call.

Hoof beats thundered on the horizon. A hundred or more horses galloped toward her. Wild and proud, their manes rippled in the wind like battle banners. Danya reached out to them, reveling in their freedom, their speed, and their sheer joy of the run.

Behind her, she heard the painted people whoop in triumph, but they kept their distance, staying back.

The herd slowed, stopping a spear's throw away. Cautious, they milled in a circle, chestnut and black, dappled and white, proud eyes staring at her. One came forward, a stallion, sixteen-hands high. Scars of triumph marked his flanks, a dark mane crowning a winter coat of dappled gray. He had a noble head and a proud curve to his neck, a king among his kind.

Danya stood and bowed low. "Thank you for coming." She filled her thoughts with warmth, reinforcing her words. "I ask for your help against a common enemy." Recalling the details from their long ride across the steppes, she showed the stallion the trail of dead horses. *Ridden to death, still saddled, left for carrion.*

The stallion reared, massive hooves pounding the turf. He snorted and bellowed, full of outrage.

"Yes, my friends and I seek the one who did this. We will avenge their deaths. Will you help?" She showed him her need for two horses, one to bear herself and the other for Zith. In her mind's eyes she concentrated on Zith's missing arm, underscoring his need for a gentle mount.

The stallion shook his head and neighed.

Danya felt his hatred for saddles and bits. "I understand. They will not be used."

The stallion dipped his head, tossing his mane, and then he stamped and whinnied.

A chestnut mare emerged from the herd. She came forward, her neck questing toward Danya, her liquid eyes warm and full of intelligence. Danya offered a hand, palm up, and waited. The mare came to her, agreeing to be touched. Smiling, Danya ran a soothing hand along the mare's silky shoulder...and then she saw the brand, and her breath caught, a horse of the octagon. The mare whinnied and nodded as if in agreement.

Danya turned back toward the stallion. "I thank you for the mare, but can we have the help of one other?"

The stallion reared, massive hooves churning the air. He bellowed a call and the herd turned and ran, galloping toward the south. Shaking his dark mane, the stallion came toward her, his head held proud.

So the king offered himself. Danya's breath caught. If only more men were half as noble. She gave him a heartfelt bow. "Thank you, my lord. Perhaps together we can end this Dark blight on the land."

The stallion stamped and whinnied and Danya knew she'd gained an ally against the Dark.

49

The Knight Marshal

King Ursus joined the marshal on the battlement. "So the Darkflamme has come to fight. Now we know why they've stayed their hand." He turned to the trumpeters. "Sound the alert. I want every man ready for battle."

A dozen horns blew a frantic call. Knights, soldiers, and archers answered, flocking to the two walls, yet the attack did not come. Twilight faded to dark, a spray of stars across the sky. Most of the men remained at their posts. Huddled beneath maroon cloaks, they leaned against the battlement, snatching a few hours of sleep, twitching awake at the slightest sound. The king and the marshal took turns walking the walls, offering words of encouragement, keeping vigil with the men.

Dawn revealed a new day. The enemy stood arrayed for battle, a long line of black shields bristling with spears, but this time, a host of cavalry waited near the front. One among them caught the marshal's gaze. Mounted on a magnificent black stallion, he wore silver armor embossed with black. His helmet was fashioned in the guise of a crowned skull, his breastplate like the ribcage of a skeleton. Even from a distance, the armor cast a fearful pall.

The marshal leaned toward the king. "Sire, do you see that one there? In the armor fashioned like a skeleton?"

The king nodded, his face grim. "The Mordant comes in the guise of the Skeleton King." His mailed hands balled into fists. "I've long thought the tales nothing more than a bard's drunken yarn. Yet it seems a legend has come to fight. Myth so often holds a kernel of truth." King Ursus took a deep breath, a glint of fire in his eyes. "By the gods, he'll learn the Octagon is equal to any legend." Reaching back, he drew his great blue sword, a gleam of sapphire raised against the dawn's light. "For Honor and the Octagon!"

The men took up the king's war cry. *"Honor and the Octagon!"* The very mountains rang with the shout, echoing the cry a thousand fold.

But the enemy was undaunted. War drums answered, pounding a furious beat. Battle banners snapped above the long dark line. And above them all, rode the Darkflamme, twelve feet of dark silk snaking against the steel-gray sky, flicking back and forth like a serpent's tongue.

A shout rose from the enemy. So many swords were drawn at once that the hiss of steel against leather could be heard on the walls.

The marshal raised his voice to a shout. "*Wait for it!*"

All along the dark line, swords pounded against shields, echoing the rhythm of the drums. The front ranks parted, revealing a massive battering ram, unlike anything they'd seen before. Made from a gigantic tree trunk, it was tapered to a point and capped with black iron shaped like a fist. But even more fearsome were the soldiers carrying it...for they were not men.

The marshal stared. "What *are* they?"

But the king had no answer.

Great hulking brutes with lantern jaws and bulging muscles, they dwarfed the men around them. They hefted the ram with uncanny ease. Clothed in chainmail and wolf skin cloaks, they looked like ogres, another nightmare sprung to life.

"*Monsters at the gate!*" The marshal reached for his sword, needing to feel cold steel in his hands. So these were the monsters the healer had warned of. The nightmare had come at last.

The ogres loosed an ululating howl and then they lurched forward, twenty monsters bearing the ram toward the outer gate.

"*Wait for it!*"

All along the wall, archers drew their bows to a crescent.

"*Wait for it!*" He let the monsters lumber five paces from the enemy lines and then he gave the order. "*Now!*" Trumpets blared and a volley of arrows hissed skyward.

The ogres churned forward, powering the ram toward the outer gate.

Arrows struck with a vengeance, a hail of feathered shafts falling on the ram. More than a few struck true, sinking into flesh and leather, but the ram did not falter.

"*Again!*" Trumpets repeated the order, loosing a storm of arrows.

"*Stop the ram!*" The marshal watched it come, rushing toward the gate like an impending doom. "*Stop it!*"

Arrows struck the ogres, a bristle of feathered shafts. Three of the beasts fell, but the others kept coming. The ram never faltered.

"*Fire arrows!*" The oil was long gone, exhausted on other assaults; but perhaps flaming arrows would stop the beasts. Trumpets relayed the command and the air swarmed with flames. A frenzy of feathered comets streaked toward the enemy. The marshal watched, willing the ram to falter. "*Stop them!*" Fire arrows thudded into the ogres, yet the ram lumbered forward. Ten feet, five feet, the great ram closed the distance to the outer gate.

And then it struck. *Kaboom!*

A giant thunderclap rocked the world.

Atop the second wall, the marshal staggered backward as if punched by a giant fist. Knocked on his back, he struggled to stand, desperate to know if the gates still stood. Gripping a merlon, he stared below.

Wood and stone flexed and groaned. Men atop the first wall screamed a warning. For half a heartbeat the gates stood...and then they disappeared, consumed by a cloud of black. When the dust cleared, the gates were gone. *They were gone!* A great hole gaped in the outer wall. Nothing remained within the gap, not rubble, not even the bodies of the ogres and their fearsome ram. Stone and wood and iron had disappeared, swallowed by a single thunderclap.

"*Magic!*" The marshal stared, struggling to understand. So this was the power of magic. But how could swords fight such a power?

Beside him, a young squire whimpered, a pitiful sound, like an animal caught in a trap. All along the wall, men stood frozen in fear, gaping at the missing gate. He had to do something.

A shout of triumph rose from the enemy.

The marshal gripped his sword and forced himself to think. The outer gates were gone. Without the walls they'd be overrun in less than a day. They needed the walls to survive...but the gate was gone. *But not the walls!* And then it came to him. "Sound the attack!"

But nothing happened. No trumpet obeyed his command.

He ran to the nearest trumpeter, a young lad with sandy blond hair. "Sound the attack!"

But the young man just gave him a befuddled look.

The marshal shot a glance at the king, relieved to see he understood.

The king towered over the young trumpeter, sunlight gleaming on his crowned helm. "You heard the Lord Marshal, sound the attack!" And the trumpeter obeyed. Other trumpets added their throats to the call. A trill of notes summoned the maroon to war.

The marshal grabbed the nearest squire, shaking the lad till the daze left his face. "Run and find Sir Mallory. Have him lead a charge of horse out through the gate. We need to hold the gap in the wall." He shook the lad again. "Do you understand?"

"Yes, Sir!"

"Then run like the devil's after you."

The squire sped away. The marshal turned and strode toward the rampart, desperate to learn the state of the battle. Out in the steppes, the enemy prepared to charge, while down in the narrow lane that separated the two walls, chaos reigned. Men in maroon abandoned the outer wall. Some of them blackened and burned, some without weapons, others unharmed, they fled the first wall scrambling for the gates of the second. All discipline was gone. To the marshal, it looked like a rout, the death knell of the maroon. Leaning on the rampart, he shouted down to them, "Heed the trumpets! Stand and fight!" but it was like yelling into the wind.

But then, in the middle of the muddy lane, a single knight stood firm. Blackened with soot, his helmet and shield lost to the fray, he raised his sapphire sword to the heavens and commanded the men to attack. *And they did!* Men, who'd been fleeing a moment before, stopped and stood with their prince. At Ulrich's command, they formed a bulwark across the gap, a ragged line of men with swords, and spears, and axes, plugging the hole in the outer wall.

The thin defense was just in time...for the enemy charged.

Like a nightmare unleashed, the horde rushed forward, a dark tide racing toward the sundered gate.

The defenders braced for the attack.

Steel clashed against steel, a mighty crash. But the outer walls still served their purpose, blunting the enemy's charge, forcing a horde of thousands to funnel down to a narrow spear of men.

The fighting in the gap was fierce. Hand to hand, men fought and died, turning the muddy gap to a churn of blood, but the maroon did not give ground.

"Loose another volley!" The marshal screamed the command and the trumpeters echoed his order.

All along the second wall, archers loosed volley after volley. Like a swarm of angry hornets, the arrows struck the attackers at the gate. But it was not enough. For every enemy that fell, two more leaped to fill the gap. Tens of thousands pressed forward, like grains of sand rushing toward the neck of an hourglass. The maroon was running out of time, the marshal needed a different plan.

"The Mordant is the key." The realization struck like lightning. The marshal raced along the wall, looking for Hadrian, the master archer for the maroon. He found him on the crown of the second drum tower, a tall blond-haired man with broad shoulders and muscled arms, an eight-foot longbow in his hands.

"Hadrian, we need to kill the Mordant."

The master archer loosed an arrow, his motions smooth as silk, and then he turned piercing green eyes on the marshal. "We need more arrows!"

"And more men, but we're not like to get either. Yet if we kill the Mordant, we may yet turn the tide of battle."

The archer grunted, gesturing to the enemy. "Which one is he?"

The marshal searched the teeming horde. "See there to the left? That battle standard, black with forked tails that look like darkness on fire? It is the Darkflamme, the battle standard of the Mordant."

"I see it."

"And nearby, mounted on a black stallion, he wears the armor of a Skeleton King."

Hadrian made the warding sign against evil. "I see him, but he's beyond the reach of my bow."

"And if you stood atop the outer wall?"

The archer gave the marshal a slow, measured look. Both men knew the risks. Hadrian nodded. "With luck and a favorable wind, I might reach him from the outer wall."

He heard acceptance in the other man's voice. Even the archers fought with the courage of knights. "Then the Light be with you."

The archer saluted and called for two of his men.

The marshal returned to the outer rampart, taking his place by the king.

"Ulrich holds them!" Pride filled the king's voice.

Below, the defenders still held the gap. Prince Ulrich fought in the center. Like a blond-haired hero of old, he roared in defiance, his blue sword cleaving a swath through the enemy. Bodies littered the gap, five black cloaks for every maroon, but the marshal knew it was only a matter of time.

The gates of the inner wall swung open and a troop of mounted knights surged toward the gap. Sunlight glinted on arms and armor, maroon cloaks streaming in the wind. Horns sounded the charge. The proud blare echoed between the two walls.

Led by Ulrich, the defenders melted away from the gap. The knights lowered their lances and charged. Hooves thundered forward, driving a maroon wedge deep into enemy lines. A cheer rose from the ramparts, a mixture of hope and defiance.

Lances couched, the knights attacked. Their charge trampled the dead and pounded into the living. Skewering the enemy, they opened a space beyond the wall. Like a maroon arrow aimed at the heart of darkness, they formed a wedge riding deep into enemy ranks. Lances shattered and broke and the charge ground to a halt. Abandoning their lances, the knights drew their weapons, swords and maces, axes and morning stars. A horn sounded, a note of pure defiance. Sir Mallory led them to the left, leading his men toward the battle standard of the Mordant. The knights fought like heroes, hacking left and right, cutting a fearsome swath through the dark horde. But just as they neared the Darkflamme, the resistance stiffened and the enemy brought their numbers to bear. They swarmed the knights. Fifty to one the black surrounded the maroon. A mob of hands reached up. They pulled the knights from their saddles, trampling them into a bloody gore. Sir Mallory was the last to fall, just two spear lengths from the Mordant.

The knights disappeared under a tidal wave of black. Even the horses were pulled down and slaughtered in a terrible frenzy of bloodlust.

The marshal stared in disbelief. Three hundred knights consumed by the horde, he saw no way to stop them.

Prince Ulrich rallied his men, setting a wall of shields along the gap.

But the horde had gained a taste for blood. They fell on the defenders, hacking and slashing, charging like berserkers.

"*Sound the retreat!*" The king gave the order. "*Open the gates for the prince!*"

The marshal knew it was the defenders' only chance, for they could not stand against the onslaught.

Locking shields, the prince and his men slowly retreated. They held the line while others ran for the inner gate. Anchoring the defense, the prince held the center, his sapphire blue sword moving in a blur of death. Attackers lurched away from the blue sword, streaming left and right, bowing the line around the prince.

"*Ulrich, get out of there!*" The king gripped the stone ramparts, staring down at the battle.

A troop of ogres surged the broken gate. Wielding massive war-clubs studded with spikes, they hammered into the thin maroon line. The ferocity of the attack proved too much. The defenders broke, running for the inner gates.

"*No!*" The king's cry carried the weight of doom.

The marshal yelled, "*Archers, protect the retreat.*"

Arrows streaked downward but they could not turn the tide.

The ogres surged forward, oblivious to the deadly rain.

The prince stood his ground, buying time for the others, dealing death with every swing of his sword. But the ogres surrounded him, attacking from every angle. The prince pivoted and whirled, a fearless frenzy of steel but he fought too many. The ogres closed for the kill. War clubs ambushed the prince, striking the back of his head. The prince crumpled under the onslaught, disappearing in a haze of blood.

"*No!*" The strangled cry came from the king.

As the marshal watched, one of the ogres hefted the prince's blue sword aloft in triumph. Hate rushed through him. "*Get him!*" But the marshal did not need to give the order. A hundred arrows thunked into the ogre, dropping him where he stood. None of the others dared claim the blue sword.

But the inner courtyard was lost. Waves of black poured into the muddy yard, pounding against the inner gates.

Beside him, the king slumped to the rampart. Clutching his chest, his face turned ashen. "My son. All my sons."

Fearing for the king, the marshal grabbed a squire. "Water, bring water for the king."

The war drums beat a ferocious rhythm.

"My lord, look!"

The marshal stared down into the courtyard. The enemy lines had pulled back opening a corridor to the inner gates. A troop of ogres emerged, carrying a second ram.

A second ram! Sweat bled from the marshal. "*Stop that ram!*"

Trumpets blared and arrows flew but the ogres did not stop. Muscles bulging, the monsters howled an unearthly scream, hurtling forward with the ram. Passing through the outer gap, they ran like demons possessed. They churned through the muddy courtyard, trampling the dead and the wounded, bearing down on the inner gate. Arrows rained like a torrent but still they came.

"*Stop them!*" But the marshal's command was lost in a mighty roar.

A second thunderclap rocked the world.

The great wall shuddered and shook, like the lashing tail of a dying dragon. Struck deaf, the marshal fell hard, the stone rampart pounding the breath from his chest. All around him, men tumbled and fell and screamed. A cloud of soot rose from the gates, eclipsing the sun.

Choking on darkness, the marshal struggled to rise. He clawed his way to the rampart and peered over the edge. The cloud of dust thinned, revealing the grim truth. The gates were gone, a great hole rent in the middle of the wall. His heart sank. Raven Pass was lost.

"*Sound the retreat!*" He did not know who would hear, but he had a duty to the living, to the last of the Octagon.

A lone trumpeter sounded the call, a mournful tune.

Men scrambled along the ramparts seeking the stairwells down.

The marshal grabbed a pair of soldiers and pressed them into helping the king. Standing in the midst of chaos, he shouted orders for any who would listen. "Take whatever supplies you can and retreat to the third wall. *Re-group at the third wall!"*

As the last of the men cleared the ramparts, he followed them down the stairwell. His hearing returned in a rush, but it did not lessen the nightmare. Dark magic had triumphed over stalwart swords. Raven Pass was lost...and perhaps the Octagon as well.

50

Blaine

A blistering wind howled across the steppes. Blaine lowered his head and struggled to keep pace with the others. Hunched beneath sheepskin cloaks, they ran into the teeth of winter. Snow pelted his face, ice crystals encrusting his surcoat, his eyebrows, and his beard. Everything blurred to white. His breath frosted to mist, snatched away by the wind. His boots pounded the frigid ground, the long grass beating against his thighs, running through a frozen hell.

Tingold, the wolf-faced scout, set a fierce pace. Blaine was determined to hold his position near the front, a matter of pride. Kath ran beside him, her two guards, Bear and Boar lumbering a pace behind. Their scouting party was eighty warriors strong. It seemed like a horde to Blaine. Kath had asked for twenty swords but other warriors kept swelling the ranks, insisting on their right to come. Blaine suspected some were glory seekers, like Brevor, the loud-mouthed spearman with the fox tattoos, while others were spies of the council, sent to witness Kath's defeat by the gargoyles. He despised the doubters, but part of him wondered if she could do it. Tales of the gargoyle gates were legendary among the Octagon, a fearsome barrier protecting the far north. Somehow Kath was supposed to defeat the gargoyles, allowing an army of painted warriors to slip past unnoticed. In the cold light of day, her plan seemed like a tale spun for small children. Blaine shook his head and kept running.

The storm eased and he flicked a glance behind. Eighty men left a trail a child could follow. Trampled grass and a stampede of footprints marked a long trail back to the Ghost Hills. If the enemy found them there'd be no place to hide, fight or flee their only choice.

The painted warriors kept their brutal pace. They slept at night, huddled together under mounds of sheepskins, desperate for warmth, and ran by day, taking short breaks to sip honey mead and munch on cold dried horsemeat. The nights were cold and the days long, filled with the endless ache of running.

Tingold raised his hand, signaling a halt. Gasping for breath, Blaine crumpled to the ground, unused to so much running. Sitting cross-legged, he put his back to the wind and chewed a strip of dried horsemeat, tough and stringy. A pity their hosts ate horse instead of riding them, but Blaine doubted the painted people knew how. A flagon of mead came his way. He took a long pull, a welcome gush of warmth running down his throat, and passed it on.

Beside him, the wolf-faced scout flashed a grin. "I told ya we'd not see much snow."

In truth, the snow was less than half a finger deep, but the cold held a terrible bite.

As if the wolf scout read his mind, Tingold slapped his thigh and barked a laugh. "In the north, 'tis too cold to snow!"

A set of smiles flashed his way. The painted people took a perverse pride in the cold, as if it was a badge of honor, proof of their manliness. Blaine pulled his cloak close; they could keep their bloody cold.

He flicked a glance at Kath but she seemed withdrawn. Dark smudges shadowed her eyes as if she hadn't slept in days. Blaine left her to her thoughts, knowing she had more than enough to worry about, but he missed the companionship of the others. Zith and Danya had both stayed behind. The old man could never have made the run and Danya had much to do before the army could march. His thoughts lingered on the wolf-girl, dark hair and an impish smile. He'd once hoped...but she'd made her feelings clear. Scowling, Blaine shook his head. Nothing ever turned out the way he expected. At least he still had his blue sword, his strength and his pride.

All too soon, Tingold signaled an end to the break.

More running, Blaine struggled to find a rhythm, his boots pounding into the frozen ground. Knights were supposed to *ride* not *run.* For the thousandth time he regretted bringing his chainmail, but he figured he'd need it in a fight. The weight tugged at his shoulders, slowing his stride. Gritting his teeth, he forced himself to keep pace. Cold air seared his lungs, harsh and unforgiving. The god-cursed steppes stretched to forever, a sea of frozen grass, pale beneath a weak sun.

Blaine forged ahead, running shoulder to shoulder with Torven, an eagle-faced warrior. The eagle looked his way, flashing a fierce grin. Somehow the blue tattoos seemed more striking in the cold, transforming the painted people into beasts rather than men. Plumes of mist streamed from their nostrils, adding to the illusion. Bundled beneath sheepskin cloaks they wore mismatched armor and scavenged weapons, mostly swords and a few spears. Nearly a third carried dented shields embossed with golden pentacles, the gleanings from past battles. Despite their ragtag appearance, they looked fierce, but Blaine wondered how they'd fight. A grim laugh bubbled out of him. Instead of fighting shoulder to shoulder with sworn knights, he was running across the frigid north with a pack of barbarians. They'd gained allies of a sort, but it remained to be seen if they could get past the god-cursed gargoyle gates.

Twelve days of running before he spied his first glimpse of the wall, a long black slash spoiling the grasslands. With each stride, the wall loomed larger. Over forty feet tall, topped with crenellated battlements, the wall cut through the steppes like a statement of power.

Tingold turned north, angling toward the wall. At midday, Blaine spied the gargoyle gates. The grim sight brought him to a standstill. He gaped in awe...till another runner bumped into him. Sketching the hand sign against evil, Blaine struggled to keep pace.

The gate was not what he expected. A paved roadway breached the long black wall. Wide enough for three wagons, the breach might have seemed like an open invitation to the north...were it not for the gargoyles. Twelve gargoyles guarded the gate, massive monsters frozen in stone. Each gargoyle was unique, beaks and claws, wings and fangs, a torment of stone so realistic they seemed poised to strike. Thrice the height of a tall man, the monsters stood perched atop pedestals, rearing over the roadway like a gauntlet of nightmares. Suppressing a shudder, Blaine clenched his fists. It was hard not to reach for his sword, especially since he knew the legend, but he would not be shamed in front of the others.

Tingold came to a halt, staying a good twenty paces from the gate.

Blaine stopped beside him, breathing plumes of frost. The others gathered round. No one said a word; they just stared at the gates. Tingold broke the silence, but he kept his voice to a whisper, as if speech might wake the gargoyles. "Keep your distance from the gates." He pinned Blaine with a warning stare. "One step on the roadway and the gargoyles will wake."

Annoyed, Blaine nodded; it wasn't the first time he'd heard the warning. His gaze roamed across the painted warriors, noting that more than a few had drawn swords, as if steel could defeat stone.

Tingold turned to Kath. "You asked for a gate. What will you have us do?"

But Kath did not say a word. Her gaze transfixed by the gargoyles, she walked towards the gate as if drawn by a spell.

Tingold leaned towards Blaine, his voice an urgent hiss. "What's she doing?"

Blaine could only shrug.

"If she steps on the roadway, the gargoyles will wake." The painted warriors stood poised to fight, but none moved to stop her.

Kath strode within a foot of the gate...and stopped. Still as a statue, she gazed up at the gargoyles.

Minutes stretched to an hour and still she did not move. The painted warriors sat on their haunches, staring at Kath. They shared a meal of dried horsemeat and mead. In hushed tones, they wagered on the outcome. A few favored Kath but most wagered on the gargoyles. Bear, one of Kath's bodyguards, gave a confident grunt, his arms folded across his broad chest. "You're all wrong. She seeks a vision from the gods and then she'll defeat the gargoyles."

Blaine smirked, more proof the painted people were little more than superstitious barbarians...but the confidence of Bear's voice irked him.

They finished their meal and still Kath did not move. Torven, the eagle-faced warrior, took charge. "We must give the War Leader the time she needs. Brevor, Tangor, Clemit and Vin, take the first watch. The rest of you get some sleep. We'll need to be well rested if the enemy comes."

Four guards loped away, taking up a square pattern around the troop, keeping watch over the steppes. Bear and Boar moved close to Kath, sitting at her back like a couple of faithful watchdogs. The others made a camp of sorts, laying bedrolls on the frozen ground. Flagons of mead were passed but they went without a fire. Blaine sat cross-legged, chewing on a salty strip of dried horsemeat. A few of the men talked, while others diced or honed their weapons, but most crawled into their bedrolls, grown men huddled together for warmth. Blaine pulled his two cloaks close, the maroon beneath the sheepskin, and kept watch on Kath. A mere slip of a girl, she was dwarfed by the gargoyles. For the thousandth time he wondered why the monks had chosen her instead of a seasoned warrior. King's blood ran in her veins but she was still just a girl and her magic seemed a pitiful weapon against the mighty statues. Perhaps their journey north was nothing more than a fool's errand.

The sun began to set and still Kath did not move. Blaine crawled into his bedroll, seeking warmth. He must have slept, for when he woke, the dawn's red light streaked a cloud strewn sky.

Torven crouched next to Blaine, offering a flagon of mead. "She hasn't moved."

Blaine tilted the flagon, taking a long pull of fiery liquor, a blaze of warmth settling in his stomach.

"It is perilous to wait near a gate. A patrol could come at any time, or worse, the gore hounds."

Blaine shuddered. "So what do we do?"

"Talk to her. Perhaps you can persuade her to move from the gate and return when she's ready."

It seemed a reasonable suggestion. "I'll see what I can do." Returning the flagon, he crawled from his bedroll. Shivering against the cold, he settled his blue sword across his shoulders and walked a few paces away to make his toilet. His piss raised a cloud of steam into the morning air, more proof the north was a god-forsaken land, not worth dying for. Finished, he turned and studied Kath. The girl hadn't moved, her two faithful guards sitting at her back.

He closed the distance, his stare roving from Kath to the gargoyles. As far as Blaine could tell, the statues hadn't moved either, but he did not trust them. The gargoyles set his teeth on edge. Cast in stone, the huge hulking brutes seemed to leer down at him, claws extended for the kill. Making the hand sign against evil, he sidled close to Kath, staying a good sword's length from the roadway. Blaine kept his voice to a hushed whisper, yet it sounded loud to his ears. "What do you see when you stare at them?"

Kath startled, as if woken from a dream. She turned and cast a weary glance toward him. "I see souls imprisoned in stone."

Blaine shuddered. "Another nightmare from the Mordant."

Kath nodded, her stare returning to the gargoyles. "Just so."

He stood at her back, not sure what to say. The silence lengthened, as if she'd forgotten him. He moved a step closer, peering over her shoulder. In one hand she held the crystal dagger, in the other, the amber pyramid. Her fingers flicked, rotating the small pyramid against her palm like a talisman or a prayer bead. Somehow the gesture worried him. "Do you know what to do?" His words sounded harsh to his ears but he couldn't take them back.

"Yes, but I'm afraid."

Her answer sent a shiver down his spine. "Afraid of the gargoyles?"

"Afraid I'll become them." She turned and stared up at him, and just for a moment, her eyes held a world of pleading.

He caught his breath, but before he could respond the look was gone, her face wiped clean, as calm as stone. Unsure what to say, he gestured back at the others. "Torven says it's dangerous to linger near a gate. A patrol might come. Or hellhounds."

Kath nodded, her face solemn. "Yes, I've run out of time." She took a deep breath. "Will you help me?"

"How?"

She pointed to the nearest gargoyle, a fearsome beast with the fangs of a lion and the wings of a bat. "I need to get up there."

"*Up* there?"

"Yes, on top of the pedestal."

Blaine did not want to go anywhere near the gargoyles. "Won't it wake?"

"It might, but it's a chance I'll have to take."

He noticed the others had drawn close, crowding behind him, judging him with their barbarian eyes. Feeling their stares he knew he didn't have a choice. "My sword is yours."

She gave him a half smile. "I don't need your sword, just a leg up," but then her face turned grim. "Don't touch the stone, don't even brush against it."

He nodded, finding it suddenly hard to swallow.

Looking past him, Kath nodded to the others. "Get back from the gate. Keep well away from the gargoyles," her voice trailed to a whisper, "for I know not what they'll do."

Bear and Boar pushed forward, their weapons unsheathed. "Let us fight for you."

She gave them a soft smile. "Loyal and brave, you'll both fight by my side in the citadel but not here. Honor my wishes and stand with the others. Swords, no matter how stalwart, cannot prevail against stone." Kath hefted the crystal dagger, holding the milk-white blade aloft. "This is the only weapon that can damage such a foe...and by the will of the gods it's mine to wield." Sunlight danced along the blade. For half a heartbeat she seemed more than a mere girl.

The others backed away, their faces fierce with blue tattoos. Hands on weapons, they stood thirty feet from the gate every stare locked on Kath.

Sighing, Kath sheathed the crystal dagger, and then turned her stare toward Blaine. Any trace of uncertainty was buried beneath a mask of stone. "This way." She led him around the back of the nearest gargoyle. "This one will do."

Even from the back the stone beast looked menacing.

"Give me a boost up but then get away. And take care, lest you touch the stone."

"What are you going to do?"

She gave him a half smile, but the smile did not reach her eyes. "What I must. End a nightmare or die trying...Tell Duncan I love him."

He stared at her, lost for words.

"It's time." She drew him toward the monster's pedestal, stopping a dagger's length from the stone.

The beast's malformed shadow loomed overhead.

Blaine's mouth went dry but he did not flinch. Lacing his hands together, he bent down as if to give her a boost onto a tall horse. Kath set her left boot in his hands and leaped up. He pushed, straining to give her extra lift.

She vaulted upward, her hands catching the lip of the pedestal.

Blaine edged away, expecting the beast to pounce, but the gargoyle remained frozen.

Kath swung up onto the pedestal, dwarfed by the stone beast.

Steel hissed from leather. Blaine unsheathed his blue sword, but the gargoyle remained lifeless.

Kath stood on the pedestal, staring up at the gargoyle. The monster reared over her, thrice the height of a tall man, a nightmare cast in stone. Kath drew the crystal dagger, her voice a whisper, "*For Honor and the Octagon!*" She touched the dagger's tip to the statue's flank. Crystal touched stone yet the gargoyle remained quiescent, nothing but a statue. Kath stepped forward and *disappeared* into the gargoyle.

"*By the gods!*" Blaine staggered backwards, his sword clutched in his fist. *She'd disappeared into the stone!* He hadn't known what to expect, but not that, *never* that! His heartbeat thundering, Blaine joined the others, his stare locked on the gargoyle.

At first he thought it was a trick of his eyes, but then he was sure. *The statue moved!* Muscles rippled beneath stone as the beast awoke. Wings unfurled and claws reached for the heavens. Jaws of a lion, claws of a dragon, wings of a bat, the great stone beast rose to its full height. Its huge jaws stretched wide and then snapped shut, as if it had swallowed something it did not like. The beast clawed at its own belly, stone raking against stone. It writhed upon its pillar, its claws making an ominous sound, but it did not roar.

And then it suddenly stilled...frozen once more.

Blaine held his breath.

The steppes went quiet, not even a breath of wind stirred.

The world seemed to wait.

The gargoyle shuddered. The great head reared back, jaws gaping wide.

Blaine thought he heard a sound, like the release of a long held sigh.

Without warning, the gargoyle exploded. Bits of stone blew in all directions. A piece of jaw thunked into the steppes. A clawed talon landed near Blaine's left boot. He staggered backwards, his hands raised to guard his face.

The rain of stone stopped.

The dust cleared.

Kath stood alone on the pedestal, the crystal dagger raised to the heavens.

"*Svala!*" All around him, the painted warriors knelt, a single word on their lips like a prayer. "*Svala!*"

They knelt, but Blaine would not bend the knee. Instead, he kept watch, his blue sword gripped in his fist.

Eleven more gargoyles remained. Blaine expected the others to fight, but instead they knelt. *They knelt,* their clawed hands extended in supplication.

Kath leaped from the empty pedestal and strode to the next gargoyle. The great beast wrapped its hand around her waist and lifted her to its chest, clasping her close as a lover. Kath melted into the statue. This time the beast did not fight. Throwing its head back, it uttered a long held sigh...and then shattered into a thousand pieces.

Kath stood alone atop the pedestal.

All around him, the painted warriors cavorted and laughed, shouting the word "*Svala!*" like a prayer or a triumph.

Blaine watched as Kath moved from one gargoyle to the next. Each time the gargoyle gently lifted her to its breast. When she entered the last beast Blaine dared the roadway, walking to the beast's pedestal. The last gargoyle shattered into a rain of stone, but somehow the pieces missed him.

Covered in rock dust, Kath stood on the pedestal, pale as a ghost, dark shadows beneath her eyes.

"You did it." He reached up to help her down. She felt light in his arms, as fragile as glass.

"Put me down." He set her on the ground and she stepped away as if she could not bear to be touched. Sheathing the crystal dagger, she stared up at him, but there was no triumph in her eyes. "They wanted to die." Shuddering she seemed to come back to herself. "Have Torven send the signal. Tell Danya to bring the army."

She turned to walk away but he couldn't let her go. "Wait." The question blurted out. "What did you see inside the gargoyles?"

She gave him a bleak look. "Hell." Turning, she took two steps and crumpled to the ground.

51

The Knight Marshal

The retreat was a ragged rout, a wild gallop half a league up the valley. Wounded limped on spears while many knights rode double. Riderless horses careened past, freed from their stalls. Baldwin carried the king's standard, a rallying point for the knights. The marshal rode in the rear, trying to bring order to chaos.

They regrouped at the third wall. A relic from a bygone age, the twelve-foot wall served as the last line of defense for Raven Pass. Crudely built from mud and undressed stone, the ancient wall spanned the valley but it offered a meager defense. Without towers, trenches, or battlements, the marshal knew it would be a bitch to defend. Little wonder the men dubbed it the Whore.

Still, it was the only wall left to them, so they took refuge behind it, counting their numbers and licking their wounds. The marshal posted a handful of lookouts but otherwise he let the men rest.

Stragglers poured in at sunset. Grim-faced, their maroon cloaks tattered and torn, they trudged to the wall, beaten but not cowed. Most told tales of fierce fighting within the hallways of the second wall, yet the enemy did not follow. The marshal figured the victors were enjoying the spoils but he doubted they'd have long before the horde came calling.

Cold and weary, he pulled his maroon cloak tight and kept moving, taking the pulse of the men. So many faces were missing; comrades and friends lost to the battle, yet his duty to the living left no time to mourn.

He found Lothar sitting around a makeshift campfire, a bandage on his head. They grasped arms like brothers, the fierceness of their grip belying their gruff words. "So you still live."

Lothar quirked a lopsided grin, "Too tough to kill."

"What happened to your head?"

"A chunk of the bloody wall up and hit me." The levity bled from his face. "I never knew stone could just disappear like that."

The marshal nodded, "Magic and monsters, just as the healer said."

"Makes you wonder what the blue-robed monk might have told us." Lothar's voice turned to a growl. "I'd like to have another chance to talk with that monk."

"And I'd like to have ten times the men, but we make do with what we have."

Lothar's face turned grim. "So you think they'll come on the morrow?"

"Aye, they'll come."

Lothar's voice dropped to a hushed whisper. "Fight or flee?"

"That's the question." He gestured to the west. "The king sits at the big campfire up that way. You can't miss it. Meet me there."

Lothar gripped his arm, worry in his voice. "The king?"

The marshal hesitated. "I've told the others he was struck by a stone when the wall sundered. But the truth is...he was shattered by Ulrich's death...his last son slain by the horde."

Lothar swore. "By Valin's sword!" He fingered his battleaxe, his gaze grim. "Will he fight?" His voice dropped to a hush. "Will he lead?"

The marshal just stared. "I have to see to the men. I need to know what's left." He gave Lothar a pointed stare and then made the rounds, taking stock of the men, their morale, their supplies, and their horses. He found more heart than he expected. Huddled under maroon cloaks, the men sat around campfires, sharpening their weapons and mending their armor. Weariness hung across them like a pall, but most refused to give up. Stubborn courage was ever the strength of the Octagon, and it hadn't failed them this day. Magic had betrayed them; else they'd still be on the walls. But he couldn't dwell on what was lost.

Toward the rear of the lines, he found the master healer working among the wounded. Somehow the pudgy healer had loaded the worst of the wounded onto a half dozen wagons, along with a smattering of supplies, cured hams and casks of ale. Because of the healer, the men ate this night.

"You did well, Quintus."

The healer looked exhausted, dark smudges under his eyes, smears of blood on his brown robe, yet he kept working. "We do what we can."

"How did you know the Mordant would come with monsters and magic?"

The healer shrugged. "All the tales say so."

"Yet, they're nothing but tales."

"Most tales carry a kernel of truth, else they're soon forgotten. All the tales of the Mordant say the same things." The healer looked up, firelight flashing golden in his eyes. "The Mordant is evil and his favorite weapons are cruelty, deceit, and magic." He shrugged. "I expect you know that." He finished wrapping a bandage on the arm of a wounded knight and then rose, wiping his hands on his robe. "But you didn't come to ask about the songs of bards."

"No. The Mordant will come on the morrow."

"Will you fight or flee?"

They all asked the same question. "What would you do?"

Quintus shrugged. "I'm a healer not a fighter."

"But I'm asking anyway."

The healer stared at him, as if weighing the question. "You won't defeat him without magic. And if you believe the Kiralynn monks, then you shouldn't even try to kill him without the crystal dagger."

"Yeah, well the gods didn't gift us with any weapons of magic, just steel and blood and courage."

"Then you'll lose."

Anger flared within him. The marshal turned away. But the healer reached for his arm, holding him back. "Fly to the hills and wait for other allies. Live to fight another day. You have more friends than you know."

"Allies? What allies?" The marshal's anger boiled to a rage. "When we stood atop the walls and faced the dark horde no other banners came to our aid."

The healer blanched and the marshal felt ashamed, the man deserved better. He softened his words. "You've served the Octagon well. At first light take the wagons east to Castlegard. You'll find sanctuary there."

"Are you saying there'll be no more wounded?"

The marshal did not answer.

"I'll send the wagons with the worst of the wounded, but I'm staying. We all have our work to do."

The marshal nodded, the pudgy healer had his own brand of courage. "As you wish." He turned away and made his way back toward the king's campfire, but his footsteps were slow and his thoughts troubled. He didn't like the healer's talk of defeat...yet the man had been right more times than not. Still, the Octagon had fared better than he had a right to hope. It was hard to tell in the dark, but he figured two thirds of his forces had survived. Tattered and weary, driven from the walls with few supplies, yet most of the men had found their way to the third wall. It seemed a miracle that so many still lived but he knew the walls were the true reason for their numbers. Without the stout walls of Raven Pass, he doubted the maroon would last a day against the Mordant's hordes. The third wall, the Whore, offered little protection, but little was better than none.

He reached the king's fire and took a seat amongst the other captains. Sir Abrax handed him a mug of tea. He sipped the bitter brew, grateful for the warmth.

Baldwin sat cross-legged beside him, polishing the king's armor. The great war helm gleamed in the firelight, silver surmounted by a golden crown, untarnished by the ragged retreat. The marshal watched the lad work, knowing the value of symbols. Courage and pride were bound deep into the men of the Octagon, but he wondered if it would be enough.

"So what do you think?" Sir Rannock asked the question, but the marshal wasn't ready to answer. Instead, he stared across at the king.

Clad in scarred fighting leathers, King Ursus cradled his blue sword in his arms, staring into the blazing fire. His silver hair was disheveled to a wild mane, his face graven with lines of grief, but his green eyes gleamed cold and keen. Perhaps the ragged retreat had shocked the king back to his senses...but the naked hatred blazing in the king's gaze left the marshal cold. He was relieved the king was back in command but he feared the blazing hatred would lead to reckless decisions.

"So what do you think, fight or flee?" Sir Rannock worried the question like a hound with a bone. The marshal might have shrugged it off but he felt the king's gaze.

Taking a deep breath, he plunged into a roundabout answer. "I figure two-thirds of our men survived the retreat, more than we have any right to hope for, but a thin defense against the Mordant. And most of them have few supplies. With careful rationing, we might have two meals before we start to go hungry. And while we have most of the horses, only half have saddles and tack. And the archers have no arrows, so we'll get no support from them." He paused to take a deep breath. "I've half a mind to send the archers, the squires, and the wounded back to Castlegard. No sense risking those who can't fight."

"I'm not going." It was Baldwin, the king's squire.

"You'll do as you are ordered."

The red-haired lad shook his head, a stubborn look on his face. "I swore to serve the king and I'll keep my oath."

Before the marshal could utter a reprimand, the king raised his hand. "Enough. Such   courage will never be turned away for it is the very bedrock of the Octagon." The king stood, his sapphire sword gleaming in the firelight. "Send the wounded and the archers back to Castlegard, but the rest will stay." He stared at each of his captains, lingering the longest on the marshal. "You'd best get some rest, for tomorrow we meet the Mordant in battle."

For the sake of the men, the marshal dared gainsay his lord. "Sire, we might do better to harry the enemy from the mountains, biting them in the flanks, chewing them down to size. We haven't the numbers for a direct assault."

The king's control cracked like fine marble...and anger bled out. "We have enough for vengeance. And by the gods, *that's* what I'll have."

No one dared say a word. The king turned from the fire, disappearing into the dark. The moon rose in the sky and still the marshal sat unmoving. No one spoke. Someone honed a sword with a whetstone, the rhythmic scrape of stone across steel sounding loud in the night, holding dread at bay. So there would be a battle tomorrow. The inevitability settled across the marshal's shoulders like a heavy yoke. He knew the other captains would not protest. The men would follow the king to hell and beyond...but he feared the morrow. True they'd have a wall to fight behind, but the Whore would provide little protection, especially against the Mordant's endless hordes. The marshal pulled a whetstone from his belt pouch and began to sharpen his sword, the sword of a dead knight, another fallen hero. There'd be plenty of blood on the morrow, but the outcome seemed assured, for the odds did not favor the Octagon. If the maroon knights fell beneath the Dark tide, then what hope did Erdhe have?

52

Blaine

Kath took two steps and crumpled to the ground. Blaine leaped forward but he wasn't quick enough. Still as death, she lay sprawled amongst the shattered gargoyles, dwarfed by the broken monsters. He crouched beside her, calling her name. *"Kath!"* Ghost-pale, her eyes were sunken and her skin cool to the touch. His breath caught with sudden fear. He grabbed her wrist, frantic for a heartbeat. "Don't leave me." A faint beat quelled his fears.

The others pounded across the roadway, a horde of blue-faced warriors bristling with swords and spears. Bear and Boar led the pack, surprisingly fleet for such big men. Bear arrived first, scooping Kath into his massive arms. "The Svala is hurt!"

Blaine was quick to put him right. "She lives but the gargoyles took their toll."

Bear pressed his hand to her neck and nodded. "She pays a price for her victory but the Svala will prevail."

Blaine sneered in disdain. Such blind devotion was just what he expected from a barbarian.

A raven-faced healer pushed his way through the pack. "Let me see." He knelt, examining Kath, holding a sprig of crushed leaves beneath her nose, but she did not stir.

"Just like Danya."

The healer turned to stare at him. "What do you know of this?"

Blaine shrugged. "I've seen it before, only not with Kath. It seems magic is a two-edged sword. Such power exacts a price. She'll sleep like the dead but when she wakes she'll be fine."

"Sleep for how long?"

Blaine shrugged. "Hard to say."

Torven, the eagle-faced warrior took charge. "We dare not linger. Feldon and Brent, we need a litter. Tingold pick ten men and do a sweep on this side of the gate. We must be away."

Tattooed men leaped to their orders, quiet and efficient. A pair of badger-faced warriors used spears and blankets to build a litter.

Blaine sidled close to Torven. "Kath said to send the signal, to call the army."

Torven flashed a fierce grin, looking more like an eagle than a man. "The Svala has gained a great triumph. None will doubt her now." He turned to the others, barking a brisk command. "Grenfir, send the signal. Let the council know of the Svala's victory."

An owl-faced warrior sped toward the nearest pedestal. Climbing to the top, he stood perched among the fractured legs of a ruined gargoyle. A small square of polished silver flashed in his hands, sending a coded signal back toward the Ghost Hills.

Torven clapped Blaine on the back. "There'll be much rejoicing in the caves tonight. It was a good day when you brought the Svala north."

That strange name again, bandied about like a title. Blaine cast a sideways glance at the eagle-faced warrior. "What does that mean, Svala?"

"It is an old word, an ancient hope, a legend from another time. One of our first Taishans foresaw the coming of a woman warrior, a champion to end the slavery of our people." He stared at Blaine, his face thoughtful. "In your words, a queen of swords."

A queen of swords! He'd heard those words before, from Sir Tyrone when he spoke of the fortuneteller on the Isle of Souls. Blaine shook his head; it was all just foolish superstition. They needed to survive the steppes. "How long before a patrol comes?"

"Hard to say. This gate is the farthest north and the least used. We might have more than a fortnight or merely hours." Torven studied the sky. "The clouds are low. We'd best hope for snow to cover our tracks."

"How many in a patrol?"

"At least a hundred spears on horseback."

A hundred was way too many, especially mounted. "Then we'd best be away."

"Aye, we must move fast and be twice as vigilant. The lands of the Mordant are fraught with danger." Torven moved among the men, urging them to their tasks.

It did not take long before Kath was tucked into the litter, wrapped snug in sheepskins. Bear and Boar claimed the right to carry her, snarling at anyone who offered to share the burden.

And then they were away, running faster than before. Blaine caught the urgency of the others, feeling the need to get far from the ruined gate. West and then south, they ran at a blistering pace, changing directions for no reason Blaine could see. He settled into a rhythm, the cold searing his lungs with every breath. Hard to believe they ran on land claimed by the Mordant. A spark of pride warmed him; Blaine doubted there was another knight alive who could make such a claim. Yet the land looked the same as the rest of the steppes, frozen grasslands stretching in all directions, a frigid hell.

The sun set in a blaze of reds and still they ran. Blaine struggled for breath, falling behind, running at the back of the pack. Sweat ran in rivulets down his back, his chainmail adding a crushing weight. He wondered how long the others could keep pace.

A painted warrior veered toward him. "Keep up or die." The gruff voice held no rancor, only a warning not a threat.

Blaine redoubled his efforts, ignoring the savage ache clawing his side.

Twilight vanished in the blink of an eye. Darkness descended like a war hammer and still they ran. Blaine sucked air through his mouth, fighting both the cold and the pain, nearly numb to both. It wasn't until he ran into another man that he realized they'd stopped. He bent double, desperate to catch his wind.

A hand gripped his shoulder. "You did well for a plain face."

Blaine didn't have the breath to respond.

"We'll make camp here." He recognized Torven's voice. "Bringold, Seigen and Tarly take the first watch. The rest of you eat and then into your bedrolls. Tomorrow will be a long day."

Blaine was too tired to eat. He picked his way through the others till he found Kath's litter. "Has she woken?"

"Not yet." Bear's gruff voice answered. "We'll keep watch over the Svala."

"As will I." Annoyed, Blaine found a spot nearby and dropped his bedroll. Shrugging his harness from his shoulders, he set his sword close to hand. He tugged off his boots but was too weary to remove his chainmail shirt. When the flagon of mead came his way, he took a long drink but he could not be bothered to eat. Desperate for rest, he curled within his bedroll, pulling his cloak up over his head. Sleep claimed him before he'd even shut his eyes.

A scream split the night.

Blaine bolted awake, reaching for his sword.

All around him, men scrambled from bedrolls, reaching for weapons and armor.

Low clouds shrouded the sky, obscuring the moon, too little light to see by. Blaine stood with his back to another warrior, his sword held at the ready, straining to find the threat.

"Where did it come from?"

"To the left."

Blaine peered into the dark, unable to tell friend from foe.

Another gut-wrenching scream, this time to the right, but there was no clash of steel. It seemed the perfect ambush.

Someone yelled, "A bloody gore hound! A gore hound's got Seigen!"

Fear spread like lightning. *The beast hunted them.* The thought shivered through Blaine's mind. He shuffled backward, needing to feel another man at his back.

A lone howl ripped the night, evoking terror in the dark.

"Stay!" The man at his back whispered a command. "It's just a diversion."

A diversion! "You mean those things *think?*"

"They think and they hate. Gore hounds hunt for the thrill of it, playing with their food before they eat. And they always hunt in packs."

And we're the bloody food. Blaine gripped his sword, straining for a glimpse of the beast.

The attack came without warning. A man screamed to his left, a bloody gurgle full of death. Blaine spun, just in time to meet a rush of fangs. He parried the fangs with a warding slash from left to right. Fear lent strength to the cut. Blue steel bit deep, a snarl of pain. Hot blood splashed across Blaine's face. A claw raked his sleeve but his chainmail held true. Blaine twisted his sword and the thing fell dead at his feet.

He wrenched his sword free and moved to a crouch, standing at the other man's back, poised for the next attack.

Terror stalked the night.

Blaine strained to see in the dark, every sense on edge.

Somewhere to the left, a man whimpered in pain. *"It hurts! It hurts!"*

Torven yelled, "Form a circle around the Svala!"

Someone lit a glow crystal, a pale beacon of light. "This way!"

Blaine shuffled toward the light, his sword at the ready. They formed a circle around Kath's litter, weapons bristling outward, a desperate defense against the beasts.

Another scream, more proof the hounds remained on the hunt.

"It's eating me!" A man's voice screeched in the darkness. *"Help me!"* The voice shrieked in terror. *"Kill me!"*

The screams preyed on Blaine's mind. "We can't just let him die!"

"Hold your ground!" Torven shouted over the shrieks, holding his men to their positions.

Blood-curdling screams turned to pitiful wails. The victims took forever to die. Snarls filled the night, the sounds of bones being crunched and men being eaten alive.

Sweat trickled down Blaine's back. Every scream conjured a fresh horror. The night seemed to last forever. Silence eventually prevailed, but the men refused to be fooled. Holding their swords at the ready, they kept their position. The vigil sapped their strength and strained their nerves, but the painted warriors held their ground, as brave as any sworn knights. The dawn light saved them. A glimmer of gold streaked the sky, giving proof that the beasts were gone.

Most of the men dropped to their knees in weariness and thanks, but Blaine staggered forward, needing to know the cost of the fight. Torven joined him, giving names to the dead. Seven men killed, one of them half eaten from the boots up. Blaine looked away, a horrible way to die.

Torven knelt, closing the eyes of the mangled corpse. "Sebold was my friend." He eased a dagger from the dead man's hand. "Such torture is deliberate. The cursed gore hounds are nothing but pure hate."

Blood spattered the trampled grass, most of it human. Amongst the slain they found only two gore hounds. The creatures reeked of evil. Everything about them was wrong. Snout like a wolf and teeth like a saber cat, the cursed hounds were the size of a small horse. Strong and vicious, the twisted beasts were clearly designed to kill. Kicking one with his boot, Blaine made the hand sign against evil.

"I heard you killed one."

Blaine nodded.

"Good fighting for a bare face." Torven moved on, scouting the battlefield, Blaine a shadow by his side. The eagle-faced warrior knelt among the trampled grass. "Too many paw prints. We've caught the attention of a hunting pack." His face turned grim. "They'll be back."

"What about the dead?"

"Food for ravens."

Blaine's disapproval must have shown on his face.

Torven scowled. "It's our way."

Others were already moving among the dead, scavenging weapons and food.

"So how do we fight them?"

"With steel and with guile. These are no ordinary beasts." Torven raised his voice to a shout. "Tarly and Pren, skin the hounds. We'll rest an hour and then move out."

No one argued. The two painted warriors set to work skinning the beasts. Blaine sat huddled with the others, gnawing on a strip of dried horsemeat. No one talked. Their faces said it all. Streaked with weariness and grim determination, they'd pit swords against the terrors of the night. He wondered how many would survive. The battle for the north had begun, but instead of soldiers they fought nightmares that prowled on four legs, making meals of men. Blaine shuddered, thankful for his blue steel sword.

53

Duncan

Darkness swirled overhead, shadows darting among the stalactites. Chained to the floor, Duncan drifted in a haze of agony. Knives studded his body, a hundred stabs of silver. So much pain, it seemed as if his body was nothing but hurt. He begged the gods for death, or perhaps he'd already died, dead and gone to hell, trapped in an eternal nightmare, the torment of the damned.

A sibilant voice whispered at the back of his mind, the voice of the Mordant. Fear struck like lightning. Duncan raised his head and searched the chamber, but only the shadows remained.

A foul oily taste crept into his mouth and then he remembered. He was alone yet it was happening again. A shout sprang to his lips, *"No! I won't let you use me!"* Braziers erupted in flames, tongues of fire licking the stalactites. A thrum of power filled the cavern.

"Not again!" Duncan shrank into the floor, trying to seal his mind.

Tentacles of darkness descended from the ceiling, as if searching for his warmth. Cold as midnight, they slithered across his skin, seeking out his wounds.

He thrashed against his bonds but he was held tight, shackled to the floor, an unwilling sacrifice.

Darkness seeped into him, like acid in his veins. A scream roared out of him, too much to contain. Magic thrummed through him, dark and terrible. Words shuddered through his mind, whispered in the voice of the Mordant, spoken in a language long dead. The words held no meaning yet they rushed to be born, erupting from his mouth like vomit. He thrashed and bucked, caught in the grip of evil. Something answered. Shadows crawled across his skin. A relentless darkness pressed down on him like a smothering hand. It poured into him, forcing its way down his mouth. He choked and gagged and still it came. Just when he thought he would drown in darkness, a roaring filled his ears. A single clap of thunder and the darkness was gone.

Duncan lay naked on the stone floor, gasping for breath, like a drowned man tossed on a stormy shore. Exhausted, he opened his eyes, half afraid to look. The shadows were gone, retreated back amongst the stalactites, waiting for another chance to pounce. The cavern stank of fear and piss, his fear, his piss. Shuddering against his fate, he closed his eyes, desperate to sleep, but all his dreams held nightmares.

Something poked his side.

Groaning, he opened his eyes. A pair of black-robed priests hovered near like hungry vultures. At first he thought he was dreaming, but then one of the priests knelt and forced a thin reed into his mouth. A spurt of warm liquid gushed down his throat, a revolting taste of boiled blood and herbs. He gagged but the foul flood kept coming. He swallowed more than he wanted, gasping for breath when the reed was withdrawn.

Priests knelt on either side of him, sponging him clean, tending him like a babe.

"Just let me die." But they ignored his words.

"Why? Tell me why?"

Finished with their work, they turned and strode from the cavern. The copper door shuddered closed, sealing him in with the shadows.

Duncan lay chained to the floor, a single tear running down his cheek. "Why?" The word was a whisper, a question for the Light. "Why did you let this happen to me? What have I done to deserve this?" He stared at the nearest brazier, willing an answer from the light, but it never came, not even the hint of an echo. A deadly silence reigned in the cavern. He heard his heartbeat and willed it to stop but even that prayer went unanswered.

Cursed and forsaken, he closed his eyes, enduring the pain, waiting for the next assault.

He must have dozed, or else succumbed to a haze of misery, he couldn't tell the difference anymore, but then he heard the voice, a faint whisper scratching at his mind.

Listen to me!

Duncan jerked awake, afraid the Mordant had returned. He cringed against the stone floor, his heartbeat thudding loud in his ears.

You must listen. I've little time.

The voice came again, a subtle whisper, small and naked, without the frightening power of the Dark. Duncan struggled to understand. "Who are you?" His own voice echoed against the stalactites, "you...you...you."

I'm a prisoner like you.

Duncan raised his head, staring into the gloom. Perhaps it was a ghost, the shade of another prisoner come to taunt him...or perhaps the pain had finally forced him to madness.

No, I'm trapped inside the Mordant.

A bolt of fear struck Duncan. "You've come to trick me." He shrank inside of himself, bracing for the next assault.

No, don't close your mind to me. You must listen.

Duncan waited for the tendrils of darkness to attack but they never came. He risked a thought aimed at the other voice. *Can you hear me?*

Yes, a whisper at the back of his mind. *My name is Bryce. I was studying to become a Kiralynn monk when the Mordant took me. He stole my body and trapped my soul. Like you, I'm a prisoner of the Mordant.*

Shock and surprise rippled through Duncan's mind, but he was afraid to trust. *I don't believe you.*

Trust your own senses. Do I feel like Darkness?

The question made him think. He fought his own pain, questing within his mind, but he felt none of the oily corruption that came with the Mordant. *How is this possible?*

"Magic, a boon of the Light, call it what you will, but when the Mordant sleeps he lowers his guard. Somehow I found my way to you, like sneaking beneath a locked door. But we must be quick. I've eavesdropped on the Mordant. I know his plans to conquer Erdhe. The southern kingdoms are in grave danger. You must get my words to the others."

"Others?" Duncan barked out loud, an explosion of rage and frustration. "I'm chained in this god-forsaken place, pierced with a hundred knives! You've picked the wrong messenger!"

The cavern mocked him, "messenger...messenger."

But the voice was undaunted, *And I'm chained within the Mordant, unable to speak, or touch, or smell, a lost soul condemned to watch a monster use my body. I'd willingly trade my hell for yours.*

His reply sobered Duncan like a slap in the face. Perhaps hell had many levels and he hadn't yet reached bottom. He took a deep breath, shuddering against the pain. *How can I help?*

I'm a prisoner yet I spy on my jailor. I've seen his plans. I know what he intends. You must live and you must get my words to the others, to the champions of the Kiralynn monks.

Fear struck Duncan to the core, fear for Kath and the others. For the thousandth time he wondered what he'd babbled to the Mordant.

Mustering his courage, he dared to ask the question. *"What did I tell the god-cursed Mordant?"*

Your words made little sense, your mind was swamped by pain.

The answer came like a balm to his heart. So he hadn't betrayed them, he hadn't betrayed *her*. He clung to the belief that Kath remained safe. *Thank you.*

The voice became tentative. *Will you tell me who wields the crystal dagger?*

Suspicions rose like a spring tide. It felt too much like a trap. *No.*

A sigh of sadness blew through his mind. *I understand. Perhaps it is best. The crystal dagger is my only hope.* But then the voice changed, a sense of urgency pulsing through his mind. *Our time grows short, you must listen, listen and remember.* A floodgate opened and images poured into Duncan's mind. A map of Erdhe lay spread before him, but it was unlike any map he'd ever seen. Jeweled castles and ivory walls sat amongst painted fields and forests. He soared like an eagle across the land, hearing details of the Mordant's plans, dire warnings about a place called Raven Pass, and the Kiralynn monastery, and the Queen of Lanverness. Visions tumbled through his head, a jumble of thoughts and ideas, each one potent with urgency. A strange hallway carved with demons of every description. A secret door opened to reveal a vast hoard of treasure and forgotten magic. His vision blurred and he was in a courtyard, in the heart of the Dark Citadel, yet he saw a squad of knights in silver surcoats, false knights wearing the colors of the Octagon, knights of deception. Another shift and he sat on a dark throne giving orders to men bearing tridents. An avalanche of thoughts and visions pummeled his mind. So confusing, they crashed against him, like being tossed in a storm racked sea. He struggled to make sense of the chaos. *I have questions, things I don't understand.* But the other voice retreated, leaving a whisper of fear in his mind. *You must live. You must remember!*

And then it was gone, snuffed out like a candle.

Silence struck like a thunderbolt.

Suddenly alone, Duncan shuddered against the stone floor, gasping for breath. He struggled to understand, wondering if he'd finally gone mad. Visions swam in his mind, things he'd never seen before, thoughts that could never have been his own. The Mordant was a monster, a demon in the guise of a man. And if the visions held true, then the south had little chance.

Pain threatened to swamp him, a constant companion gnawing at his sanity, but the memories of the other voice assaulted his mind.

"You must live. You must remember!" Duncan turned his head to stare up at the nearest brazier, his gaze fastening on the flickering light. "You used me." His voice sounded hoarse in his ears. He still wanted to die, still wanted the pain to end, but he changed his prayer, his voice a low whisper. "Let Kath come, let her hurry." He bit back a sob, resolved to endure the pain, for the secrets of his mind could not die with him.

54

Blaine

Strung out in a line, they shambled across the steppes, a shrinking column of weary warriors. For five nights they'd fought the hell hounds, a grim battle of attrition, and each morning they ran, needing to get clear of the dead lest the feasting ravens betray them.

Blaine forced himself to keep running. Every breath froze to a ragged plume of white, his boots pounding the ground in a jagged rhythm. Speed bled from his stride, dragged down by the weight of his armor. He fell behind the others, sorely tempted to shuck his chainmail...were it not for the hell hounds. The burnished links had saved his life more times than he cared to count...but he paid a price for the added weight. Gritting his teeth, he fought to keep running, waging a constant battle against the gnawing ache savaging his side.

Torven raised his hand, signaling a halt.

Gasping, Blaine slowed but he did not stop, needing to know how Kath fared. Bear and Boar carried her litter. Where they found the strength, Blaine did not know.

He found them near the front of the column. "Is she?"

Bear shook his shaggy head.

Nodding, Blaine crumpled to the ground, desperate for sleep. He spread his bedroll and crawled inside, chewing on a piece of dried horsemeat. No one spoke. No one had the strength to spare. The battle with the hell hounds had its own unique rhythm. Starting at first dark, the men formed a circle, a bristle of weapons surrounding Kath, waiting for the hounds to come calling. Sometimes they stood for hours, a weary vigil. Just when sleep threatened to claim them, the beasts attacked. Screams and howls filled the night, a series of short battles separated by long stretches of quiet. Nerves grew as taut as bowstrings, always listening for the next ambush. Dawn brought the only relief, revealing the cost of the night. Each morning, they tallied their dead and gathered their wounded. Poison made even minor wounds a deathblow. Anyone who couldn't keep up was given a merciful end. They left the dead behind, food for ravens, and started running, needing to escape the battlefield.

Bone-weary, Blaine stared up at the afternoon sun, wondering how much more they could endure. Eighty men whittled down to forty-three. They waged a valiant fight, but the cursed hounds kept coming. At least they hadn't yet attacked in daylight. Pulling his cloak over his head, he fell dead asleep, expecting another fight at nightfall.

Someone shook him.

Blaine startled awake, reaching for his sword.

"It's all right."

Confused, he blinked up at Torven. The sun hadn't yet set, too soon to fight. "What?"

Torven leaned close, his words a low whisper. "We need to change tactics. We can't keep this up."

Rubbing the sleep from his eyes, Blaine struggled to wake. He'd puzzled the problem on their long runs, but he'd never found a solution. "A ring of fire might hold the beasts at bay but it would also signal the enemy." He scowled, knowing they couldn't afford a fire, trapped by their own need for secrecy. "We should retreat and wait for the army."

Torven glared at him, the tattooed eagle fierce on his face. "The Svala said we should scout the citadel."

"To what end? Kath's not even awake!"

"We obey the Svala."

The painted warriors had become fanatical when it came to Kath, as if their common sense was scattered to the four winds. Frustrated, Blaine growled, "We're losing more men every night."

"True." Torven frowned "I've never seen such a large pack. Unless we defeat them, they'll ruin the Svala's battle plan. Best if we fight them before the others cross the gate."

"Each night they kill more of us than we kill of them. The night is their element and the bastards use it to their advantage."

"That's why we need to change tactics."

Something about the other man's voice bothered Blaine. "So what do you have in mind?"

"I've spoken with the other scouts and they all agree, the gore hounds avoid their own dead, as if they can't stand the stench."

"So?"

"So tonight, seven warriors will wait outside the ring of defense, hiding beneath the skins of dead gore hounds. When the beasts come hunting, the seven will rise up and attack from the rear."

"I wondered why you had the mangy beasts skinned."

"A desperate gamble." Torven's gaze went to the hilt of Blaine's blue sword. "You've killed more beasts than any other."

Blaine's mouth went dry. "And if your scouts are wrong?"

"Then each man will fight on his own."

A death sentence, a lone warrior outside the ring would not stand a chance, but Blaine refused to shirk a fight. "I accept."

Torven clasped his arm, warrior to warrior. "I knew you'd take the risk. Despite your unmarked face, you have the heart of a painted warrior. You'd make a good eagle." He raised his voice to the others. "Grenfir, bring the knight a gore hound skin."

Blaine accepted the bundle without a word, appalled by the stench of the uncured hide.

"Best choose your spot before darkness falls."

Taking only weapons and armor, Blaine moved out into the steppes, choosing an untrammeled stretch of grass. The raw hide stank of corruption, far worse than rotting flesh, yet he slung it across his shoulders, knotting the forelegs around his neck like a gruesome cape. At least the poisonous claws had been hacked off, too dangerous to handle. Unsheathing his blue sword, he lay in the deep grass, huddled beneath the skin, waiting for the dark, wondering if this would be his last sunset.

Twilight lingered, the red sun fading to purple. Thick clouds scudded across the sky, promising another dark night, another advantage for the beasts. Lying prone under the gore hound skin, Blaine scanned the steppes for movement. Night fell like a hammer, the moon a faint smudge hidden by thick clouds.

Darkness prevailed, the time when the beasts held sway.

Blaine gripped his sword, lying in the tall grass, a knight turned hunter, or was he merely bait? Hairs prickled at the back of his neck, nothing to protect him but the stink of a dead gore hound. Cold seeped up from the frozen ground, a threat of another sort. Despite his weariness, despite the freezing cold, Blaine thrummed with tension, straining his senses. *Kill or be killed,* it seemed the only law of the god-cursed steppes.

Movement in front of him, but it was only the others. The soft chink of arms and armor proved the painted warriors moved into position, preparing for battle. Hidden by the dark, yet he knew they stood in a circle, weapons held at the ready, waiting for the first sign of ambush.

The night proved still as death, not a whisper of wind.

A searing cold seeped up from the ground. Blaine fought not to shiver. Darkness pressed close, making it hard to wait, and harder to lie still. His own breathing sounded loud in his ears, every rustle of grass a threat. Time held no meaning, an eternity of darkness.

The wind picked up, whispering across the steppes. Blaine cursed the change, knowing the subtle sound would aid the beasts.

And then he heard it, *a soft chuffing*.

So close, just a few paces to his left.

Blaine froze, not daring to breathe.

A low growl to his right, *the beasts were all around him!* He lay exposed, the back of his neck unprotected, yet he dared not move. Sweat trickled down his spine. Lying statue-still beneath the gore hound hide, Blaine gripped his sword, praying the beasts would pass him by.

He felt them circling, snuffing the air. One padded close...close enough to hear its harsh breath. Blaine gripped his sword, frozen beneath the hide. The beast chuffed, a low snorting sound, and was gone, a soft rustle of frozen grass.

Blaine breathed again, a brief reprieve.

A scream broke the night. The battle was begun.

Blaine stood, his sword held at the ready. He padded forward, searching the dark. Sensing movement, he leaped forward, slashing with his blade. Steel connected with flesh, a howl of pain. Even wounded, the beast whirled, lashing at Blaine's chest. Claws raked across his surcoat but his chainmail held. He parried the beast, slicing through sinew and bone, severing the paw. The hellhound howled, an unearthly sound, but still it came, fangs snarling in hate. Blaine staggered backward and then whirled to the left, trying to flank the creature. Sensing an opening, he put all his strength into an overhand blow. His sword bit deep, crunching into bone, a lethal stroke.

Something struck him from behind. Powerful as a battering ram, it knocked him to the ground. He lost his grip on his sword. Turning, he got his left arm up. Saber fangs lunged for his face, a snarl of hate. He forced his arm deep into the beast's mouth, holding the fangs at bay. Teeth clamped down in a painful grip but his chainmail held. The beast snarled, a rage of hot drool dripping into Blaine's face. Desperate for a weapon, he struggled to reach the dagger at his belt. The beast shook him like a rag doll. Groping blind, Blaine found the dagger, plunging it deep into the beast's belly.

The hound snarled but the jaws refused to release. Once, twice, three times he stabbed the beast before he found the heart. Blood spurted over him, a gush of warm gore. The creature shuddered and then lay still, pinning Blaine to the ground.

Gasping for breath, he pushed the beast away, trying to avoid the fearsome claws. He checked his arm. His fingers still worked but his arm ached horribly, too dark to see if the chainmail was broken.

Screams split the night, proof the battle still raged.

Someone wailed in pain, *"It's eating me! Get it off!"*

Nightmares lurked in the dark. Blaine knelt in the grass, frantic for his sword.

Something moved to his right, but he only had a dagger. Drenched in sweat he searched the grass. And then his hand touched steel. He gripped his sword and rose to a crouch. Guided by sounds, he eased to the right, hoping to take a hellhound from behind. Sensing movement, he swung his blade to the left, but his sword found only air. The beasts were too clever by half.

A low growl came from his right...and another to his left. They had him surrounded, taunting him with snarls, playing with their food. Drenched in sweat, Blaine pivoted left and then right, but the darkness favored the beasts. He cursed the night. Staying in a crouch, he waited for the first attack, vowing to take at least one with him.

But then the gods lent a hand. The wind picked up. A cold blast from the north opened a swath in the cloud-shrouded sky. Moonlight bathed the steppes in a silvery light. And then he saw them. Black and brown, the beasts stood out against the silvery grass. A shout of triumph rose from the other men. Slings whirled, a whisper of death hurled into the night.

Blaine leaped forward, charging the nearest gore hound.

The beast whirled, a snarl of fangs as sharp as sabers, but Blaine had the advantage of reach. The great blue sword swept forward like vengeance unleashed. Steel struck the beast's head, sundering the skull in two. He wrenched the blade loose and turned to find another. But the battle was already won.

Dead gore hounds littered the trampled grass.

Moonlight brought their first triumph.

Raising their fists and howling to the moon, the painted warriors celebrated a primal victory. Blaine joined them, sharing a flagon of mead. Bathed in moonlight, they danced and clapped and sang, raising their weapons to the heavens. And in the midst of the revelry, Kath woke.

Perhaps the gods had not abandoned them after all.

55

The Knight Marshal

The sun rose in a blaze of golds, too glorious a morning for such a grim day. The marshal watched it rise, wondering if it would be his last.

All along the Whore, the men took their positions, waiting for the horde to come calling. A lone battle banner flew overhead, the king's blazon, maroon silk embroidered with a golden crown. Saved by Baldwin in the mad dash from the second wall, the banner was tied to a broken lance. The lone standard snapped proud in the cold morning wind, like a mailed fist defying the terrible odds.

The king stood beside his banner, his crowned helm and silver breastplate polished bright, his great blue sword looming over his right shoulder. A single sunbeam broke from the clouds, anointing the king. Gleaming like a star set in a long line of maroon, he stood tall and indomitable, a fabled hero clad in sun-kissed armor. The sunbeam seemed a sign, like a blessing of the gods. A cheer roared from the wall, a burst of pride from the men.

Clouds blew in from the north, shrouding the sun.

And then it began to snow. A flurry of snowflakes pelted down, turning the land sepulcher white. Winter had come, the ally the king had hoped for...but too late to save the maroon.

The marshal pulled his cloak close. Turning his back on the winter wind, he walked the wall, trading words with the men. A few muttered prayers, others bantered jokes, but most were stoic, minding to their armor and weapons. The grim truth reflected in their eyes, yet he knew they would not waiver. Without archers, the battle would be a bloody. The ancient wall offered little protection. Short and stubby, the Whore would blunt the enemy's charge, but at a height of only twelve feet he expected the ogres to scale it in a single bound. And only the gods knew what other foul magic the Mordant hid in his arsenal. But one thing was certain; the courage of the knights would not falter. Pride swelled through him. He wondered if a bard would ever sing the tale, so few standing against so many. But bards' songs went to the victors. The marshal scowled, all his thoughts full of ashes. He drew his great sword, Sir Tyrone's sword, comforted by the feel of cold steel.

The waiting proved hard, always the worst part of any battle. The sun climbed the sky and still they did not come. Not until midday did they hear the drums, the steady beat of doom.

Men tensed along the wall, readying their weapons. They strained to see the horde.

When the enemy finally came, it was only six riders. Bedecked in plumed helms and dark armor emblazoned with gold pentacles, they sat on their horses and waited fifty yards from the wall.

The marshal joined the king. "Perhaps they offer terms."

The king scowled. "The Octagon never surrenders."

"True, but perhaps we should hear them out."

The king agreed, so they called for their horses.

Six men waited so six rode out from the wall. The king led, resplendent on his white war stallion. The marshal rode on the king's right. Baldwin rode on his left, bearing the king's banner. Two champions and a captain came close behind: Sir Abrax, Sir Rannock, and Sir Lothar.

They stopped two spear lengths from the enemy. The king's white stallion snorted and pawed the frozen ground, as if eager for a fight. The maroon battle banner snapped overhead, a subtle reply.

The marshal studied the enemy. Four were mere soldiers, muscles bulging beneath armor, but the other two were older, their armor more elaborate, embellished with gold. He judged them to be generals, come with the Mordant's terms.

The center general, the one with the most gold on his armor, spoke first. "My name is General Haith, and I speak for my lord, the Mordant." His horse shied left and he quelled it with a tug of the reins. "Your men fought bravely but they were outmatched. Against our numbers, against our magic, none in the south can stand. Yet the Mordant does not wish to spend his men needlessly. He offers terms."

The king's voice was a low growl. "The Octagon does not surrender."

"But will you fight?" The general lifted a mailed hand, forestalling the king's reply. "The Mordant offers to settle this contest by single combat."

"Single combat?" Flummoxed, the king shook his head, sunlight glinting on his armor.

Sir Abrax muscled forward. "*I* will fight for the Octagon! Give me the honor, Sire!"

Sensing a trick, the marshal interposed. "What are the terms?"

General Haith nodded, his gaze fixed on the marshal. "Single combat to determine the outcome of this battle. The loser retreats with his army, ceding Raven Pass to the victor."

Sir Abrax gasped, but the marshal stilled him with a glance. It was a fantastical offer, especially given the enemy's numbers, yet it reeked of lies. The marshal pressed for details. "If the Octagon wins, you'll take your army back to the north and leave the southern kingdoms in peace?"

"Hardly," the general's voice dripped with disdain. "If the Octagon wins, our army will retreat and find another way south. Raven Pass is not the only gap in the Dragon Spine Mountains."

"And how do we know you'll hold to the terms?"

"You have the word of the Mordant."

It was a measure of discipline that none of them scoffed.

"I need your answer."

The king seemed to consider. "Single combat?"

"To the death."

"Our champion against yours?"

General Haith flashed a grim smile. "No, you misunderstood. Our *king* against yours."

A premonition of dread flashed through the marshal. "Sire, it's a trick! You cannot do this."

The king's voice cracked with anger. "Osbourne, hold your tongue. This is a *king's* decision."

The marshal bit back his words, fearing a disaster.

The king stared at the general. "So the Mordant will fight?"

The general gave a terse nod. "This afternoon, in three turns of an hourglass, midway between our two armies."

"No, it will be here, within sight of the third wall, where all my men can bear witness."

The general hesitated but then he agreed. "As you wish."

"And the weapons will be swords."

"Agreed."

"And we'll fight afoot."

"As you say."

The king nodded, his face solemn. "Then I call upon the gods to witness this agreement. For the sake of the Octagon, I will meet the Mordant in battle."

The general smiled. "So be it." He began to turn his horse but then stopped. "Oh, the Mordant bade me to give you this." One of his escorts threw a long bundle wrapped in bloodstained maroon to the ground.

"In three turns of the hourglass, the Mordant will meet you in mortal combat. To the victor goes the spoils." The general turned his horse and put spurs to flanks.

They watched as the enemy galloped into the north.

"Sir Abrax, the package."

The king turned his mount and they galloped back to the wall. The other captains waited near the campfire. The men pressed close, yearning for news.

Sir Odis, the champion of the lance, broached the question. "What news, my Lord?"

But the king ignored him. "Sir Abrax, the package."

The king sat by the fire, using a dagger to cut the bindings. The bloodstained cloak fell away revealing a gleam of sapphire blue. The king's breath caught. "My son's sword." He lifted the great sword, "Mordbane!" a sheen of blood still coated the blade.

A hushed silence fell on the men.

The marshal took a deep breath. "Sire, the sword is a weapon aimed at your heart. More proof of the Mordant's treachery."

Rage smoldered in the king's green eyes. "He mocks me by returning Ulrich's sword. As if it has no value."

"Sire, he seeks to cloud your judgment. By returning the sword he goads you to battle. He goads you to rage. I implore you, for the sake of the Octagon, do not accept these terms."

"For the sake of the Octagon, what else am I to do?" The king rounded on the marshal, a spray of spittle flying from his mouth. "Would you have me hide behind my men, letting his army slaughter us to a man? Or should I take this chance, this *one* chance, to wrest victory from the Mordant?" The king glared, his mailed hands balled into fists. "It's not just the fate of the Octagon at stake. Nay, the fate of the entire southern kingdoms lies at risk. You're the knight marshal of the Octagon. Can you see another way to victory? Can you?"

The marshal had no answer.

"This is an offer I *cannot* refuse. Not and keep my honor." The king's voice turned winter cold. "Or do you doubt my skill at arms?"

Aghast, the marshal shook his head, "Sire, no, never that."

"The Mordant is not trained as a knight, nor does he wield a blue sword. He will not stand against me."

"Not in a fair fight, no." The marshal struggled to put his fear into words. "Sire, I cannot believe the Mordant will take the risk. Since when does the Dark Deceiver fight from the front?"

The king's gaze narrowed.

The marshal pressed the attack. "Sire, there's some trick here that we do not understand."

"Enough!" The king's voice carried a cold rage. "It is done. I've given my word. In three hours time, I will meet the Mordant in single combat." A gasp of awe rippled through the men. "As the gods are my witness, I shall slay the Mordant, claiming victory for the Octagon and vengeance for my sons. So help me, Valin."

The marshal bowed before the king's will. "May the gods make it so," but in his heart, he feared the Mordant's treachery.

56

Blaine

It took the better part of the day for Kath to recover. She asked a torrent of questions, while ravenously devouring their meager stores. "Tell me again about the hellhounds."

So Blaine told her everything while Bear and Boar sat nearby, urging her to eat. He told her a tale of running during the mornings, sleeping in the afternoon, and then fighting all night. The hardest part was explaining the hounds' fiendish cleverness, how they always waited till the men were bone weary and how they used diversions, hunting as a pack. And then he told her about Torven's idea to use the dead hides to ambush the hounds and about the battle in the moonlight.

Kath listened hard to every word. When he finished, her face was thoughtful. "I never thought they'd be so many." She looked at him, a trace of fear in her eyes. "I wonder what other surprises the Mordant has in store?"

It was a question none of them could answer.

"Do you think there are more hounds out there?"

Bear answered. "Most likely."

Kath nodded. "Then the battle's not over."

"Svala, we have a gift for you." Blushing red beneath his blue tattoos, Bear nudged a large leather pack toward Kath, a pack he'd carried all the way from the Ghost Hills.

"A gift?" Kath smiled, her face a mixture of surprise and pleasure.

Bear nodded, gesturing to Boar. "We traded for it. We thought it might be yours."

"Mine?" Kath pulled the pack toward her, fumbling with the buckles.

The other warriors crowded close, come to watch Kath.

She opened the pack and gasped, pulling out a small octagonal shield, the same shield she'd borne from Cragnoth Keep, the one they'd abandoned after the battle on the steppes. *"My shield!"* Blaine marveled how her face lit up, as if someone had given her the moon.

Bear said, "It was badly battered, but Gren has a way with fixing shields."

She ran her hands across the polished wood. "My thanks."

The big man blushed. "There's more, Svala."

Kath reached into the pack and removed a chainmail shirt. The tightly woven links flashed silvery bright in the morning light, a small shirt, suited to a squire or a girl. "My mail shirt! I never thought to see this again."

Blaine gaped in surprise, amazed that the big warrior had carried the extra weight all the way from the Ghost Hills.

Bear nodded, his face solemn. "It was scavenged from a battlefield where more than a hundred of the enemy lay slain." He dipped his head toward her. "The same battlefield that brought you to us."

Kath shrugged the chainmail over her head. It fit like a tailored shirt, a bright gleam of silver.

Blaine's breath caught. He'd seen her in mail before but somehow this was different. In the depths of the Mordant's domain, she suddenly seemed like a warrior princess touched by the gods. But then the clouds dimmed the sun and the spell was broken.

Kath ambushed Bear with a hug. The big blond warrior flamed bright red. And then she did the same to Boar, settling a quick kiss on his tattooed cheek. "You both have my thanks."

The others hooted and laughed, making good-natured sport of the two men.

Bear and Boar looked away, their faces crimson, but then Bear said, "There's one more thing."

"Something else?" Kath reached into the pack and then her face turned solemn, tinged with sadness. She pulled forth a knight's maroon cloak. "This is not mine, never mine."

"But Svala, is not maroon the color of Castlegard? And are you not born of the great castle?"

She smoothed her hand along the cloak's soft wool, a wistful look on her face. "Yes, but a maroon cloak must be earned. It is a high honor, a mark of knighthood." Her voice caught. "And never meant for the likes of me."

Blaine watched how she fingered the cloak, the look of longing etched on her face, and he thought of the many times she'd stood against the enemy, daring to come north while so many knights stayed safe behind stone walls. He found himself standing, taking the cloak from her hands. "Rise, Katherine of Castlegard."

She stared up at him, a look of wonder on her face, and then she stood, her lower lip trembling.

"Most knights earn their maroon cloaks in the Octagon Trials," Blaine did not know where the words came from but they felt right, "but you've earned yours in true combat. There can be no better way to earn a maroon cloak." Swirling the cloak, he settled it across her shoulders. "Wear it well."

Pride shone from her sea-green eyes, pride and astonishment.

And then Blaine knelt. "Katherine of Castlegard."

All around, the painted warriors knelt, their voices raised to a shout. "Svala! Lead us to victory!"

She stared at them, as if memorizing every face, and then she unsheathed her sword and raised it to the heavens. "For the Light!"

"For the Light!" The men echoed her cry. Weapons raised, they danced around her as if victory was assured.

Laughing, Kath moved among them, offering a word and a smile. And just for a moment, she reminded Blaine of the king.

But then her laughter changed and she looked at him, an impish grin on her face. "It's too long!" She lifted the cloak and pivoted. More than a foot of maroon dragged on the ground.

Blaine shared her laughter. "Let me." He cut a notch in the wool and then tore a wide swath from the bottom. He handed it to her. "Better?"

"Better." But then her face changed, like quicksilver, suddenly growing solemn. She stared at the men around her and they caught her mood, becoming quiet.

A hush settled over the warriors, a gleam of expectation in their eyes.

"You've all shown your valor, daring to fight the hellhounds instead of retreating, keeping me safe while the magic claimed me." Her voice dropped to a whisper. "Will you share my pride and wear my colors?"

A resounding, *"Yes!"* echoed from every man.

They crowded close, watching as Kath cut thin strips from the cloak's remnant. Bear was first. The big man insisted that Kath tie the maroon strip around the bulging muscles of his right arm. Boar and Torven came next. One at a time, they accepted the strips of wool as if they were symbols of valor...or holy talismans.

Blaine stood aside, watching their faces. With a strip of cloth, Kath claimed them for her own, a troop of warriors who'd fight to the death, no matter the odds. And he marveled again at what a mere girl could do.

57

Blaine

Running, always running, they pressed on, into the steppes. For five grueling nights they played cat and mouse with the gore hounds. On moonlit nights, they became the cat, hunting the hounds. On cloud-shrouded nights, they stayed in a defensive hedgehog, fending off the beasts. But even on cloudy nights, they fought back, for the mice had gained fangs. Kath changed their tactics, putting the slingers inside a ring of swords. When the hounds came hunting, the slingers cast stones at any sound, confident they'd not strike a companion. After five nights of fighting, the hounds came no more.

"Do you think we've finished them?" Kath nudged a dead hound with her boot, pulling her throwing axe from the beast's ugly maw.

Blaine shrugged, his sword held at the ready. "Either they're all dead or they've learned to fear us."

"Let's hope they're dead, else Danya and the others will have a tough time of it." She stared up at the waning crescent. "Three more nights till the dark of the moon," she gave him a wolfish grin, yet he could see her worry in every line of her body. "It's past time we caught a glimpse of the Dark Citadel."

The Dark Citadel, the name alone conjured nightmares, a bastion of evil. Blaine wiped the gore from his sword and sheathed it. "When we came north I never truly believed we'd attack the Mordant's lair."

"Nor I, but we've gained allies, just as the monks said."

"But will it be enough?"

She stared at him and he saw the nightmares crowding her eyes. "It has to be."

"You think Duncan is there."

Kath made the barest of nods, but then she looked away, her voice a whisper. "He has to be there...else he's dead."

He wanted to say something reassuring but the words eluded him.

Torven found them, keen eyes staring from an eagle's face. "Time to leave before the ravens find us. Shall we head for the citadel?"

Kath nodded. "It's time."

They ran across the frozen north, the morning sun rising at their backs. Kath kept pace beside him, her throwing axes strapped to her back, the small octagonal shield on her left arm, the maroon cloak billowing in the cold wind. Blaine smiled to see the cloak, knowing how much it meant to her. Strange how the impulse had come over him, but then he scowled, wondering what the other knights would say. He doubted the king would approve, or the lord marshal, but such worries were leagues away, as distant as another lifetime.

They settled into a loping run, boots pounding the frozen ground, each breath a plume of frost. Having grown accustom to the pace, Blaine stayed near the front with Torven and the scouts. Of the original eighty men, the hounds had chewed them down to thirty-four swords. The painted warriors paid a steep price for their audacity, yet they never faltered. Their ways were strange, and often unfathomable, but Blaine had come to trust their courage. Hard fighters, tough and stubborn to the core, yet they were wild and undisciplined. He wondered how they'd fair in a real battle against stone walls and trained soldiers. A grim laugh bubbled out of him. They ran *towards* the citadel. He'd soon know the answer, for better or worse.

Torven led them out of the grasslands and into fallow fields, a flat crust of snow stretching in every direction. The fields surprised Blaine. Somehow he didn't think of the Mordant as ruling a bunch of farmers, yet he supposed they had to eat.

Just before noon, Torven called a halt. Weary from running, they dropped to the ground, spreading bedrolls across the frozen field. Blaine stayed close to Kath, chewing strips of dried horsemeat and handfuls of dried berries. No one bothered to talk. He finished the meager meal and crawled into his bedroll, falling fast asleep.

All too soon, someone shook him awake. Blaine lunged for his sword but a whisper stayed his hand. "Time to run." Groaning, Blaine stretched and made his toilet, and then they were running again, across the fields and into the setting sun.

The crimson sunset drew them west like an ill omen, and then he saw it. A black fist jutted up into the bloody sky, rampant and strong, a malevolent fortress bristling with battlements. *The Dark Citadel*, the name thundered through Blaine's mind like a curse. With each stride it loomed larger. Somehow seeing it was far worse than anything he'd imagined. As much a city as a fortress, tiers of dark stone wrapped around a massive monolith. He'd expected a simple walled city guarded by a castle, not this monstrous beehive of stone. The citadel's dark ramparts defied his worst nightmares. Blaine shuddered, refusing to think how many soldiers lurked within its walls. *"We're going to take that?"* The question burst out of him, but no one answered.

Torven signaled and they dropped flat onto the frozen land. "We dare not draw closer. Not till darkness falls."

Hiding beneath their sheepskin cloaks, they appeared nothing more than a smudge of cream against the snowy expanse. Blaine and Kath huddled on either side of Torven, studying the citadel from afar. Still leagues away, yet the details of the mighty fortress were clear as daylight. Blaine counted nine rings of battlements stretching toward the clouds, no telling how many men walked those dark walls, or what weapons lay in wait, catapults, trebuchets, and other engines of war. A host of warnings whispered through his mind, reminding him that this was the lair of the Mordant. Beneath his sheepskin, he made the hand sign against evil. A fear deeper than swords gripped him. If the legends proved true, then the Mordant was a master of magic. *Dark magic*, weapons he couldn't even begin to imagine. Back in the caverns, he'd agreed with Kath's plan, naming it bold and imaginative, but in the shadow of the citadel it seemed insane, a vain conceit run amok. Riddled with doubt, he stared at Kath. "How in the nine hells are we going take that?"

Her voice was calm, not a hint of fear, but her eyes told another story, shadowed with worry. "It all depends on how many men the Mordant took south. The fact that we haven't run across a patrol is a good sign. He left the gore hounds but I'm betting he took most of the men south."

"You're *betting* with our lives."

"I know, but it's our best chance." She met his gaze. "Remember, no matter the numbers, we're counting on deception and surprise to win the day. Danya will provide the deception, and this," she pulled her stone gargoyle from beneath her chainmail shirt, "will provide the surprise."

Blaine's frustration boiled over. "But your plan is all sleight of hand, a house of straw! Once we're inside those walls, we could face a hundred thousand men or more! The odds are staggering!"

"We take the north gate...and then we hope the people rise and fight." She stared at him, as if willing him to believe. "We seek surrender not a bloodbath."

Surrender! He nearly spat the word. Surrender was the wet dream of every commander who'd ever lived, yet it seemed to Blaine that it rarely happened, especially when the enemy held the walls. And *these* walls were formidable. He bit his lip and kept his doubt to himself. "What are those things over there?" Five leagues to the east of the citadel, a series of wooden towers reared into the sky like malformed dragons.

Torven answered. "That's the lip of the Pit."

"The Pit?"

Torven scowled. "It's the worst of the Mordant's domain, worse than any dungeon. Those wooden structures lower cages down into the Pit, the only way in or out." He pointed to the left of the towers. "And over there are the soldiers' barracks for the Pit guards, and next to them, the stables." His voice deepened, revealing a touch of pride. "Come the dark, Fanggold will lead a war party against the barracks when Danya brings the others."

Blaine prayed the wolf-faced leader brought enough men to take the barracks, else they'd have swords at their back as well as in front. One mistake and Kath's plan would turn into a deadly trap. His gaze was drawn to the citadel. He brooded on the tiers of dark battlements, ramparts nested within ramparts. Like a Castlegard of the north, it seemed a daunting task, nigh on impossible. His stare slid toward Kath. "Still time to change your mind?"

She shook her head, a stubborn look on her face. "This is our best hope, our one chance to strike a blow against the Dark. It must be done now, while the Mordant marches south."

Conviction filled her voice, yet it did not ease his doubts. It seemed to Blaine that too much depended on luck and magic. He'd rather put his trust in good solid steel.

"Look over there!" It was Bear, pointing toward the east. A dark smudge flew through the twilight. Like an errant storm cloud, it flew straight for the Pit.

"Danya's done it." Kath's voice rang with a mixture of relief and pride. "She's called the ravens!"

A flock of ten thousand ravens bore down on the Pit. Blaine shivered beneath his cloak. "It's unnatural." He couldn't help sketching the hand sign against evil. The dark cloud circled overhead and dove into the Pit.

The painted warriors shared a grin, laughing and pointing toward the ravens, but Blaine could not share their joy. To him, the ravens had always been an omen of death, the scavengers of the battlefield. "Ravens are the heralds of death. Now the enemy knows we're coming."

Kath glared at him, steel in her green gaze. "Only if they know the symbols of slaves. This message is for our friends."

"Friends?" Blaine barked a laugh. "Depend on the swords you know."

Kath did not answer. They kept watch on the Pit. The cloud of ravens eventually remerged. Soaring out of the Pit, they circled the citadel. Round and round, they rode the wind, releasing a chorus of caws, and then they turned east, departing in one massive cloud.

Blaine shivered. "No one could ever see that as natural."

Kath gave him a barbed stare. "Then perhaps they see it as an omen of defeat."

Blaine looked away.

It took forever for the sun to set. Huddled beneath sheepskins, they shared a scant meal of dried horsemeat and honeyed mead, keeping watch on the citadel. The sun sank in a blaze of colors, gold and red streaking across a winter sky, but the glorious display was fleeting. Darkness descended like an executioner's axe. Torches appeared on the dark walls. *Too many torches,* proof the walls were not abandoned. Blaine took the first watch, but doubt gnawed at his mind. In three nights they'd storm the citadel. He couldn't help but think they were destined for doom.

58

Mara

Mara trudged through the mud, a wicker basket riding on her back. Brown clouds boiled overhead, sealing the Pit like a cauldron's lid. She glanced up anyway, longing for a glimpse of blue. Every spring she stood in line, desperate for a chit to work the farms, but her face always betrayed her. Youth and beauty chained her to the Pit. She worked on her feet during the day and on her back at night, a miserable existence, but she never stopped longing for a glimpse of sky, for a taste of freedom.

At least she no longer worked in the mines. After the rebellion, her uncle had gotten her work at the dung heap, but still her beauty betrayed her.

"Come and see me tonight." A guard leered at her, making a poking gesture with his right hand. "Ask for Harit in the barracks of the First Fist."

She ducked her head and hurried on. "Cursed be the Dark Lord and all those who serve him." It was only a whisper but the words eased her burning heart.

A hard frost covered the ground but her weight was enough to break the crust. Cold mud oozed between her bare toes, another blight of the Pit. Pulling her cloak close, she trudged through the muck. Mara reached the gates and a familiar guard waved her through. The dung heap was a landmark of the Pit, a brown mountain leaning against the western wall. Shoveled from the stables above, the dung formed a massive brown cone, a scree slope of waste. Old men in tattered rags scurried like beetles across the steep slope, gleaning the dung from the dross. Horse dung was precious in the Pit, the only source of fuel. Strange how the waste from above became the treasure of those below.

A horn blast sounded from above.

Someone screamed a warning.

A brown avalanche fell from the clouds, tumbling down the sheer rock wall. Workers scrambled to avoid the rush. Mara stopped and stared, unable to look away. An old man stumbled and fell, buried beneath the brown slush. Mara closed her eyes, such a terrible way to die.

A guard poked her with his spear butt. "No time to gawk. Those who work, eat."

Mara lurched forward, following mud-churned footprints. A brown mist clung to the air, the pungent scent of fresh manure. The tumble of waste slowly settled, adding a fresh layer of dung to the mountain. Workers scurried up the slope, hoping to find treasure buried among the dross.

Oblivious to the drama, a dozen old women knelt on the frozen ground, kneading straw into dung. Their hands beat a steady rhythm, forming the mixture into flat patties suitable for cook-fires. Stacks of patties dried in the weak winter sun, worth a small fortune to the overseers. Mara eased the empty basket from her shoulders and bent toward the nearest stack.

A toothless old crone scurried to her side, her back bent, her hands stained brown to her elbows. "Mara let me help." Thessala touched her hand, the old woman making a deft exchange. Mara risked a quick peek. A small comb carved of bone, only a few teeth missing, nestled in her hand.

Thessala flashed a snaggletoothed smile. "It's good, isn't it? Found it yesterday. Some soldier probably carved it for his sweetheart, lost among the stable's dross."

Mara slipped the comb into her pocket. "It should fetch a good price, an extra ration at least." She tucked her blond hair behind her ears and reached for another patty.

The old woman worked beside her, helping to fill the basket. "You're a good girl, Mara. With your face, you'll get a good price."

Her face, a blessing and a curse, but Mara just nodded, knowing the crone meant no harm. Forty patties filled her basket, a seller's allotment. Mara knelt, slipping her arms through the straps. Bending forward, she slowly rose, taking the full weight on her shoulders, just another beast of burden. She waved to Thessala and trudged toward the gate.

Mud squished between her toes, cold and slippery. One step at a time, she made her rounds, delivering the patties. Two tokens bought a single patty, enough to heat a pot of stew. A few women haggled for a better deal but the price was never hers to set.

Dirty faces peered from mud huts and thatched hovels, everything brown and dreary, a misery that leached into her soul. Nothing ever changed in the Pit...except for him, the man with the mismatched eyes, the one who'd dared to start a rebellion. She'd helped him in the mine, and helped herself to revenge. Her fist tightened, remembering the feel of the dagger, the sweet nectar of justice, but the rebellion was short-lived. She didn't even know his name...but she'd never forget his face, or the way he'd made her feel, like a woman with choices instead of chattel. At least she no longer served in the mine, gaining a dung sellers' basket by the grace of her great uncle, but she never forgot that brief taste of rebellion. A shame the gods didn't favor the uprising. Six men condemned to death, the soldiers hung them from the standing stones, a lesson for others. She'd kept vigil in the crowd, needing to witness their fates. The man with the mismatched eyes remained stoic in his pain, but the others began to talk, especially Clovis, calling the people to rebellion. His words kindled a fire in her heart. She'd sought out the council of elders, adding her voice to the others, begging them to rise up. But old men are slow to action, debating while brave men died.

A shadow fell across her face. The standing stones stood empty, the rotting bodies finally put to rest, but the call of rebellion still roiled in her heart. She leaned against the stone, wondering if the gods ever listened.

Something hard struck the back of her head.

She whirled to find the culprit...but no one was there.

Suspicious, she waited.

A stone clattered against the standing stones.

Astonished, Mara stared skyward. Another pebble fell from the sky. Piercing the thick brown clouds, it bounced and skittered, landing in the mud. *A stone from the sky*. And then she saw another. She stared open-mouthed.

The sky rained stones.

People emerged from their huts to stare. A hail of pebbles clattered into the Pit, a brief storm and then it was over.

Dark wings glided down from the clouds. Mara's breath caught at the rare sight. A single raven soared in a circle and then came to land at her feet. It dropped a pebble and then glared up at her, as if expecting something. "*Caw!*" Feathers ruffled, it stared at her with smoke-colored eyes. "*Caw! Caw!*" Dark wings stretched wide and the raven took flight, beating for the sky.

"Fly free, little brother." She made the words a prayer. Mara watched till the clouds swallowed the dark bird and then she knelt to claim the pebble. Just a small gray stone till she noticed the symbol etched on one side. Her fingers traced the carving. She couldn't read but every slave knew the symbol for rebellion. Her heartbeat quickened. She turned it over and saw three scores on the other side, a message from the gods.

Elated, she rushed to the nearest knot of people. "Do you see it?"

Three of them held pebbles. They all bore the same markings.

Mara smiled, "It's a message from the gods!" Rumors started this way, but she didn't care. She found herself running, suddenly fleet of foot, all the way to the large hut that served the council of elders. A small crowd had already gathered, a murmur of voices in the muddy lane. Shrugging the basket from her shoulders, she wormed her way to the front. A single guard blocked the doorway, a big man with a Taal's sloped forehead. He looked intimidating but Mara knew him from childhood. "Braith, let me in!"

He shook his head and stamped his foot. "No one passes."

Standing on tiptoes, she whispered in his ear. "Uncle Elswin asked for me."

Braith grinned a lack-wit's smile. "Okay, just you."

She slipped through the doorway, always surprised by the sudden warmth. A dung fire glowed in the center of a large circular room, the smoke rising to the peaked roof. The elders took their ease around the circular hearth, leaning on pillows, sipping cups of cha served by a handful of women. Thirteen elders ruled the slums, all of them men, their hair respectable shades of silver, gray, or white.

Mara clung to the shadows, slipping along the wall till she reached her great uncle, the only one she dared approach. She crept forward to kneel by his side. "Honored Uncle," she kept her voice to a hushed whisper, her head bent in respect, "I have something you should see."

He turned towards her, a rounded face framed by a wealth of silver hair. A necklace of polished red beads hung from his shoulders, the symbol of his council seat. "Mara, child, you should be working." He reached out to caress her cheek with a six-fingered hand. "You've a pleasing face but you disturb the council chambers all too often."

"But Honored Uncle, you must see this." She pressed the pebble into his hand. "Stones are falling from the sky. It's a sign from the gods."

"What?" Surprise flitted across his face. "You bring me a pebble?"

She struggled to contain her excitement. "I bring you a message! All the stones bear the same symbol!"

He fingered the pebble, a flash of annoyance on his face. "You bother me with nonsense."

"No!" She fought to keep her voice a whisper. "A rain of stones fell from the sky, all bearing the same message! It's a message from the gods! They mean for us to follow the words of the prophet, to rise up and claim our freedom."

"Quiet!" His voice hissed. "Talk of treason will get us all hung from the Stones." He dropped the pebble as if it had stung him. "Forget this nonsense. It took a fist full of favors to get you a dung sellers' basket. Now get back to work before you lose your place."

She shook her head, baffled by his disbelief. "But I saw you in the crowds. You heard the prophet. Everyone knows Clovis had the third eye. And now stones fall from the sky, giving proof to his words!"

He pounced, grabbing her arm, pulling her close, the smell of rancid milk on his breath. "You little fool." His face twisted to an ugly sneer. "*Dung* falls from the sky! Do you name that a miracle?" His long fingernails bit into her flesh. "Now be gone, or you'll find yourself chained in the brothels, nothing more than a broodmare for soldiers."

Horror pierced her heart, wakening her deepest fear. Snatching up the pebble, she scuttled backwards, fleeing the cruelty of his gaze. Desperate to be gone, she fled to the doorway, but the entrance was clogged with people, a barefoot mob chanting for answers. *"Lead us! Free us!"*

Braith struggled to open a space, his towering bulk pressed against the mob. "No one passes." He waved his arms like clubs, forcing the crowd from the doorway.

Spying an opening, Mara ducked beneath his arms. Clutching the pebble, she joined the crowd, just another dirty face in a sea of brown. The crowd's chant beat against her, waking the anger in her soul. *"Lead us! Free us!"* The chant rolled through the people like a rumble of thunder.

Movement at the council doorway. A space cleared and her uncle emerged, his hair glinting silver in the sunlight, his necklace of red stones adding authority to his broad shoulders. He raised his hands for silence, six fingers spread wide on each hand, proving to the people that he was one of them.

An expectant hush settled over the crowd.

Mara shuffled to the left, anxious to see, but not to be seen.

"Be calm, my friends," her uncle wore a paternal smile. "Return to your work. All is well."

"But the stones!" A tall man near the front dared to argue. "Surely it's a sign from the gods!"

A murmur rose from the crowd.

Her uncle raised his hands for quiet. "Think, my friends. Everything that comes from above does so by the will of our overlords." The crowd began to protest, but her uncle shouted above the murmur.

"Hear me! The stones are a test devised by the priests! A way of sorting the rebellious from the loyal."

Mara gaped, knowing it was a bold-faced lie. "*Ravens* brought the stones." It was only a whisper, but others repeated her words, an undercurrent of hope threading through the crowd.

Other councilmen emerged to stand behind her uncle, a show of authority. "Do not be deceived by the stones! Return to work and all will be well."

A dark-haired woman raised her voice in protest. "But what of the words of the prophet? Clovis had the sight! And now the gods have given us a sign!"

Anger flashed across her uncle's face. "Clovis *died* on the Stones and the gods did *nothing*. Don't be misled by false prophets." He glared at the crowd like an angry father disciplining a wayward child. "You have a duty to yourselves and your families. Life in the Pit is simple. You work and you eat. You work and you stay warm. You work and you live." He waved his arms in dismissal. "Be gone from here. Forget the stones and return to work before the soldiers come to claim the rebellious."

Mara stared at her uncle with fresh eyes. For the first time she noticed all the councilmen wore boots. *Boots!* Cold mud oozed between her toes, a reminder of her station in life. She realized the overlords set the councilmen apart from the people. Coddled by luxury, the council would never heed the gods' call. Mara stared at the pebble, flipping it from one side to the other, *rebellion in three.* But three what? And then she understood. Three nights till the dark of the moon, the perfect time for an uprising. The meaning burned with certainty in her heart, proving the truth of the message.

The council retreated to their chambers and the crowd began to thin. Most shuffled away with their heads bent, yoked once more to the will of the overlords, but a few knots of discontent remained.

Rebellions grew in the shadow of misery. Mara smiled, gripping the pebble in her fist. She'd seen the raven and she understood the message. Perhaps a pretty face could sway others to the truth. She tucked her blond hair behind her ears and moved toward the nearest knot of conspirators. Three days to make a difference, she swore to the gods she'd not be counted among the sheep.

59

The Knight Marshal

Three hours to prepare for mortal combat, yet the king seemed at ease, passing the time with his captains. The marshal sat at the king's right hand, sharing meat and mead by the fire's warmth. They supped on a light meal of roast ham, hard biscuits, and bread pudding, the best their meager stores could provide. Baldwin fussed over the king's armor, making sure every belt and buckle was secure, but there was no need to sharpen the king's sword, for blue steel never dulled.

King Ursus was in high spirits, regaling the men with tales of heroes from the Octagon's past. All the heroes triumphed, vanquishing their foes with keen swords and dauntless courage. The marshal listened but he could not share the revelry. A feeling of doom pressed down upon him, obsessed with the riddle of the Mordant's challenge. He stared into the fire but found no answers.

The healer came begging a word, but the king dismissed him and the marshal ignored him. Neither man could stomach more words of warning.

All too soon, the time was gone. The marshal claimed the honor of armoring the king. Greaves and gauntlets, breastplate and bracers, he made sure each piece was tightened and secure, everything polished to a silvery glow. On the king's head he placed a crowned helm, and for his left arm, a massive octagonal shield made of stout oak and beaten metal. Few men could wield a great sword and a shield, but the king did it with ease, a boon of blue steel.

Last of all, the marshal reached for the king's great sword, *Honor's Edge*. Five feet of peerless blue steel, the monk's crystal freshly set in the pommel; it was a mighty blade, a king's sword, forever honed to a silk-cutting edge.

"Not that sword." The king's voice was a low growl. "I'll take my revenge with Ulrich's sword, *Mordbane*." His voice softened. "The name always seemed a son's conceit but now it proves prophetic." His voice hardened. "I'll wield *Mordbane,* the perfect sword to claim a blood debt from the Mordant."

A shiver of foreboding raced down the marshal's back. "But Sire, for such a fight, you should use your own blade, the sword that best knows your hands."

"Give me *Mordbane,* for I'll use no other."

The king's voice was implacable. Bowing, the marshal unsheathed *Honor's Edge*, handing the great sword to Baldwin for safe keeping. Retrieving Ulrich's blue blade, he sheathed the sword and settled the harness across the king's shoulders.

Finished, the marshal bowed to his lord. "May Valin guide your blade."

The king smiled and gripped the marshal's arm, brothers-in-war once more. "Osbourne, guard my back."

It was the highest praise one warrior could give another. The marshal's voice caught. "Always, Sire."

A troop of knights brought the king's warhorse, Snowmantle, freshly curried and caparisoned in maroon and silver. Such splendid finery was unexpected. The men had clearly scavenged among the other mounts to outfit the stallion in the best the maroon had to offer, a gift for their king.

King Ursus openly admired the stallion and then he swung into the saddle like a man half his age. Unsheathing *Mordbane*, he raised the sapphire sword to the heavens. "For Honor and the Octagon!"

The men answered with a thunderous roar. *"Honor and the Octagon!"* They drew their weapons and beat their shields, giving the king a warrior's acclaim.

As if in reply, a rumble of drums announced the enemy. A dark line appeared on the horizon. A thicket of spears and shields clogged the snow-cloaked valley, yet the horde kept their distance. As before, only six riders approached the Whore, but one was the Mordant. Distinctive in his skeleton armor, he rode a massive black stallion caparisoned in gold. Overhead, the Darkflamme fluttered and snapped like a serpent slithering in the wind, announcing his presence.

The marshal shivered with foreboding, but it was too late for words.

The king rode out to meet them. The marshal and four champions rode at his back, a keen set of weapons protecting their liege, the one precaution the king had agreed to. They stopped fifty yards beyond the wall, waiting for the enemy.

Six men rode toward them...led by the Skeleton King.

His armor glistened with a baleful light. Helm and breastplate, greaves and gauntlets, the silvery armor was patterned to resemble a lich king. The breastplate showed a skeleton's ribs, the helmet fashioned into a fearsome skull. A whisper of terror spiked the marshal, his gaze shying from the Mordant's armor. It reeked of wrongness, as if evil were somehow annealed into steel. A sudden queasiness gripped his stomach. A part of him wanted to rip the helm away and judge the enemy by his eyes, but another part expected a red-eyed ghoul to stare from the helm, a living dead encased in armor, a nightmare sprung from the pits of hell. Doubt gnawed at the marshal, as if the king faced an invincible foe. He shuddered and looked away. "Sire, you cannot fight that."

"I gave my word." The king swung down from his warhorse, a blaze of silver and maroon.

The marshal's horse stamped and shied, fighting the bit as the enemy drew near.

Six riders stopped a bowshot away, the Darkflamme snapping overhead. The Mordant dismounted and walked forward alone.

The marshal swung down from his horse and gripped the reins, studying the enemy with veteran eyes. The skeleton helm hid the Mordant's face but he was most likely the younger man. Quickness and perhaps stamina would be to the Mordant's advantage, but the king had a lifetime of experience, a seasoned warrior, a master at the sword. And the king stood slightly taller and heftier than the Mordant, giving him the advantage of reach and strength. The Mordant carried no shield, but that was to be expected. Only blue steel allowed a great sword to be wielded in one hand, another advantage to the king. But the skeleton armor proved hard to look at, as if some dark magic ensorcelled it with an aura of dread. *Steel against magic,* he liked it not. The marshal made the hand sign against evil, sending a desperate prayer to Valin.

The king met the Mordant halfway. Whatever words were exchanged, the marshal could not hear. The combatants moved apart, putting two spear lengths of snowy ground between them.

King Ursus drew his blue sword, a gleam of sapphire in the afternoon light. *"For Honor and the Octagon!"*

The Mordant remained silent, slowly drawing his sword. The great sword had the same length as the king's, but *the blade was black!* Dark as sin, it seemed to swallow the light.

"What sorcery is this?" The marshal's words were a hiss.

Beside him, Sir Rannock growled, "We swore not to interfere."

The marshal ground his teeth, "Sorcery was not part of the bargain!" but the battle was already joined. The king sprang forward, attacking with an overhand cut. The sapphire sword sliced down with a deadly whistle, a mighty overhand cleave, but the Mordant glided sideways, evading the blue sword. Pivoting, the king chased his opponent with a powerful diagonal cut, but once again the Mordant slipped away, almost as if he anticipated the king's moves. Attack and evade, the battle fell into a maddening rhythm.

"He's toying with him, trying to wear the king down."

"But look at his footwork, the bastard glides like a veteran."

And it was true, the Mordant fought like a seasoned knight. The marshal's mind screamed a warning, yet he could only watch.

Stroke and evade, they circled like a pair of scorpions wary of each other's sting. The king's footwork began to slow, and the Mordant leaped to the attack. The black blade slashed down in an overhand cut. The king was quick to parry. For the first time, the two blades met in a fearsome clash...but the sound was wrong. Instead of a metallic clang, the swords loosed an ear-shattering screech.

Blue steel screamed in pain! The sound scraped across the marshal's soul.

The king staggered backwards, but then he recovered, aiming a fury of blows at the Mordant's head. The black blade parried each blow...and each time the steel screamed.

The combatants broke apart, slowly circling, testing with a series of feints. Fatigue slowed their footsteps, but both kept their swords raised. It seemed as if both men waited for an opening, but then the king did something unexpected. He hurled his shield at the Mordant, making him stumble. Leaping forward, the king attacked with a mighty two-handed blow, a great overhand cleave. Keening a deadly whistle, the sapphire sword descended like righteous vengeance. The blow should have cut the Mordant in two, but somehow the Skeleton King raised his dark sword. Black steel parried the blue blade, releasing a deafening screech.

And then the king's blade broke.

Blue steel sheared in half! Ulrich's sword failed!

The marshal gaped in horror. *"Impossible!"*

The king staggered to a stop, staring at his broken sword, little more than a hilt in his hands.

The Mordant attacked, sending a vicious cut to the king's head.

Weaponless, the king jerked backward, trying to avoid the blow...and then he tripped and fell. The Mordant leaped forward. Placing his boot on the king's chest, he held him at sword point. The

Mordant removed his helm. "Behold the man who claims the life of a king! Vengeance is mine this day!"

The marshal gasped for he knew the face. Not a ghoul, not a lich, but a man with broken octagons branded deep into his cheeks, Raymond, the traitor-knight of Castlegard. The marshal's great sword leaped to his hand as if it belonged there. Rage drove him forward, a scream of defiance on his lips. *"No!"*

The traitor lifted the black sword in a two-handed grip, the tip held poised above the king's chest.

The marshal redoubled his speed, desperate to save the king.

The black blade plunged down. An unstoppable force, it sliced through steel and leather, flesh and bone. The king screamed as if burnt.

"NO!" Two strides and the marshal swung. His great sword took the traitor at his throat, cleaving the head from the body. Blood gushed from the severed throat. Headless, the skeleton staggered for two steps and then crumpled to a bloody heap.

The marshal glared at the Mordant's guards and they chose to flee rather than fight, running for the enemy's lines.

A great shout rose from both armies, but the marshal did not care. He knelt by his king, grief struck. "My lord!"

The king still lived, clutching the dark blade embedded in his chest, but it was a mortal blow, and they both knew it.

A sob broke from the marshal. "My lord, they lied, it was not the Mordant."

The king's eyes locked on his. "Sound...retreat."

Chaos erupted around him. The other champions surrounded the king with a ring of steel. And then a wagon rumbled near. The healer held the horses to a tight turn. Baldwin crouched in the wagon bed, his face chalk white. Quintus pulled the wagon to a stop. "Put him here!" They bent to lift the king.

The healer shouted a warning. "Remove the sword and he'll die!"

They laid the king in the wagon bed, the dark sword still protruding from his chest. Baldwin cradled the king's head, crying a river of tears. The healer cracked the reins. The wagon jerked forward, the horses lashed to a gallop.

The marshal grabbed the reins of his stallion and vaulted into the saddle. He threw a glance toward the far end of the valley. The enemy roiled in a froth of confusion. Putting spurs to his stallion, the marshal galloped back toward the Whore. "Sound the retreat!" Standing in his stirrups, he yelled above the din. *"Sound the retreat!"*

A single trumpeter obeyed, but it was enough. The call stirred the maroon to action. Like angry hornets flung from the nest they scrambled beyond the third wall, seeking mounts and supplies.

The marshal spied Lothar in the confusion. "Get the men away. Tell them to split up and ride for the hills. If we leave a thousand trails, the enemy will never bother to follow. We'll regroup at the Stonehand in a fortnight."

Lothar nodded. "And you?"

"I'm with the king." Heedless of anything else, the marshal put spurs to his horse and followed the wagon tracks toward the hillside, desperate to reach his king.

60

Duncan

Pain pierced every part of his body, a hundred stabs of agony. Chained to the stone floor, lying spread-eagled beneath the gibbering shadows, madness reached for Duncan yet he fought to keep his sanity. He needed to remember, he needed to live, holding onto the hope that Kath would come...yet he feared for her to dare the Mordant's stronghold.

Kath! Her name alone was like a balm, yet he tried not to think of her, afraid the shadows would invade his mind, tricking him into a betrayal. Yet sometimes he could not resist. Succumbing to daydreams, he clung to her easy smile or a flash of her leaf-green eyes, imagining all that could have been. Such dreams were sweet but fraught with danger. So he locked them tight in his heart, longing to know that she was safe.

On worse days, when nightmares plagued his mind, he lived in dread of the Mordant's return. Three times the Mordant had reached through his pain, using him as a scrying vessel to speak with the Dark Lord. Always it started with a foul, oily taste in his mouth, a prelude to agony. Even from afar, the Mordant inflicted torment, flaying his body with Darkness, using him like a whore, a sacrifice to the Dark Lord. Each ordeal seemed worse than the last, leaving him shuddering on the cold stone floor, gagging on the foul taste of Darkness. Duncan wondered how much more he could endure.

Naked and chained to the cavern floor, he struggled to survive the slow drip of time, nothing to do but suffer and wait. But then one day, he perceived a change. High among the stalactites, the shadows broiled like angry wasps; perhaps something spoiled the plans of the Dark Lord. Duncan took it as a sign of hope, watching the shadows through hooded eyes.

Later, much later, he learned the truth.

A small voice came to him in the back of his mind. *Are you there?*

Yes! He grabbed for the voice like a drowning man lunging for a piece of driftwood.

Listen to me! The voice of the monk whispered through his mind. *A great battle has been fought*"

His heartbeat quickened, thinking of Kath and her sword, but then he forced the image away, striving to listen.

Raven Pass has fallen; the Mordant's hordes sweep south. The Octagon is defeated but not broken, not humiliated. A traitor was revealed, spoiling the Mordant's plans. Ever the Deceiver, the Mordant laid a trap for the knights, hoping to defeat the Octagon with their own honor. But the knights escaped the trap, scattering into the mountains. Even in defeat, there is still hope!

What about the north? He longed for some word of Kath yet he dare not reveal too much. He still did not trust Bryce, not with his most precious secret.

The Mordant's gaze is fixed on the south. Urgency spiked the monk's words. *You must tell the others. The crystal dagger must come south!*

Where are you? Tell me more

Fear flashed through the whispered words, *The Mordant wakes. I dare not linger.*

And then the monk was gone, like a door closing in the back of his mind. Duncan was once more alone, trapped within his own nightmare. He rattled his chains and glared at the shadows, but within his mind he savored the words of the monk. *Even in defeat, there is still hope.* The words gave him strength, a way to fight back, making him a warrior once more. Laughter bubbled out of him, a wild berserker's laugh. Duncan stared at the shadows and roared his defiance. "You shall not win!" From the depths of the cavern, his words echoed back to him, as if a thousand ghosts took up his war cry. "You shall not win!" But the grim chorus could not shake his conviction. Even in this desolate hell, Duncan knew there was more to the world than just darkness.

61

Katherine

Poised for battle, Kath and her band of warriors hid within the shadow of the citadel, waiting for the dark of the moon. *The dark of the moon,* that fallow time of the month when all life held its breath and the dead drew near. A time of superstition and fear, when honest folk sought shelter and nightmares held sway. Even the sea birds sensed the coming dark, stilling to a hush as twilight fled.

Kath made the moonless night her ally. Dark and forbidding and laden with omens, it was the perfect setting for a deceit of swords.

Twilight deepened. The dark was nearly upon them. Hiding beneath a sheepskin cloak, a smudge of cream against the snow, Kath led her small band toward the dark walls. Silent as death, they crept within the very shadow of the Dark Citadel. Needing the assurance of cold steel, Kath drew her sword and stared up at the monstrous fist of stone, the lair of the Mordant.

Nightmares lurked within. She felt it in the marrow of her bones, yet she refused to turn back. More than a fortress, the citadel was a bastion of evil, a source of power for the Mordant. She swore to deny him that power. But oh, the risks. The painted people had come to believe in her, naming her their Svala, the wearer of their War Helm. Without reservation, they lent her all their strength, every warrior, young and old, male and female, committed to a single battle. If they failed...if *she* failed, a proud people would be left defenseless before the Mordant's soldiers. She could not fail. Yet despite the risks, she would not turn back. In the depths of her soul, she believed this was their one great chance to strike a blow against Darkness. And she believed her plan would work. Kath prayed to Valin like she'd never prayed before.

A soft rustle at her back. Beside her, Bear whispered, "They come."

Pride rushed through her; she'd never doubted it.

More than three thousand painted warriors crept across the frozen fields. Hiding beneath sheepskin cloaks, they seemed a part of the landscape, a wild force of nature. Approaching from the north, they lay in ambush behind her, waiting for her signal.

Kath planned to attack from the north, from the direction least expected. While the bulk of her army moved into position, another smaller force of eight hundred, led by Fanggold, was making its way up from the south with Danya. The citadel was an imposing fortress but it had two weaknesses, two gates, a main one on the south side, and a smaller sea gate in the north. Like swordplay, battle was all about feints and misdirection. If her plan worked, the forces of the citadel would rush to protect the southern gate while she attacked from the north. But much would depend on Danya and the dark moon.

She leaned towards Bear, keeping her words to a whisper. "Call a runner."

The big man cupped his hands to his mouth and made a soft whirring sound, imitating a bird of the steppes.

A few moments later, a youth clad in white sheepskin crept near. In the fading twilight, Kath could just make out the fierce fox tattooed on his face. "Your name?"

"Tannin, Svala."

"Tannin, I need you to get a message to Fanggold. Tell him to attack the barracks at the Pit, release the horses from the stables, and then set them aflame. And tell him to raise a loud noise, for I want the enemy to hear the battle. The citadel needs to be convinced that a great army lies beyond its southern gates." She stared at him. "Can you do that, Tannin?"

"Aye, Svala, I will." And then he was gone, scurrying across the frozen fields like a mouse evading a hawk, his sheepskins blending into the snow.

Kath prayed he wasn't seen.

Blaine leaned toward her, his face darkened with streaks of mud, just like her own. "What now?"

"Now we wait for Danya."

Darkness fell like a scythe, slaying the last of the twilight. Kath huddled beneath her sheepskin cloak, desperate for warmth. Time seemed to crawl. Waiting proved hard, giving her too much time to think. Nightmares plagued her mind, memories from inside the gargoyles, images of hell. Souls bound for centuries inside stone statues, trapped in unspeakable torment, a fate she could have shared. Shuddering, she gripped her sword hilt, fighting to banish the memories. She needed to focus on the battle ahead. So many things could go wrong. The biggest risk was the enemy's numbers. She had no way of knowing how many soldiers lurked within the dark walls. But if her army breached the gates and fought within the narrow streets of the citadel, then the numbers might be negated. And then there was Duncan, a worry of another sort. She prayed her dreams were only nightmares, not a warning from the gods.

The night wore on and the darkness deepened, not a sound upon the land. Even the stars were reluctant to shine. Valin gifted her with a moonless night, so dark and absolute that the sky seemed like the vault of a grave and all the world a tomb.

"Svala, look!"

And then she saw them. Lights crept across the land, thirty thousand or more, moving up from the south. Spread out across the fields, they swept forward like a tide of starlight, as if a vast army marched toward the citadel, each soldier holding a lighted taper.

Blaine gripped her arm. "It works! Danya's done it!"

"The awesome power of a Beastmaster." Kath could only imagine the strength of Danya's magic to hold so many to her will. She'd asked the wolf-girl to bring the mountain sheep out of the Ghost Hills and march them across the steppes. Thirty thousand sheep with glow crystals tied to their horns, they moved across the steppes like a vast eldritch army. Superstition and the dark moon completed the illusion, as if an attacking horde swarmed toward the citadel. The ghost army gave Kath the deceit of numbers she so desperately needed. "Now we wait to see if they believe it."

Huddled at the base of the citadel, Kath was close enough to hear the cries of alarm raised along the walls. Horns blared from the ramparts and drums pounded a warning. Shouts rang out, echoing against the stone walls. The distinctive whump of catapults and trebuchets shook the night, hurling boulders into the steppes. And all the boulders fell toward the south.

Blaine's voice leaped with eagerness. "You've done it! They've bought the ruse!"

"Wait." Kath held her forces back, giving the citadel time to shift the bulk of their men toward the southern gate.

Out on the southern fields, the army of lights kept their distance, a bright swarm dancing just beyond the reach of the defenders, yet the rain of boulders never slowed.

A clash of steel shattered the night, the distant battle sounds heightening the sense of danger. Flames erupted to the east, tongues of fire licking the barracks. A bright orange glow lit the massive wooden structures of the Pit, making them seem like flame-breathing dragons. "Fanggold." Kath released a long held breath. "Almost time."

The time for battle was nearly upon them, but she was not afraid, as if she'd finally found her true destiny.

"Stay low and keep quiet." Kath led her band of thirty-four warriors toward the northern gate, the same men who'd battled the hellhounds, every one wearing a swath of maroon tied to their sword arm. To a man, they'd insisted on following her into the citadel. If they failed, the rest of the army had orders to retreat.

Faces blackened, they crept across the frozen ground to the stone ramp, a broad roadway leading up to the northern gate. Torchlight flickered along the battlement but the ramp remained sheathed in darkness. Kath shed her sheepskin cloak, leaving it in the snow, trusting the maroon cloak to hide her against the dark stone. Slow and stealthy, she crept up the ramp, a thin line of marauders following behind. Halfway up, her shoulder blades itched. Fearing an arrow or a crossbow bolt, she hugged the ground, afraid to breathe. When no bolt came, she scurried forward, relieved to reach the ironbound gate.

The gate was immense, timber reinforced with iron plates, thrice the height of a tall man. Wood was impervious to her magic, so Kath avoided the gate, seeking the stone wall on the far side of the gatehouse. Slipping around the corner, she pressed her back against the cold stone. Blaine, Bear and Boar kept close. The others hugged the darkness, an ambush waiting for an open gate.

Kath reached for the amber pyramid lodged deep in her pocket. Breaching the wall would be risky. Anything could lurk on the other side, including a legion of soldiers. Kath knew she was just as likely to walk into a trap, as to succeed, but it was too late for doubt. She sidled close to Blaine. "If I don't return, take the others back and warn the painted people."

Kath held her breath, expecting another argument, but he just gave her a curt nod. "I'll be waiting for you."

She gripped his arm in thanks. Sending a quick prayer to Valin, she looked at Bear and Boar. "Ready?"

Both men nodded, gently easing their swords from their scabbards.

"Then take a deep breath, and whatever happens, don't let go."

She stood between them, linking her arms through theirs, pulling them close. Taking a deep breath, she summoned her magic and stepped into the wall.

Evil assaulted her. Like plunging headfirst into a frozen sea, she writhed in shock. Stone surrounded her, seeking to steal her breath, pulling her down like a dark malignant tide. Panic threatened, like nothing she'd ever experienced. The stone itself was corrupt, imbued with evil. Kath flailed against the dark current, desperate to keep her bearings. Disoriented, her lungs burned with need. She tightened her fist on the small amber pyramid. A light flamed within her mind and the panic eased. Forcing herself forward, she battled against the dark tide...and then she was through, stepping into air. Gasping for breath, she doubled over, convulsing like a drowned sailor.

Firm hands seized her arms.

She looked up, relieved the two men had made it.

They pulled her back against the wall, into the shadows. Her mind snapped back into focus; they were *inside the citadel*. Excitement laced with fear shivered through her. She'd half expected a legion of soldiers to be lurking just inside the gate but the street was nearly empty. She strained to listen for the tramp of boots. Drums and trumpets echoed through the night, but the sounds were distant, somewhere toward the southern gate.

Torches fluttered along the far wall, drawing her gaze. Kath gasped in shock, recognizing the small statue carved into the wall like a wayfarer's shrine. Three creatures sitting in a row with rounded ears and long tails, but the carvings had very human gestures. One covered his ears, another his eyes, and the third his mouth, a crude version of the statue in the Kiralynn monastery. The creatures seemed to mock her. She staggered back against the wall, there was more evil here than she'd ever imagined.

"Are you all right?" Bear gripped her arm, staring into her face. "You're as pale as death."

Kath nodded. "I'm fine," but she knew she wasted valuable time. She gripped her sword, desperate to clear her mind. A pair of guards patrolled the gate, but otherwise the street was empty.

A door burst open and a dozen armor-clad guards emerged, half of them carrying crossbows. They clattered up the stairs to the barbican over the gate.

Kath shook her head. "We need more men." The plan called for her to slip back into the wall, ferrying her men through two at a time. She shuddered, reluctant to re-enter the stone, but she had no choice. "Wait here."

Taking a deep breath, she gripped the amber pyramid and stepped back into the wall. Evil struck like a cold wave, battering against her, but this time she was ready. Holding her breath, she forged a path against the dark tide, refusing to be swept away. Head down, she battled forward, holding a blaze of light in her mind. And then she was through, staggering into the air.

Hands caught her, strong and sure, pulling her back against the wall. "Svala!"

Blaine and Sidhorn stared down at her, big men bristling with weapons.

Just for a moment, she sagged against them, gulping air and warmth, and then she took a steadying breath. "You're needed on the far side."

They did not hesitate. Linking arms with her, they turned to face the wall. Kath wished she had their certainty. Taking deep breath, she sent a prayer to Valin and plunged back into the dark stone.

Thrice more, she made the perilous passage. Each time, the men were unaffected, but the dark stone took its toll. Shaking, Kath leaned against the inner wall. "No more," she shook her head, "I can't do it again."

Blaine took charge. "Then we'll have to make do." He whispered orders to the others. Bear and Boar would open the gate while the rest charged the stairs, attacking the bowmen on the battlement. "Kath, can you take out the two guards with your axes?"

Her hands shook. "Not yet." She hated admitting the weakness but she'd not spoil the plan, not when they were so close.

Bear said, "We'll take them with our slings."

Kath grinned at the irony. The simplest of weapons would open the gates to the Dark Citadel.

Blaine nodded to the big warrior. "When you're ready."

Kath slipped her sword from its scabbard. They crouched in the shadows, tensed for battle. Bear and Boar loosed their slings, a quick whirl followed by a sharp crack. The two guards dropped, felled in their tracks, and then everything erupted in a blur of motion. Bear and Boar raced for the gate while Kath guarded their backs. The big men put their shoulders to the massive crossbeam, straining to open the gate. Blaine led the others up the stairwell, attacking the archers on the barbican.

"Who's there?" A shout rang from the ramparts, followed by a scream.

A crossbow bolt whistled into the courtyard, but it struck only stone.

"*Hurry!*" Kath stood in a crouch, holding her blade at the ready, searching the shadows for enemies.

Boar grunted, struggling to lift the massive beam.

Shouts rang from the ramparts. A man screamed and a body tumbled from the walls, landing with a thud on the cobblestones. Kath flicked a glance toward the corpse, relieved to see a stranger's face. *"Hurry!"*

A door crashed open and more guards poured out.

"They're coming!" Kath tensed, tightening her grip on her sword and shield.

A troop of guards raced towards her, their weapons bared.

Behind her, the massive beam crashed to the cobblestones. The gates creaked open.

"They're coming!" And then the fight was upon her. She parried the nearest sword thrust. Steel clanged with a fearsome clash. The brutal blow shuddered down her sword arm. Kath pivoted away, slashing toward her opponent's knees. A second sword flashed towards her neck. Spying the blow from the corner of her eye, she pulled away at the last moment. Sweat erupted beneath her chainmail. Badly outnumbered, she lurched backward, keeping her shield raised, too many to fight. Slash and turn, she gave ground, trying to blunt their attack.

And then the others came. With a wild howl, her painted warriors poured through the open gate. They roared into the guards, pushing them back, leaving a trail of death in their wake.

The battle swept past Kath. Sheathing her sword, she ran to nearest torch. Wresting it from its bracket, she leaped towards the gate. Standing in the open mouth, she waved the torch back and forth, once, twice, thrice.

A howl erupted from the steppes. Her army was coming. Tossing the torch aside, she unsheathed her sword and ran to join the others. *"For Castlegard and the Light!"* She raced up the cobblestone street, torchlight glinting on arms and armor. The battle for the Dark Citadel was begun.

62

Katherine

The night became a confusion of swords, a running battle fought in the streets. The cobblestones ran slick with gore. Kath fought in the vanguard, struggling to push the guards up hill. One step at a time, they claimed the street, a bloody clash of steel.

A sword stroke rushed towards her face. Kath took the blow on her shield and then lunged forward. Her sword found an opening, severing a guard's hand. Another guard leaped to take his place. All around her, swords rang to a furious beat. Men in sheepskins battled men in armor. Her rag-tag band of painted warriors fought like demons, pushing the soldiers back, their fury defeating discipline. But Kath knew fury was fleeting. She urged her warriors forward, desperate to break the guards.

Beside her, a painted warrior slumped to the cobblestones, a feathered bolt lodged in his back. More bolts rained down. The street became a deathtrap. *"Push them back!"* She redoubled her effort. They needed to get away from the gate.

Feathered bolts hissed among them. More warriors fell. Some clutched arms and legs but there was no time for the wounded. Once begun, the battle was to the death.

The fighting was fierce, a desperate struggle on both sides. Men yelled and screamed. Wounded crawled away, trailing slicks of blood. Horns blared, adding to the confusion. Kath screamed her battle cry, *"For the Light!"* Bear and Boar fought beside her, a sword on her right a spiked mace on her left. The big men dodged in front, taking a blow aimed at Kath. Fighting like lions, they forced the guards to give ground, but not fast enough. Crossbow bolts hissed from the wall, bleeding their ranks from behind.

Somehow Blaine found her. Screaming his battle cry, *"For the Octagon!"* he pushed his way to the front, cleaving a path through the enemy. His blue sword cut like a scythe, driving the enemy back, but still the guards did not break.

Footsteps thundered from behind. Painted warriors poured through the gates, joining the fray, their tattooed faces savage in the torchlight. Like a relentless tide they pounded up the street, adding their numbers to the vanguard, a battering ram pushing from behind. The line surged forward, trampling the wounded. The guards gave ground...and then they broke and ran.

"*For the Light!*" Kath led the charge.

Her painted warriors gave chase, howling like banshees.

The cobblestone street curved upward, taking them beyond the reach of the deadly crossbows. Houses crowded close, creating a canyon of stone. Doors slammed shut all along the street. Grim faces peered from half-shuttered windows. The people of the citadel neither hindered nor helped. A smoldering rage erupted in Kath. She longed to drag the watchers from their homes and convince them to fight, but she dared not stop. The tides of battle were fickle. The advantage had swung to her side and she needed to ride the wave all the way to the top.

Someone howled like a wolf and the others took up the cry, as if a rabid pack stalked the citadel. Stone walls echoed the sound, multiplying their numbers. Tattooed faces leered in the torchlight, hungry for vengeance.

Their savagery had the intended effect. All resistance melted away.

The guards fled, disappearing into side alleyways. Kath kept her men together, refusing to be lured into rabbit warrens. Weapons held at the ready, they pounded up the main street, a relentless army of savage-faced warriors grinding their way toward the top.

The street curved around a bend, spilling into a second courtyard. Another gate blocked the way, a gleam of armored soldiers on the ramparts. But the torchlight revealed an obstacle of a different sort. Brown-robed citizens clogged the courtyard. A frightened mob pounded on the gates, demanding sanctuary. A black-robed priest stood atop the barbican, exhorting the people to fight. "Stay within your tier! Protect your homes! Take up arms and fight! Kill the invaders and your reward shall be great!"

Kath's army slowed to a crawl, crowding the mob from behind. She leaned toward Bear. "Can you reach the priest with your sling?"

"Yes."

"Then wait for my word." Kath raised her voice to the crowd. "Why do you listen to the priests, when they are your true enemy?"

The crowd milled in confusion, frightened faces staring back at her.

"We've come to save you not to fight you! Join us! Kill the priests and take the citadel!"

The priest's face twisted into a mask of rage. "Kill the invaders!"

Kath hissed, "Now!"

Bear's sling whirled.

Crossbow bolts hissed from the walls, striking warriors and citizens alike. Kath took a bolt on her shield, staggering under the blow. A woman shrieked and children wept. Screams erupted through the courtyard, a massacre in the making.

Bear's aim struck true.

The priest tumbled from the wall, a flutter of dark robes landing on the cobblestones. The mob surged forward, attacking the priest and the gate.

More sling stones whirled through the air, striking the guards atop the wall.

Crossbows answered with a rain of death.

The courtyard became a deathtrap. Kath had to break the stalemate. Choosing a handful of warriors, she led them into a side alley. "We need to open the gate!" Left and then right, she made her way toward the wall. Bear and Blaine kept pace at her side. She gripped their arms, and they ran for the wall. "Don't stop!"

They leaped into stone. Darkness clawed at Kath but she barreled forward, never breaking stride. The inner walls were not as thick as the outer. They stumbled into air...and found themselves in a bedroom. A woman shrieked, clutching sheets pulled to her chin. Beside her, a naked man blustered.

"We mean you no harm." Kath made for the doorway, Bear and Blaine pounding behind. They tumbled through a kitchen and then another door, before reaching the street.

The sounds of battle drew them toward the gate.

Torches lined the barbican, a halo of light against the crenellated battlement. Soldiers crowded the walls, but they stared the other way, loosing bolts at the mob. Only four guards barred their path to the gates.

Surprise was their best ally. Quiet as death, they raced toward the gate. Kath hurled her twin axes at the nearest guards. Blaine leaped forward, his blue sword held high. One guard fell, an axe embedded in his throat. Another staggered backward, taking an axe in his shoulder. Before they could raise an alarm, Blaine reached the two remaining guards, attacking with a head-high swing. Blue steel keened a deadly whistle, cleaving straight through flesh and bone, taking two heads with a single blow. Bear dispatched the wounded guard and Kath retrieved her axes. "*Hurry!*"

The two men ran to the gate while Kath stood guard. Putting shoulders to the crossbar, they struggled to lift the massive log.

"*Hurry!*"

Groaning, they heaved the log from the braces. The massive beam crashed to the cobblestones and the gates creaked open. Shouts rang from the barbican but it was too late to stem the tide.

Kath and the two men retreated back up the street. Ducking into a side alley, they crouched in the dark.

The gates swung wide and the mob poured through.

Peering from the alley, Kath studied the people they'd come to save. Small and slight, they seemed stunted and malformed. Dirty and dressed in drab rags, they looked like a pack of starving urchins, yet the rage on their faces was fearsome to behold. Fists raised, the mob raced up the street, howling like a pack of harpies loosed from hell. One carried a spear impaled with the priest's severed head. The grisly trophy waved back and forth like a battle banner, spattering the crowd with blood. The mob cheered, seething with hate. Kath wondered what type of whirlwind she'd unleashed.

Blaine and Bear stayed close, their weapons held at the ready. They hid in the alley while the mob thundered past.

Moments later the army followed. Howling like wolves, the painted warriors ran through the street like a pack loosed to the wild hunt.

Kath stepped from the alley, standing within a ring of torchlight. The painted warriors raised a great cheer. "*Svala!*" Their shout shook the citadel. "*Svala!*" She drew her sword and led them forward, feeling the weight of destiny at her back.

63

The Knight Marshal

The marshal pushed his horse to a frothing gallop. The wagon proved too easy to follow. Twin ruts carved a path into snow, an easy signpost for friends or foes. Their best defense was confusion. With the maroon in retreat, the marshal hoped they'd leave too many trails for the enemy to follow, a scattering of thousands disappearing into the foothills, like mice scurrying to countless bolt holes.

Horns echoed up from the valley, a desperate blare repeating the retreat, but his only care was for the king. He gained the hilltop and skirted a stand of cedar, deep green against a forest of winter branches, a crust of snow covering the ground. The hillside dipped into a hidden valley, a small hollow nestled among the pines. Somewhere in the heights an owl hooted, a lonely sound. He spurred his horse forward, praying he wasn't too late.

The wagon stood at the heart of the hollow, horses lathered and blowing, hobbled within their traces. A massive oak loomed overhead like a marker, bare branches stark against a winter sky. Shadows crowded the hollow, the first touch of twilight. The marshal shivered, pulling his maroon cloak close, too many portents of death.

Three champions guarded the king, their weapons unsheathed. Sir Rannock, Sir Blaze, and Sir Abrax stood sentry around the wagon, grim-faced veterans, alert and wary, but they lowered their weapons when he rode into sight.

The marshal swung down from the saddle before the horse even came to a stop. His gaze sought out Sir Rannock. "Is he still...?"

Sir Rannock nodded, his face tense. "Just."

Sir Abrax growled, "Did you see his face? A traitor hiding beneath the Mordant's armor," he hawked and spat, "treachery and treason combined."

Sir Rannock said, "If the arrogant bastard hadn't lifted his visor we might have honored the terms."

But the marshal had no time for idle banter. "You three stand guard at the top of the rise. The wagon paints too clear a trail. We dare not be surprised."

The men saw through his words but they obeyed, mounting their horses with a swirl of maroon.

"And take Baldwin with you. I must speak with the king."

Dazed with shock, the red-haired squire obeyed. He swung up behind Sir Blaze, gripping the knight's maroon cloak.

Sir Rannock saluted. The horses whirled, a clatter of hooves on stone.

But the marshal was already focused on the king. Drawn like iron to a lodestone, he strode toward the wagon. The king lay sprawled across the flatbed, his face pale, his silver hair matted with sweat, his breastplate skewered by the dark sword. They'd removed most of his armor, but not the breastplate. The hilt of the blade jutted up from the king's chest, dark and obscene, proof of treachery and treason.

The marshal flicked a questioning glance to the healer. "Still alive?" The words were nearly a sob but the healer gave the barest of nods.

The marshal forced out the other question. "Can you?"

Quintus shook his head, his face lined with sadness. "He is beyond my skill." The brown-robed healer knelt by the king, gently easing a poultice under the breastplate.

"Osbourne...is that you?" The king's hand reached out.

The marshal climbed into the wagon. Kneeling, he gripped the outstretched hand, so cold the king seemed already dead, one hand reaching from the grave. "Stay with me, my liege."

"Blue steel...failed."

The marshal rushed to reassure his lord. "It wasn't the fault of the sword, or the wielder." Pride leached into his voice. "You fought like a legend, sire. But the dark blade is surely cursed, another trick of the Mordant. At least the traitor is dead, I promise you that."

Pain ripped across the king's face. "It burns, Osbourne. It sucks the life from me. Pull it out."

He yearned to rip the cursed blade from his king's body yet his gaze sought the healer.

Quintus whispered a warning. "Remove it and he dies all the quicker."

He gripped the king's hand, willing him to live. "My lord, there is something I need ask."

"The men?"

"I sounded the retreat and ordered the men to scatter. We'll regroup in a fortnight and harry the enemy from the rear." Stubborn pride filled his voice. "Be assured, my lord, the Octagon fights on."

"Good." The king sighed, as if a great weight eased from his shoulders, but then his face twisted in pain. "The sword, Osbourne! It burns!"

The marshal dreaded asking the question yet it needed to be done. "My lord, the Octagon needs a king."

The king stared up at him, a bubble of blood at the side of his mouth. "Five sons...dead."

"Yes, my lord." The marshal could not imagine another man wearing the octagon crown yet he persisted. "Who will you name as your successor? One of the champions or a younger captain, someone who can take the Anvril name and wear the crown? Perhaps Sir Abrax or Sir Blaze or Sir Ademar?"

The healer intervened. "My lord, you still have an heir of your body."

The marshal rebuked the healer with a sharp stare but Quintus persisted, his voice low and urgent. "Princess Katherine is the rightful heir to the Octagon."

The marshal reared back in shock. "A mere girl?"

"She proved herself at Cragnoth Keep, defeating Trask and the other traitors. And she lit the signal fires calling the Octagon to war. And she dared go north when others would not listen."

The marshal felt the weight of the great sword strapped to his back, another man's sword, taken from the ashes of the signal tower. "True knights fought at Cragnoth, Sir Tyrone and Sir Blaine, how dare you ascribe their deeds to a mere girl."

Anger rode the healer's words. "You're as blind as the others. The gods choose Katherine. *She* is the true bane of the Mordant."

"A mere girl cannot wear the octagon crown."

"Does...Katherine...still live?"

The king's question stilled both men.

The healer answered. "Sire, she must, else our best hope is lost." Quintus bent toward the king, conviction in his voice. "She is your true heir, a warrior and a leader."

Blood frothed at the king's mouth. "Only...a girl."

Frustration rode the healer's words. "Trust to your blood if nothing else. She is the last of your line. An Anvril, born and bred to the sword!"

"My sons...were born to...lead."

"And all of them are dead!"

The king gasped for breath, making a painful gurgle.

The marshal heard death lurking beneath the sound. "My lord, speak but a name and they will wear the crown." He leaned toward the king, desperate for an answer. "Will you have Katherine as your heir? Or will you name another? One of your champions or a younger captain?" He held his breath, willing the king to speak.

The king's stare moved from the marshal to the healer and then toward the distant heavens. "*My...sons!*" Blood frothed at his mouth...and then his face went slack as death.

"*My lord, no!*" The marshal gripped the king's hand, but there was no life left. Sorrow warred with rage. A scream ripped out of him. "*My king!*" He stood and yanked the cursed sword from the king's body...*and the hilt burned his hands!* Like cold fire eating through mail and leather, it stung him. He hurled the cursed blade into the woods. "*It burns!*"

The others heard his shout and came riding at a gallop.

He stood in the wagon, consumed by grief. "The king is dead."

They milled on their horses, staring up at him, shock writ large across their faces, yet they waited for a single name to be proclaimed. But he had nothing to give them. Instead he said, "Time to honor our king. He earned a hero's cairn."

The others bowed their heads in acceptance.

The marshal shot the healer a silencing glare.

They washed the king and bound his wounds. One last time, the marshal armored his lord, greaves and gorget, bracers and helm. They laid him on the crest of the hill, where he could keep watch over Raven Pass. The marshal arranged the king's maroon cloak so it covered the hideous rent in his breastplate. King Ursus looked as if he slept, his skin as pale as alabaster, yet he would never again wield a sword or lead the maroon into battle. Grief choked the marshal's throat.

They raised a cairn of stones over him, working late into the night. The healer offered to help but the marshal sent him away, keeping the honor for the maroon.

Working in silence, they scavenged stones from the hillside. The marshal set the last stone on the shoulder-high cairn. A great sadness descended upon him. There should have been trumpets and drums and a long recitation of honors, but there were only four knights and a squire attending the grave. The marshal drew his sword in a final salute. A ring of steel came from the others. He raised his sword to the heavens. "For Honor and the Octagon!"

The others echoed his cry. "*Honor and the Octagon!*"

The marshal stood at the head of the cairn, remembering his king. "Here lies Ursus Anvril, a valiant king, a staunch warrior, a man of honor; he gave his life defending the southern kingdoms, the last great king of the Octagon."

He felt the other's stares but he had no more words to give. One at a time, they sheathed their weapons and bowed toward the cairn and then they drifted away, but the marshal kept vigil with his lord. Twining his gloved hands around his sword hilt, he stood guard over the cairn, watching the stars span the winter sky. The world seemed a lonely place, impossibly empty without his king.

Something white glided through the trees. Silent as a ghost, it came to rest just beyond the cairn. "*Whoooo?*" A giant frost owl stared up at him, golden eyes glowing in the faint starlight. The owl seemed to ripple and stretch and then a blue-robed monk stood in its place.

The marshal staggered back a step. "So it's true!" The monk looked older, dark rings beneath his eyes, more than a touch of gray feathering his long hair.

"My sorrow for your loss." The monk gestured to the cairn. "It seems I've come too late. But perhaps all is not lost." Aeroth raised his right hand, palm held outward, revealing the blue tattoo of a Seeing Eye. "For the third time, I come bearing warnings to the Octagon. The king has fallen and shadows threaten all of Erdhe. Time grows short. Will you listen?"

The marshal gripped his sword, suddenly realizing all the decisions were now his to bear. "Speak your words."

"A great king dies without naming an heir."

The marshal gasped, the meddling monks knew too much.

But Aeroth gave him no time to respond. "It is best if the Octagon remains headless."

"Why?"

"So that the Mordant's gaze is kept elsewhere, away from the rightful heir."

His mind seemed to be stuffed with wool. "The rightful heir?"

The monk gave him a piercing stare. "Katherine of Castlegard."

He gaped to hear the name. "Just a girl." But sometimes he wondered...ever since the battle at Cragnoth Keep...but it could not be. It went against everything he believed. "Just a girl."

"The king's true-born daughter, born and bred to the sword, yet she is far more than just a warrior."

A girl wielding a sword, the image was unsettling. "Why does the octagon crown matter to you?"

"It matters to Erdhe."

Anger boiled within him. "So now the truth is revealed. Your Order is nothing but a bunch of bloody kingmakers."

The monk shrugged, but the intensity of his gaze never lessened. "We've been called worse." He gestured to the cairn. "One age is ended but another begins. Born of blood and deceit, the new age threatens to be full of Darkness unless a few dare to make a difference." The monk stared at him, as if peering into his very soul. "Will you dare to be among the few?"

"I'll hear your words but I'll make no promises"

"My Order takes the long view. Unlike the king, you know our warnings are worth heeding."

The marshal waited, unwilling to answer.

"Name no heir, at least for now."

He could have laughed, or cried, for he had no heir to name. For the thousandth time this night, he wished the king had spoken a name, just one name, any name, taking the awful weight from his shoulders. "I'll wait...for now."

The monk nodded, his face solemn. "And be wary of the dark sword, for it is not meant for the hands of men." And then the monk was shifting, blurring, changing, till a giant frost owl took wing into the night.

"Wait! I have questions." But the owl was already gone, soaring over the treetops.

The marshal swayed on his feet, suddenly struck with a profound weariness. Too much had happened this day, too much loss, too much pain. The night tightened around him, dark and cold and quiet...and full of loneliness.

Torchlight glimmered in the valley below. A river of torches moved south, too many to count. The enemy rallied, claiming Raven Pass. The way was open to the south, nothing to stop the Mordant's hordes. The Octagon had failed.

Defeat, the word tasted sour in his mind. Weary and disheartened, the marshal leaned on his sword, standing guard over the cairn. His king was gone and the world had changed. His soul rang with sadness. Perhaps the monk had the truth of it. Perhaps it was a new age, full of magic and darkness, full of tricks and deceit, but for the sake of his king, he would not give up. He raised his sword to the night sky and made his pledge before the king's cairn. "For Honor and the Octagon!" And it seemed the mountains echoed his cry, as if the gods accepted his word. Perhaps honor and valor still mattered in a world turned dark. The marshal clung to the hope, for it was all he had left.

64

Katherine

The fighting was fierce, a brutal plod through the cobblestone streets. The Dark Citadel proved a stone beehive full of stinging traps. Each level was guarded by a gate and each gate marked a different battle, a logjam of death, yet the fighting never seemed to end.

Corpses littered the street, the dead mingled with the dying. They left a bloody trail behind them, racing the ever-tightening death spiral toward the clouds. Resistance stiffened as they neared the top. Kath supposed the wealthy had more to lose but she refused to be bogged down in a siege. Urging her men forward, she used her magic to take most of the gates, but each level grew harder, weariness sapping her strength.

The numbers of her army waxed and waned with each spiral. Painted warriors fell in battle and brown-robed citizens emerged from houses to take up their swords. Kath led a wild-eyed swarm of tattooed warriors and starving urchins bent on vengeance. Her makeshift army stormed ever upward like a force of nature refusing to be denied. They showed no mercy. Even if she wanted to, Kath could not have stopped them. Every priest was doomed to death, torn to shreds by the mob, their grisly heads mounted on pikes like war trophies. Kath assumed they'd earned their fate, that evil begat evil, but the gory heads seemed like an ill omen, a barbarous act mocking the goodwill of the gods. She sent a swift prayer to Valin, hoping she never lost his favor.

Dawn streaked the eastern sky and still they fought.

Weariness assaulted her. Exhaustion became a second enemy, yet they dared not stop lest the soldiers regroup. Tired beyond the telling, Kath rounded the final bend, shocked to realize they'd reached the last gate. "Of course it's gold." Tall and imposing, the golden gates portrayed scenes of evil, cities destroyed, people enslaved, a fitting entrance to the palace of the Mordant.

Beside her, Blaine leaned on his blue sword, blood spatters marring his silver surcoat. "Can you?"

Kath shook her head. Countless passages through the dark walls had taken their toll. "I dare not, not without rest. My magic is spent. If I enter the wall I will not leave it."

Blaine nodded. "Then we'll do it the old fashioned way." He raised his voice in command. "Bring the ram!"

A dozen burly warriors carried the crossbeam from the last gate. The massive beam served as a makeshift ram. Her painted warriors raised scavenged shields above the ram, forming a protective shell of gold and black. Like an armored turtle, the ram bore down on the golden gate. Spears and crossbow bolts rained death from the wall but they could not slow the turtle. Bristling with feathered bolts, the ram barreled toward the gate.

Beside her, Blaine whispered, "Almost there!"

But the sense of victory eluded her.

Once, twice, thrice, the ram knocked against the golden gates. A great boom echoed through the street. And then the ram broke through. The golden doors buckled and broke. The way was open. They'd breached the last tier, reaching the palace of the Mordant.

A great cheer swept through her army. With a roar, they rushed forward, eager to claim the ultimate prize, but Kath entered with dread, all of her nightmares crowding close.

The gates opened onto a vast circular courtyard. A royal palace dominated the far side, like nothing Kath had ever seen. Gilded steps led to a great crescent-shaped palace adorned with golden columns and black marble. Grand and imposing, it reeked of power and opulence. Kath wondered what horrors lurked within.

Steel clanged against steel. Small battles raged across the courtyard, pockets of guards making a desperate stand, but they were soon cut down. Her army swept across the yard like a tidal wave, an unstoppable force bent on victory.

Kath followed at a measured pace, her sword in her hand, Bear and Boar at her back. And then she noticed the detail beneath her feet. Dark runes marred the silvery granite. Carved from black marble and inset in gray granite, the runes spiraled inward toward the courtyard's heart, like a trail of dark magic, a curse writ in stone. The runes seemed to writhe with evil, daring her to read them, a dark incantation waiting to be woken. She followed the runes, drawn toward the center. At the heart of the runic spiral, the peak of a dark monolith thrust up through the courtyard like a primal force. And on the side of that monolith was a doorway, a dark cleft in the stone.

Kath shuddered in fear. She'd seen that doorway in the worst of her nightmares. It called to her like a fate that could not be escaped.

She crossed the courtyard, oblivious to the fighting.

A wounded soldier reared up in her path, a sword in his hand, an ugly leer on his face. "You're mine, witch."

"*Svala!*" Bear leaped in front, crossing swords with the soldier.

A hand grabbed her ankle, but Boar attacked, severing the grip.

Swords clashed across the courtyard, yet she did not care. Kath walked past, drawn toward the doorway. She entered the cleft, a chill spearing her soul. Steep stairs spiraled down, torches lining the rough-hewn walls. The very air reeked of evil.

Blaine called to her, but she did not answer.

She took the stairs two at a time. Cold and dank, the shadows flitted around her like swarms of bats. Sensing steel would be of little use, she sheathed her sword and reached for the amber pyramid. Light glowed in her mind like a shield. Down and around, the stairs delved deep, as if she descended to the very pits of hell. Even the air tried to strangle her, so thick with evil she nearly choked. Fighting her own dread, she raced down the steps, desperate to prove her nightmares wrong.

Footsteps followed behind, a fading echo. Friend or foe she did not know, but she could not wait. A bonfire of urgency burned through her blood. Kath raced the darkness into the depths.

Down and around she followed the last spiral, and then the stairs opened to a small chamber. A massive copper door blocked the way. Two guards startled alert. Bristling with spears, they leaped toward her. But Kath never slowed. She reached for her axes, two whirls of death. The guards died where they stood, clattering to the stone floor.

Kath stood before the Door.

Incised with runes, the great copper door was green with age. Round like a portal, it reeked of time and death and evil, a prelude to nightmares. Kath gripped the amber pyramid, wondering if she dared even touch the rune-covered copper.

The Door shuddered open.

Moving of its own accord, it gaped like an invitation...or the maw of a trap. A rotting stench poured out, the smell of sulphur and blood and death, a taunt of fear. Kath whispered a prayer to Valin and then plunged through the Door.

She entered a cavern carved from nightmares. Red stalactites hung from the vaulted ceiling like drops of frozen blood. Braziers belched flames, tongues of fire licking the ceiling. Shadows capered across the cavern walls. And there, at the heart of the chamber, chained to the floor like an offering...*Duncan!*

"No!" The scream tore from her heart. *"Not you!"*

He lifted his head. "Kath?"

She raced toward him, kneeling by his side, overcome by the sight of his broken body. "What have they done to you?"

Fear shimmered in his eyes. "Are you real or an illusion come to tempt me?"

She touched his face, covering his mouth with a kiss. "I'm real, beloved."

He gasped, staring up at her, as if drinking in her face. "I knew you'd come." Love shone from his eyes, tearing at her heart.

She longed to take him in her arms and hold him close, to feel his heart beating against hers, but oh the daggers. Pierced by a hundred silver knives, they'd ruined his magnificent body. She shuddered to think of the pain, wondering that he still lived. "We need to get you out of here."

Words tumbled out of him, full of urgency. "I never told him about you. He does not know what you carry. Your secret is safe and so is Danya."

"Later, tell me later, but first your chains."

Fear flickered across his face. He threw a glance toward the ceiling. "Beware, the shadows listen."

She followed his gaze and saw it was true. Shadows broiled across the ceiling, taking sinister shapes. Horns and tails, claws and faces, the shadows took the form of demons, staring down at her like a ravenous horde of nightmares. A sibilant hiss whispered through the cavern. *"Give us the Quickner! The power is ours!"* Shadowy claws stretched towards her.

Kath ducked away.

Duncan convulsed in pain. "It's a trap! You must go!"

"Not without you!" She tugged on his chains, desperate to free him, but he was bound tight. Drawing her sword, she attacked his shackles. Steel clanged against steel, drawing sparks, but the shackles did not break. Desperation lent her strength. Again and again, she struck with all her might, but the sword did no damage, as if the dark metal was spelled against harm. Kath sobbed, "It won't break!" She clawed at the chain, frantic to win his freedom.

The shadows grew bold, darting toward her. *"Give us the Quickner!"*

Huddled on the floor, she slashed at them with her sword, but steel could not pierce shadows. Her hand crept to the crystal dagger, but a sixth sense warned her to keep it hidden.

Emboldened, the shadows grew close.

Duncan yelled, *"Run! You must run!"*

And then Blaine appeared in the doorway. Like a hero of old, his silver surcoat shimmered in the torchlight, his sapphire sword in his hand.

The shadows shrieked, retreating to the stalactites.

"Blaine! Your sword!"

Her command conquered his shock. Blaine rushed forward, lifting his sword in a two handed grip. He struck at Duncan's shackles. Sparks flew and metal screamed. Blue steel blazed bright like a sword of legend. Once, twice, and the dark metal shattered, releasing the first shackle.

Shadows broiled overhead, a flock of angry demons.

Blaine attacked the second shackle.

Duncan howled in pain, his face contorted like a thing possessed. *"He's come! The Mordant comes! Don't let him see you!"*

Fear pulsed through the chamber.

The shadows gibbered overhead, dark claws reaching down like a flock of starving vultures.

Kath stared at Blaine. "Get him free! No matter what happens, get him out of here!"

Blaine struck a mighty blow and the second shackle crumbled to dust.

Duncan writhed against the floor, his face a mask of pain, his mismatched eyes clouding with an inky Darkness. *"He comes! Get back!"*

The force of his warning drove Kath backwards, deeper into the chamber. She crouched on the floor, willing Blaine to hurry.

Blaine leaped to the third set of shackles, his blue sword flashing against the darkness. Metal screeched as if in pain and the third shackle sundered.

Overhead, the shadows *laughed.*

Duncan convulsed on the floor. His back arched, his mouth stretched impossibly wide, as if he swallowed darkness. And then his voice changed. Another voice, deeper and full of malice, filled the cavern. *"I see you, knight of the Octagon!"*

Blaine froze, his blue sword held poised above his head.

Kath gaped, knowing she heard the voice of the Mordant.

"You breach my citadel but the prize is hollow. The battle for the south is already lost. The Octagon is broken, scattered before my army. And your king lies dead, spitted upon my sword."

Father! Kath stifled a whimper, a splinter of pain piercing her heart.

"You come here at the bidding of the Kiralynn monks. Yet you follow a doomed cause. They have deceived you. The monks will fail, condemned to a terrible end just like the Octagon. I alone will rule all of Erdhe."

Kath's hand crept toward the crystal dagger...but this was Duncan not the Mordant. Yet what if this was her one chance to slay evil? A chance to defeat the Mordant within his very lair? But her heart cried against it, she could not harm Duncan.

"I alone am the one true power of Erdhe." The Mordant's voice boomed through the chamber, full of dark seduction. *"Serve me and you shall live. Kneel to me and I will raise you up, granting you powers you cannot imagine!"*

Kath stared at Blaine willing him to strike, but the knight remained still as stone, an odd look on his face.

The Mordant's voice grew in strength. *"Swear your sword to me and you will have more than one lifetime of pleasure! Kneel to me and become much more than a base-born knight!"*

Blaine shuddered, as if released from a spell. *"No! Never!"* His blue sword struck true. Sparks flew and the dark metal shattered. The last chain broke into a thousand pieces.

"You've failed, knight. Remove him and he dies! He's mine or nothing!"

Blaine yelled, "Go to hell!"

"Then feel my wrath!"

Tremors shook the cavern. The earth began to shudder and shake, as if a slumbering dragon sought to emerge. Shadows gibbered across the ceiling, claws and fangs reaching down. Stalactites crashed down, hurled like stone spears. Blaine stumbled and fell, a sheen of blood on his forehead. Kath lurched forward, desperate to reach Duncan.

Something grabbed Kath's hair, yanking her back.

Something else grabbed her ankle, a cold, searing touch.

Kath fell to her knees. *The shadows had gained substance!* Darker and somehow more dense, the shadows pounced. Icy fingers poked and clawed, trying to pull her to the ground.

Kath whirled away. Drawing her sword, she slashed at them.

They evaded her blade, as if the touch of steel somehow hurt. Slashing left and right, she pushed them back, her blade becoming a blur. Steel proved unable to kill them, yet they shied away, lurking just beyond reach. Making a final slash, she turned and ran for Duncan. Grabbing his arm, she began pulling him from the pentacle.

The shadows attacked, clawing at her, a searing cold. She struck at them with her sword, struggling to pull Duncan with just one hand.

The cavern rumbled and shook, a powerful tremor. Stalactites crashed to the floor, releasing a hail of dagger-sharp chips.

Shadows swooped towards Blaine, too many to count. His blue steel sword slashed through them. Gibbering screams, they whirled away.

Kath sheathed her sword, desperate to pull Duncan to safety.

Bear and Boar appeared at the doorway.

"Help me!"

A stalactite crashed down, nearly impaling Duncan. Rock chips flew in all directions, a storm of stone. The floor tilted and shook like the back of a mighty beast. Blaine struggled to his feet, his blue sword clutched in his hand. The others leaped to help.

Overhead, the shadows howled in rage.

Bear and Boar lifted Duncan to their shoulders. Staggering like drunks, they bore him from the chamber, narrowly avoiding the stone spears. They raced up the long spiral of stairs, climbing as if demons chased them. Kath followed, fearing for Duncan. The earth shook like an angry beast yet the passage remained open. The stairs stretched to forever, but the dawn light finally appeared at the cleft.

They stumbled from the doorway.

Tremors shook the citadel, but these were mild compared to the nightmare below.

"Put him down!" They laid Duncan on the courtyard. Kath cradled his head. "Come back to me." She covered his mouth with a kiss.

His eyes flashed open, one golden and the other sapphire blue. His mismatched gaze was clear, without any taint of Darkness. "I knew you'd save me."

She bit back a sob.

His gaze roved to the open sky, toward the dawn light. Seagulls circled overhead, releasing a mournful cry. He took a deep breath and then his gaze sought her face, like a man seeking a long lost sanctuary. "I longed for green, only to find it in your eyes."

His words lodged in her heart, a searing mixture of joy and pain. She almost cried, but forced the tears back, drinking in his voice, his mismatched stare, every detail dear. "Stay with me."

A stolen moment stretched to forever but then he gasped and the pain returned, and with it duty. "Beloved, there's much I must tell you."

"Let me find a healer first."

"No, you must listen." Agony washed across his face, but he fought through it, forcing the words out. "The monk, Bryce, still lives within the Mordant. He spies on the Mordant. He knows his plans. Somehow he spoke to me while I was trapped in the chamber." He flashed a weak smile. "And the Mordant thought I was no threat."

A sob escaped her. "You spoiled his plans, my love."

Someone handed Kath a water flask. She held it to his lips. Her gaze traveled the length of his body. Every dagger wept blood, as if the spell keeping him alive was broken. Tears crowded her eyes, but she held them at bay, determined to be brave for him.

"You must listen. You must remember." His voice trailed to a whisper.

She huddled close, her ear bent to his words.

A flood of warnings poured out of him, dark tidings and grim plans. He spoke of Lanverness, and the Octagon, and the Kiralynn monastery. He told her about a dark sword and a hallway carved like demons. He warned her of Taals that looked like ogres and dwarves that could sniff magic. Some of the warnings made little sense, a confusing jumble of images, but she listened to it all, struggling to memorize every detail.

Finally his words trailed to silence and his eyes closed.

Fear gripped her throat; she thought he was gone. "Duncan, don't leave me!" She cradled his head, willing him to live.

His eyes opened, full of light, and he smiled up at her. "I'll never leave you. But you must promise me two things."

"Anything."

A spasm of pain crossed his face, but his eyes remained opened. "You must put an end the Mordant. I've learned that evil is real and it must be stopped."

Hate boiled within her, an easy promise to make. "I promise."

His hand gripped hers. "And you must promise to live."

Tears crowded her eyes.

"Promise me." His voice sank to a whisper. "Promise me and I'll wait for you on the edge of the Light."

Her heartbeat quickened. "You'll wait for me?"

"Yes."

"I promise."

He smiled up at her...and then he was gone.

"NO!" She stared up at the heavens, challenging the gods with her cry. "Heal him! Heal him or I will not forgive you!"

Seagulls roiled overhead, screeching a mournful cry...but no miracle came.

"Svala!" The word was a murmur coming from a thousand voices. The courtyard was crowded with her army, a thousand tattooed faces staring at her. They drew their swords and knelt. They'd gained a great victory...but she'd lost her heart. Kath closed her eyes and the world dissolved into tears.

Dear Reader,

Thank you for following Kath, Duncan and Blaine, through the kingdoms of Erdhe. Their adventures continue in the fourth book of the saga, The Poison Priestess. More excitement awaits, so I hope you will read on.

I'd love to know what you think of my books and what you'd like me to write next (The Silk & Steel Saga is finished!). So tell me what you liked, loved and even what you hated. You can contact me at k_azinge@hotmail.com or on Facebook at Karen Azinger.

I'd love to hear from you.

And now I have a favor to ask. Readers have the power to make a book or a saga successful. The fate of The Silk & Steel Saga rests in your hands. Please support my books by posting a review on Amazon or Goodreads or any other social network. Even a one sentence review matters. I'd love to see my books on the silver screen, but that will only happen if you show the world you care. Thanks for your time and your support, I write for you. For Honor and the Octagon!

APPENDIX

CASTLEGARD

Three hundred years after the War of Wizards decimated the kingdoms of Erdhe, a group of knights banded together to protect the southern kingdoms from the ravages of the north. They claimed Castlegard, the great mage-stone castle left empty after the War of Wizards, as the seat of their power. Adopting the shape of the great castle as their symbol, they became known as the Octagon Knights.

To bolster their cause, the knights were ceded land running along the length of the Dragon Spine Mountains. Stretching from Castlegard all the way to the Western Ocean, this land became known as the Domain. A series of castles, keeps, and walls were built along the Dragon Spines, allowing the knights to control the mountain passes and deny access to the southern kingdoms. The Domain also includes the only iron ore mine in all of Erdhe to yield blue ore, the rare ore required to forge the knights' fabled blue steel swords.

As a sworn brotherhood of elite knights, the candidates forsake their lineage and their past when they win their maroon cloaks. Their symbol is a maroon octagon emblazoned on a silver shield.

KING URSUS ANVRIL, King of Castlegard and the Knights of the Octagon, Lord of the Domain, hero of the Battle of Raven Pass, bearer of a great blue sword named *Honor's Edge*.

    -his wife, **QUEEN PHYLA**, died giving birth to their only daughter

    -their children:

    PRINCE ULRICH, First-born son of the king, a sworn knight of the maroon, commander of the wall at Raven Pass, bearer of a great blue sword named *Mordbane*

    PRINCE GRIFFIN, Second-born son of the king, a sworn knight of the maroon, commander of Dymtower

    PRINCE GODFREY, Third-born son of the king, a sworn knight of the maroon, commander of Shieldhold

PRINCE TRISTAN, Fourth-born son of the king, a sworn knight of the maroon, slain while leading a patrol into the steppes

PRINCE LIONEL, Fifth-born son of the king, a sworn knight of the maroon, commander of Cragnoth Keep, slain by Trask

PRINCESS KATHERINE, Sixth child of the king, also known as the Imp or Little Sister or Kath. As a female, the Octagon symbol of Castlegard is forbidden to her. Instead she uses the Anvril's ancient heraldic symbol of a red hawk attacking with talons outstretched on a field of white.

-his sworn knights and retainers:

SIR OSBOURNE, The Knight Marshal of the Octagon, right hand of the King, a one-eyed man with a scar-crossed face, he wields a saber as his weapon of first choice, but then takes up Sir Tyrone's great sword from the signal tower of Cragnoth Keep.

SIR LOTHAR, knight-captain of the Salt Tower, wields a battleaxe, close friend to the knight marshal

SIR BORIS, knight-captain of Holdfast Keep

SIR DALT, knight-captain of Ice Tower

SIR GRAVIS, knight-captain of Sword Keep

SIR ABRAX, knight of the maroon, champion of the sword, guard to King Ursus, he wields a blue steel sword named *Protector*

SIR RANNOCK, knight of the maroon, champion of the morning star

SIR ODIS, knight of the maroon, champion of the lance

SIR BLAZE, knight of the maroon, champion of the mace

SIR ADLEMAR, knight of the maroon, champion of the claymore, wields a blue steel claymore named *Stalwart*

SIR TRASK, knight of the maroon, champion of the battleaxe, assigned to Cragnoth Keep as a punishment posting, slain at the battle of Cragnoth Keep

SIR TYRONE, knight of the maroon with skin the color of ebony, often referred to as the 'black knight', he wields a great sword, companion to Princess Katherine, a hero slain at the battle of Cragnoth Keep

SIR MALVOY, a fresh-sworn knight of the maroon

SIR MARIN, a knight of the maroon

SIR AMBROSE, a knight of the maroon

SIR WINTON, a knight of the maroon

SIR VARDINE, a knight of the maroon

SIR MELLOT, a knight of the maroon

HADRIAN, master archer of the maroon

BALDWIN, senior squire of the maroon, serves the King

BROCK, squire to Prince Ulrich

EMMETT, young squire

STEWARD MALT, Steward of the armory of Raven Pass

OTTO, the Master Swordsmith of Castlegard's forge, responsible for the forging of all blue steel weapons

QUINTUS, the Master Healer of Castlegard

VAL, a stable lad of Castlegard

SIR RAYMOND, branded as an unmade-knight of the Octagon, exiled from the Domain of Castlegard on penalty of death

THE KIRALYNN MONKS

Founded over two thousand years ago by a group of scholars, knights, and wizards, the Kiralynn Order has always presented an enigmatic face to the world, a face that is open yet closed. One hundred years before the start of the War of Wizards the monks withdrew from the southern kingdoms, retreating to their monastery hidden deep in the Southern Mountains. As if erased from the minds of men, the location of the monastery disappeared from the maps of Erdhe. The memory of the Kiralynn monks has slowly faded, becoming little more than legend and myth. Yet select rulers of the southern kingdoms still receive scrolls sealed with the symbol of the Order. History has proven that these scrolls contain an uncanny prescience. Kings ignore the advice of the Order at their own peril.

The symbol of the Kiralynn monks is a Seeing Eye in the palm of an Open Hand. Their seat of power is their mountain monastery. The motto of the Order is "Seek Knowledge, Protect Knowledge, Share Knowledge".

THE GRAND MASTER, the leader of the Kiralynn Order, his/her identity is a closely guarded secret
-monks and initiates of the Order:
>   **MASTER RIZEL**, a Master of the Order
>   **MASTER GARTH**, a Master Healer of the Order
>   **BRYCE**, an initiate of the Order, he studied to take his vows to become a monk and a healer but was subsumed by the Mordant's Awakening, becoming a prisoner in his own mind
>   **MASTER AEROTH**, an ambassador monk sent to the kingdoms of Erdhe
>   **MASTER ZITH**, a Master of the Order, accompanies Kath as one of her companions

-visitors to the monastery:
>   **PRINCESS JORDAN**, a princess of Navarre, sent to the monastery for her Wayfaring, she remains locked in a healing coma, felled by the treachery of the Mordant

DANYA, a young woman who sought sanctuary in the monastery with her mountain wolf, **BRYX**

THE DARK CITADEL

The Dark Citadel is a forbidding fortress-city in the far north. Perched atop three-hundred-foot cliffs that overlook the Western Ocean, it is built upon a huge monolithic boulder. The tiered city has nine layers spiraling upward around the stone monolith. Each layer holds a distinct class of people, with the palace of the Mordant at the summit. The stone monolith contains steps leading to a cave, the ancient source of Dark power.

The Mordant's domain also includes the steppes, a vast sea of grass that serves as a desolate greensward for the Dark Citadel, a barren killing field. The northern steppes are divided from the south by a dark wall studded with ten Gargoyle Gates.

The domain also includes the Pit, a massive crater with near vertical glass-sheer walls. Slaves live within the Pit, toiling within the Mordant's iron mines. Female slaves are forced to serve as whores for the Mordant's army. Residual magic in the Pit results in the massive abnormalities of newborns. Two new sub-races have been born and bred in the Pit: the Taals, an ogre-like sub-race with massive strength and limited intellect, and the Duegar, also called the Hounds of the Mordant, dwarves with the ability to scent magic.

The symbol of the Dark Citadel is a gold pentacle emblazoned on a field of black. The Darkflamme is the Mordant's personal battle banner, twelve feet of black silk ending in two silken tails of bright red flecked with gold, creating the illusion of darkness on fire

THE MORDANT- With over a thousand years of life, he is the oldest of the Harlequins, the god-king of the north, the ruler of the Dark Citadel. He wields the Staff of Pain, an iron scepter with a red crystal at the top.
    -his officers and priests:

> **HIGH PRIEST GAVIS-** High Priest of the Pentacle, Keeper of the Trials Return, the ruler of the Dark Citadel in the absence of the Mordant

GENERAL HAITH- General of the army of the Pentacle, witness to the beheading of the Mordant in his prior life
GENERAL MARRIS- commander of the cavalry
BISHOP SIFF- Administrator bishop serving the High Priest
DOLF- Master Assassin of the Ninth Rank
BISHOP TYNES- bishop of the border guards
SIR RAYMOND- branded as an unmade-knight of the Octagon, exiled from the Domain of Castlegard, sworn to serve the Mordant
CAPTAIN LORNID- captain of the citadel guard
CENTURION CAYLEX- commander of the third border guard
TAVOS- priest of the border guard
FENTHANE- priest of the border guards, serves Bishop Tynes
JAMIS- a guard of the Door, witness to the beheading of the Mordant in his prior life

-Emissaries to the Citadel:
MERCHANTER TIMOTH- emissary from the MerChanter Sea Lords, vassals to the Mordant

Lords and people of the Pit:
LORD SLEGHORN- the self-styled lord of the Pit and the iron mines
GRACK- a one-armed Taal turnkey, guard of the lower mines
CRIBB- guard of the Pit
HARIT- guard of the Pit
MARDAK- Taal guard of the upper mines
HONORABLE ELSWIN- leader of the slave's Council of Elders, he has the deformity of six fingers on each hand, he is Mara's uncle
BRAITH- a slow-witted slave Taal, serves as the guard to the Council of Elders
MARA- a serving girl assigned to the upper mines, the niece of Honorable Elswin
THESSALA- patty woman working the dung mountain

Prisoners of the upper iron mine:

KRELL THREE-EYE- prisoner/leader of the upper mines, a massively strong man with the deformity of a third eye in the center of his forehead

NAGA- dark-skinned prisoner of the upper mines

MARCUS-prisoner of the upper mines

Prisoners of the lower iron mines:

CLOVIS- also known as **CLOVIS FARSEERER**, born of the Pit he became a guard of the Citadel before being condemned to the iron mines, he has a hidden deformity, the hidden eye, the third eye of prophecy

BROCK- prisoner/leader of the lower mines

SETH- prisoner of the lower mines, has rocklung

BRUCE- prisoner of the lower mines

HAL- a slow-witted Taal prisoner of the lower mines

GREN- a Duegar dwarf prisoner of the lower mines

BREDON- prisoner of the lower mines, born with a third eye in his forehead

NEF- prisoner of the lower mines, has six-fingered hands

TRELL- prisoner of the lower mines, has a clubfoot

BRENT- prisoner of the lower mines, is a hunchback

SIMEON- prisoner of the lower mines, is a hunchback

FELDON- prisoner of the lower mines, has rocklung

STAN- prisoner of the lower mines has a cleft lip

BREDAN- prisoner of the lower mines, has a third eye in his forehead

THE PAINTED PEOPLE

An ancient people, forgotten by most of Erdhe, the Painted Warriors are the descendents of escaped slaves and runaway soldiers. Living in the shadow of the Dark Citadel, the Painted People have forged a fiercely independent warrior culture that spans a thousand years. Outnumbered and poorly equipped, they strike back at the Pentacle in lightning raids across the steppes, reaping steel and armor from their enemies. They make their home in a secret labyrinth of caves hidden in the Ghost Hills. Deeply spiritual, they invoke the power of nature by tattooing their faces with the images of beasts and birds, a spiritual melding of man and animal. Divided into dens marked by their tattoos, they are guided by the Ancestor, a shaman of mystical memories, and led by a Council of Leaders made up of representatives from all the dens. A secret and forgotten people, few in the southern kingdoms have ever heard of them.

THE ANCESTOR- Also known as the Keeper of Memories, the Old One. The Ancestor is always a woman, following a matriarchal line of mystical seers that stretches back for nearly a thousand years. As the spiritual leader of the painted people she is respected and revered but she does not rule as a queen. Instead she guides the council of leaders.

VALDUR- a Taishan of the mountain lions, a vision-hunter lost on a quest in the southern steppes. Attacked and left for dead by soldiers of the Pentacle, a patrol of Octagon knights found him and took him to Castlegard where he died in Kath's arms.

ROYCE- warrior leader of the mountain lions, leader of the Council

THERA- leader of the ravens, master healer

SHAGRITH- warrior leader of the eagles

BRANT- leader of the boars

FANGGOLD- warrior leader of the wolves

ANTON- fox-faced warrior patrol leader

TORVEN- eagle-faced warrior patrol leader

BEAR- a bear-faced warrior assigned to guard Kath, he refuses to reveal his true name, adopts the name of Bear and becomes Kath's personal guard and friend, wields a sword

BOAR- a boar-faced warrior assigned to Kath, refuses to reveal his true name, adopts the name of Boar and becomes Kath's personal guard and friend, wields a mace
NEVEN- a wolf-faced warrior smitten with Danya
TINGOLD- a wolf-faced scout
BEARANT- a bear-faced warrior
TIGE- a hawk-faced warrior
BREVOR- a badger-faced warrior
TANGOR- a badger-faced warrior
CLEMIT- a wolf-faced warrior
VIN- an eagle-faced warrior
GRENFIR- an owl-faced warrior
TARLY- a boar-faced warrior
PREN- a bear-faced warrior
SIDHORN- an eagle-faced warrior
TANNIN- a fox-faced youth serving as a message runner

The Front Cover artwork was done by the Australian artist, Greg Bridges. Greg's artwork has appeared on the book covers of many well-known fantasy authors. His cover perfectly captures the dread of The Skeleton King. To see more of his art or to contact Greg, visit his website at http://www.gregbridges.com/

The Maps and the Back Cover artwork were done by a graphic artist from Oregon, Peggy Lowe. Her illustration of the two maps helps to bring the kingdoms of Erdhe to life and the screaming candles convey the horror of the Mordant's domain. Peggy can be contacted at her e-mail address, peggy@portfoliooregon.com

Other books by Karen L Azinger

Hungry to learn more about the kingdoms of Erdhe? Then consider reading my short story collection, *The Assassin's Tear*. The first story, *Prophecy's Twist*, explores the start of the War of Wizards, and the second signature story, *The Assassin's Tear*, explores the Dark Citadel from the perspective of a young thief.

The Assassin's Tear- Explore the medieval kingdoms of Erdhe, raid the tomb of the first emperor of China, survive an apocalyptic event Down Under, time travel to learn the secret of a famous scientist, and unravel the enigma of Dark Space in this collection of fantasy and science fiction tales from the author of *The Silk & Steel Saga.*

Power Writing: Make Your Genre Fiction Soar! **-** Fans of *The Silk & Steel Saga* will peek behind the curtain, gaining insights into the author's imaginings. Revisit the wonders of Erdhe with the author as your tour guide. Writers will learn how to color outside the lines and write bold genre fiction that will enthrall your readers and make your stories soar. *Power Writing* provides insights into many unique topics rarely discussed by other writing books. You'll find tips on writing magic, fortune telling, making maps and writing great battle scenes. Learn how to spice it up with romantic subplots and how to write with iconic images and tropes. Examples are drawn from genre masterworks like Tolkien's *Lord of the Rings*, Martin's *Game of Thrones*, Herbert's *Dune*, Rowling's *Harry Potter*, and the author's own *Silk & Steel Saga*, as well as examples from silver screen blockbusters like *Star Wars, Star Trek, Braveheart* and *Gladiator*.

ABOUT THE AUTHOR

KAREN L. AZINGER has always loved fantasy fiction, and always hoped that someday she could give back to the genre a little of the joy that reading has always given her. On a hike in the Columbia River Gorge she realized she had enough original ideas to finally write an epic fantasy. She started writing and never stopped. *The Steel Queen* is her first book, born from that hike in the gorge. Before writing, Karen spent over twenty years as an international business strategist, eventually becoming a vice-president for one of the world's largest natural resource companies. She's worked on developing the first gem-quality diamond mine in Canada's arctic, on coal seam gas power projects in Australia, and on petroleum projects around the world. Having lived in Australia for eight years she considers it to be her second home. She's also lived in Canada and spent a lot of time in the Canadian arctic. She lives with her husband in Portland Oregon, in a house perched on the edge of the forest. Her seven book epic fantasy, *The Silk & Steel Saga,* is finished! This saga includes: *The Steel Queen, The Flame Priest, The Skeleton King, The Poison Priestess, The Knight Marshal, The Prince Deceiver,* and *The Battle Immortal.* Karen also published a collection of short stories, *The Assassin's Tear,* including two stories set in the kingdoms of Erdhe. She also published a book on writing, *Power Writing: Make Your Genre Fiction Soar!* You can learn more at her website, www.karenlazinger.com or at her Facebook page for The Steel Queen.

www.ingramcontent.com/pod-product-compliance
Lightning Source LLC
Chambersburg PA
CBHW020926020726
47495CB00002B/364